By Force

of

Patriots

BY
CAMERON REDDY

J NY NE P OR DIE

Published by White Feather Press. (www.whitefeatherpress.com)

ISBN 978-161808-024-0

Printed in the United States of America

Cover design created by Ron Bell of AdVision Design Group (www.advisiondesigngroup.com)

Interior flag photo ©iStockphoto.com/ HultonArchive

White Feather Press

Reaffirming Faith in God, Family, and Country!

Dedication

I'd like to thank everyone who listened to me wax and ramble (I'd like to think it was poetic but I'm a realist about such things) about this story and who, despite my obliviousness to their boredom and discomfort, gave me advice and encouragement.

Regrettably, due to my ever decreasing memory capacity and the passage of so much time (I finished the original version of this story in 1999) I am certain that I have forgotten a few people who spent time with me or my manuscript. To those I can only offer my deepest apologies and I ask your forgiveness.

So, in no particular order, I'd like to thank Dan Rosen who was with me on this story from the beginning, read every word, and offered tons of advice; Dave Felbeck who did yeoman's work on editing the entire manuscript in an earlier form, James Christy who read the latest version with the eye of a former FBI agent, Kip Allen and Sara Christensen who read with such analytical eyes; Arcadio Ramirez who talked at length with me when I was getting started back in the 90s; my neighbor Joe Dougherty who often put me on the right track on computer issues; Al Zuckerman for his fabulous book, "Writing The Blockbuster Novel," without which I'd have been lost; Writer's Digest Criticism Service and Martha Stoner who gave me valuable encouragement and writing advice; The Honorable Debbie Stabenow for finding my novel on my website and writing me a most encouraging personal letter; Skip Coryell for spending his money to publish this opus; and Mary Mueller, Lee Ann Walker, and Peggi Zahn for editing my latest version and finding errors I would have never found.

This is a work of fiction. However, astute readers will notice that my story is peppered with actual events, facts, and figures. These anchor the story with today's reality of a federal government that could scarcely have been imagined by the founding fathers. So anchored, I believe many of the issues raised, be it racism, abortion, immigration, gay rights, modes of constitutional decision making, the

Second Amendment, the Commerce Clause, regulatory authority, depression, loyalty, or sex, will stir the reader to consider, and hopefully more deeply understand, what we must do, as Americans, to form a more perfect union. If we do not so engage our minds and our lives, we may soon be at that place where our nation will be formed, again, by force of patriots.

April, 2012.

Cameron Reddy

BY FORCE

OF

PATRIOTS

CHAPTER I

THOUGH THE OAK AND PINE TREES WERE THIRTY TO sixty feet tall, deep foliage made Jeff Kreig nearly invisible. He was looking across a small clearing that extended some thirty yards before the woods and brush became dense again. The trees were full, and though the sun was brilliant that day, and high in the sky, shade engulfed the entire opening. All around, birds chirped in a symphony-like cadence. Overhead, two squirrels scurried from branch to branch.

Jeff inhaled deeply. From the spicy aroma of witch hazel to the aromatic perfume of white pine, everywhere was the sweet fragrance of life and beauty. For a moment his conscience objected to the irony that his intent, his purpose, his great effort, was to kill.

The thought quickly passed. He could see his prey through the trees.

Jeff's pulse quickened. His muscles tightened. His breathing became rapid and deeper. *Relax*, he told himself.

Hours on the practice range. Months of anticipation. Hundreds of dollars on lodging, gas, and greasy-spoon meals. And hours of stealthy movement through these woods...

All for this moment.

His prey took another step and was standing at the far edge of the clearing in the apparent belief that there was adequate cover.

It was time to kill.

Carefully, Jeff raised his left arm, making sure to not stir the surrounding brush; any visible or audible movement could warn his prey. Silently, he drew back the arrow toward his right ear. The arrow's razor-sharp point glistened in a thin band of sunlight that pierced the overhead tree cover. A drop of perspiration snaked its way down his forehead to his eyebrow, where it filtered through and spilled into his right eye. The salty tear stung, and he fought the urge to blink.

Jeff's muscles easily pulled the 80 pounds of tension in the compound bow. At close to 350 feet per second, the arrow would cover the distance in less than a second. If properly aimed, it would rip into its target with all its force concentrated on its razor-sharp edges. If unimpeded by bone, the arrow could slash all the way through the body and emerge out the other side.

Jeff trained the arrow at the precise location necessary to strike directly in the center of the breast—now!

He let the arrow fly.

The combined sounds of the vibrating bow cord and the acceleration of the arrow raced to the target about three times faster than the arrow itself. Instantly sensing danger, the victim's eyes darted toward the sounds.

He looked right at Jeff. His eyes were big, watery, and sullen.

The arrow plunged into the center of the deer's chest and its eyes went wide in confusion. A moment later its nervous system registered the damage. The leg muscles gave way and the deer collapsed to the ground.

"You got him!" Miles yelled, his voice piercing the quiet of the deep woods.

Jeff swallowed hard. "I guess so."

"Gee, don't sound so excited. Did you see? He looked right at you!"

That, of course, was the problem.

The deer's eyes had seared into his mind. This was his first try at bow hunting. His churning stomach was telling him that it might be his last.

"Looks like an eight-pointer, Jeff! Come on! Let's make sure he's dead." Miles pushed his way through the underbrush and into the clearing.

Jeff hesitated. He had thought about the possibility that his first shot might not kill the deer. That possibility was now real—and those beseeching eyes! How could he finish him off? Jeff hadn't accounted for those damned eyes. A lump formed in his throat and he thought he might be sick. Reluctantly, he pulled himself up and trudged after Miles with one hand to his stomach.

Miles and Jeff had become best friends while competing on the wrestling team in high school. Now, both 22 years of age and a shade under six feet tall, they had maintained their muscular builds and six-pack abs. Jeff's round face, blond hair, and boyish blue eyes contrasted sharply with Miles's chiseled face, curly black hair, and brown eyes. Where Jeff seemed young and confident, though quite harmless unless you noticed his muscular neck and forearms, Miles looked tough as nails, with a massively thick chest and broad shoulders which rose up in a distinct "V" shape from his waist.

Jeff reached the deer. Miles was already on his knees, working to free the arrow. It had been a perfect shot and the deer was quickly expiring. But there it was—a huge animal still so warm its body steamed in the cool air. Its chest was heaving, fighting for its last breaths. *Lord,* Jeff thought, *This is a nightmare, a living—no, a dying nightmare.*

Jeff shook his head. "I'm done."

Miles turned away from his efforts with the arrow. "What?"

"I'm never killing anything again."

"Oh, come on. You'll get over it once you taste this meat." Miles went back to work on the arrow. "There, got it." He raised the bloody arrow as if it were a trophy. There was still bright red flesh trapped in the web of the arrow's tip.

Jeff's stomach went sour and he felt dizzy. He dropped to one knee for support. "No, really, I think—" A noise caught Jeff's attention and he stopped speaking in mid-sentence. He turned his head in the direction of—

His heart instantly leaped into his throat. Out of the corner of his eye he saw that Miles had also turned and looked up. They were both staring at the business end of what appeared to be a Colt M16A2 gas-operated 5.56 mm select fire assault rifle.

"Who the hell are you?" demanded the gunman, whose six-foot four-inch frame towered over both Jeff and Miles. He wore camouflage fatigues, complete with military-style black leather boots.

Jeff's mind began to race. He and Miles had discussed the possibility that they might have inadvertently wandered onto private property; apparently, they had. And it was shaping up to be a very big mistake.

On the other hand, Jeff quickly analyzed, a landowner would not likely shoot them on his own property—incriminating blood and guts are not the things one would want strewn about. So, this guy was probably just bluffing with his... *Wait a minute.* What in the heck would he be doing with a military assault rifle? This was not making any sense: a nasty-looking gun, a face chiseled out of rock, and eyes that glowed with an eerie coolness... Clearly, this was one mean dude.

The gunman moved forward and motioned with the M16 for Jeff and Miles to stand. With a scarcely visible smile, the gunman jammed the barrel of the rifle into Jeff's chest. The gunman kept a hold on the pistol grip of the M16 as he frisked Jeff with his free hand. Jeff looked down at the gun's flash suppressor that was pressed into his coat. He could smell gun oil mixed with the faint odor of spent gunpowder.

Already nauseous and dizzy from the deer, Jeff started to panic. Faced with a deadly threat, his body was inexorably shifting into a fight or flight response. Suddenly, his eyes could see nothing but the gunman—nothing past or to either side—as though everything else had ceased to exist. And what he couldn't see, he couldn't hear. Instead of the comforting sounds of rustling trees and the chatter of birds—there was deathly silence.

Jeff shook his head to force his senses back into operation. The gunman smiled, as though he could read Jeff's mind and knew he was struggling to maintain awareness.

The gunman pulled Jeff's hunting knife from his belt pouch. Apparently satisfied, the gunman pulled the gun from Jeff's chest and jammed it likewise into Miles and frisked him.

The gunman stepped back, eyed Miles and said, "We ought to have a little coon hunt."

Jeff glanced over and saw Miles's eyes go as big around as silver dollars.

The gunman laughed.

Miles stood motionless; he seemed to be holding his breath.

Jeff battled to gain awareness; somehow he cut through the panic-induced fog. *If this jerk would only put his gun barrel back on my chest…* In his senior year, Jeff had placed third at the Michigan High School Wrestling Championships. He was still very strong and fast. All he needed was a fraction of a second…

The gunman was a bit more relaxed, apparently satisfied that Jeff and Miles were now unarmed. He was standing only a gun's length away as he again raised the M16 toward Jeff's chest.

That was all Jeff needed.

As the M16 came up, Jeff reached out with both hands and yanked the barrel toward himself and to his side, pulling the gunman off balance and forward. Jeff stepped into the forward motion of the gunman and wrapped his left hand around the back side of the gunman's right arm, just below the shoulder. Taking advantage of the gunman being off balance and falling slightly forward, Jeff lowered his center of gravity and shot his right arm into the gunman's crotch. This folded the gunman at the waist and effectively positioned him across Jeff's shoulders. Jeff then pulled down hard with his left arm and raised his right shoulder deeper into the gunman's crotch, pulling the gunman off his feet and suspending him across Jeff's shoulders, as if the gunman were being carried out of a burning home by a fireman.

Jeff continued his move by rotating his shoulders: the left, down; the right, up—cartwheeling the gunman to the ground. The M16 jammed into the turf, twisted out of the gunman's grip, and fell harmlessly to the side.

In competition, Jeff usually followed his fireman's carry with a half nelson to pin the opponent's shoulders to the mat. Instead, he threw the gunman to his stomach and promptly drove the gunman's right arm up behind his back. Jeff slowly raised the gunman's wrist until he started writhing in pain. At that point, Jeff knew he had, at least temporarily, resolved the matter. He raised his head away from the gunman's back as much to get his nose away from the stench of stale cigarettes as to locate Miles.

Miles had grabbed the M16 and had it trained in their general direction, but with the barrel pointed safely toward the ground. Jeff leaned into the gunman, applying a little more upward pressure on the wrist. It elicited another wince of pain and caused the gunman to arch his back in an attempt to ease the strain on his arm and shoulder.

Jeff tried to sort things out, but his heart was pounding between his ears so hard and fast he could barely think. He needed a few moments, so he leaned a little harder into the gunman. The problem, Jeff realized, was that once a wrestling match was over, the opponent shook your hand and walked off the mat. This match was over—but letting this guy up would be a very different story.

Suddenly Jeff realized that the protrusion he felt around the man's waist underneath the camouflage jacket was a holstered gun. It made him wonder…

"Miles, point that thing at this jerk's head while I check him for another gun."

"Gladly." Miles moved closer and put the flash suppressor to the gunman's temple. Jeff noted with satisfaction that Miles had his finger off the trigger but alongside the trigger guard. For their high school graduation they had both received a week-long training course at the famed Gunsite Training Academy, where they had quickly learned that the finger goes inside the trigger guard only upon a decision to discharge the weapon.

Keeping upward pressure on the gunman's arm and wrist, Jeff pulled the gun out of the holster at his waist and began to search.

"Miles!" Sure enough. There was another gun—this one in an ankle holster. Jeff tossed both guns into the bushes several feet away.

"Hell!" Jeff pulled a small radio transmitter from a deep pocket on the gunman's pants.

Miles choked, "What if he used that before we got him?"

"He did," came a voice from the woods.

Miles wheeled around in the direction of the voice. Jeff frantically scanned the bushes but saw nothing.

Again from the woods: "Drop the gun before we blow your head off!"

This time Jeff could tell the voice came from behind Miles, and as Jeff strained to see through the bushes, several men appeared, dressed in the same fatigues as the gunman they had disarmed. Each one had an M16.

They were approaching from all sides.

Miles cast a defeated glance at Jeff and, without further prompting, he let the M16 drop to the ground.

One of the men spoke, "Well, lookie what we got here." Jeff figured he was the leader.

Another said, "I didn't think spooks had any brains. But this one was smart enough to toss the gun." They all laughed.

Jeff counted five men.

The leader motioned his M16 at Jeff. "Why don't you get off our friend before I blow your damn head off?"

Jeff wondered whether that might occur anyhow. As he got up, he tried to create some space between himself and the man he had taken down. The guy would be pretty pissed, and with all his buddies around he might come up swinging, or worse.

Jeff felt himself pulled from behind. He saw black hands wrapped around his waist.

One of the men shouted, "Hey, Sambo! Smart of you to pull your friend back. Leonard would probably like to rip his head off!" The armed men laughed.

Leonard stood and began rubbing his right shoulder. "Let's just get these punks back to the lodge." He retrieved his guns from the bushes.

Several men nodded in agreement, and one of the men stepped forward. "Just turn around and head toward that clearing and then left along the tree line." The man motioned the M16 in the direction he wanted them to go.

Miles and Jeff turned around and began walking. Miles was in front and a gunmen followed Jeff. Suddenly Jeff felt a hard jolt to his back, followed by a searing pain just below his shoulder. The man had apparently slammed the barrel of his M16 into Jeff's back. Jeff lurched forward from the impact, lost his balance, and stumbled into Miles. He grabbed Miles's coat to stay up. Jeff moaned as he straightened himself and moved forward in silence. His back and shoulder started to throb. *Oh God*, he thought, *this is just the beginning...*

❧

THE GREAT HALL WAS PART OF NATE SMITH'S HUNTING estate. Deer racks covered the walls, and at one end of the huge room a mammoth stone fireplace rose 20 feet to the apex of the cathedral ceiling. The lodge, built with indigenous stone and rough-hewn logs, some up to 14 inches thick, was the largest of several structures on the huge hunting estate. It once served the fancy of a railroad baron who passed it to his granddaughter, Catherine, whose husband, Nate, appreciated the property's remote and secluded location. It now served as Nate's home and as Headquarters for the American Patriots.

The patriot movement got its start in the early 1970s at the Hayden Lake, Idaho, compound of the Aryan Nations, but it didn't gain much force until the Bureau of Alcohol, Tobacco, and Firearms (BATF) asked Randy Weaver to infiltrate the Aryan Nations as an

informer. When he refused, the BATF targeted him in a sting operation with the hope that, facing federal firearms charges, he could be
persuaded to turn informant. The sting operation (a federal agent
posing as a civilian seeking to purchase sawed-off shotguns from
Weaver) eventually went so badly sideways that an armed assault on
Weaver's Ruby Ridge home in northern Idaho commenced in 1992.
In the confusion and arrogance increasingly typical of such federal
operations, an FBI sniper fired a shot at a retreating Randy Weaver.
The shot ripped through the door to Weaver's cabin and killed his
wife, Vicki, who had been standing inside holding a baby in her
arms.

Six months later, the ranks of the patriot movement grew at least
tenfold when the BATF attempted to execute a search warrant at the
Branch Davidian compound near Waco, Texas. After a 51-day siege,
Attorney General Janet Reno authorized an armed breach of the
compound. Seventy-six people died in the resulting fire, including
21 children and two pregnant women, along with Davidian leader
David Koresh.

Nate had gone through his own hell with the federal government
and had begun planning revenge. Eventually he found his target in
the Alfred P. Murrah Federal Building in Oklahoma City. Timothy
McVeigh and Terry Nichols were his front men, and it was a damn
shame that McVeigh got the electric chair. He was a true patriot.
But neither ever betrayed Nate's involvement nor his planning and
explosives expertise that made it possible—and successful.

It frustrated Nate that so few in the patriot movement were willing to go on the offense—to use violence for revolution. Everyone
wanted to train with guns; that was fun. And everyone was willing to shoot to defend their family, home, or nation. But very few
were willing to take the next step—the step made necessary by the
radical transformations brought about by unhindered illegal immigration and massive increases in the size and power of the federal
government. Regrettably, too few were willing to use violence to
take back their culture and country. Some of the men who called
themselves "leaders" even thought Oklahoma City was a mistake!

Well, getting so many children caught up in that... Even now, thinking about it, Nate's heart knotted up. The more he read the Bible... Jesus talking about children—*so damn many little smiles and squeaky voices...* Nate shook his head to break a train of thought that was taking him somewhere he didn't want to go. The idiots, the liberals, the talking heads on all the major networks, couldn't tell the difference between Oklahoma City and the Arab attacks of 9/11 and 8/24. A bunch of towel heads killed a million Americans. Oklahoma City— well, that simply didn't compare. It was totally different. *It* was the beginning of a justifiable revolution.

Nate was standing at the back of the hall, finishing off a 3 Musketeers candy bar and waiting for the meeting to begin. Virtually every leader in the American Patriots was there. Each leader represented from a few hundred to 10 thousand—and more— regular members, drawn from every state in the union. Everyone was in full military dress. Everyone was armed with at least one handgun. Presently, most of the men were still standing and milling about. Over a hundred gray metal folding chairs spread in concentric rows away from the small plywood stage with a podium standing in its center. There was an aisleway from the podium to the back of the room that effectively split the gathering into two sections.

With his right hand resting on the butt of his .45 caliber 1911, Nate was studying faces for signs of weakness—for signs of a willingness to break from the ranks. His six-foot frame gave him a good vantage point, while his cool eyes moved from face to face, occasionally catching a return glance that was, more often than not, giving back a measure of allegiance. *Excellent*, Nate thought. His pulse quickened.

Oklahoma City had turned out to be a disaster for Nate. In a hastily called election, just two months after the bombing, Nate had lost his command to the man who was about to speak: Hartman, the wimp-ass "Commander."

With his left hand, Nate silently opened and closed his custom-made Kasper fighting knife. He worked the Damascus blade in total silence, wrapping his middle finger around the jeweled titanium

handle to ease, and hush, the locking action of the frame spring.
He ran his large, callused fingers along the wide, flat handle, which
ensured good purchase should the knife need to be thrust, palm
down, blade horizontal, into some s.o.b.'s chest, followed by
immediately pivoting the elbow down, thus twisting the blade to
vertical, and slashing the knife down the chest and across the abdo-
men, eviscerating most everything in the gut.

Patience, Nate thought. Must be patient. Isaiah 40:31 came to him
and he whispered under his breath, "but they who wait for the Lord
shall renew their strength."

Yet, the sooner he could get rid of Hartman, the sooner he would
be able to turn people his way. With the nuclear attack fresh in
everyone's mind, and San Francisco obliterated, those less inclined
to violence were beginning to feel that Hartman was taking too
much time.

The meeting was about to commence. People were talking and
laughing, and generally seemed to be in a festive mood. Nate was
watching Hartman pace back and forth at the head of the hall.
Seemingly preoccupied, Hartman hadn't noticed that everyone
was waiting for him to speak. Some people were beginning to look
around in confusion.

Instantly, Nate knew he could not pass up this opportunity.
Excitement raced through his body. But what should he say? For
a moment he panicked. Nothing would come to him and he was
afraid Hartman would wise up and begin. He had to say something.
Anything. Please God, give me the words!

The words came.

Nate's voice cut through the air. "We need to act decisively—
now! The government is killing us. You're all driving suv's and
trucks at least five years old—because they can't make 'em anymore.
Do you remember when your kids could play tag during recess?
How about the last time you saw a Christmas decoration on public
property? Remember when abortion was illegal and we had a death
penalty for terrorists? They said it's inhumane to terrorists, yet
they've passed laws allowing live-birth abortions?"

Nate paused. His heart was pounding. Heads had turned when he started. Now, more and more patriots were beginning to look and listen. The cornucopia of talking and laughing had hushed, replaced by a muted rumble of "he's right" and "that's right."

Nate ran both hands through his hair and continued, "Don't forget how Obama did it—instigating an economic crisis like we have never seen in our lives, and then promising 'change' to the brain-dead masses. There is no other way this country would have elected a Muslim, Marxist revolutionary as president. Then he let in millions of illegal immigrants and gave them voting rights. Then he let ACORN 'find' hundreds of thousands more voters. And look at the results. The government owns and centrally plans our major industries. Gas is close to 10 bucks a gallon! Ten bucks! Remember when you could just drive up and fill up? When you could drive as many miles as you wanted? When gas stations didn't have a compliance official standing there to punch your gas ticket?"

The murmur of approval was now silent. This was a seriously sore spot for Americans generally, and patriots in particular. Obama had been a disaster for American energy production. After closing down all coal-burning power plants, he and Maxine Waters had nationalized the oil industry and shut down all domestic oil exploration. The resulting spike in the cost of all forms of energy was well beyond anything Americans had ever imagined possible. Per gallon federal gasoline taxes were now more than the total cost of a gallon just a few years before. And to ensure no one used more than his "fair share," the federal government posted a Gas Compliance Official, know as a "GCO," at every station to punch a monthly allotment ticket. The government was saving the world against "climate change," the moniker now used to describe a globe that wasn't warming.

"Our country has turned against us," Nate continued. "We're the bad guys! The world is ass backwards. The feds aren't looking for real terrorists. They are strip-searching grandmas wearing Depends. Meanwhile, the public is cooling off over San Francisco. Even now, you don't see any TV pictures of the destruction. 'It will only make us angry at Muslims,' they say. Well, screw that!"

A chorus of cheers erupted. Nate tried to pause for effect, but it was like trying to obey a stop sign in the middle of nowhere; he touched the brakes and drove on through. "You've seen the videos produced by Homeland Security where they are trying to get citizens to report suspicious activity. They depict whites as terrorists and the actual terrorists as the good guys. We need to act before FBI infiltrators make significant inroads into our command structure. We won't remain secret forever."

Nate ran his hands over his face and then again through his hair. This was going so well that he felt a stab of shame for doubting that God would see him through. Psalm 40:1 came to mind: *"I waited patiently for the Lord; he inclined to me and heard my cry."*

Nate forced himself to slow down. This time, he spoke in a low, dark tone. "We can't even be sure they don't have someone in our command structure now."

Nate glared out over everyone. Several in the crowd began to shift about nervously. He had struck another cord. Faces were rapt with attention. They were leaning his way. He could see it and feel it. Nate again ran his hands through his hair, which had, over the years, become permanently parted. God really *was* with him.

Nate slammed his fist on the closest table, causing everyone nearby to flinch. "Are we going to let these people…" He held out one hand and with the other grabbed one finger, and then another, as he ticked off each group: "…the 'I-want-my-share' nee-grows, the A-rabs, the libs, the feds…" Then he thrust his hand up high with all five fingers fully extended, "…and every damned special interest group destroy our country and our God-given rights—our constitutional rights?"

Nate again slammed his fist on the table—this time so hard that his hand began to throb. Many were nodding in agreement so he slammed the table again. Pain flashed up his arm. Sweat began to drip from his forehead. *Saint Paul knew worse,* he thought, and he slammed the table again. He reached into his back pocket with his throbbing hand and retrieved a small sheet of folded parchment. Gingerly, lovingly, he slowly unfolded the piece and set it on the table.

It was in his own handwriting, drawn with meticulous attention to detail. The flowery letter forms had been a source of wonder to him as a child, and he had dedicated hour upon hour to learning them. The beloved document's importance was second only to the Bible. He really didn't need to refer to the now-unfolded sheet before him to recite the words, but he felt a certain reverence for the document's ideals and a level of comfort with having it spread before him.

He began to speak in measured phrases:

"... when a long train of abuses and usurpations,
pursuing invariably the same Object,
evinces a design to reduce them under absolute Despotism,
it is their right,
it is their duty,
to throw off such Government,
and to provide new Guards for their future Security."

Everyone seemed to agree. Several dozen cheered and threw their fists into the air.

"Let's hear from Hartman," yelled someone, apparently straining to be heard over the increasing clamor of support for Nate.

❧

WHEN NATE BEGAN TO SPEAK, HARTMAN WAS JOLTED OUT of his self-absorbed state. He cursed under his breath and immediately headed to the podium. Unfortunately, by that time everyone had turned toward the back of the hall and to Nate. They were listening intently.

Hartman was six feet of lean muscle, with charcoal hair and a prominent, square jaw. He had the look of a man who had been there, done that, and who could take care of things. He waited for the right pause in Nate's delivery and then, thank God, someone asked for his opinion.

Nate had been amazingly good, so Hartman knew he had to begin with something clever—something that would catch everyone off guard.

He had an idea and he screamed at the top of his lungs, "Nate is right!"

The room fell silent. Some of Hartman's closest supporters glanced at each other with raised eyebrows.

"Our country *has* turned against us. The FBI *is* trying to infiltrate. We do need to act." Hartman paused and leaned out over the lectern so he could look directly into as many eyes as possible. Nate Smith stood at the back of the room. His face was drawn and his eyes were riveted. He was massaging something in his hand.

"But we need to act at the right time. Not sooner. Not later. Thomas Jefferson knew. The colonial leaders knew."

Hartman stepped off the stage and began to walk along some of the rows, here and there squeezing between two chairs to get to the adjacent row. He wanted eye contact—full, frontal, "in your face" contact. He had to match Nate's performance so he directed his comments toward one leader, then another, and then another. As he walked, people turned and twisted in their seats to watch.

Truth was, he lived for this. Speaking before so many true patriots who loved this country so much. Nothing matched it. All his life he had wondered what he was born to do. And now he knew.

It had been a challenge to wrest power away from that madman Nate Smith. What he had done was beyond the pale. No true patriot would sanction killing even one innocent American, let alone scores of them. It was true that the country needed to learn a lesson only patriots could teach it, but killing innocent civilians didn't need to be part of the lesson. And surely the lesson didn't need to include blowing up a building full of children.

As Hartman talked, he ended up near the back of the room, and something made him walk toward Nate. As he approached he noticed Nate make a quick movement with his right arm. The guy was a former Navy Seal, so who could know what he was up to? All Hartman could see was the back of Nate's hand. Was he holding something?

Now was not the time to back off. Nate had challenged him and he had to respond. Hartman continued toward Nate until they stood nose-to-nose. Nate's eyes were cool, calculating. Small beads of perspiration had formed around Nate's mouth and forehead. Hartman could smell his breath. He could hear his breathing, which seemed, oddly, to be quite rapid for a man standing still.

Hartman was contemplating whether he should try to embarrass Nate by pointing out how panicky he looked when he noticed Nate's eyes suddenly dilate. Alarm bells rang in Hartman's head. He recalled that Nate had been holding something—a knife!

Hartman reflexively thrust both hands out in a blocking motion and simultaneously threw his body backward, away from an anticipated knife thrust—that never came.

Hartman knew instantly he'd been played like a fiddle. He felt foolish as hell and was sure he looked as if he were doing some kind of weird dance. His face reddened with embarrassment, and his scalp prickled as the muscles contracted from the back of his neck to his forehead.

Nate broke into a smile and began to laugh. Others followed.

Momentarily stunned, Hartman stood gawking at Nate and the others who were laughing. After a moment he regained his composure and turned away. Nate was just trying to upset his speech, and Hartman had played right into his hands. Hartman strained to think of something that would allow him to regain control. He scanned the room and was pleasantly surprised. Most of the leaders were frowning and shaking their heads. They seemed to take the little episode for what it was. Only a few seemed to think it was great fun.

Then an idea struck that he couldn't resist. He abruptly turned toward Nate and in a flash drew and snapped open his own custom made Kasper Fighting Knife. It caught Nate off guard and *he* flinched.

The entire hall erupted in laughter. It was Nate's turn to flush with embarrassment.

Hartman turned back to the audience and raised the knife into the air. As he walked to the front of the room and the podium, he said, "We have formed the most formidable patriot organization the world has ever known. And with this knife…" He paused in his step and turned from one side of the room to the other, holding the knife high above his head. "We shall carve out from this intrusive, power-grabbing, anti-constitutional president our own life, our own true, constitutional government."

Cheers erupted. High-fives spread awkwardly around the room. Not everyone was on board, and a few hands that raised to high five were ignored or even answered with an angry glare. For the most part, however, it was clear to Hartman that his supporters vastly outnumbered Nate's. He felt the warm glow of success and broke into a wide smile as he took the last few strides to the front of the room and stepped back to the podium.

Someone said, "But, Hartman, how long do we have to wait?"

Hartman gave the man a quick nod of approval. This was a question he had asked himself more than a thousand times. He put his hands on the podium, gripped its edges and leaned over it toward the audience. He pushed himself further up and over the podium by rocking his feet forward so he was standing on his toes. "The colonial revolutionaries took years to get going. Had Adams and the others acted sooner, the revolution wouldn't have gained enough popular support. Just getting and keeping men under arms was a problem."

Hartman lowered himself off the podium and stood to its side. "Yet, had they waited longer—the British might have crushed them." He paced from one side of the small stage to the other. "This is the question all revolutionaries have faced: When to act? From Machiavelli to Castro, to Obama, the big question has always been timing: when do we begin?"

Someone else said, "But this isn't colonial America. We have a Big Brother government that has grown from within. Not one imposed from England."

That was a good point, but it wasn't relevant to when they could safely go forward. "Soon we can act," Hartman promised. "The government has grown drunk with its power. Americans all over are waking up. We're so close. And think of it: we have one hundred million gun owners, and 90 percent of them are with us, or will be."

The place was brimming with excitement. Dozens thrust their clenched fists into the air and yelled various versions of "Yeah, baby!" Hartman cleared his throat and continued, "Mark my words. This business of arresting nuns will continue. It will spread. The PC police, this Bureau of Socially Correct bull crap, will not be able to restrain itself. It's a roaring beast, slashing and tearing at its tether, and the rope is starting to fray. And when it breaks free, in all its savage fury, the big federal beast will terrorize America. Then. At that point. It will be time to move."

Several people here and there stood and started clapping their hands. Hartman smiled, stepped off the stage and started shaking hands and chatting with various leaders.

At that moment, the rear doors to the Great Hall burst open and everyone turned to see Leonard Williams come in and quickly make his way to the podium.

Leonard said, "I found a couple of spies in the woods. I'm telling'ya we better do something before we're found out!"

Several of Nate's supporters immediately began pounding on their chairs and shouting, "Screw Hartman! We can't screw around! We move now! This is bullshit!" A few of Hartman's supporters responded by shouting back and, within seconds, all hell had broken loose. A chair flew from one side of the hall to the other and crashed against the wall, knocking into a huge, life-sized portrait of George Washington. The massive painting tilted and then slid down the wall. It hit on a corner with a thud, and crumpled to the floor. A few people began pushing and shoving. Hartman tried speaking above the clamor, but it was no use. His voice was a drop in a raging river.

Hartman looked around. He thought about putting a chair on a table and standing on it. But that would make it too easy for someone to knock him off. Yet, just thinking about what to do was allowing things to get further out of hand. There was more pushing and shoving.

He got an idea. Hartman looked up to the ceiling. It was arched and composed of solid logs. He really had no choice. With lightning speed, Hartman pulled his Glock 27 from his inside-the-waistband holster and aimed it straight up.

He pulled the trigger twice.

The sound and shock waves from two 135-grain COR-BON .40 caliber cartridges were tremendous, even inside the large hall. Several men threw themselves to the floor. Others ducked behind chairs and drew their own weapons. The sound had reverberated so much that no one, except those closest to Hartman, seemed sure who had fired the shots.

There were surprised faces. A few guns were held at the ready.

But there *was* quiet.

Well, that sure as hell worked, Hartman chuckled to himself as he made his way back to the podium.

Hartman had everyone's attention, and in a show of displeasure, he cast his eyes downward and shook his head. "I am very disappointed. We have come to this point—a unified force—because we do things in an orderly manner. We must not get caught up in emotion—even against our enemies. Our response must be rational, calculated, and determined. We can't do that by flying off the handle." Hartman let that simmer.

One by one, men holstered their sidearms. Others nodded in agreement. Most of those who had led the boisterousness looked down at their feet, while others wore pained expressions on their faces. Hartman glanced at Nate, who was still at the back of the room.

The bastard was smiling!

Hartman felt a sudden chill.

Remembering what had started the ruckus, Hartman said, "Now let's go see if these two intruders are spies or just lost hunters who happened to stumble onto our property."

God forbid, Hartman thought, *that they might be spies or government agents...*

❧

JEFF HAD FOLLOWED BEHIND MILES ALL THE WAY TO A SMALL shed some 50 yards from the lodge. It looked to be an old tool shed. The walls were old, highly distressed one-inch by six-inch boards that had warped in the harsh seasonal changes. In some places the gaps between boards were up to an inch wide. Peering between the boards, Jeff could see someone just outside the door. The man was holding an M16.

During their walk to the shed, Jeff and Miles had discerned from the discussions among the gunmen that the man they had disarmed was the leader of this security detail. His name was Leonard Williams, and his buddies had gently chided him about being disarmed and subdued. To Jeff's relief, Leonard did not seem interested in meting out any sort of revenge. He was, instead, rather professional about the whole matter.

This Leonard Williams was more concerned, to Jeff's utter surprise, in questioning them about being spies for the government. Of course, Jeff and Miles explained that they were nothing of the sort. Unfortunately, they had unwittingly shot the deer within a few hundred yards of a very secluded and apparently secret lodge. That alone made them worthy of suspicion.

"What's going on out there?" whispered Miles as he and Jeff stood with their faces pressed to gaps between the moisture-rotted boards.

Jeff said, "Some kind of meeting. Sounds pretty heated—*Holy Shit!* Did you hear that! Sounded like gunshots!"

Miles mumbled something Jeff didn't understand, and he let it go; far more interesting was what was happening in the lodge. He could see only part of it since his line of sight was partially blocked by another log building. It was late afternoon, and the sun was setting over the top of the surrounding trees and the lodge.

Jeff's heart skipped a beat as he suddenly became aware of several people—it looked like three, maybe four—emerging from the lodge. The sun's glare obscured his view and hid their faces. At least two of the men carried rifles.

Miles saw them, too. "What's going on? They're coming here!" Jeff didn't say what he felt: this group of asses was probably going to torture Miles before killing him.

As the men neared, every muscle in Jeff's body tensed. He picked up individual voices, growing ever louder—one he recognized as Leonard Williams. He'd heard talk of "spies" and "government pukes." But it made no sense. What would they by spying on? It was so ridiculous that it didn't seem real or possible.

The men were close now. Another voice sounded familiar but was so out of context that its owner didn't register. Miles started to say something but abruptly stopped at the sound of the men directly outside the door.

Jeff and Miles pressed themselves along the wall opposite the door. Jeff could hear nothing but the pounding in his ears. His eyes focused on the door, which would open outward…

The latch moved, and the door swung out. There were voices, but they seemed muted and indistinguishable. Miles started to say something, but he stopped as the barrel of an M16 appeared. The gun seemed to pause, and hang, suspended in the doorway.

Time stopped.

Jeff knew his life was about to end.

☙

HARTMAN HAD FOLLOWED LEONARD WILLIAMS AND TWO other men out of the lodge. He had been watching the heels of Leonard's black boots as they stepped ever closer to the shed. With every step he prayed that the prisoners were just unlucky hunters who had stumbled onto the property.

There was no question what would have to happen if they were spies; they would be taken off-site, executed, dismembered, and buried very deep in the woods.

Yet, if they really were hunters, how would they be able to prove it? A hunting license wouldn't do it; real spies would certainly take the precaution of obtaining licenses as cover. The absence of wires to transmit signals wouldn't do it; real spies often relied on their sight and hearing to record events. Hartman's stomach turned as he realized it might be impossible to prove their innocence.

They reached the shed and Leonard went in, gun first. Hartman paused to let the other men go in, guns at the ready.

Please be hunters, he thought. He took a deep breath and stepped around the corner—and gasped.

Jeff, Miles, and Hartman stared at each other, mouths opened wide in disbelief.

Jeff spoke first.

"Dad!"

❧

CHAPTER 2

JEFF'S SPIRITS SOARED; IN A FLASH HE WENT FROM BEING sure of death to outright joy. He rushed forward and gave his dad a big, powerful hug. Hartman returned the hug, but without the gusto Jeff expected. Then, oddly, Jeff felt his dad's arm drop to release him even while Jeff was still holding fast. Something was wrong.

Hartman took Jeff by the shoulders and held him at arm's length, as he had done so often when Jeff was growing up and something serious needed to be said—except this time he said nothing.

Hartman finally let go and ran his hand over his face. He looked at the patriots and said, "This is my son and his best friend, and I want to talk to them in private."

Leonard Williams said, "We are supposed to bring them right in."

Hartman impatiently snarled, "I'll bring them right in. Just get the hell out."

Leonard threw a glance at the other men and growled, "We won't be far."

The three men filed out and Jeff started to speak, but Hartman held up his hand for him to quiet. Hartman peered through a wide crack in the wall and watched the men walk over to a picnic table and light up for a smoke. He turned to face Jeff and snapped, in a very harsh whisper, "What the *hell* are you doing here!?"

Jeff blinked. He didn't know what to say.

Miles said, "We were hunting."

Jeff said, "Dad, what's going on?"

Hartman seemed to be calculating what to say. "Jeff, you and Miles have walked into a hornet's nest. These people are none too happy about you being here and…" He paused as if to think. After a moment he lowered his tone. "And your lives are at risk."

Jeff felt a flash of heat rise from his neck and run across his scalp to his forehead. His mouth felt suddenly dry. Their lives at risk? How could this be? What had he and Miles done?

Hartman said, "We don't have much time. You will have to trust me." He nervously glanced back and forth at Jeff and Miles.

Jeff's mind was racing. His dad had just said they might be killed, and he seemed scared. Apparently, there was some question about who was really in charge here. Or, at least, there were limits to his dad's control. What in God's name had they gotten into?

Hartman read his mind. He took a deep breath and released it with a plaintive sigh. "Okay, look, this is a meeting of the leaders from every patriot unit in the United States. The FBI has tried several times to infiltrate, so any stranger is suspect."

Jeff wanted to say that he wasn't a stranger (to his dad), but he understood the point.

Hartman continued, "Anyhow, to get you out of here with your lives, I've got to come up with a story." He paused to think. "Are you two still into computers and hacking?" It was a reference to "The Mother Of All Hacks" as Jeff and Miles liked to describe it.

Years ago, Jeff and Miles had been going to hacker meetings when, during their sophomore year in high school, someone had given them a CD that someone else had pulled out of a dumpster outside an IBM facility. No one had been able to access the data, as the disk was scratched up. Jeff and Miles had taken the disk home and, together, they spent a full year writing a program that finally made the disk readable.

Readable it was; interesting it wasn't. Until, that is, they stumbled into one sector that seemed out of place with the rest of the information. This sector was most likely a remnant of something else that had been incompletely overwritten and therefore no longer showed up on an index of data on the disk. So the last person to use the disk likely had had no idea he or she was tossing in the garbage a treasure-trove of passwords and login codes.

"Have you guys kept up with the latest in secure cellular phones?"

Jeff nodded and Miles gave a reserved, "Yeah... I know it."

Hartman shot Miles a concerned look, and his eyes lingered on him as he continued, "We have been working to develop our own communications system on Apple iPhones so we can utilize all its features in the field. We have some people who were C3I experts in the military; but those guys are a bit close to Nate Smith, and I want people I can trust. You know that stuff?"

Miles frowned, but Jeff decided to forge ahead, hoping that whatever reservations Miles had he would keep to himself until they got out of this mess. He said, "Yes, Dad, we know it. There's hardware and software solutions. Hardware is best, but you have to be able to manufacture integrated circuits. We can do that in relatively limited numbers. It's pretty easy, actually. Miles and I have both made custom flashlights with integrated circuits that do some pretty cool things. Security is a bigger topic; it's more complex—requires a lot more code. It's no big deal. Of course, by itself, software can do a lot, too, but it's not as—"

Hartman cut him off with a wave of his hand, apparently satisfied with the explanation of their knowledge. "Okay, I'm going to introduce you as computer experts." Hartman again paused to think. Miles cleared his throat to speak, and Jeff held his breath. Miles said, "There is no way I'm going to help these racists."

Jeff's heart sank. This was not the time for Miles to have a chip on his shoulder, justified though it certainly was.

Hartman was now staring at Miles, apparently also wondering what to do. Hartman said, "I don't give a damn what you do when you get out of here—ah, except you will not speak to anyone about this. But you are in serious trouble here, and the only thing I can think of right now is to have you two offer your technical skills."

Jeff was having a hard time getting his head around the circumstances. Secure cellular phones were hard to get since the new regulations had gone into place, but they could still be had on the black market, for a price. But, even $10,000 for a pair of phones wasn't that much if you were really serious about it. Surely the patriots could afford a couple of expensive phones. So something was simply not making sense. He said, "Why do you have to get us involved? All we were doing was hunting! Just tell them we're not spies!"

"I'm going to do that, Jeff, but I need to establish your value. Some of the people in there want to cut you into little pieces and bury you in the woods."

Jeff still couldn't fathom what his dad was telling him. "They would just kill us?"

Hartman replied, "If they believe you were hunting and stumbled in here, probably not—at least not here and now. Someone like Nate Smith might take you out later. So, to protect you, we need to establish the coincidence *and* your value. Because you are my son it's believable that you would agree with us and help."

Jeff glanced at Miles, who still looked determined.

Hartman said, "Miles is a little different story. It's a problem that he's black, so it's especially important to establish his value."

This is not good, Jeff thought. Of the two of them, Miles was the one who really needed to show he would help. Yet, based on what had happened in the woods… Jeff turned to Miles. "Miles, you've got to deal with it, man."

Miles's look softened. He was obviously working out in his head how he could justify agreeing to help people who threatened to hunt him down like a coon. After a few moments, he sighed. "To get the hell out of here… *okay*, all right."

Jeff looked to his dad, "Do you think they will believe us?"

Hartman shrugged. "I think so. But don't be surprised if someone watches you." Hartman looked at Miles. "And especially you." Miles shifted uncomfortably. Hartman continued, "Okay, now when we get in there and they start asking you about your hacking skills, for God's sake tell them about 'The Mother Of All Hacks.'"

They both nodded.

Hartman said, "Well, these guys think IBM is the end-all of computer geeks. So, you beat IBM at its own game, and that should establish your *bona fides*."

Miles smiled and Jeff relaxed a bit.

Suddenly there were voices from outside, and all three of them put their faces to the largest cracks in the shed's walls. Hartman said, "Nate Smith is coming." Hartman stepped away from the crack in the wall and said, "Show time."

A second later, Nate Smith and Leonard Williams were standing at the opening to the shed. Their eyes glared with anger. Both had the checkered wood grips of handguns protruding from strong-side holsters at their waists. Nate's gun stood out because it had stunningly beautiful grips: mirror-polished cocobolo with deep red and black grain which contrasted brilliantly with streaks of cream-colored sapwood. It even looked as if there was some engraving on the frame.

Was Leonard's hand lingering over the grip of his gun? Or was it was just the way Leonard naturally stood? Jeff wondered if his dad had noticed. He wanted to point it out somehow, but he couldn't figure a way to do it without being obvious. Instead, he simply found himself staring at Leonard's gun, which was, Jeff knew from his Gunsite training, a 1911 single action that Leonard obviously liked to carry with a round in the chamber, hammer cocked, and safety in the "up" (locked) position, known by the cognoscenti as "condition one." This was one of the guns Jeff had tossed into the woods. At the time, he hadn't noticed that it was in condition one.

Jeff quickly glanced back at Nate and saw the same thing: hammer back and apparently in condition one. He checked his dad's waist. He hadn't previously noticed the rather smallish black grip of a handgun tucked into his dad's inside-the-waistband holster. It was one of those mini-guns made so popular during the Clinton years, when the Brady law outlawed high-capacity magazines. Might as well make smaller guns, manufacturers decided, and it turned into the golden era of smallish guns suitable for concealed carry, much to the chagrin, of course, of the Brady anti-gun bunch.

Hartman glared back at Nate, whose right hand was fingering—almost massaging—what appeared to be a folding knife. Jeff was glad he wasn't itching to go for his gun—or so he hoped, anyhow.

Hartman and Nate were glaring at each other. Nate stopped massaging the knife and he clipped it back to the inside of the right-hand pocket of his pants.

What the hell was going on? Jeff wondered.

Hartman started forward, directly toward Nate, who was standing in his path to the door. Leonard put his hand on the grip of his handgun. For a moment, Jeff was afraid shots would be fired.

Hartman drew up to Nate, virtually nose to nose.

Jeff held his breath…

And Nate stepped aside—his eyes full of rage. Jeff had thought Leonard Williams looked like one mean bastard; this Nate Smith was just as intimidating, if not more so.

Hartman turned back to Jeff and Miles. "Let's go."

Without any further prodding, Jeff and Miles hurried after Hartman. Jeff staggered slightly at first, then his legs stiffened and he moved quickly along. As he passed Nate, he caught a glint of light that must have been the extended blade of the folding knife.

❧

Big Sky News
Missoula, Montana

Ninth Circuit constrains Heller decision
by Tom Bridger

PASADENA, CA – It was a cool summer night in Seattle, Washington, when Frederick Jones returned home to find his wife on the living room couch, naked from the waist down, throat slashed, and oozing life. With her last breaths, Melinda Jones pointed to the bedroom of their 14 year old daughter.

Sounds coming from the bedroom made Fred Jones's blood turn to ice. His daughter, Melissa, was gurgling as though cries for help were bubbling through a severed throat; her bed was creaking and the headboard was knocking into the wall in a quickly repetitive cycle. Fred Jones raced down the hall and recovered a .357 Magnum revolver hidden in a utility closet just outside his daughter's room. He turned the knob on her bedroom door and rushed in.

A year later, Frederick Jones was convicted and sentenced to ten years in prison for using a six-shot .357 Magnum revolver to kill Abdul Saeed who had been granted amnesty citizenship just ten days before. The law in effect prohibited ownership or use of any firearm that could hold more than four cartridges in its magazine or cylinder or fire a bullet farther than 75 yards. The maximum penalty had been 25 years, but the circumstances of the case augured for the lighter sentence. Mr. Jones's appeal was upheld, and six months later, his attorneys filed a federal lawsuit against the state's Attorney General, Rolando Bouchard, maintaining that the law under which he had been convicted violated the Second Amendment as interpreted by the United States

Page 2, Big Sky News
Ninth Circuit, Cont.

Supreme Court in *District of Columbia v. Heller*.

Today, in *Jones v. Bouchard*, the Court of Appeals for the Ninth Circuit ruled, 10-1, en banc, for the State of Washington, agreeing that its "police powers" allowed its legislature to craft reasonable regulations on gun ownership to curb rampant gun violence. In its somewhat obtuse 261 page ruling, in which seven of the judges combined in three concurring opinions, and the lone judge voting in the minority wrote a 67 page dissent, the Court noted that *Heller*, by its own terms, applied to only restrictions enacted by the federal government. States, Bouchard said, were free to weigh the competing benefits of laws restricting the use and ownership of privately held firearms, and so long as the decision it reached was in good faith and abided by the appropriate legislative rules, the Court was in no position "to strike down such a democratic decision."

Jones had argued that the features required for a gun to be lawful (that it hold no more than four cartridges in its magazine or cylinder and fire a bullet less than 75 yards), do not exist in the market or, if they did, would render the gun ineffective for self defense. The Supreme Court's 2008 ruling in *Heller* had found that a ban on handgun possession in the home, as well as storage requirements that rendered rifles and shotguns inoperable for immediate self-defense, violated the Second Amendment's guarantee that the right to keep and bear arms shall not be infringed. In the case at bar, Jones argued, the facts were essentially identical to *Heller*; in both, the laws effectively banned armed self defense.

Two curious footnotes to the majority opinion appear to be aimed at providing additional grounds to support the ruling if, as is expected, the case is appealed to the Supreme Court. In the first, the Ninth Circuit indicated that *Heller* incorrectly read the history of the Second Amendment's drafting, and that Justice Stevens "got it right"

Page 3, Big Sky News
Ninth Circuit, Cont.

when he concluded, there in a dissenting opinion, that the founding fathers intended to protect only the military use of personal firearms. In the second footnote, a rambling two-page discussion about international law, the Court found it "persuasive that the United Nations Department of Disarmament Affairs has proposed exactly this type of limitation on gun ownership."

The attorney for Appellant Jones, Frank Layton Jr., confirmed that his client would appeal. He said that, according to *Heller*, "The enshrinement of constitutional rights necessarily takes certain policy choices off the table." "The Supreme Court" he added, "will see this scheme for what it is: an effective ban on self defense, the most fundamental right inherent in the Constitution."

Wilber Terrapin, attorney for Washington state, said, "I think the court was impressed with Justice Stevens's reasoned dissent in *Heller*, and further agreed that it's wholly proper to utilize the opinions of international bodies to guide interpretation of the Constitution."

Second Amendment scholar and firearms expert, Professor of Law David Couples, when reached at his office by telephone, noted that, "Any gun useful for self defense will of necessity fire a bullet much farther than 75 yards." He agreed that states have a right, according to their police powers, to impose reasonable regulations on firearms. "But what's reasonable," he asked, "about requiring the use of something that doesn't even exist, or if it did, wouldn't work?" When asked about the court looking to the United Nations to interpret what our founding fathers intended when they wrote the Bill of Rights, Couples quipped, "it's worthy of the mad hatter."

<<<<>>>>

Dearborn Daily Chronicle

NEWS FOR ARABS IN AMERICA

Local Police Beat
Two cases of new law in action: offensive acts

by Abdul Rahman

DEARBORN, MICHIGAN — Agents from the Bureau of Socially Correct Activities arrested two Catholic nuns today as they were distributing Christian Bibles at a local mosque. The women, white members of the Sisters of Saint Sebastian, were taken into custody after complaints by members of the mosque that the nuns' activities were offensive.

The nuns were arrested for violating felony provisions of the Religious And Cultural Sensitivity Act (RCSA), recently signed into law by President Jared Wallmire. According to Ragib Ahmed, Special Agent in charge of the Bureau's Detroit office, the RCSA prohibits uttering or publishing statements that offend or oppress minorities.

"You can follow whatever religion you like," Agent Ahmed said. "However, handing out Christian Bibles like this is an attack against Muslims. Under the RCSA, acts of such hostility constitute felony hate speech."

The women arrested were identified as Merideth Polaski, 58, and Susan McCann, 62, of Hamtramck, Michigan. Both face up to seven years in prison and a fine of up to $50,000, Ahmed said. It was not known whether the nuns had retained legal counsel. An African-American nun, passing out Bibles with her white Sisters, was not arrested due to a provision in the RCSA that exempts minorities from arrest and prosecution under the law.

In a separate incident, Bureau agents also arrested two people today for making offensive hand gestures at school children outside a Muslim elementary school last Wednesday. The school's surveillance cameras showed a man and a woman making the gestures

Page 2, Dearborn Daily Chronicle
Local Police Beat, Cont.

from inside a large sport utility vehicle. According to one source who's seen video footage of the incident, the driver leaned out an open window and, in a threatening manner, thrust his arm, middle finger of his hand extended, toward the victims. After images of the attack were published in the Chronicle and other local newspapers, citizens came forward and identified the perpetrators as Jim Gallagher, 48, and his wife Beth, 44, of Canton, Michigan. Both will be charged with violating felony provisions of the RCSA, and face up to 7 years in prison and fines of up to $50,000, according to Ahmed. Jamison

Diegle, the Gallagher's attorney, refused to comment on the case.

The arrests of the nuns and the Gallaghers were met with demonstrations where hundreds of people marched on the Federal Courthouse in Detroit, demanding more aggressive enforcement of the RCSA. Hate crimes against Arab-Americans occur daily, and have increased in virulence, since the Al-Qaeda nuclear attack on San Francisco last year that killed almost one million Bay Area residents.

CHAPTER 3

HIS CAPTORS HAD DRIVEN ONE LARGE SPIKE THROUGH both of his legs. His hands were nailed to the wooden beam. The pain must have been unbearable. And to think that His Father had given him up for this horror...

Nate wondered how long it had taken for Jesus to die. Probably much longer than Nate had been praying bedside on his knees and thinking he was pious for doing so. He stood and rubbed his knees; they'd been grinding on the hardwood floor for a good 20 minutes, and they hurt.

Nate gazed at the picture of Jesus on the cross. He had seen this image a thousand times in his lifetime, and he had never thought much about it. Lately, however, it had begun to weigh on his heart.

Nate's wife, Catherine, had come home one day three years ago with a Bible and a small Christian pamphlet in her hands. They had both grown up in God-fearing families, and both had fallen away from God in their young-adult years—Catherine from the general pull of modern, secular society, and Nate from the senselessness of two bank robbers one sunny day in Lincoln, Nebraska.

Nevertheless, when Catherine suggested they go to a Bible study, Nate couldn't come up with a reason why they shouldn't; and since that time they had both been growing in their individual walks with the Lord.

Oddly, as Nate thought about it, he had been drawn back to God from an event as senseless as that which had pushed him away so many years ago: a bunch of Muslims had piloted jets into the Twin Towers, the Pentagon, and a field in Shanksville, Pennsylvania to kill 3,000 innocent Americans in the name of their false god.

It had to be a false god.

Nate stared at the picture of Jesus on the cross. God had given His Son as the ultimate sacrifice. In return, He asked only that we believe.

Only that we believe!

There was no command for a murderous attack on nonbelievers. There was no promise of victory for one and defeat for the other. There was only the option—the choice, really—to believe that Jesus Christ died for our sins.

The depravity of the Muslim religion was becoming more and more clear. No God would order the death of innocent civilians, and certainly not on the massive scale that was becoming the stock-in-trade of Islamic Jihadists, even if a good number of the million dead in San Francisco were gays and sexual deviants. God had destroyed Sodom and Gomorrah only after he found that there were just four righteous inhabitants in the entire population. San Francisco was bad—but it wasn't *that* bad.

Deep in the recesses of his mind, Nate was beginning to have a sense that, perhaps, blowing up the federal building in Oklahoma City had not been the right thing to do. Revenge could be had—he was still pretty sure of that. But unnecessarily killing innocent people… Well, it just didn't square with the picture before him.

So, what to do about Hartman Kreig, the commander of the American Patriots? The man simply didn't understand the situation. He didn't understand that an inferior race and a monstrous religion had taken control of our society, had diluted our European heritage, and had polluted our minds with political correctness and racial equality. He didn't understand that our societal rush to eliminate race, Christianity, and appropriate discrimination based on intellect and character was the crumbling cornerstone of our collapse into socialism.

And it was that damn Obama who had turned our economy, and with it our entire society, into lapdogs of the government, looking to it for jobs, education, health care, and the permission to wipe our asses with three sheets of reusable toilet paper.

Just thinking of Obama was making Nate angrier by the second... Suddenly the memory of Hartman embarrassing him in the Great Hall pushed itself to the fore of Nate's mind. That bastard had humiliated him in front of everyone. It would be more difficult, now, to regain his leadership position. That bastard was going to pay. And if Nate knew anything, he knew how to extract revenge— big time.

Alfred-P-Murrah big time.

Nate's anger was now in full bloom. His Bible was sitting on the floor and had somehow been pushed partially under his night stand. He reached down to pick it up but a corner caught on the underside of the night stand and it flipped out of his hand and tumbled open on the floor. A three-by-five card slid from its pages. He picked up the card.

The card had come from a Bible study and on it was a carefully written note in Nate's elaborate, Declaration of Independence cursive:

Deuteronomy 32:35: "To me belongeth Vengeance and recompence; their foot shall slide in due time: for the day of their calamity is at hand, ..." kjv

The guilt of wishing to take his own vengeance hit him like a ton of bricks. His mind began to fight with itself, trying to resolve the anger he felt with the words he read.

An idea struck; surely it was from God!

What if God sought to use Nate as his vessel to extract revenge? Indeed, how *else* would God effectuate his desires? Surely, God could strike down Hartman with some accident or disease... But might it be possible that God could implant, in Nate, the desire and the means with which to bring about Hartman's calamity?

That had to be a possibility—even a probability!

The question he needed to resolve, then, was how to tell whether his desire was selfish or from God. After a few moments' reflection he decided it had to be the means. He would know if God provided him with the *means*.

Nate realized he had been standing in one spot for a while, and it was time to get moving. He glanced at his wrist and gazed lovingly at his Swiss watch that made a Rolex look like something from Walmart. On a trip to Paris, after Catherine had inherited her money, Nate had become smitten with the most incredible watch he had ever seen: a $100,000 Patek Philippe chronograph perpetual calendar that could, by means of over 350 dials, sub dials, arms, and cams, keeps track of the actual number of days in each month, even through leap years. The salesman had carefully explained that this watch was unlike all other mechanical calendar watches, which must be manually corrected after every month with fewer than 31 days. The perpetual calendar ran, instead, on a cycle of 1,461 days and needed human intervention only on years that were evenly divisible by 100 but not by 400, or some such. He never could get it straight in his head. All he knew was that the next date his watch could not handle was March 1, 2100. He figured to be long gone by then.

It was two minutes and 36 seconds past seven in the morning and Catherine was no doubt already out taking her morning walk. The sun was just breaking through the trees. He glanced out the window above his bed and decided it was a perfect day to continue fashioning custom ammunition for his main carry gun, a beautifully customized Ted Yost .45 caliber 1911, complete with a black anodized and hand-engraved frame and slide, exquisite cocobolo grips, and every exotic component he could order. He even had a specially forged barrel that could withstand the extra pressure of his hot-rodded (called "++P") load. Nate smiled, thinking about the gun's hand-polished sear and hammer that allowed the trigger to break crisply at four pounds of pressure.

Nate reached under the bed and pulled his gun out from under an old issue of *Shooting Magazine* and slid it into his beautiful, hand-boned, cordovan leather, Mitch Rosen holster. He opened the night-stand drawer and retrieved five additional eight-round Wilson Tactical magazines, renowned the world over for their ability to make even troublesome 1911s feed with absolute perfection. He smiled as he slid the magazines into special leather pockets on his belt. He loved having the best of everything, though in this situation, having the best was essential; it would do no good to find himself with a need to make the gun go "bang," only to have it go "click," instead. On his way to his range, Nate ducked into an outhouse.

Having an outhouse on the property was not unusual in the Upper Peninsula. Having one that disguised an underground room, was.

Nate was pretty happy that he had had the foresight to construct his underground ammunition manufactory and to stock it with sufficient quantities of top-quality Barnes all copper, XPB hollow-point bullets, Remington +P nickel-plated brass, primers, and various types of gun powder to make a quarter of a million rounds of .45 ACP handgun ammunition. He figured he had enough stock to see him through many years of the Dianne Flamsteal and Harriet Blead Ammunition Registration and Tax Act, which outlawed all "cop killer," a.k.a. "hollow point," bullets, barred the military from selling used brass to non-defense contractors, and established a total prohibition on the unlicensed making and reloading of ammunition for rifles above .17 caliber and pistols above .22 caliber.

The only thing odd about the outhouse was that it was larger than necessary to sit on the crapper and do your business. Someone really quick on the uptake might recognize it and wonder. The extra room was so Nate could stand to one side, as he did now, and lift a false floor that opened to a set of stairs wide enough to carry in and out reloading equipment and cases and cases of bullets, brass, primers, and powder. Nate headed down the first several steps and closed the false floor behind him. As soon as the floor closed up he was in total darkness. He reached out with his right arm to the place where he had installed a light switch. He flipped it and the cavernous room blinked up with dozens of high intensity fluorescent shop lights.

Back in the days when gun enthusiasts were allowed to purchase more than 50 rounds a month, they usually kept expensive store-bought ammunition (something like Federal Hydra-Shok or the newer, more effective HST) in their guns and in several back-up magazines until it was time to practice. Then, for cost reasons, they would swap out their good stuff for relatively inexpensive, but much lower-powered, ammunition made in some sweat shop overseas.

Regrettably, this seriously hampered training and violated Nate's first axiom of lethal confrontations: be prepared to rapidly put follow-up shots on target. To do that, one needed great familiarity with the gun's action and recoil. Often in the history of close-quarter gun fights, the ability to manage recoil meant the difference between putting follow-up rounds on target or dying in the attempt.

Nate had seen this play out when he was a witness to a bank robbery as a young boy. The lesson was burned into his mind as if it had happened yesterday…

He had been walking down the sidewalk in Lincoln with his dad after getting ice cream cones. They were enjoying the afternoon when, suddenly, two armed men burst out from a bank and brushed by Nate and his dad as the men ran into the street. They were both carrying what, at the time, seemed like absolutely humongous silver revolvers.

At that moment a police car came to a screeching halt and nearly ran into the robbers as they crossed the street. Both officers jumped out of the car with their guns drawn. The two robbers, now on the other sidewalk, seemed to sense they were in the open and vulnerable; they turned and faced the officers. In that instant Nate realized there would be gunfire. He froze.

The police fired first, and both robbers twisted slightly, as though the rounds had hit home. Nate could see their faces wrench in anguish—but only for a split second, as they quickly recovered and leveled their guns on the officers. Nate could see the backs of the officers; he knew they were firing, but he couldn't see their guns. It didn't occur to him that he and his dad were in the robbers' line of fire.

The guns of the robbers barked and jumped repeatedly and both officers went down…

Nate found himself face down on the sidewalk. He was in a pool of blood, and his first thought was that he must be cut, because it seemed as if someone had turned on a faucet of blood. As he regained his senses he came to the realization that his dad had pushed him out of the line of fire and was lying on top of him. He asked his dad to get off, but nothing happened. He pushed his hands into the blood flowing all around him on the sidewalk, and he rolled to one side and out from under his dad. Then he saw why his dad had not responded. Blood was still oozing out of a hole in his head that used to contain an eye.

Weeks later, Nate learned that the robbers had been caught when they tried to get medical attention for their single gun-shot wounds. Each officer had scored a hit with his initial round, just as it had appeared to Nate, but not with any of the 12 subsequent rounds that each one fired (they had 12 round magazines and their guns held one round in the chamber). In both cases, the bad guys had hit each officer five times, killing both. Only two rounds missed: the one that killed his dad and the one later found on the sidewalk behind where he and his dad had been standing. The bullet had shattered when it hit the brick on the front of the bank.

For years afterward, Nate seethed with anger at the robbers, the two dead police officers, the police department, the county that ran the police department, the state, and ultimately his country. And he seethed at a society made weak by placing these two obviously incompetent (he was sure they were there via affirmative action) African American officers in a position of supposed strength. It was a sickening travesty. The events convinced him that affirmative action did no one any good. Better-qualified officers, he was sure, would have placed those follow-up rounds on target, and the two African American officers, who would probably have been relegated to a less demanding role, would be alive. And his dad would be alive. So, as Nate did the math, affirmative action had killed three innocent people and hadn't killed the two guys who needed it.

Nate shook himself out of the memory and found what he'd been looking for: a box of 3 Musketeers candy bars, a tray of 50 custom .45 ACP cartridges, earmuffs, and an electronic chronograph—a device that looked like a radio with two triangular shaped antenna spaced eight to 10 inches apart and through which one could fire a bullet. The chronograph was used to measure the speed of a bullet as it exited the barrel of a gun. And Nate was looking for speed; he wanted a bullet screaming down range. But he did not want too much speed, which would indicate that his customized load of gun powder was too powerful.

Nate ripped open a 3 Musketeers bar, crumpled the wrapper and tossed it toward a trash can in the corner. The wrapper bounced off the back wall and missed the trash; it landed next to four other crumpled wrappers of 3 Musketeers bars. Nate stared for a moment at the wrappers on the floor. It always annoyed him that he could never seem to make a basket. He turned away and headed up the stairs and out to his group of ranges located in a small, heavily wooded valley about a half mile from his main lodge. He had cleared out a 50 yard handgun range and a pair of rifle ranges, the first at 100 yards and the second at 300 yards. He headed over to a table set up about 20 yards out on the handgun range.

Nate had been working on developing custom 1911 ammunition for one reason: there were only a couple of companies that still had the courage to produce ammunition that approached the pressure limits of the guns for which the ammunition was made. Like most businesses in the United States, ammunition manufacturers were terrified of frivolous lawsuits. This caused them to make ammunition to the capabilities of the weakest gun in each caliber. It was obviously thought that people were not capable of selecting ammunition that was suited for their particular gun. No! No! No! They had to be treated like babies unable to read and reason. Consequently, Nate had been frustrated in his attempt to find a round chambered in .45 caliber that took advantage of the strength of his particular gun. In this case, his barrel was hammer-forged out of an exotic steel that could supposedly handle a several thousand pounds per square inch more than a standard 1911 barrel.

So far, he was getting his combination of gun powders to throw a 230-grain copper-jacketed hollow point down range at an average of 975 feet per second; that generated 485 foot-pounds of energy. With the finest reloading equipment and brass casings, he was slowly working up his load a tenth of a grain at a time. His goal was to get the bullet to reach 1,050 feet per second, which meant that he could deliver over 560 foot-pounds of energy. This was nothing compared to the stopping power of a truly big handgun, such as the renowned Dirty Harry .44 magnum, which could fire a 310-grain bullet down range at 1,325 feet per second to achieve 1,200 foot-pounds of man- or beast-stopping power. And even the .44 Magnum was trifling compared to Nate's favorite gun of all time, the WORLD WAR II M1 Garand, firing the renowned .30-06 cartridge, which produced fully twice the stopping power of the .44 magnum.

As Nate set up on his range, he lined up a firing position that would position his gun immediately behind the chronograph's antenna yet be aimed at a target at the back of the range. Satisfied, he sat at the table and stretched out his arms to bring the gun's barrel up close to the first of the two triangular antennas. He pulled on his fancy new electronic earmuffs that amplified quiet sounds, such as conversation, yet blocked out the blast of the exploding cartridge, and began firing.

Nate promptly put five rounds into a two and one-half inch circle at 15 yards, though it was not without more than a little effort.

"Woo hoo!" Nate yelled. "These babies jump!"

Even in Nate's strong, reactive grip, the muzzle of his 1911 snapped up and back nearly 45 degrees from horizontal—before the brace and spring of his grip pulled the muzzle back to level.

Nate was in the middle of a five-shot drill when a warning sounded on his phone. Wha-da-ya-know! His new security system really worked! The phone, tied into his security system with its several sophisticated detectors that could filter out squirrels and deer, told him a person or vehicle was approaching along the private road to his lodge. It was almost certainly Leonard (in his car). Nate quickly fired the last rounds in the magazine, and the slide locked back as the last round was spent.

Most of Nate's training was conducted as though he were in a fight, where one of the last things he wanted to see was his slide locked back, indicating he was out of ammo—and out of the fight—for as long as it took to reload. So, while his left hand moved to his belt to retrieve a full magazine, his right thumb fingered the magazine release. The empty magazine and the full magazine passed each other in the flash of an eye; the empty, falling magazine, on its way to an inglorious landing on the ground, and the full magazine smartly on its way into the beveled opening of the magazine well.

Nate's left hand slammed home the full magazine into the grip of the gun and a millisecond later his right-hand thumb reached and activated the slide release: the slide raced forward, pulled the top cartridge off the stack in the magazine, and rammed the cartridge into battery. The gun was ready to go, and Nate immediately brought his sights back in line with the down-range target.

From slide-lock to back-in-the-fight: barely a second.

Nate was not in a fight, however, so what came next was not as hurried. His right thumb flipped the safety up to lock the hammer from falling. He holstered the gun, and with his right hand he fingered the magazine release. The magazine slid out towards his backside, and with his right hand he scooped up the magazine as it was exiting the gun's grip. With his left hand, he retrieved a fresh round from his reloading box and he examined it to see that the bullet and primer were seated neatly and snugly in the shiny nickel-coated case. Satisfied, he took the round and slid it into the magazine just pulled from the gun.

Most people hated this part, but not Nate. When he was off the range line it was time to relax, even if it did involve the messy, even unpleasant, part of shooting. He always chuckled when he watched newbies trying to insert cartridges into their magazines; the last couple rounds could be testy. It's a task often not appreciated by those who think it will be cool and fun to go shoot for a few hours—most of which time will not be spent shooting, but reloading the magazines, one cartridge at a time.

And then, of course, newbies are usually stunned to learn that all that spent brass has to be picked up!

By hand.

One shell at a time.

And the brass shells are covered with gun powder residue that gets all over everything. It amused Nate to no end to watch city folk on a serious range for the first time. The looks on their faces when they realize they have to pick up all those dirty shells, many of which are, by now, after an hour or two of walking around and shooting, mashed into the ground and require a finger dug into mud or snow to leverage them out. Yes, those were always happy times for Nate.

When the eighth round was fully inserted, he shoved the magazine back into the gun and again thumbed at the safety, this time to ensure that it was up. Satisfied, he went off to check on his visitor.

Leonard apparently saw Nate, who was standing behind a thick stand of pines along the entrance to the lodge. Nate cursed under his breath. He would have to be more careful when surreptitiously checking out visitors. That damn' Leonard was pretty observant. Nate waved and Leonard stopped his truck. Nate walked to the road and jumped in the passenger side.

Leonard started talking before Nate had pulled the door shut. "Nate, did you hear about yesterday's argument in the Supreme Court on *Jones v. Bouchard*?" Then, without waiting for an answer, he went on to explain that six of the justices had been openly hostile to the *Heller* decision. Leonard had driven the couple of hundred yards to the main parking next to the lodge and were in Nate's kitchen with a fresh pot of coffee brewing before he stopped talking.

Nate sat at the kitchen table and simmered. He had known it was coming. The only question was when. The *Heller* decision seemed ages ago, back when conservatives still had a majority on the Supreme Court. But now, with the Obama and Wallmire appointments, the Constitution was in for a whole lot of hurt. Nate glanced up at Leonard, who was looking at him with an expectant expression.

Leonard said, "Well, what do you think? This bullshit or what?"

Nate glanced at the coffee maker to see whether he could grab a cup. He didn't want to talk about it. It didn't matter to him. He had enough guns and ammo to get where he was going. This would just help his plans, that's all. It was good news, actually. He looked up at Leonard and said, "I've been thinking about Hartman—"

Leonard interrupted, "We've gotta take him out. No doubt. But what do—"

Nate cut him off. "Damn it, Leonard, I don't want to talk about that Arab- and liberal-filled court. We knew it was coming." He glared at Leonard, who averted his eyes and looked down at his coffee.

Leonard said, "Yeah, you're right, Nate. I was just telling ya since you hadn't heard." He looked at Nate with despondent eyes.

Nate grunted and said, "No big deal."

Leonard seemed relieved. He chirped, "So what about Hartman?"

Nate gave him a long look. "Well, I've been thinking."

Leonard looked confused. "What's to think about? The guy's gotta go."

Nate got impatient and went to the counter to pour another cup of coffee. He could feel Leonard's gaze and understood why he would be confused. Until this morning, Nate had been of one mind about Hartman. But now he wasn't so sure. He took a sip of his coffee. Ah... the aroma... a wisp of steam rose from the surface of the dark brew. And it tasted great. Dark, oily beans made wonderful-tasting coffee.

Leonard offered hopefully, "I have an idea, Nate. Been thinking about it for a while, too."

"Yes?" Nate was curious. Leonard was a country bumpkin, but he was not an idiot.

"Let me follow him and learn his routine. I know some people who might do us a favor."

Nate waited for more, but Leonard was apparently finished. Impatiently, he barked, "What the hell are you talking about?"

Leonard's eyes went wide. "Take it easy, Nate. I have some friends who are looking at a couple of banks. Hartman probably goes to his bank. If the timing works out for them, maybe Hartman could be in the wrong place at the wrong time." Leonard took his right hand to his head and mimicked an execution shot.

Nate was stunned. "That's a great idea, Leonard!" Romans 11:33 jumped into his mind: *"Oh, the depth of the riches of the wisdom and knowledge of God! How unsearchable his judgments, and his paths beyond tracing out!"*

This was God showing him the means. It meant his desire to kill Hartman wasn't selfish; it was implanted by God! He felt an immense sense of pride. God was using him. Directly! The implications were profound: he could trust that his desires were God's desires. He excitedly said to Leonard, "What do you think they will want?"

Leonard scratched his forehead. "Not certain. But I did a couple of jobs for them a while back, so they owe me. And if you are willing to pay in advance—" He looked up expectantly. "I know they are hurting for some new stuff."

Nate's excitement was tempered. He didn't like the idea of providing serious weapons to people he didn't know. The last thing he wanted was for bad guys to end up with his guns. On the other hand, this was the means God had provided. He closed his eyes and recited from Proverbs, though he couldn't remember the exact citation, and he made a mental note to look it up and redouble his efforts to commit scripture to memory:

> *Trust in the Lord with all your heart, and lean not on*
> *your own understanding; in all your ways acknowledge*
> *Him and He shall direct your paths.*

Nate said, "Fine. Talk to them. See what they want."
Leonard's face brightened.

✦

JEFF AND MILES DROVE IN SILENCE FOR THE FIRST TWO
hours on the way home from the Upper Peninsula. They had just
crossed the Mackinac Bridge and were heading south on I-75. Jeff
was thinking about developing the secure communication system
on Apple iPhones. He was sure it could be done; he was just as sure
he'd need Miles's programming and manufacturing skills with
embedded systems.

Miles broke the silence. "I don't think I can do it, Jeff. I mean,
help those racists?"

The muscles in Jeff's neck tightened.

Miles continued, "Your dad and the others we met were fine.
I even sympathize with them. I'm conservative, after all. I don't
believe in the nanny state or big government any more than you
do."

Jeff glanced at Miles. "But?"

"I even blame the Democrats for pushing that minority fair
housing crap on banks and then allowing Fannie Mae and Freddie
Mac to bundle those mortgages in securities that they told the market were investment grade. That's what started the 2008 crisis—
no question about it. And everything Obama did after that. And
General Motors and Chrysler. He suckered us; and now, with all the
immigrants we let in, and with ACORN finding voters in the inner
cities, Democrats will never get voted out of power."

That, of course, was not the entire story. Leftists had killed two
Supreme Court justices, and that had enabled Obama and Wallmire
to appoint four liberals to the Supreme Court. Every appeal challenging Obama's qualifications as a "natural born" citizen had been
denied *certiorari*. It didn't matter that his "original birth certificate"
had been shown to be a forgery. Millions of illegal immigrants were
now citizens and on the dole, and several hundred thousand voters
had been "counted" from inner cities based on "estimates" of who

ACORN thought should be there, despite the fact that no one had been able to actually identify and speak to any of these new voters. Democrats thus had majorities in key urban areas that swung red states to blue, and darkened to deep navy the states that had already been blue. In short, Democrats elected anyone they wanted and passed any law they wanted.

Jeff said, "A nation of laws has become lawless."

Miles shook his head in disgust. "I'll never forget the moment when I realized the stock my mom bought for us in General Motors was simply given to the UAW. We lost everything."

Jeff replied, "I'll never understand how he did that. It was a pure violation of contract law. The UAW put little and got the lion's share of the deal."

Miles grunted. "Bastard."

"So it sounds to me like you are talking yourself into helping."

Miles sighed. "Yeah, maybe so…" He shook his head. "I don't know, Jeff. A coon hunt?"

Jeff swore. "I mean, what the hell?"

Miles smiled and nodded. "Ah, mean'na tell'ya." It was Miles's best ghetto-talk.

Jeff laughed, and said, "Well?"

Miles contemplated for several minutes, then finally spoke. "I guess it'd be better to watch the racist jerks from the inside…"

Jeff raised an eyebrow. Miles had just lumped Jeff's dad in with the nasties. Miles screwed his face as if to say that that hadn't come out as intended. "Ah, ah done messed dat up…" He looked at Jeff and they both broke up laughing.

When the laugh calmed to a minor chuckle Jeff knew the deal was done. He took his eyes off the road to glance at Miles. Jeff was fighting off a big grin because he didn't want to make it seem as though he had won and Miles had lost. Miles met his eyes and said, "Yeah, yeah. Don't be so smug. I'll be damned if I'm going to let Leonard Williams and company run around free as jail birds. I'm going to make dang sure we can keep tabs on everything they say on those phones. Everything they text. Every picture they take. Hey.

What do you want to bet we'll end up tracking Leonard to a whore-house or something?"

Jeff shot Miles another raised eyebrow.

"I'm not kidding, Jeff. You watch. That racist jerk. He'll get his prick into some nasty places. You watch."

They drove in silence again for a good 30 to 40 miles. Jeff wondered what it would be like to be African American, to be in Miles's shoes. The threatened coon hunt had been terrifying—insulting—over-the-top racist.

Jeff couldn't fathom it. They had considered Miles an animal that would be *fun* to hunt. Jeff wondered how a human could deal with being hunted. What would the mind do? Would it shun the horror? That seemed an easy "yes." But would it also embrace the horror in order to seek solutions for survival? A tug of war of sorts—pushing away the reality of a coon hunt while also pulling it in to find a way to live…

Jeff shuddered, and he decided that was enough about that.

A couple of huge trucks threatened to box him in and he gunned the engine to get past, swerving in and out of the lanes to maneuver. Jeff smiled. He loved the power of his v-8 powered Shelby 5.0 Mustang. It was a relic and highly non-PC. You had to buy a commercial truck nowadays to get this much power.

Jeff fondly recalled the driving lessons his mother had given him at a local race track in Waterford, Michigan. How to clip the apex of a corner; how to look up the road, trusting your sense of where the car was, when you skimmed past the pylons in a salmon course; how to slide the car through a corner and steer with the accelerator. Jeff picked it up pretty quickly, but he never had the knack his mom had. She was truly a gifted driver. Her father, his grandpa, had once been a BMW club racer who believed his daughter should know the finer aspects of driving fast. Grandpa had always been unconventional like that.

Miles broke his silence. "I've been thinking. We can write the code to send us everyone's private key, or generate a flawed algorithm on certain copies of the program, or maybe have the program cache the passwords and link somehow with the cipher text. We should be able to keep tabs on whomever we want, including our racist friends Leonard and Nate. If something looks as if it might get out of hand, well, we could do something. Possibly avert another Oklahoma City. It's worth it for that."

❧

CHAPTER 4

ANNE KREIG COULDN'T BELIEVE IT. "THREE THOUSAND six hundred dollars! You're out of your mind!" Anne punched the "off" button and slammed the cordless telephone into its base on the wall. Both of her miniature Schnauzers, Cara and Roni, who had been playing under her feet, hastily scampered away, toenails scraping and skittering on the hardwood floor. Anne slumped her head to the counter top. Her heart pounded. She locked her fingers behind her neck. Her nose flattened into the mirror-finished, navy-blue tile; with each breath her nostrils emitted tiny, ephemeral plumes of condensation.

Anne's large blue eyes accented her fair complexion. She stood a well-proportioned five feet five inches, and her shoulder-length, naturally light-brown hair made her a youthful 43. When she smiled, it was wide and friendly. When she was happy her eyes sparkled like blue sapphires.

Her eyes hadn't sparkled in years.

Anne was sitting on one of three maple stools at the breakfast bar of her large country kitchen. Pastel-colored drapery hung gently over the large kitchen window. It had taken years of hunting and poking around summer art- and pottery-fairs to assemble the many contrasting accent pieces, such as the artist-signed navy fruit bowl at the end of the breakfast bar, the hunter green, oversized, kitchen clock with big Roman numerals and a second hand that snapped off each second with big, authoritative movements. The clock hung over a small desk built into the inner-most wall. Delicately embroidered burgundy table linens added the finishing touch as they adorned the solid-mahogany kitchen table.

The kitchen was a cook's dream. A pedestal butcher block with a deep, smooth indentation in its center from years of use stood next to the island that held one of the kitchen's two white porcelain sinks. Above the island hung numerous pieces of copper cookware. Each pot hung on a black metal hook attached to a lustrous brass rack. All of the cookware bore flame and heat marks from numerous Thanksgiving feasts and on-the-run meals. Across from the main sink stood a double-wide stainless steel Sub-Zero refrigerator. The focal point of the kitchen was the massive Wolf stainless steel griddle that could make, time and again, perfectly cooked and uniformly round pancakes (Jeff's favorite meal). Next to the griddle was an eight-burner Wolf range top with oversized, black-enameled, cast-iron grates. Below, running nearly the full width of the range top and griddle, were deep, side-by-side Gaggenau convection ovens. Spanning, and rising above the ovens, range, and griddle, was a huge, stainless steel hood equipped with infrared lights to heat food on racks at its back. At this particular moment, Anne was heating water for tea, so the hood's powerful fans hummed gently in the background.

It was a shame that Anne hated to cook.

In years past she had loved her kitchen. Now, it did nothing for her.

Jeff still happily used the griddle for his mouth-watering pancakes. For Anne, however, there was no "happily" anything.

"What in the heck was that about?" asked Linda Larson, Anne's best friend. Linda was 44 and a registered nurse at the University of Michigan Hospital. Linda's face was full of sharp angles that accented her decisive manner. Her tightly curled, dark-brown hair was medium length and nicely shaped around her face. Long hours on her feet kept her trim and shapely. Linda was also sitting at the breakfast bar, her eyes glued to the back of a cereal box. Linda was a bit of a health nut and she studied ingredients lists and nutritional content with a vengeance.

Anne's head still pressed into the tile counter top. She grimaced and ground her forehead into the tile. It was going to leave a big red mark, she was sure. But who the hell cared?

She didn't.

God didn't.

She spoke without raising her head. "I'm getting screwed. Again."

Linda replied without looking up. "Who? What are you talking about?"

Anne raised her head and touched her forehead. *Oh for cripes's sake.* It wasn't going to be just a red mark. She had dug into the grout so hard her skin was torn like a piece of cloth. It was also bleeding pretty good. She saw that Linda's face was still buried behind the cereal box.

This was great. Just great. Anne's heart tied itself in a knot.

Tears began to collect on the lower lids of Anne's eyes. She grabbed a Kleenex and dabbed her eyes and forehead. She noticed a large carving knife on the counter and stared at its razor-sharp edge.

"Some collection agency says I owe over three thousand dollars."

Linda set the cereal box down, but her eyes lingered on it as she began to speak: "For cryin' out loud, woman. How do you get yourself into these situations? You have the money. How—" She finally looked at Anne and saw the blood. "My God, Anne! What are you doing? You are hell bent on self-destruction. Just look at yourself!"

Tears rolled off Anne's cheeks and splattered on the countertop's glossy tile. They mixed with the blood already there.

Linda got down from her stool and regarded Anne before she stepped forward and put her arms around her. "I'm sorry, Anne."

Anne let herself melt into Linda's arms. *Thank God.* This was what she needed. They embraced for several moments. Slowly, the knot in Anne's chest loosened. She wiped her eyes with the backs of her hands and dabbed her forehead. The bleeding was slowing to a trickle.

Linda seemed to tense as if caught in a conflict of ideas. She released Anne and sat back on the stool. Anne grabbed a fresh Kleenex and began to swab the tears and blood on the tile. She was so thankful for Linda's comfort and strength. Anne sensed Linda's gaze and looked up.

Linda's eyes were suddenly angry. She snapped, "If you ever got up in the morning."

Anne blinked and subconsciously held her breath. A flash of heat enveloped her face and gave the sensation of dozens of little pins pricking her in swirling waves.

Linda went on, "Face it, Anne, you are going to have to get out of bed before 11 in the morning. Or is it later?" Linda paused, scrutinizing Anne. "Do you ever get out of bed before noon?"

Anne got suddenly dizzy and she thought she was going to pitch off the bar stool. Reflexively, she grabbed the edge of counter top with one hand. Her head felt so hot and heavy. She steadied herself and again found her eyes focusing on that big, sharp, kitchen knife. A deep ache rose up in her heart and tears began again to flow. She swallowed; her throat was suddenly dry and sore.

"Anne, I'm sorry. It's just hard to sympathize with someone who can't seem to meet the world on its terms."

Anne grabbed a Kleenex, blew her nose, and coughed from all the congestion of crying. The cough grated her throat like sandpaper. She tried to put some resolution into her voice. "I get up and have a cup of coffee, sit on the toilet five times. A couple of hours later, I'm so sleepy I take a nap. It's not until four in the afternoon that I'm really up. But then, you know, I get a migraine and—" Anne looked down and saw her face in the tile. The reflection was like something in a carnival fun house; the small squares of tile made her face appear twisted and misshapen; the jagged gash in her forehead, magnified and grotesque.

Anne glanced over to the kitchen knife. She clenched her jaw and had the sudden urge to carve jagged gashes all over her *God damned* face.

Anne's mind raced. Everything was a nightmare; no one was on her side; no one really cared; everything always turned bad; it just wasn't worth doing anything; no one would want someone who had already lost *one* husband; she was defective and the next man would eventually discover her flaws and leave…

As a result of this non-stop, internal monologue Anne rarely got to sleep before three in the morning, which meant she rarely got up much before noon—at which point she would start the drawn-out routine that constituted getting ready. In simple terms, Anne struggled to get out the front door before the business world rolled up its sidewalk. More specifically, doctors' offices resisted making appointments after four in the afternoon; the bank closed by five; the cleaners by six. Sometimes, in the winter, it was getting dark outside before Anne was out of her pajamas. And when she arrived somewhere that had just closed… well, it just reinforced what she already knew: *she was a failure.*

Anne glanced up into the mostly blue sky, saw a cloud that looked like a car, and remembered what she had been talking about just a few minutes ago. She turned to Linda. "When I turned in my Shelby GT 300 at the end of its lease—"

Linda cut in cheerfully, apparently glad to change the subject, "I loved that car, Anne. You looked so good in it—though you did get quite a few speeding tickets, Ms. Lead Foot." Linda smiled and sat down on one of the stools.

Anne nodded. There were still tears around her eyes and she wiped them with the back of her left hand. "I was sorry to turn it in, underpowered as it was." She rued the EPA regulations that made its 3.0 six cylinder the most powerful engine allowed. "Anyway, I got a letter from the leasing company—it wasn't Ford—I can't remember who it was."

"Why didn't you pay?"

Anne cleared her throat. "They claimed all kinds of things: a chip in the windshield, a few door dings. I don't know, there might have been some others. I got the letter and called. The man said it was my responsibility. I didn't get anywhere." *And it just proves I'm a loser,* she didn't add.

"So, why do you believe you shouldn't have to pay?"

Anne stepped over to the breakfast bar and picked up the cereal box to see what Linda had found so interesting a short time ago. She tried to read and talk but couldn't. She set the box down. "Because I shouldn't owe it. A lease is supposed to except reasonable wear and tear. They should expect minor door dings and some small stone chips. And the so-called chip in the windshield was nothing more than a tiny scratch that didn't go any deeper than the surface." She shoved away the cereal box, wrinkling up her nose. The new federally mandated format for the nutrition section still confused her. They kept trying to make the information more understandable for the uneducated, with the result that it was counterintuitive for the educated.

"Harder to figure out, isn't it, since the government went and improved the information in the nutrition section… *again?*" Linda chuckled at her own comment. Anne felt a smile try to rise up; and it almost—but not quite—made it to her face. Linda became serious again. "So now there is a collection agency after you? Surely there is someone you can talk to, or some appeals process. Maybe you can still work it out."

That hit a painful chord. The thought of trying to appeal was overwhelming. Her chest tightened. No way would it do any good.

There had been a process, and Jeff had helped by writing a letter that itemized the various charges she disputed. Still, despite Jeff's letter, the agency maintained that its charges were valid and that they had no alternative but to turn the file over to collection. Rather than explain all of that to Linda, however, Anne said, "If I was a lawyer, maybe…"

"And if I was president." Linda rolled her eyes. "Oh, hell, Anne, let's go back and feed your horses."

Relief flashed through Anne's body. "Good idea."

Anne went to the cabinet and popped one of her several prescription drugs. *I'm so screwed up,* she thought, *these damn pills hardly do any good.* She picked up the carving knife.

Linda gave her a quizzical look.

Anne set the knife down and headed out to the barn.

Anne had planted dense shrubbery along the walk which led to the barn that sat behind and to the side of the house. The shrubs had grown to about shoulder height and were pretty good at blocking the worst of the harsh winds that blew across the open, gently rolling fields. It was an autumn day and the crisp, cool air bit into her face. When they reached the sliding door to the barn, Anne lifted the latch and began to pull on the rusty handle. The door reluctantly moved in small, screeching jerks.

Anne said, "Sometimes I'm still awake when Jeff gets up and leaves for work around five—damn this door!" Anne started yanking at the handle. She gave it a big pull and said in a strained voice, "It won't budge."

"But Anne, insomnia is a symptom of your depression, and you won't cure it until you do something. Get a job; go to school; write a book; volunteer."

Anne mused, *if only it were that simple.* She had thought about going back to school, but she couldn't imagine what could get her out of the house every day, let alone out of the house at a "normal" hour. She just didn't want to do anything. Even the piano, her first love, held little appeal. She hadn't played it in months, and very few times in the past several years.

Anne began to put her weight into the door handle.

Linda said, "If you are going to get something done, then you have to act. It's that simple. You are 43. You just have to dig deeper."

Anne held her hand to her forehead, which was ready to burst from internal pressure. This was not the help she needed. She felt so weak, tired, and helpless. She was powerless to solve the current dispute with the leasing company—correction, the collection agency. The nasty man on the telephone had explained that they would be reporting her delinquency to nationwide credit-reporting agencies, and that her credit would be damaged. How could they have such power? How could they ruin her credit for a bill she shouldn't have to pay?

Anne grabbed the rusty handle of the barn door and gave it a great heave. It opened about two inches and then stopped. Suddenly, Anne glared at the door and started to yank violently on the handle, throwing her whole body to and fro. Then, with one extra-hard pull, Anne let out a teeth-gritting, primal scream.

The door didn't budge.

Anne drooped her head to her arms. She still had a white-knuckled grip on the door handle. But she was utterly defeated. With that last effort all of her strength seemed to flow out of her arms and body—until there was none.

Linda moved around to the edge of the door and with both hands pushed with all her might against its edge. Slowly, the door squeaked the rest of the way open. She stood with an expectant smile.

Anne ignored her and stepped into the barn. Linda raised her eyebrows at the slight, and followed.

In the dark coolness of the barn, the pressure in Anne's head and chest eased. The barn was illuminated only by the light cascading in through the tall door, two tiny windows at the apex of the east and west walls, and from an undersized electric lamp fastened to one of the rafters. Straw covered the floor in many areas. One side of the barn contained several horse stalls, and the remainder of the open area contained horse feed, old farming implements, and Jeff's hot-rod dune buggy under a cloth covered with bird droppings. The loft was full of hay.

Anne headed toward the horse stalls. The thought came to her of a scene from a movie, where a bomber in WORLD WAR II got peppered by gunfire until its systems were shot up and malfunctioning. Leaking oil and billowing smoke, the bomber was going down… It hit and burst into a fireball.

How nice.

Anne measured out the horse feed. She hadn't even done this in several weeks, and doing it now only accentuated her lack of interest. She mumbled under her breath, "Poor things would die of starvation and lack of exercise if Jeff didn't take care of you."

Linda was standing somewhere out in the middle of the barn and spoke loudly enough for Anne to hear. "It's too bad you don't ride the horses anymore, you—"

Anne heard Linda's voice break off at the same time she heard a distinct metallic clank. Those sounds were followed by a scream, a thud, and a grunt. Anne stepped away from feeding the horses and saw Linda on the floor of the barn, rubbing her elbow.

"Are you okay? My God! I should have warned you about that knob!" Anne rushed over to Linda.

"My elbow!" She rubbed the bend in her arm, dislodging small pieces of straw and dirt. "It hurts!"

"I trip on that blasted thing all the time. It's always covered with straw. Do you think it's broken?"

"That blasted thing or my arm?" Linda pointed at the metal ring in the floor—and smiled.

Anne shifted her weight from one foot to the other and jammed her hands into her sides. She didn't think this was funny.

Linda chuckled. "I think it's bruised a little. What's it to?" She continued to rub her elbow as she got to her feet.

"It's Jeff's fort. It used to be a fallout and storm shelter years ago. It was actually just outside the foundation of the old house that burned and was replaced by this barn. The new farmhouse—our house—was relocated to take better advantage of the southerly sunlight, or so the realtor told us. Years ago, Jeff and Miles made this into a fort."

"So *that's* the fort Miles always talked about," Linda exclaimed. Then, appearing to be momentarily lost in thought, she somberly added, "I'd forgotten. He always wanted to show me."

Their eyes met. Linda's eyes began to build up a moist, slightly puffy, *I-just-might-cry* look. Anne felt the sudden urge to break Linda's train of thought. Quickly, she said, "Here, let me show you.

I'm curious myself. Haven't been down there in years." Anne hurriedly brushed aside the straw from the wood trap door and pulled on the metal ring. The wood plank door opened with an eerie "creak." The ambient light cascaded just far enough down the shaft to reveal a blanket of spider webs and swirling dust.

Linda jumped back. "Oh no! I hate spiders."

Anne almost smiled. The tough nurse was afraid of spiders—my goodness. Anne walked over to the corner of the barn and retrieved a broom. She shoved it down the darkened hole in the floor and swept it around. "There, sissy." Finally, Anne smiled.

Linda made a face and stuck out her tongue as she slowly crept forward. Ever so carefully, she leaned toward the hole and studied the darkness, apparently in some effort to evaluate the horrible dangers that lurked below. After a moment, she turned to Anne. "Is it safe? That ladder looks pretty flimsy."

Now Linda was getting irritating.

Linda said, "You first."

Anne blurted, "Oh for goodness sake," and headed down the ladder. She'd gone down just two rungs when a thought gripped her: what if she just slipped and fell the rest of the way? It would be so easy. Just let go…

Before Anne knew it, she was standing on the floor of the fort. She couldn't remember climbing down the rest of the rungs. She took one step forward and felt something brush her face. Instantly, her heart jumped into her throat. After a moment of panic she realized it was just the cord for the light switch. Mildly chagrined at having abused Linda for being afraid of spiders, she pulled the cord.

Linda came down the ladder and glanced about. "Well, look at this."

Anne felt as though she had been transported back in time. Inside this "fort," which was actually a 10-foot by 10-foot cellar, were numerous personal items left behind by Jeff and Miles. On Anne's right, above a workbench that ran nearly the length of the wall, shelves were stuffed with tattered softball gloves, hockey skates with rusted runners, and toy models of race cars and WORLD

WAR II airplanes. A pellet gun stood in a corner; a stack of framed pictures in another. Jeff's old chemistry set sat on a small table, and like everything else, it was buried in dust.

Anne walked over to the pictures and dusted off the tops of the frames and picked up the tallest one. It was a framed glossy of her first nightclub promotion. There she was, sitting at the piano—a svelte figure in an ankle-length black dress that seemed, now, just a little too tight. The dress had a plunging neckline but covered her arms to her wrists. She remembered that diamond necklace, sparkling in the accent lights. It had been borrowed, but she couldn't remember from whom. Anne's heart began to pound as her mind raced back…

Anne had excelled at voice and piano in college and, upon graduation, studied dance in New York. A multi-talented artist, she played the piano and sang in a trio with an acoustic bass and an electric guitar. They toured jazz clubs around Detroit and Windsor, playing old favorites such as "Frim Fram Sauce" and "I'm an Errand Girl for Rhythm." Like Diana Krall, who followed her, Anne's favorites were the Nat King Cole classics.

Anne met Hartman the weekend she had a gig at the Bird of Paradise in Ann Arbor. She had gone to a University of Michigan football game on a Saturday afternoon before a performance, and Hartman ended up sitting in the next seat. He was there with a couple of buddies and, as evidenced by his red eyes and cheeks, had obviously been tailgating for some time before the game. As Anne sat in her seat, Hartman turned to her and his first words were, "You're pretty, and I'm drunk." He wore a big smile.

Hartman was social, even amiable, when drunk, and so he was friendly and courteous toward Anne even in his drunken haze. It was a blistering cold day and, perhaps because he had already consumed plenty of antifreeze, Hartman gave her his heated seat cushion. After a little while he offered whiskey from a flask.

Michigan lost that day to Michigan State, thanks to one fearsome Bubba Smith. To Anne's surprise, however, the loss did not seem to touch off any hostile reaction in Hartman who, Anne had decided, was quite cute. Without much forethought, and as the clock ticked down to end the game, Anne invited Hartman to her performance that evening at the Bird of Paradise.

Two romantic months later they were married and, within a month of that, Anne was pregnant. Years later, Anne began to wonder how they could marry with virtually no discussion of managing two careers. Anne assumed that she would simply work her career around raising her baby, and Hartman would continue running the discount copy center he had started after college. Ruefully, Anne recalled, Hartman had talked of opening up several more copy centers across the city. At the time, however, Anne never anticipated that she was a part of those plans.

To Anne's surprise, and eventual horror, Hartman demanded that she do the bookkeeping and handle the administrative affairs for one, then two, and ultimately five copy centers. At first she balked, but Hartman became so angry she feared for the marriage if she didn't relent. So, she tried to make the best of the situation and channeled her artistic drives into the new task. She even picked up a couple of thick textbooks and taught herself cost and financial accounting. But as time went on, she began to long for her artistic pursuits. She tried to do a few weekend gigs but found she was far too spent to perform even close to her potential. And soon, there was so much to do in the business that she often worked a good many hours on the weekends.

Anne loved her son and husband, and she desperately wanted to support the family business, but resentment and anger began to smolder under the surface—and it went unabated for years. Eventually, Anne found herself more and more depressed, and the anger started bubbling to the surface. Her casual drinking became more frequent and heavy. Fights with Hartman became the norm. The marriage was soon subject to the powers inherent in a bottle of vodka.

Anne was startled from her recollections by the faint sound of Jeff's Mustang coming up the driveway and parking on the grass adjacent to the barn. She turned to Linda, who was examining the pellet gun. "I hear Jeff's car. I missed him last night when he came in from his weekend of hunting with Miles. I wonder if they got a deer."

"They didn't. I saw Miles this morning. Though that's all I got out of him. He was in a funny mood. Wouldn't talk at all about his weekend. I was really surprised. I think he said he'd planned on coming over to your house after work to watch a hockey game with Jeff—but he said it in a way that made me wonder if he was going to do it. Maybe they got into a little tiff over something."

"Well, let's get them together. They are never mad at each other for very long. We can make them something for dinner. I rarely have the gumption to cook anymore, but if you come over—"

"That would be fun. I don't have to work until tomorrow afternoon."

"It's settled. Just tell Miles we are making dinner. I've never known either of the boys to pass up a meal. And we'll get them to tell us about their weekend."

❧

JEFF PULLED HIS CAR UP NEXT TO THE BARN. HE TURNED THE key and the big engine quieted, oddly, with a slight shudder. Or was it him? He had been unnerved since the weekend. Several times at work he had gotten the shakes for no apparent reason. And each episode of the shakes had been followed by a pounding in his chest. It was happening now. Jeff put his hand to his chest and felt the thump, thump, thump of his heart. His head seemed too heavy for his neck.

The weekend had been an emotional roller-coaster. There was the thrill of shooting the deer, then the dread of seeing the huge beast die. There was the terror of staring down the barrel of a military assault rifle, then the intense emotion of successfully taking down and disarming Leonard Williams. There was the horror of being recaptured and locked up, then the shock and relief of seeing his dad walk into the makeshift prison. Finally, there was the sobering recognition that, in agreeing to help the patriots and in

PAGE 64 • CAMERON REDDY

scheming to tap into the secrecy of their communications, they were potentially risking their lives. *Oh hell*, he thought. There was no "potentially" to it. They *were* risking their lives.

His temples started to throb. He touched one side of his head with his fingers; the blood vessels in his forehead were pounding. He wondered if this was how his mother sometimes felt.

After a moment's reflection he decided it was probably exactly the way she felt.

Jeff headed up the back steps of the house and heard his mother call. He turned and saw her coming from the barn, Linda right behind. Anne tried to project her voice as she walked briskly. "Jeff! How was the weekend hunting? I'm sorry I missed you this morning."

Jeff groaned. That was the last thing he wanted to discuss. He tried to put on a normal face. "It was okay. I'm starved. Miles is coming over for the Red Wings game. Want me to order a couple of pizzas?"

Anne was out of breath when she got up to him. She held her hand to her chest as if to slow her breathing. Between breaths, she could only manage broken phrases. "Linda and I… were just talking about fixing… something… for you and Miles… The four of us could have a nice dinner… Watch a movie?" Anne took a big breath, her chest expanding way out, apparently to catch up. *Cripes*, Jeff thought. He would have to get her into a workout schedule.

Linda hadn't hurried and came up behind his mother. Linda noticed Anne's heaving and seemed to want to say something. Instead, she turned to Jeff. "Hi, Jeff. Sorry you guys didn't get a deer. Anne and I—" Anne took another big, chest-expanding breath. Linda quickly glanced at Anne and then rolled her eyes for Jeff. "If she ever recovers from her run, or doesn't collapse right here and now—we would have fixed you guys some nice venison burgers." Anne gave her a nasty glare.

Jeff said, "Yeah, we almost got one. Boy, that would have been nice."

Anne said, "Well?" There was an edge to her voice that Jeff figured was from Linda's last comment.

"Yeah, Mom. Sounds great. I think Miles wants to watch the Red Wings, but it's supposed to be a blowout, so maybe he won't mind. If you two want to watch a movie—" Jeff shrugged his shoulders, raised his eyebrows just slightly, and tilted his head to one side. It was his way of saying "anything you want."

Linda said, "Did you two get into a little argument?"

Jeff tensed slightly and hoped it didn't show. "Not really. It was just a long way to go to come home empty-handed."

Linda said. "Oh, I guess so." But her eyes told Jeff she thought differently. Her career had made her pretty perceptive, and she was obviously onto the fact that something unusual had happened. Thankfully, however, she appeared willing to accommodate his reluctance to talk about it. She said, "I'll call him to pick up a movie. Anything in particular?"

Jeff shrugged.

By the time Miles had picked up a movie and made it over, Linda and Anne had burgers on the Wolf range and a giant Caesar salad on the table. After dinner everyone headed to the living room. Jeff decided to catch the early news while Miles fussed with cleaning smudges off the DVD. Jeff punched the TV remote. CNN was just switching to what the announcer said was a previously taped interview.

The picture came up and there were three men seated in a semi-circle. Behind them was a light blue studio backdrop.

"… Senator Kennison, now that we have the Religious and Cultural Sensitivity Act that establishes the new Bureau of Socially Correct Activities under the Justice Department, and since the president just appointed you director of that new agency, what changes do you think will occur here in the United States? Oh, and that's a 10-year term, am I correct?" asked Brett Claymore, the CNN anchor.

Elmer Kennison flashed a smile to the camera. He had been a senator (D) from Massachusetts until a week ago when his appointment had been confirmed by the Senate. He was dressed impeccably in a black suit with a red silk tie that accented his silver hair and heavily lined, square face. He said, "Ah, yes, I serve a term of 10 years. Yes."

Brett quipped, "So we better get used to your face, right, Senator, or, ah, I'm sorry, Director. It's going to take me some time to get used to this." The camera switched to a close-up of Kennison, but Brett could be heard chuckling in the background.

"It's okay, Brett, you can still call me Senator."

"Okay, thank you... Senator."

"Anyway, to answer your question, Brett, I would say not much. Only those who seek to harm the less advantaged will be affected. It's only patriotic to support our president." Kennison wagged his finger in accusation. "We have given a message that Americans are proud and willing to protect the downtrodden from un-American thugs."

"Well, Senator, my question is what type of harm, as you say, are these people protected from? Is a politically incorrect comment—is that harm?"

"Look, Brett, just a few days ago, in Detroit, I think it was, several radicals were distributing hate speech all around a peaceful Mosque. That was despicable, and they were arrested and charged under the new law."

"Yes, Senator, we covered that story. It was handled efficiently. But I wonder if you think that the Bibles they were handing out aren't protected by the First Amendment?"

"Absolutely not, Brett. This wasn't a question of free speech; this was hate speech, pure and simple. It was designed to, and it did in fact, offend and oppress law-abiding Muslims. We simply cannot tolerate resistance by white Americans to the diversification of their society. Christians will have to tone down their offensive sermons and actions." Again, Kennison flashed his broad smile for the cameras.

"Professor Fletcher, your comments on the situation." The CNN cameras switched to Bradley Fletcher, Professor of Law at the University of Michigan Law School. His handsome, neatly arranged face—with crystal blue eyes, light brown hair, cut and parted conservatively to one side, perfectly proportioned nose and ears—were at odds with his slapdash attire. His bow tie determinedly resisted repeated on-camera attempts to keep it from tilting off to one side or the other. The shoulder pads in his olive sport jacket appeared broken down from years of wear—as they unevenly humped up over his neckline. One collar of his badly ironed shirt was intent on breaking free from the confines of the coat's lapel.

"With all due respect to the senator, I believe we have just opened the door to massive assaults on the First Amendment."

"That's nonsense! This was hate speech!" blurted Kennison.

The camera momentarily switched to Kennison and his flushing red cheeks, and then went back to Professor Fletcher.

Unaffected by the outburst, the professor continued, "Senator, I find it stunning that you would characterize nuns passing out Bibles as 'radicals' committing a hate crime. I find it hard to believe that a nun is even capable of hate. In any event, this is an example of what happens when we allow political correctness to become codified into law. It's the most blatant attack on the First Amendment in our history—and we have institutionalized it in a federal regulatory agency."

Brett Claymore asked, "Professor, don't you think it is right that we should be protecting minorities from hostile treatment?"

"Well, Brett, that begs the question of what constitutes hostile treatment. I certainly agree that no one should be allowed to physically harm another. We also have had defamation and harassment laws already on the books that have worked pretty well to protect the well-being of all citizens, white and black, Christian and Muslim. But to merely have a piece of paper handed to you that reflect a different religious point of view… well, first off, you don't have to hold your hand out and take it. But if you do take it, just throw it away. I simply do not see the harm."

Senator Kennison interjected, "Professor, come on. These radicals knew the Muslims would be offended. And that is their crime. And you conveniently forgot to mention important facts about the other situation, where the man made threatening gestures out of a huge SUV, and he and his wife did that to a bunch of helpless children. How can you sit here and say those people should not be punished?"

The CNN anchor asked, "Professor?"

"Brett, and, again, with due respect to the senator, we have started down the proverbial slippery slope. I wonder what's next. What we are doing here is casting aside the First Amendment to attain a result some people would like. This is what totalitarian regimes have done throughout history. The ends justify the means to these people. The United States we grew up in is gone. This is now pretty much a socialist country that is turning pretty rapidly, mind you, towards the dictatorial governments that always come to power when individual liberties are thrown under the bus. Now that there is a far-left majority on the Supreme Court, I'm waiting for the *District of Columbia v. Heller,* which held that the Second Amendment applies to individuals, to be constrained or even overturned. *Jones v. Bouchard* was just argued in front of the Supreme Court and I'm afraid we will see very shortly the end to our right to keep and bear arms."

Brett said, "Well, Professor, I read Justice Stevens's dissent in *Heller,* and it's pretty clear to me that the founding fathers didn't intend for citizens to own dangerous guns for self-defense. Even the United Nations favors prohibition of guns that hold multiple rounds and can shoot so far they endanger bystanders. That's just sensible. *Heller* clearly got the history wrong, as Justice Stevens made clear. But, I want to get back to how you think the Religious and Cultural Sensitivity Act is an attack on the First Amendment."

Flummoxed, Professor Fletcher stared at the reporter. Finally, he said, "This is why people are starting to call you advocacy networks instead of news networks. I mean, did you read the majority opinion?"

Brett smiled but his eyes glared. "I'll ignore the advocacy comment. And, no. I didn't need to read the majority opinion. As I said, Justice Stevens tore it apart. But let's get back to the issue."

Senator Kennison was waving his arms furiously, and the camera zoomed in. He said, "I read the majority opinion, and it's clear that *Heller* was decided by a bunch of right-wing judges and should be overturned, and will be overturned, now that we have a majority on the court." He wagged his finger at the professor. "The United Nations Treaty is clearly the right thing to do. Guns kill people. And little children. And innocent mothers. You would have them all die just to keep a dangerous instrumentality for personal, selfish reasons?"

The camera zoomed out to show all three men.

Brett said, "Okay, back to the issue. Professor?"

Professor Fletcher gave a long look at the Senator and then turned back to Brett and continued, apparently unperturbed by the personal attack, "Okay, prior to this, if somebody uttered words that were offensive to someone, the threshold question was whether the act was a form of free speech—"

Jeff blurted out, "Did you see that? They wouldn't let the professor respond!"

"Shhhh!" Anne protested. "I'm listening."

Professor Fletcher continued, "Now, if you say anything that anyone thinks is offensive, you will be arrested and possibly thrown in jail. And fined an unconscionable sum."

Brett interjected, "It's up to $50,000 isn't it?"

"Yes, it is. It's just absurd. And this whole thing started just before Obama's first inauguration. Some schools banned any speech that was derogatory of then President-Elect Obama. It caught on and expanded to any speech offensive to Arabs, African Americans, and Hispanics. The important thing to remember is the legality of the speech is determined by how the victim perceives it. So my question is, what if a minority walks by a Republican rally and is offended by conservative issues being discussed? Can they call the police, shut down the rally, and have the speakers arrested? How about arresting people in the audience if they nod in agreement?"

Brett said, "That's pretty absurd, Professor." Senator Kennison was vigorously nodding in agreement.

"Really? Is it?" Professor Fletcher paused, apparently to let that sink in. Kennison began an obviously exaggerated throat-clearing. Professor Fletcher continued. "The truth is, no one knows what arguments will be made to outlaw speech, opinions, or even groups that irritate whoever is in power."

The CNN cameras switched briefly to a profile of Senator Kennison, who was shaking his head in almost violent disagreement. His jowls were really rattling. The camera again focused on the three men.

Brett said, "That would cause a stir, wouldn't it?"

Anticipating a reply from the professor, the camera switched to a close-up of his face.

Deadpan, Professor Fletcher said, "It would cause a revolution."

❧

Detroit, Michigan

"DAMN RIGHT!" DERRICK ROBINSON SLAMMED THE POWER switch to the television. There *was* going to be a revolution. That was for sure. It just wasn't going to be what that whitey professor thought. He walked out of the room and down the hall to the large assembly room where African American leaders from all over the country were assembled.

Derrick had mellowed somewhat from his early days as a Black Panther. But his mellowing from militancy was about the same as saying President Clinton had changed from his "I never inhaled" days of draft dodging and free sex. In other words—not much.

Derrick was the leader of this conference because he had successfully begun the new organization, Blacks for Affirmative Action Today. "BAAT," as it was called, had recently come up with a clever slogan, and "GO TO BAAT 4 RIGHTS" bumper stickers were being handed out by the tens of thousands. They were showing up everywhere: across storefront windows, on the sides of busses, across the front windshields of parked cars. It was clear that the organization was taking off and promised to be one of the most successful of its kind.

At this conference of a thousand gathered leaders of his movement, Derrick was to announce that the finishing touches were complete on a plan for mobilizing. Assisted by ACORN's manpower and money, as well as by a bill passed in the last days of the Obama presidency creating the Agency for Advancement of Affirmative Action (AAAA), the plan included the following actions:

» an education campaign that would be instituted in all K-12 schools across the country by William Ayers, head of the United States Department of Education,

» dispatching of legal defense teams to counter challenges to federal, state, and local set-aside programs,

» encouraging African American executives to take a portion of their AAAA pay-equalization supplement to raise more money for BAAT's coffers,

» utilizing ACORN to harass members of Congress opposed to writing the AAAA pay supplement into a constitutional amendment.

Derrick walked into the assembly room and the place erupted in cheers. Derrick smiled and walked down the center aisle to the stage. The applause increased and became deafening as he mounted the stage and walked toward the podium. He stopped at the podium, looked out at the assembly cheering him wildly—waiving ACORN, BAAT, and AAAA flags. He suddenly shoved both fists high into the air.

The assembly hall shook with thunderous applause.

☙

Big Sky News
Missoula, Montana

More Dissidents Arrested
BY TOM BRIDGER, BSN STAFF WRITER

MISSOULA—THE local office of the FBI today announced five more arrests of alleged members of the Mountain Men Militia. Arrested as a result of a grand jury investigation into dissident activities, the men are accused of plotting to blow up the local IRS office as well as the home of a local Democrat congressman. The FBI declined to provide further details, and referred questions to the local office of the Department of Homeland Security (DHS), which is coordinating the investigation.

In a shocking but related incident, sheriff's deputies from Missoula County reported making several arrests and cordoning off an area adjacent to the Capitol Building to protect thousands of supporters of the Mountain Men. The supporters were setting up a public address system when several people, identified by witnesses at the scene to be employees from the local DHS and IRS offices, began cutting the wires, tearing down the speakers, and beating several workers. One IRS employee at the scene, who claimed he was not involved in the melee and who refused to identify himself, told the *News*, "These people are full of nothing but illegal hate speech, so we have a right to shut them down. No one wants to hear what they have to say." When asked why government employees felt it was their place to make such decisions, the IRS employee said, "We have moved past the day when people can do their own thing. The people work for us. Capitalism didn't work—Obama proved that. People don't understand what's good for them. That's why we make the decisions now."

<<<<>>>>

Page 2, Big Sky News
Ninth Circuit, Cont.

HELENA (AP)—Three members of an anti-government group have been arrested on charges of first-degree murder, conspiracy to commit murder, tax evasion and weapons possession, United States Attorney for Nevada Askari Khaleel said Friday. The men were arrested after a month-long manhunt following the death of a school superinten-dent who was accused of rap-ing a high school prom queen. The men claimed that the rape occurred because the school offi-cial believed his religion gave him permission to rape Christians.

Khaleel said the men are members of Unintended Con-sequences, a group which seeks to overthrow the government with targeted assassinations. The arrests are part of an ongo-ing investigation and follow a grand jury indictment in Helena naming Chris Powell, 45, and James Powell, 20, of Eden, Idaho; William Style, 47, of Helena; and Michael Smith, 36, of Bozeman.

Chris Powell is a national leader of Unintended Con-sequences, whose members believe all federal laws passed by the Obama administration are invalid. Powell is a lawyer devoted to anti-government teaching, and Style, a fired FBI agent, leads the Mountain Men Militia, a group affiliated with Unintended Consequences, Khaleel's office said.

<<<<>>>>

NORTHERN POSSE

COMITATUS

Copper Harbor, Michigan

by Annikki Karvonen

Copper Harbor, MI. Concerned Citizens for Representative Government held a meeting today at the local VFW hall. Eino Amslad, President, presented findings that showed the continuing trend of the federal government and Michigan to ignore the plight of the Upper Peninsula and its hardworking residents. Amslad called for members to explore the feasibility of secession from the union whereby the Upper Peninsula would become the nation of "Superior."

Amslad stated that he has communicated with the Ottawa government, which expressed regret for the circumstances but a willingness to pursue advantageous economic relationships with the nation of Superior.

Many Canadian companies have developed new mining techniques and want to open up our copper mines and return them to profitability. The Environmental Protection Agency (EPA) as well as the Michigan Department of Natural Resources (DNR) have steadfastly rejected the new techniques as potentially damaging to local plant and animal species.

Outside the hall, hundreds of supporters carried homemade signs and shouted slogans. One sign read "EPA, DNR—OUT OF OUR MINES!" Another said, "SUPERIOR NATION!"

A number of supporters also voiced concern over the federal government's steady onslaught on our right to keep and bear arms and the federal government's demand that the state rescind its "shall issue" concealed weapons law. "They won't let us open our mines so we can afford to buy good meat, and then they want to take our guns so we can't

Northern Posse Comitatus, Page 2

by Annikki Karvonen

shoot for fun, hunt, and defend ourselves," said Iida Pöyhtäri, one of the supporters. "They are going too far. Just way too far," she added.

Stan Smith, another supporter, also voiced concern over what he called the government's "gun grab." He said, "There is no way me and my family are going along with some treaty with the United Nations. And none of my neighbors are, neither."

We here at the Posse keep reminding our wonderful readers that the environmental and mining regulations imposed by Lansing and the federal government keep our copper mines from becoming competitive. With everything going on, it's no wonder our residents are so excited about secession.

CHAPTER 5

ANNE KREIG SAT AT THE BREAKFAST BAR, PHONE TO HER ear, head slumped between her shoulders. The afternoon sun was streaming through the skylight and shining in a distinct rectangle on the floor's terra-cotta tile. She half-muttered, half-cried into the phone, "How can you do this to me? My car was in excellent condition."

The woman on the other end of the line spoke without emotion, "Speak clearly. I did not understand you."

Anne raised her head from her shoulders and strained to speak more resolutely. "My car was in nearly perfect shape. How can you do this?"

"Your leasing company sent you a Bill of Particulars. You did not pay, so they turned the account over to a collection agency. That agency contacted you on several occasions, and I see here—" Anne could hear papers rustling. *Oh God.* They had a whole file on her! "—that you had one conversation with them. Our records show that you have been provided the documentation required by state law. Your delinquency has already been referred to a credit-reporting agency which, apparently, was not enough to compel you to pay. That leaves us no choice. We have been hired to file suit on behalf of the leasing agency, and we are making this courtesy call to hopefully avoid litigation that will be costly and embarrassing, insofar as your delinquency and this lawsuit will become public record."

Anne said nothing. It was no use.

"Ms. Kreig. Again, please speak up. I can't hear you... Are you all right?"

That last comment had a human tone. It came too late, however. The call was already making Anne sick to her stomach. Her head felt as if it weighed 50 pounds. Anne took a deep breath and tried to summon enough strength to reply. Her voice cracked as she spoke. "No. I'm fine. I'll try to speak up... I don't understand how a leasing company that sends me a bill full of exaggerated damages... now that bill is like some law or something, that I'm a criminal if I don't pay."

"Not a criminal, Ms. Kreig. We will file a civil lawsuit to collect. We are very careful to not imply criminal action, as to do so, in concert with our attempt to collect the debt, would constitute extortion. This is civil, only." Anne almost quipped that it didn't sound too civil to her, but her heart was just too heavy. The voice went on, "—that is, unless you pay. Of course, you have the option of defending the suit in court. You can do that yourself, but I can pretty much assure you that I would beat you. So I strongly suggest you hire—"

Anne pressed "off" and let the phone drop out of her hand and fall to the floor with a crash. Anne watched, without feeling, as the battery cover flew off and the two "AA" batteries bounced out of their clips and rolled in opposite directions on the floor. She couldn't take this. It was a royal screw job. There was nothing to do but pay the bill. She knew that a lawyer worth his salt would want a $5,000 retainer, which was quite a bit more than $3,600 she owed. The leasing company knew its game.

Jeff walked in and sat at the breakfast bar. He was just home from work. He appeared to study her. "Mom, you okay?" He noticed the phone and the batteries. "What happened?" He got down from the stool and gathered the phone and its pieces.

"Nothing. I'm fine," she lied.

He didn't seem totally satisfied with her answer—and his gaze lingered. He put the phone back together, hung it in its cradle, and went to the refrigerator. After a moment, he grabbed his choice for the afternoon, a frosty cold bottle of Bell's Pale Ale. He sat at the breakfast bar, popped the cap, took a long swig, held the bottle out to admire its contents, burped under his breath, and smiled. In days past, Anne would have smiled back. Instead, she ignored her son's bit of comedy, got up, and brought the coffee pot back to the breakfast bar.

Jeff said, "You sure you're okay?"

Anne tried to give him a convincing nod. She really wanted to dump her emotional demons on him.

Jeff chirped, "Anyway, I have a question for you. If the Supreme Court's decision in *Heller* gets overturned and they ban ownership of handguns, would you turn yours in?"

Anne studied her son. How could he be so cheerful? What in the world was there to be cheerful about?

"Hello, Mom, you there?"

Anne was startled. "Oh, I'm sorry, Jeff. I was just thinking of something. What was your question?" She poured a cup of coffee.

Jeff repeated the question.

Anne said, "Where did that come from?" Jeff seemed quite animated, and it struck her as a little odd, at least over a subject such as this.

"We saw that interview with a professor and senator about the cultural sensitivities crap and the professor said the government might try to reverse the Supreme Court decision on the Second Amendment and pass a law banning gun ownership. And that CNN anchor said, 'Of course that's a good idea,' or some such."

Anne took a sip of her coffee. This was all too much. The lawyer on the phone, lawsuits, banning guns... She could feel a headache coming on. "I don't know, Jeff. I've never thought about it."

Jeff shifted impatiently on the stool. "Well? Cripes, you seem so preoccupied today."

"I'm sorry, Jeff." Anne put her hands to her head to relieve the pressure. She doubled down her effort to interact with her son. She pictured her custom Adventurer from Bill Laughridge of Cylinder & Slide, a miniaturized 1911 handgun that had been a present from Hartman. Beautifully made, she treated it like a piece of fine jewelry.

Hartman had taught her how to shoot and had insisted she carry a "big bore" .45 for its stopping power.

And a good thing it was to carry it, Anne recalled with a chill. Twice she had brandished her .45 to good effect: once when she was approached by two knife-wielding youths in a parking lot at night, and once in the store when a young man began to pull from under his coat a big hunting revolver. In both instances, the miscreants had been understandably surprised by Anne's swift draw from a concealed holster. The youths ran and the man with the big hunting gun didn't even have it fully out from his jacket by the time Anne had him in her sights. He slowly put the gun back in his coat, smiled, and said, "Oops, nobody never 'splained it ta'me that way befo." He backed out of the store, one careful step at a time, reaching behind with one hand to find his way. He never took his eyes off the muzzle of Anne's .45.

Anne held the coffee cup to her mouth but didn't take a drink. She said, "No way I'd ever give up my .45."

Jeff's eyes twinkled, and he nodded his head with big, sweeping movements. "I wouldn't, either. Dad just gave me a couple books—" Jeff stopped mid-sentence and his face began to redden.

Anne was intrigued. She sipped her coffee. "Where did you see your dad?"

Jeff appeared to be thinking and Anne got the distinct impression that he was sorry he had mentioned his dad. He said, "Miles and I bumped into him in the U.P."

"The U.P.? What was he doing up there?"

"I think he just likes it up there, Mom. Anyhow, he gave me two pretty interesting books that I've been reading. *Democracy and Distrust: A Theory of Judicial Review,* by a law professor named John Hart Ely, and *Liberty and Tyranny,* by Mark Levin."

Hmm... Anne thought. *That was evasive.* Clearly he did not want to talk about his dad—bad memories about the divorce, probably. Maybe they got into a tiff. *Well, okay. Fine,* she thought. She would honor his feelings. "*A Theory of Judicial Review?* Sounds pretty intense."

"Yes, it is. But it's also pretty interesting. Ely says that the Founding Fathers had good reason to put law-making authority into a legislative branch while refusing to give that power to the executive. And the reason is distrust."

"What?"

"We distrust the executive making laws because it is not representative of the nation. It's only one party, and in the case of the president, only one person. And the Founding Fathers rightly distrusted its, or his, ability to adequately consider all perspectives. And considering all perspectives is the *sine qua non* of an elected body."

Anne made a face at Jeff's fancy language and Jeff seemed to read it. He smiled and added, "Like I said, the guy who wrote this is a law professor."

"But sometimes," Anne replied, "the elected body chooses one group of people over another, such as when gay marriage used to be against the law."

"Correct. The choice it makes isn't the point. That the elected body *considered* the desires of a minority—that's what's important. Even when gay marriage was *not* recognized, some of the representatives were themselves gay, and so it's impossible to say that gay rights were not considered."

"Okay, so what's your point?"

"Well, Mom, it explains what happened to our printing business."

"What?" Anne was interested in hearing this. She poured another cup of coffee. The federal government's shut-down of the family business had started in motion the events that eventually destroyed her marriage and ended in her depression. But how did that have anything to do with this—executive—legislative—consider everybody's feelings—stuff? He was really stretching.

Jeff tapped his fingers across his chin in a wave-like motion he often used when thinking. "The Founding Fathers gave the power to make laws to the legislative and they *withheld* it from the executive exactly for this reason: the executive is not representative. We cannot trust it to make appropriate laws. It's one person or one party. There's not even the pretense of being representative."

"Okay, I buy that. But what does that have to do with the government running us out of business?"

"I'm getting to it. First off, can we agree that the executive branch should not be making law? Its job is to *enforce*—not make."

"Agreed."

"So, how would you feel if most of the laws in this country were made by the executive branch?"

"Well, that can't be. The Constitution won't allow it."

Jeff smiled. "But what if that's what's happening?"

That was easy, Anne thought. "There would be a revolution."

Jeff's smile grew and his eyes lit up. "I can show you that that *is exactly what's happening.* Right here. Right now. In this country."

Anne's face wrinkled in disbelief. "Right," she said. Her son was bright... but there was simply no way it could be as he was implying.

"Have you heard of the Federal Register?"

Anne shook her head.

"It's the official publication that catalogs, on a daily basis, all of the rules, proposed rules, and notices of federal agencies. During President Roosevelt's last year in office the government printed 2600 pages of rules, notices, and proposed regulations. It was 40,000 pages per year for Reagan. Now, with all of the regulatory agencies and new federal employees by Obama, the new rules and proposed rules run over 100,000 pages per year. The actual Code of Federal Regulations, which lists all of the regulations once they are final, is something like 220 volumes."

Anne shook her head. "That's a lot of regulations. But what's the point?"

"Well, the regulations are law. That's the first thing to realize. People, companies, state governments—all have to abide by these regulations. And they are made by agencies in the *executive* branch—the Department of Transportation, Education, the EPA, etc. There isn't even any real congressional oversight!"

Of course Anne knew of the main regulatory agencies, but she hadn't ever really considered that these agencies were in the executive branch of government. This was getting interesting.

Jeff continued, "You might not know it, but nowadays you can't get your kitchen remodeled if any of the paint on the walls is from the 1970s. Well, you can have it done, but it costs $20,000 more than it used to because they have to come in with hazmat suits and expensive HEAP vacuums and air filters to make sure no dust from the paint gets into the air. It's driven many remodeling companies out of business. And that has shut down custom cabinet makers, wood shops, and companies that make and sell wood-working tools and machines."

"That's insane. But it sounds like what happened to us."

Jeff smiled. "See, I told you."

Hmm... Anne thought. *So he had. The little whipper-snapper was getting big for his britches.*

"And get this—the Consumer Product Safety Commission once did a five-year study and published a 101-page report suggesting that manufacturers deliberately build water buckets that leak so that infants falling into the buckets would face less risk of drowning. That was Clinton's brilliance. Fortunately that didn't become a law. But they thought about it!"

This was truly frightening. Anne wondered why she didn't get any of this on the news.

Jeff continued, "Then, once all the proposed regulations become actual laws they are published in the Code of Federal Regulations. And that, like I said, is, like 200+ volumes! That's hundreds of thousands of pages of laws that were written by the executive branch. Not Congress. *The executive!*"

"So how in the heck did this happen? I mean, isn't all of this against the Constitution? Can't someone challenge these laws in court?" Anne knew at least that much. Surely these laws could be challenged.

"Hold on a second and let me get it." Jeff rushed out of the kitchen and headed back to his room. Anne sipped her coffee as she waited. He was obviously excited about this. In a moment he returned with a couple of books and several reprints of articles. Triumphantly, he held up his copy of *Liberty and Tyranny*. "Mark

Levin says it all got started with the 1942 Supreme Court case of *Wickard v. Filburn*. Let me find it…"

Jeff nosed through the book until he put his finger on a spot on a page. He looked up. "First off, one of the main reasons for the Constitutional Convention was to eliminate protectionist barriers that the states had erected to the free flow of goods. The various states were in commercial warfare with each other and the fighting threatened to pull the union apart. The Constitution was written, therefore, to give Congress the power to regulate that portion of commerce that flowed from one state into another. That's *interstate*—as in *between the states*—commerce. And it makes sense. You don't want Ohio enacting a law that says trucks carrying goods into Ohio must deliver those products *in* Ohio. That would prohibit trucks from traveling, say, from Michigan to Kentucky by way of Ohio."

Anne nodded. "Right."

"Importantly, though, at the time of the founding, 'commerce' meant trade. It did not mean manufacturing, or agriculture, or mining, or even retail sales. So, the goal was simply to give Congress the power to prohibit *barriers* to free trade across state lines.

"I'm following you," Anne said.

"The question is, how did we get from *that*—to what we have today, with the federal government controlling virtually every aspect of our economy. How is it that the federal government can limit our shower heads to a specific flow rate, our toilets to .6 gallons per flush, our light bulbs to twisty fluorescents, and so on?"

"I have no idea. My understanding is that the government can do anything it wants."

"Right, and *this* is how it got there." Jeff held out his copy of *Liberty And Tyranny*. "Mark talks about a Supreme Court ruling in the forties called *Wickard v. Filburn*. There was a farmer, Filburn, I guess, and he grew more wheat than was his quota under some federal law. The government imposed a penalty on him and he said, 'Wait a minute. How in the heck can you do that when I wasn't engaged in *any* commerce?' He said, 'Look, none of my wheat was sold to anyone and none of it even left my property. We ate it, for God's sake. And used it for our cattle. And we stored some of it to eat later.' Mom, the court even acknowledged that the— hold it. Let me find the quote in my article… Here. The court said, and I quote, '… this Act extends federal regulation to production *not intended in any part for commerce*, but wholly for consumption on the farm.'"

This is incredible, Anne thought. "So how in heck did the court claim it could regulate, under the Commerce Clause, wheat that was not ever in commerce? It's a no-brainer. You can't do it." Anne shook her head in disbelief and added, "How can the government tell someone how much wheat he can grow for private consumption?"

"By ignoring the clear intent of the Founding Fathers and the Constitution. How else?"

"What year did you say this decision was?"

"1942."

"Hmm…" Anne murmured. "So how did the court justify its ruling?"

"It said if everyone grew their own wheat and ate it, there would be less demand in the market, which would reduce prices, and *that* would have a substantial effect on interstate commerce in wheat."

"Well, that does sound correct, doesn't it?"

"Yes. True. But it would be just as easy to say that having a baby affects the number of people and if lots of people give birth there will be more goods bought and sold—having a substantial effect on interstate commerce. Under this way of thinking, the federal government could tell you can have only one child, or that you must have three, or whatever… See? You can argue that just about any human activity, taken in the aggregate, has an effect on interstate commerce. So, if we can agree that the Constitution was intended to limit federal power…" Jeff let his voice trail off, as if waiting for a reply.

Anne nodded. "Yes, I agree." Without knowing much about the Constitution, she did know it was supposed to limit federal power.

Jeff smiled. "So, clearly, that *'in the aggregate'* concept cannot be the right analysis."

"Unless," Anne jumped in, "your goal is to rewrite the Constitution."

"Exactly."

"So read me the Commerce Clause."

Jeff thumbed through a few pages. "'The Congress shall have the power to regulate Commerce with foreign Nations, *and among the several States,* and with the Indian Tribes;'"

"Well, that seems pretty clear. 'Among the several states.' That's a limited field of authority."

Jeff nodded vigorously. "The Founding Fathers distrusted the federal government."

Anne laughed. "I'd say that was prescient."

Jeff chuckled. "Well, Barry really made that clear." Barry was a reference to Obama's first name—at least the one by which he had been known for most of his early life. "And that's why we *don't* live in a democracy." Jeff really accented the "don't." He continued, "We live in a *republic of 50 states.* Powers not granted to the federal government are reserved to the states. And the people in each state have their own constitutions, where they grant whatever powers they want to their respective state governments."

Anne wasn't sure her coffee was strong enough for all this. "One thing at a time. Let's get back to that Filburn case. I can't believe the Supreme Court actually acknowledged Filburn's wheat was not in commerce, let alone commerce *among* the several states..." Anne paused. This was starting to look like a wholesale breach of the constitutional confines that were supposed to limit the power and reach of the federal government. And it was getting scary. Obama had demanded that everyone *buy* health insurance. So now the question was, what else could the federal government force you to do? Anne could see these wacko environmentalists demand that people take no more than three baths a week. But what if they told you that *you must take* at least two showers a week? The use of water, soap, and shampoo, would have, under the aggregate test, a substantial effect on interstate commerce. So clearly such a demand would be constitutional...

Anne said, "The only thing stopping an administration from going that far is—" Anne couldn't finish the sentence. The fact was, she didn't know what was stopping the Democrats from making all sorts of demands.

Jeff finished her unspoken statement. "Only their gall."

Anne looked at Jeff and he seemed to read her.

He continued. "Their hubris. The only thing stopping them from forcing us to do all sorts of crap is that they are afraid to try. They know they have the *power* to do it, based on current Supreme Court decisions. The only thing stopping them is they know if they push too far we will revolt. And they know we have lots of guns."

Oh God, Anne thought. *This is getting really scary!*

Jeff said, "So this is the case that established federal regulatory authority over virtually all activity—and it opened the floodgates to what is now over one thousand federal agencies and departments that make and enforce regulations. Mark says here that the federal workforce, and mind you this book was written way back in 2009, the federal workforce is nearly two million people with an annual budget of over three *trillion* dollars. And the regulations they produce! Here, let me read one..." Jeff thumbed through another one of his articles.

Anne recalled something Nancy Pelosi had said when asked if the Constitution gave Congress the power to impose a mandate to buy health insurance. She'd said, in her most derisive tone, "Are you kidding?" Now, she was beginning to see what had caused the Tea Party to rise up seemingly out of nowhere.

Jeff found what he wanted. "Diane Katz has a great series of articles about absurd federal regulations. This one is my favorite and was written for the Heritage Foundation. She points out that the Department of Energy has regulations for how much energy is used by virtually every appliance in our homes. And now, she says, the DOE is regulating how much energy a microwave oven uses when it's *not* in use.

Jeff looked up. "You get that? When it's *not* in use!"

"What?"

"Exactly." Jeff smiled. "Check this out:

> … [I]f the microwave oven is equipped with a manual power on/off switch, which completely cuts off power to the appliance (i.e., removes or interrupts all connections to the main power source, in the same manner as unplugging the appliance), the microwave oven would not be in the "off mode" when the switch is in the "off" position. … But DOE revises its determination … and tentatively concludes that zero energy consumption due to activation of an on/off switch would be indicative of off mode rather than a disconnected mode."

Anne said, "My head is spinning."

"Well, just imagine what the manufacturers are doing with this. How do you comply if these morons in government can't even define what they mean by 'off'?' Mark Levin says that most federal regulations are written in exactly this type of dense and confusing language and that it costs businesses over a trillion dollars to read, understand, and comply. Look, here's one I found…"

Jeff shuffled through his papers and held up one titled, "Subpart A." "Get this Mom. Here are the federal regulations on bicycles. It's 11,000 words and there are all sorts of test apparatuses that you have to build to run all sorts of tests. Here is the regulation for grip size. Can you believe this? Consumers cannot be expected to select a bike with grips that fit the buyer. *No-No-No.* We have to have the federal government research this with morons who obviously know nothing about bikes and then write this garbage:

> The grip dimension (maximum outside dimension between the brake hand lever and the handlebars in the plane containing the centerlines of the handgrip and the hand brake lever) shall not exceed 89 mm (31/2 in) at any point between the pivot point of the lever and lever midpoint; the grip dimension for sidewalk bicycles shall not exceed 76 mm (3 in). The grip dimension may increase toward the open end of the lever but shall

PAGE 88 ❧ CAMERON REDDY

not increase by more than 12.7 mm (1/2 in) except for the last 12.7 mm (1/2 in) of the lever. (See figure 5 of this part 1512.)"

"Or, how about this one, dictating the width of the chain guards:

The minimum width of the top area of the chain guard shall be twice the width of the chain in that portion forward of the rear wheel rim. The rear part of the top area may be tapered. The minimum width at the rear of the guard shall be one-half the chain width. Such chain guard shall prevent a rod of 9.4 mm (3/8 in) diameter and 76 mm (3.0 in) length from entrapment between the upper junction of the chain and the sprocket when introduced from the chain side of the bicycle in any direction within 45° from a line normal to the sprocket."

"Now think about that. How in heck can you test that last part? A rod, which is presumably a stick, can't get trapped between the upper junction of the chain and the sprocket when 'introduced.' What the heck does 'introduced' mean? Thrown at it? Shoved in there? And at a direction, oh, excuse me, '*any* direction within 45 degrees from a line normal to the sprocket...' This is all gibberish."

Anne had to admit—it was exactly that. And the product was something as simple as a chain guard. *My God,* Anne thought. *What in the heck do they write for nuclear reactors?*

Jeff wasn't done. He said, "And for reflectors. You won't believe this. Before they test how reflective it is they have to... well, I'll just read it:

Warpage conditioning. The reflector shall be held in a preheated oven for at least one hour at 50° ±5 °C (122±5.4 °F).

How about that? The regulations require that you put the reflector in the oven at precisely 122 degrees, plus or minus exactly 5.4 degrees. Then, after passing other obtuse tests, they finally get to measure the reflectivity of the thing. See if you follow this." Jeff held out the article as if a nobleman reading the proclamation of his Lord:

> "The observation angle is the angle formed by a line from the point of observation to the center of the reflector with a second line from the center of the reflector to the source of illumination. The entrance angle is the angle between the optical axis of the reflector and a line from the center of the reflector to the source of illumination. The entrance angle shall be designated left, right, up, and down in accordance with the position of the source of illumination with respect to the axis of the reflector as viewed from behind the reflector when the plane of the observation angle is vertical and the receiver is above the source."

Jeff ended his nobleman act and looked to Anne. "Get that?"

Maybe the coffee was *too* strong. Anne's head wasn't just spinning, it was whirling like the Tasmanian Devil in a Looney Tunes cartoon. 200,000-*plus* pages of this stuff for everything from the size of bicycle grips to how much electricity a turned-off microwave uses to run a digital clock? It was amazing that America had any industry at all. This was certainly not the right way to run a country. It seemed more like a way to destroy a country. As if a federal bureaucrat knew more about designing a chain guard than a bicycle manufacturer. This was all insane and it was only a few pages out of more than 200,000. It truly was mind-numbing.

Jeff continued, "Obviously, the costs are astronomical. So what happens is—we have all these federal congressmen and women who would be ashamed to publicly vote for these laws—and instead they create federal agencies to make them. And from there, the agencies hire hundreds of thousands of bureaucrats, do five-year studies on putting holes in buckets and on microwaves with a running clock and draft literally hundreds of thousands of pages of regulations."

Anne said, "How many people have even heard of the Federal Register, or could find it if they had, or could read it if they found it?"

Jeff added, "Two notable regulatory actions were the prohibition of off shore drilling and the fines they imposed on coal burning that shut down coal-fired energy plants. Together, they destroyed thousands of jobs and an entire drilling-based economy. And they have driven gasoline and other energy prices into the stratosphere. We've been in a depression or a severe recession since 2008! And there is no end in sight. But here's the problem, Mom: the people who write the regulations are not elected. They are just employees of the executive branch—union-protected bureaucrats who can't be touched, so they develop an arrogance of power. The Fannie Mae and Freddie Mac bureaucrats destroyed the housing market and with it our whole economy and then took millions in bonuses! And look what has happened with the Bureau of Socially Correct Activities. That administrative agency is making its own laws that the FBI is using to investigate and prosecute nothing more than mildly offensive words and even something as stupid as flipping the bird to some Arab. Public employees are making stuff a crime. Where is this going to end?"

Anne hadn't heard about the Bureau of Socially Correct whatever until she had seen that interview on TV with a senator and a terrifically handsome law professor—Fletcher something, she recalled. But, she also hadn't heard about people getting arrested for this stuff. She asked, "People really got arrested?"

"Sure did, Mom. And the investigation was even done without any warrants. No need to go to a judge and establish probable cause by sworn affidavits. No. No. No. Just get a statement from the 'victim' and go make the arrest."

Anne was again stunned. She took a sip of coffee that was now cold. She topped off the cup from the carafe. This couldn't be. Why hadn't someone challenged it in court? Surely—

Jeff had a knowing look on his face. "Remember the law Obama passed a few years ago offering money to state courts to increase the number of judges in state courts? Lots of states refused it, but others took the money. The catch was, if they accepted the money, the states had to establish judgeships that Obama filled with his judges.

With that, and nearly doubling the number of federal judges across the nation, all of which were appointed by Obama and Wallmire, our courts are little more than a rubber stamp for the president."

Anne was dumbfounded. This simply couldn't be happening in America. She said, "That's not right," and immediately realized how stupid that sounded. Embarrassment mingled with anger. At the same time, she was startled by the knowledgeable and lucid nature of her son's explanations. Of course, he was no dummy. But still, this was quite impressive—a surprising show of interest in a subject he had only occasionally mentioned. Anne felt Jeff's enthusiasm rubbing off. She added, "And I suppose it's useless to vote the representatives out of office, because that won't reach the union-protected bureaucrats writing the laws. And we'll never elect a congress willing to dismantle all our socialist agencies. Obama made sure of that with allowing so many millions of Arabs and Mexicans into the country and putting them on welfare with full health benefits."

Jeff said, "In effect, we're screwed."

"We were." Anne recalled the lawsuit that had brought an end to their printing business. A bit of adrenalin rushed through her body. This conversation was bringing her alive even as it was making her dizzy. "You know, I recall your dad saying that federal agencies screw everybody—"

Jeff cut her off and for the first time in memory Anne was impatient to speak. Jeff went on, "I think many people are beginning to see that. There seems to be a growing opposition to government."

Anne jumped in, "I suppose, Jeff; but the funny thing is, I'm upset with society in general. Everyone is trying to screw you. You have to be a lawyer to protect yourself. The jerks out there are smart enough to nickel and dime you, knowing that it costs more to hire a lawyer than to just pay them. It's bullshit!" Anne was glowing inside. It felt great!

Jeff raised his eyebrows.

Oops, Anne thought. *That slipped out.* She disliked swearing but decided, in this case... "Come on, Jeff, you've heard me swear." She picked up the cup of coffee. It was cold again—but this time she didn't care.

"That's not it, Mom. It's been a long time since I've seen you so worked up about anything."

Anne held the cup to her mouth. "Maybe I'm getting tired of getting the raw end of the deal." She took a long sip of her coffee. It was worth it to buy Zingerman's coffee. It was good even cold. She held it in her mouth to savor the flavor.

"Maybe you should go to law school."

Anne spit the coffee all over the counter and started hacking and coughing uncontrollably.

"Mom! You okay?"

Anne struggled to control herself. She put one hand out toward Jeff to signal him to stop and the other hand went to her throat. "Down the wrong—" She was suddenly overtaken by hiccups. Jeff got up and started patting her on the back. After a minute, she finally settled down. She grabbed a stack of paper napkins, swabbed up her mess, and blew the coffee out of her nose.

Jeff sat back down. He was obviously trying hard to keep from laughing. She smiled warmly. It was, after all, quite funny. And, she decided, he couldn't be serious about her attending law school.

Jeff said, "Anyway, you could protect yourself and maybe even fix the damn government. Cause if the politician's don't fix it, someone will fix it for them."

The tickle in her throat was driving her crazy. She forced a cough to get rid of it. Nevertheless, she had strained to concentrate on what Jeff was saying. She was a little unnerved by the implications of his line of thought, but she couldn't quite put her finger on where it led.

Jeff lowered his voice in emphasis, "I was also serious about you going to law school."

As far as Anne was concerned, the law school idea didn't even merit a reply. She was more intrigued with their discussion. She studied Jeff's face. "I didn't realize that you were so opinionated about this stuff." She regarded him for another moment and laughingly added, "Don't tell me you've joined the militia."

→

B EADS OF PERSPIRATION BROKE OUT ON JEFF'S FOREHEAD. He was stunned by his mother's seeming joke about the militia. His face flushed and he turned as if to casually glance around the room. He couldn't let his mom see his reaction. Then, to his great relief, there was a knock at the door. He jumped up to answer it.

Heading to the door gave him the needed moment or two to formulate a response. He toyed with simply lying and saying no. But this was a troublesome issue for Jeff. Up until a few minutes ago, when he had skirted the full truth, he couldn't remember ever having told a lie—to his mother or father. Yet, he certainly couldn't acknowledge his involvement. He had sworn to secrecy and remembered too well the image of Leonard Williams's M16. He was starting to feel a knot develop in his stomach. Possibly, he could just ignore the question and maybe she wouldn't follow up. That was possible. As he reached the door and let in Linda, he decided to ignore it. That was his safest course. Jeff followed Linda into the kitchen. Anne's face was blank. That was good; she had probably already forgotten her question.

Anne looked at Linda and said, dead-pan, "Jeff's in the militia."

Jeff's scalp contracted and he felt a rash of heat spread across his entire head. This time, he knew there was no hiding the redness of the blood that he could feel rushing to his face. He was nailed and saw no escape. The only thing he could do was try to laugh it off. He tried to come up with something—anything—he blurted out, "Yeah, I've even got an AK47!" which was an absurd statement on two counts: one, no true American patriot would favor that Russian-designed piece of garbage, and two, virtually every semiautomatic rifle made was now banned under the new and more expansive Brady "assault weapons" law. He held his arms in a mock shooting stance and made a "ra-ta-ta-ta-ta-ta" sound to mimic firing the gun. Linda broke out in laughter. Anne watched with a detached air. Linda pulled up on a stool next to Anne at the breakfast bar.

Anne said, "Jeff, are you feeling okay? You look all flushed." She waved for him to step closer. She put her hand to his forehead. "You seem a little warm."

He was burning up. With an effort to ensure his voice sounded relatively normal, he said, "Gee, Mom, I might be a little warm. I'm okay, though."

Linda had something she wanted to tell Anne and the two were quickly immersed in conversation. Relieved, Jeff's first inclination was to walk out of the room. He had even started to lean that way when he decided it would look best if he stayed. He sat at the kitchen table and watched his mom and Linda talk. His mind wandered… What would his mom have thought had she actually believed he was in the patriot movement? Much of the country was beginning to embrace the patriots' goals—even if people didn't realize their desire to turn back the Obama-Wallmire socialism was exactly what the patriots aimed to do. His dad had become the perfect candidate for the patriots. Jeff wondered, why not his mother? After everything she had gone through…

Jeff cringed as he recalled how the government had destroyed their printing business and, indirectly, the marriage of his parents. His mom and dad had worked hard, slowly building the business from scratch. The long hours frequently made them irritable. His mom eventually became an automaton. She performed the accounting and administrative tasks for the business—and the home—but without really being there. She was present in body, but absent in mind. Then she started drinking.

The lawsuit. That was the turning point. A tremor of anger swept through Jeff's body. The clinical law program at the University of Michigan Law School helped several people file lawsuits to force handicap accessibility. It was designed as a learning experience for the students.

All five of the Kreig's printing outlets were in tiny rentals spread around the city of Ann Arbor and the University of Michigan campus. The rentals were located above street-level businesses in old apartments no longer habitable under federal housing codes. The spaces in three of the Kreig's copy centers were barely large enough for a high-speed copy machine and a cash register. Ingress and egress were accomplished by long climbs up narrow staircases. The lighting was marginal, the paint on the walls dirty or chipped, and always the carpeting was stained and frayed. But the rent was cheap and the Kreigs passed the savings along to the students.

However, federal regulations had recently expanded the scope of the Architectural Barriers Act (ABA), which had previously required compliance with federal standards by all buildings and facilities constructed or altered with federal funds, or leased by a federal agency, but which now required compliance by all *private* buildings and facilities used in interstate commerce.

For the Kreigs, it was a physical impossibility unless the buildings could be completely remodeled, which was out of the question from an expense and practicality standpoint.

With a bitterness that made his mouth dry, Jeff remembered the most galling thing about the whole lawsuit. During the process of discovery, the Kreigs learned that the law students had *recruited* several handicapped individuals to be plaintiffs.

Jeff recalled the first time he walked through the metal detectors guarding the Federal Courthouse. Armed guards stood along the walls. As he walked, his footsteps echoed down the long corridors of polished tile. There was an incessant clamor of talking, punctuated by the sounds of briefcases snapping open and clicking closed.

Walking into the actual courtroom had been another experience. The judge sat high above, behind a massive, ornately carved wood desk, gavel ominously within reach. He was flanked by court officers and United States flags. Behind was the crest of the United States of America. In contrast to the commotion in the hall, the courtroom was filled with muted voices and careful, hushed movements. Lawyers moved about without speaking and put their fingers over their briefcase latches so they wouldn't open with a head-turning "snap." Knowledge of where to sit, when to stand, and how to talk was solely within the province of the lawyers. Everyone seemed afraid of offending the almighty judge.

Jeff clenched his teeth as he recalled the pivotal moment in the trial.

The student lawyer for the plaintiffs, Cassandra Rose, was a tall brunette with dark eyes and a bright, sexy smile. She called William Adams, one of the recruited handicapped plaintiffs. He rolled his wheelchair up a makeshift ramp to take the witness stand, which had also been modified to allow all the plaintiffs to remain in their chairs to testify. The witness was sworn and turned to face Rose. His smile was confident.

Ms. Rose quickly got to the heart of the matter. "Mr. Adams, what is your physical challenge?"

"I was wounded during Desert Storm. My spine was severed and I am paralyzed from the waist down."

"I'm very sorry to hear that. Were you decorated?"

"Purple Heart."

Just great, Jeff recalled thinking. *What a perfect plaintiff.*

"Are you a student at the University of Michigan?"

"Yes."

"Have you had the occasion to have copies of documents made by process of what has generally become known as a copy machine?"

"Yes."

"Do you own a copy machine?"

"No."

"How is it, then, that you obtain copies?"

"I have to go out to a copy center."

Ms. Rose paused and flipped the page in her notes. "What copy centers do you frequent?"

"There are several along South University. That's a road through a small downtown area that is basically a part of the campus."

"What do you pay for copies?"

"Usually eight cents per page."

"Do you seek the lowest prices available for copies?"

"Yes. Eight cents is the lowest price that I can obtain." The witness put on a mournful look. He turned his head down.

"Do you know if there is a copy center that charges less?"

"Yes," he said, head still down.

"And who is that?"

Now, with defiant eyes, he glared up at the Kreigs. "The defendants' copy center charges only six cents per copy. But I can't use them. They are located at the top of a long staircase that is not accessible to me or anyone in a wheelchair."

The student lawyer smiled and turned to the Kreigs' lawyer. With a smirk, she said, "Your witness."

The Kreigs had hired their business lawyer, Terry Elliott. Despite the fact that he was not an expert in litigation, he seemed, from Jeff's perspective, to do an excellent job. His impeccable dark suits with power red ties, complete with his graying sideburns and side-parted black hair, certainly gave off an aura of professionalism.

"Mr. Adams. My name is Terry Elliott and I represent the defendants. I have a couple of questions for you."

"Fine."

"Mr. Adams, how long have you been a student at the University of Michigan?"

"Four years."

"When you first came to the university, did you then have occasion to have copies made at a copy center?"

Ms. Rose jumped up. "Objection. What the plaintiff did when he first came to the university is irrelevant."

Federal District Court Judge Julianne Stoner looked to Attorney Elliott, who said, "Your Honor, the plaintiffs have made an issue of their purchasing habits. I believe we are entitled to establish whether, and to what extent, those habits have been consistent or have changed. The testimony bears directly on this plaintiff's assertion that he would have chosen to use the defendant's facility if there had been access."

Judge Stoner tapped her pen on her desk for a moment. "Overruled. You may proceed."

Terry Elliott readdressed the witness. "What was the best price you were able to obtain?"

"I said, eight cents."

"No, Mr. Adams. What was the best price at the time that you first came to the university?" Terry stepped closer to the witness stand and put his hands on the wooden ledge. To Jeff's surprise, the witness started to sweat and had to pull out a tissue and dab his forehead. Terry repeated his question and remained perched at the witness stand, his head only a foot or two away from the witness. After what seemed like an interminable delay, Mr. Adams finally answered.

"Ten cents."

Terry said, "Exactly." He turned to the jury and asked, "When did the price drop to eight cents?" Glancing back to the witness, but staying near the jury, he said, "That is, when did the lowest price at which you were able to obtain copies drop to eight cents?"

"I don't recall."

Terry smiled and turned away from the witness and walked toward the defendants' table. Just before he reached the table he said, still facing away from the jury and the witness, "Well, Mr. Adams, was it some time after the defendants opened their facility on South University?" Again the witness dabbed his forehead. And this time he also looked over to the plaintiffs' table. Terry turned suddenly and faced the witness. He spoke in a surprisingly stern voice. "Mr. Adams?"

The witness seemed startled and mumbled something Jeff couldn't hear. Neither, apparently, could anyone else. The judge spoke in an annoyed voice, "You will have to speak up, Mr. Adams."

"I said, about two weeks after they opened their center."

Terry Elliott turned sharply and sat at the defendants' table. He lifted his notebook from the table and studied it for a moment. "Thank you. I have no further questions for this witness."

Jeff knew they had won. He watched the dejected witness wheel himself from the stand. Terry Elliott had just made it clear that their business caused prices to be lowered at competing copy centers.

Their business was a significant benefit to the handicapped even though the handicapped couldn't actually use them. And wasn't it the goal of the law to assist handicapped people? How could they lose?

The problem, as Jeff learned, was that common sense too often has no place in the law.

After three days' worth of witnesses on both sides, the judge ruled that the federal regulations made no exceptions for the possibility that a non-complying entity might provide other, tangible, benefits. It didn't matter that all prices had been lowered to eight cents. What mattered was that the people who climbed the narrow stairs to the Kreigs' outlets obtained a price of six cents. That, as a matter of law, was a disparate impact. The case never even made it to the jury.

The Kreigs had few choices. They could raise their prices. They could provide access. They could spend tens of thousands more in battling the law students through an appeal. Or they could close down.

Raising prices wasn't in the cards. Hartman knew that would just send his customers to the fancy, nicely lit copy shops all over campus. Spending more on the lawsuit was too distasteful. And the landlords had already indicated that they would not contribute any money to remodel since the Kreigs' use had created the problem.

Hartman's only solution was to give up and close down.

And then an interesting thing happened. Virtually every copy shop in town raised prices.

Jeff mused at how the law worked. The handicappers got rid of the odious disparate treatment, all right. And they also got rid of the lower prices. Now, everyone charged 10 to 12 cents a copy. It was a fitting end to a bullshit lawsuit.

Afterwards, Jeff recalled, his dad began to spend more and more time away from home. His evenings and weekends, Hartman told everyone, were for hunting or fishing, depending on the time of year.

Anne reacted differently to the closings. Jeff had thought she might go back to singing and playing the piano, maybe even do a few gigs. Instead, she seemed to retreat from her life even more. Her drinking increased, as did her hostility. Her fights with Hartman seemed to get more vicious.

When Hartman filed for divorce, it threw Anne into such a depressed state she simply stopped functioning. She began to develop all sorts of ailments that only seemed to reinforce her tendency to do nothing.

Jeff heard Linda say something that snapped him out of his recollections. Whatever he had heard apparently surprised Anne as well.

Anne said, "What?" She was sitting straight up, her back stiff as a board.

Linda said, "Then why don't you go to law school? You said yourself that everyone is trying to screw you. Look, we've talked about you going back to school. Why not law school?"

Jeff could hardly believe it. He had just suggested the same thing. Maybe this would finally jolt his mother back into the world. He burst into their conversation. "That's what I just told her!"

Linda seemed surprised but quickly nodded approval. Then she glared at Anne. "First, those law students destroyed your business. Next, you have this dispute with the leasing company." Linda pointed at the telephone. "And now you are going to get sued. A while back your insurance company refused to pay for that diamond ring you lost because they said it wasn't on their records." This time Linda pointed and shook her finger at Anne's left hand, which was minus that beautiful ring. "Remember?"

Jeff wanted to cheer her on. Linda was on a roll. Jeff could see that his mother was listening. He remembered that one about the ring. His mother had sent in the appraisal but didn't keep a copy. The insurance company claimed it had never received proof of the ring's existence or value. Typical.

Linda thrust her fists to her hips and stamped with her right foot. "In all of those situations, had you been a lawyer, I'll bet you could have changed the outcome!"

Jeff was startled by Linda's determination. He began to study her as she continued her verbal assault, complete with animated body English. Truth was, he really admired Linda. She had never made a secret of her desire for Miles to go to medical school, and she had done everything to make it possible. Jeff knew they had lived hand-to-mouth for years. She worked full-time jobs while Miles was in school. During the summers she took odd jobs such as baby-sitting and house-cleaning so that Miles could be with her while she worked. When she scraped together enough money for her own school, she attended night classes and took Miles with her. Eventually, it all paid off. She had a good job and a Bachelor's degree from Wayne State University School of Nursing. And even with going to school and working, she had provided Miles with a stable environment; his high school grades had been good and, at times, spectacular.

Recently, Linda had been on a campaign to get Anne out of the house and doing something—or at least playing the piano in the house. But nothing had worked. Jeff was struck by the irony of the reversal in stereotypes. Of course, Jeff knew that wasn't fair to his mother. She suffered from major depressive disorder. She wasn't normally lazy. But it made Jeff wonder if "disadvantaged" African Americans suffered in the same way. Could it be that the "Race-Gap" was, in some measure, the result of African Americans' depression about society and their inability to get ahead?

And Obama and Wallmire were only making it worse. The new "Great Society" was further ingraining a welfare mentality that was destroying incentive and simultaneously raising expectations. Jeff figured heightened expectations were good, so long as people realized hard work, not handouts, were necessary to reach them.

The more Jeff thought about it, the more convinced he became of the correctness of the patriots' goals. The country needed something dramatic to happen to get people to shake off this destructive pattern.

❧

CHAPTER 6

RALPH MARTENASS WAS AN INCORRIGIBLE NOTRE DAME Law School graduate and football fan who never missed an opportunity to lord the school's prestige and victories over graduates of more pedestrian schools. The widely acknowledged office jerk, Ralph, was smiling and reveling in his latest antics. Just yesterday, in the employee cafeteria, Ralph had succeeded in getting an entire table full of coworkers to laugh with him. It had been just wonderful, looking at everyone laughing, pointing fingers—and seeing the look of anguish on the face of the person who was the target of Ralph's ridicule.

Ralph's target was a new employee with some sort of physical deal that caused his arm and head movements to be really strange. Ralph had never seen such a dork. While eating, for example, the retard held his fork with a bowed arm and slowly moved it toward his mouth while tilting his head and opening his mouth extra wide. Ralph had gotten everyone to laugh by mimicking his odd physical movements.

It was a wonderful time. Ralph just loved to make people laugh.

At other people.

And when Ralph made fun of people, everyone *always* laughed. It was great being the boss.

Ralph was the middle-aged, overweight Director of Fissile Materials Disposition at the United States Department of Energy/

National Nuclear Security Administration. The United States was, by order of Presidents Obama and Wallmire, hastily disposing of its nuclear arsenal by shipping the warheads for disassembly and disposal to the B&W Pantex facility just outside Amarillo, Texas. Ralph was in charge of coordinating and scheduling those shipments and had fallen behind by a couple of months. The heat was on from the White House and, for that reason, Ralph had decided to schedule a few shipments from home.

For the last dozen or so years, telecommuting with laptops and "air cards" had become all the rage for Department of Defense (DOD) and related employees. Laptops were chosen over desktop computers because, in cases of sensitive or classified information, laptops could be locked in a home safe when not in use. And cellular air cards from the DOD had full encryption capabilities.

Unfortunately for the United States of America, the weak link in the chain remained, as had been the case for 25 or so years, what has become known as a "TEMPEST" attack. "TEMPEST" is generally understood to mean Transient Electromagnetic Pulse Surveillance Technology. The basis of a TEMPEST attack is the fact that fluctuations in electrical current generate fluctuating radio waves. Those waves can be read at some distance and then fed into software that can discern the patterns that caused those wave fluctuations.

Up until the mid-1980s, it had been assumed that a TEMPEST attack would require tens of thousands of dollars worth of equipment and considerable expertise. Thus, the government never really considered it to be much of a risk. That changed, however, when a Dutch researcher named Wim van Eck spent all of $15 on equipment and demonstrated that he could reproduce the text from a computer monitor by reading only the emanating electromagnetic pulses (radio waves).

Consequently, for more than a few years the DOD had been concerned about TEMPEST attacks. Fortunately, and at least as far as it is known, no serious TEMPEST attack ever materialized, and as time progressed, and budgets shrank, and as the demand for easy-to-use laptops increased, the risks started to look smaller, while the solution started to look more and more expensive.

It turns out that virtually every component of a computer emits telltale electromagnetic pulses. Monitors, keyboards, and even the wiring in and outside the computer are all ripe for attack. Research began to show that even running a "red" wire, meaning a wire carrying classified information, next to a "black" wire, one which does not carry classified information but which is exposed to the outside world, ran the risk of giving off—to the black wire—readable electromagnetic pulses that could be exploited. So, quite unfortunately, the task of separating all red and black wires, and shielding each and every component, began to be seen as a $500 dollar solution to a 50 cent problem.

The DOD's 50 cent solution was to deal with potential TEMPEST issues in the same way that it dealt with terrorist IED (Improvised Explosive Device) threats: with space and distance. Except in rare cases, all classified processing was to be performed in a fenced and patrolled installation. Only very senior folks such as the Director of the CIA, the Secretary of Defense, the Director of the National Security Agency, and the war fighter in theatre, were supposed to perform classified processing off-installation.

Today, however, Ralph was at home; and while he regretted missing out on making more fun of the new dork, he couldn't wait to get a bit of work out of the way, including scheduling a couple of shipments that were over 60 days late, and head out to his private golf club. The forecast was for sun and he couldn't wait to try out his new Callaway driver.

What Ralph didn't realize, primarily because he had not paid attention during any of the security training seminars and briefings, was that TEMPEST surveillance devices had advanced in the last 25 years and were now much more sensitive and sophisticated than Wim van Eck's $15 toy.

⭮

Big Sky News
Missoula, Montana

Wallmire Fills Ranks of Domestic Defense Force
by Tom Bridger, BSN Staff Writer

Washington, d.c.—President Jared Wallmire today announced activation of the Domestic Defense Force (DDF), the outlines of which were created during the Obama presidency. Diya al Din Wasem, Director of the White House Military Office (WHMO), commands what will be a force of 1,250,000 men and women soldiers when fully equipped sometime late next year. Congress has placed the DDF on an equal footing with the other branches of the military in obtaining the latest military technologies to the extent such are relevant to, and necessary for, its mission of fighting domestic terrorists. It is not expected, for example, that the ddf will have a need for b2 long-range bombers, aircraft carriers, or intercontinental ballistic missiles.

Controversy had surrounded the issue of who would fill the ranks of this military force. Some Democrats wanted soldiers from the United Nations, while others, backed by the Wallmire administration, wanted to utilize a portion of the millions of formerly illegal aliens who have been granted amnesty over the past several years but who have found integration into American society difficult. A compromise was reached earlier this year whereby the officers will be provided by the United Nations and the enlisted soldiers will be supplied by a lottery system from government records of formerly illegal immigrants. Preference will be given to Arabs, as they represent the smaller percentage of the population and, according to sources,

Page 2, Big Sky News
Wallmire Fills Ranks of Domestic Defense Force Cont.

will be most willing to carry out actions against natural born, white Americans.

It remains an open question how hastily trained, virtually uneducated, Spanish-only and Arab-only speaking, formerly illegal immigrants can be expected to cooperate as well as operate the vast range of complicated weapons, communications, and transportation systems they will be given. Since the only reporters given access to the president are from the advocacy networks, this question has not been asked.

<<<<>>>>

CHAPTER 7

ANNE FOUND HER FAVORITE JEANS IN A PILE OF DIRTY clothes, and she cursed herself for again neglecting the laundry. It took some rummaging through her closet but she finally found a clean pair of black stretch pants. She slipped them on and looked in the full-length mirror that hung on the inside of the closet door.

The panty lines were just not going to do.

She stripped off the pants and the panties and tossed the latter into the overflowing dirty clothes basket... Well, there was a basket under there *somewhere*. She turned her back to the mirror and frowned.

Oh, things were nice and curvy all right. Curves around a freaking mountain, she rued.

She glanced at the pile and saw what she wanted: just peeking out from the pile, near the bottom, was the yellow sleeve to a favorite black and yellow Spandex tank. She pulled on the sleeve and, to add insult to injury, the rest of the top remained firmly buried under the cumulative weight of the pile. *What the hell*, she thought, as the sleeve stretched and stretched, doubling in length to a long, thin tube... Finally, just when she thought she might tear a seam, the rest of the top finally snapped out like a rubber band, bouncing a couple times in her hand as it resumed its original shape.

She gritted her teeth and furrowed her brow. This was really unacceptable.

Turning around, she held the tank in front of her naked torso and looked in the mirror, debating whether to wear a bra. Her breasts were still quite firm, *thank God*, and rode high and proud, even if they were a bit small.

But at the moment they were also broadcasting the temperature. She'd need her "No one will know it's there" bra from Victoria's Secret.

She looked at the huge pile and the muscles across her forehead went taut. That bra was in *there*.

Screw it. She was just going to pick up some information. No one would recognize her anyway.

A woman on the phone had told her that a copy of the LSAT/LSDAS (Law School Admissions Test/Law School Data Assembly Service) information packet could be picked up in the admissions office at the University of Michigan Law School, so she put her hair into one of Jeff's baseball hats, with a ponytail out the back, and headed downtown.

The University of Michigan Law School is the "Ivy League" of the Midwest. Consisting of two massive structures, the original quadrangle completed in 1933, and a new commons and classroom building completed in 2011, the buildings are densely covered in ivy and exhibit Gothic, Tudor, and Elizabethan architectural influences. The original William Cook Law Quadrangle, known as simply "The Quad" by law students, consists of a Legal Research Library which houses over one million volumes; the Reading Room with 50-foot ceilings and full-length stained glass windows; Hutchins Hall, home to the classrooms and administrative offices; the Dining Hall; the Lawyers Club; and student dormitories, many of which have massive stone fireplaces. The exteriors of all the buildings are intricately detailed in seam-faced granite and Indiana limestone. Indeed, to make the 2011 building match the 1933 Quad, the quarry for the original limestone had to be reopened to obtain stone of the exact color and texture. Slabs of heavy slate in various sizes cover the steeply pitched roofs.

Stepping inside the main entrance to the Quad, one is awed by the arched junction of three corridors, rising a full two stories. Voices reverberate and heel strikes ring out with biting sharpness, their sounds echoing and then decaying as they are lost in the high ceilings and long hallways. Inscriptions adorn the walls: *Honeste vivere alterum non laedere suum cuique tribuere* and *Fiat justitia ruat coelum,* exhort law students "To live honestly; to not harm another; to give to each his due," and to "Let justice be done though the heavens fall."

Yet the intimidating aura is broken up with humorous (some say Satanic) gargoyles and painted glass windows depicting oddities such as two football players under whom the word "mayhem" appears. Interestingly, "mayhem" is defined by the American Heritage Dictionary as, "A state of violent disorder or riotous confusion…" and so the meaning arguably applies to the game of football *and* the law.

Slate walks crisscross the inner courtyard of the Quad, where some of the nation's brightest students relax in the sun or hurriedly rush off to class with extra-thick law texts under one arm, and sometimes even both!

As Anne drove up State Street, on which part of the Quad sits, she noticed, with frustration, that the Fall Art Fair was in full swing. Famous throughout the Midwest, the Ann Arbor Summer Art Fairs attract thousands of shoppers and hundreds of artists, whose display booths clog the entire downtown. The newly established Fall Art Fair was quickly developing a similar reputation. With the grimace typical of "townies," who grudgingly endure this overrunning of the city, Anne realized that she would not be able to park close to the law school. She smiled as she recalled the famous poster that politely claims, "Welcome to the Art Fair!" while below that heading, all manner of crudely made signs proclaim, "No Art Fair parking!"

The battle over parking always cracked Anne up. It was a much-beloved Ann Arbor tradition.

One mile away was the closest Anne could get to the law school. She squeezed into a parallel spot on one of Ann Arbor's numerous one-way streets. The surrounding area was full of homes from the 1930s and 1940s. Some of them were run down for her taste, but were probably considered great by the students who were glad to be away from their parents. Stepping up to the curb, Anne walked around an old, tattered couch some student had decided he or she no longer needed in the house.

It was a bright and warm October day; as she got closer to the downtown and the law school she noticed more and more of the weirdos, or "pinheads," as she preferred to call them, who always seemed to come out of the woodwork during Art Fair weeks. Dressed in a strange mix of 60's psychedelic and the latest craze of wearing pants with the waist down around the bottom of the butt cheeks, most of them looked as if they had fallen out of an airplane and landed, face first, into a jewelry store.

Walking up Liberty Street, Anne stopped at a bookstore to relax with a cappuccino and take a quick look at the *New York Times* bestsellers. She pushed past the crowd around the front door and headed toward the back of the store, where stairs led to the second floor and a deli. She passed the display of bestsellers; none looked familiar.

Upstairs, waiting in line at the deli counter, Anne noticed that all the employees behind the counter had apparently fallen out of the same plane and into the same jewelry store. The man who took her order had a ring the diameter of a 50-cent piece in each nostril. Anne was afraid to look too closely—just in case he was not particular about hygiene. She didn't even look at him when he handed her the double cap and her change. She just turned and made her way to a nearby table.

She sat at small table and recalled the excitement she used to feel when she came downtown to this spot when it was a Borders Bookstore. Then, she often experienced a sense of wonderment and exploration; she often took the stairs to the deli two at a time, so anxious was she to get her deli drink and browse the shelves or just sit and watch the intelligentsia of Ann Arbor mill about with their learned book selections and exotic coffee drinks.

Today, she felt no such enthusiasm.

Anne sighed, resigned to her new reality; depression took the enjoyment out of anything and everything. She finished her drink and headed downstairs. As she passed a table with books spread out in neat piles one caught her attention. She picked it up. *"Learning To Tell Myself The Truth"* by William Backus. It was a six-week guide to freedom from anger, anxiety, depression, and perfectionism. *Hmm...* she wondered. It couldn't hurt. She bought it and headed back out to Liberty Street. A beggar aggressively stepped right in her face and asked for change. Anne looked him in the eye and sidestepped past. How could he work so hard at begging and yet not get a job?

Anne turned right on State Street and crossed over to the "Diag," which is a walkway that cuts, obviously, diagonally across Center Campus. It was slightly out of the way to the law school, but she hadn't been through there in years, and she wanted some time to think. She needed to figure out what in the hell she was doing.

A few things came to mind. For one, she was mighty pissed about that impending lawsuit over her car. She wanted to shove those suit papers right down that lawyer's throat. Another big thing was the disappointment she felt over what she had done, or more precisely, not done, with her once-promising artistic career. And there was, of course, the tremendous regret for the drinking and all that followed, with the attending effect on her son. Anne's stomach turned, and her head suddenly felt heavy. She stopped walking and leaned against a nearby tree for fear of toppling over.

So, why was she heading to the law school? Was it out of a desire to study the law? That was possible. The law did seem interesting— and wouldn't it be something if her mind were again opening up to new desires and interests?

A young couple passed by going in the opposite direction. They were holding hands and ogling each other. They seemed in a hurry. Young lovers in a rush... probably headed to one or the other's dorm room. Anne sighed, and walked on.

She got closer to the center of the Diag and had to thread and even push her way past a student rally for affirmative action. "GO TO BAAT FOR RIGHTS" bumper stickers were being handed out by a group calling themselves "Blacks for Affirmative Action Today." She remembered seeing something on TV about them. And, come to think of it, Jeff had even mentioned the organization.

That was odd.

Anne passed the Graduate Library and turned toward the Law School. She rounded a corner and there, across the street, the facade of the Law School suddenly appeared. Anne stopped and quickly drew her hand to her mouth. A shiver ran down her spine.

Anne had passed by the Law School hundreds of times. But here, now, from this angle of view, under these circumstances, it suddenly had a power she could feel. Its massive and magnificent architecture took her breath away. Here was something so majestic it brought forth a sense of intrigue, of mystery. Anne felt drawn to the school as if by magnetic force.

She headed across the street with a jump in her step.

❧

JEFF AND MILES WERE DRIVING TO DOWNTOWN ANN ARBOR to meet with Hartman to discuss details of creating and implementing a secure communication system. Jeff didn't yet fully understand what Hartman wanted the iPhones to do, and he and Miles had to know at least that before they could even begin planning and writing software.

Jeff finally found a parking spot about a half mile from Sweetwaters Cafe, one of the very popular exotic coffee and cappuccino hangouts in Ann Arbor. Hardly a word had been spoken on the drive into town, and now they walked in silence. Clearly, Miles was not totally comfortable with getting involved and utilizing his electronic and programing skills for people who had wanted to hunt him down like an animal.

Inside Sweetwaters, paintings, sketches, and some excellent photography, all from local artists, adorned sandblasted, red-brick walls. With a white maple floor and black wooden tables and chairs, and overstuffed love seats scattered here and there, the atmosphere was an artistic blend of rustic and modern. Jeff and Miles spotted Hartman at a small table directly under a colorful abstract painting, next to a large picture window. Hartman was already working on what appeared to be an espresso. Miles and Jeff got in line and were about to order when Jeff reached into his pocket and pulled out his wallet.

"Damn. I need to hit a money machine."

"It's okay. I'll cover you," Miles said.

That was cool. Maybe Miles was coming around. Jeff nodded a thanks. "Double latte please." Jeff eyed a Zingerman's chocolate brownie. He never ate candy bars and pure sugar treats like fudge—a throwback to his wrestling days, where calories he consumed had to have nutritional value—but a Zingerman's brownie was an experience to behold. He decided against it.

Miles said, "Double cap for me." He smiled to the woman behind the counter and handed her a ten. "Keep the change."

That drew a curt smile from the woman. Miles hadn't purchased a coffee drink in some time, so he was unaware that the change would be less than 50 cents. Reading the situation, Miles quickly pulled another dollar out of his wallet and pushed it into the tip jar.

The woman behind the counter smiled. "Thank you," she said.

Jeff and Miles picked up their drinks at the end of the counter and headed over to Hartman. Jeff paused before he sat down and looked at the small card underneath the painting on the wall. He was surprised to see a name he recognized from high school. He was also surprised by the $1,600 price tag for what looked like a big mess of colors strewn about.

Then something else caught his attention out of the corner of his eye. A car flashed past the picture window and the front passenger appeared to be putting a stocking or something over his head. The car was moving fast and it was quickly out of Jeff's field of vision.

Jeff sat down, "Did you see that?"

Hartman looked up from swirling his espresso. His blank expression answered the question. Miles, already seated, turned around from looking at someone standing in line for drinks. He said, "What?"

Jeff frowned. "I think I just saw a car go past and someone was putting pantyhose over his head." Hartman said nothing, but Jeff noticed that he seemed to reach behind his back to make sure something was there—like checking for a wallet.

Miles said, "I think all this patriot stuff is getting to you. Pretty soon you will be seeing black helicopters."

Jeff felt a tinge of anger at the sarcastic remark. But he had to admit—it was a strange thing to see, and he had only caught a quick glimpse. Miles was probably right. Jeff said, "I must have been seeing things. Probably someone just pulling a sweater over his head. Okay, lets get started."

The meeting went well until Miles mentioned his plan to write a Trojan Horse into the software on the chips put into the phones that would be given to Nate Smith and some of his allies.

Hartman said, "How can I agree to do that and have a straight face when telling people about the hypocrisy of America's legislators, judges, and past presidents."

Miles shot an incredulous look at Jeff; he clearly wanted Jeff to jump in and help him out. This was going to be a problem. Jeff had gotten Miles to agree to be involved largely on the basis of their ability to write something into the software that would enable monitoring conversations of Nate and his closest allies.

Jeff looked at his dad and said, "Because sometimes you have to step beyond the rules you would impose in order to create the world in which your rules can exist. I mean, what good are your rules, if by following them, you can never have the society in which they can be implemented?"

"We can't compromise on our principles. The ends do not justify the means. This is an old, old argument. If I can't do it the right way, within the law, then screw it. I'll toss in the towel on America and move to… I don't know. I'll move *somewhere*."

"But Dad, taking over a part of the country forcibly, isn't that illegal?"

"Yes and no. To protect constitutional liberties, we are using means that are technically illegal only because of the unconstitutional laws that violate constitutional liberties."

"Ah, sounds kind of circular to me."

"Not at all. Break it down. If I promise I will never ground you so long as you follow certain rules, and you follow the rules, and then I ground you anyhow, wouldn't you feel like I had improperly restricted your liberties?"

"Yes, but parents have the right to change the rules."

"Ah, yes—but not our government. They have to keep within the boundaries of the Constitution. If they ground us using laws in violation of the Constitution, than we have a right, we have a moral duty, to breach those rules and reinstitute laws consistent with the Constitution. Even Abraham Lincoln said that one of the most cherished rights we have as Americans is to throw off, and violently if necessary, a non-responsive, paternalistic, dictatorial government such as we have."

"So, why do you feel the need to limit yourself to the boundaries of the law when dealing with a rogue like Nate? What's the difference?" Jeff thought he had him. Hartman was willing to violate laws to fix those laws, as had our Founding Fathers, but he wasn't willing to violate the privacy rights of Nate Smith to insure that he didn't kill innocent people. It just didn't make sense. When faced with an adversary who had no rules, only a fool would bind himself to rules he made for bad guys—when those rules had been made on the assumption that the bad guys had rules. In other words, the bad guys, by their actions, choose which rules will govern the fight. If they protest peaceably instead of suicide-bombing innocent people, or even if they declare war on you but fight you within certain rules that retain some level of humanness, then you keep to the rules yourself. If they wantonly kill innocents, then the bets are off.

Hartman paused, as if stumped. Then he said, "We cannot step aside from the law and say that the ends justify the means. That is pure socialism and communism crap. This is the United States of America!"

"But Dad, what if you can't defeat them precisely because you limit yourself to your rules while they play by their rules. Why let them make one-sided rules? This is exactly what the Islamic Jihadists all over the world do to us, because they know they can hide behind our Constitutional protections. Screw that! Those protections were designed by Americans, for Americans. We have a different way of valuing the world. We value the integrity of the individual. Our concept of a citizen is a free individual entrusted to operate on his own, assume his own. In our world individuals assume their own responsibilities. They have every opportunity to exploit their potential. Wallmire and his communists hate that idea; the Jihadists *kill* us for that idea."

Jeff was on a roll. This was a winning argument and he knew his dad would come around to his point of view. "And Nate is no different. Something went wrong in his head. He wants to kill innocent people. We can't—we just can't let our own laws bind our ability to stop such predators. Look, there are too many Americans who will rise up if any group gets out of hand, be it the government or even the patriots. But who is going to object to bending a law to save innocent lives?"

Hartman smiled. It wasn't the response Jeff was expecting, and suddenly his confidence was shaken. Hartman said, "You just made the liberals' point about gun control. They have argued, if it will save just one life, then it's worth ignoring a silly, outdated, constitutional provision such as the Second Amendment. The ends, saving lives, justifies the means, trenching on the Constitution."

"But the libs ignore the fact that the Bill of Rights lists inviolate guarantees. And more importantly, they are wrong on the facts. Citizens exercising their Second Amendment rights save more lives than are lost by accidents or law-abiding citizens going berserk. The people who cause gun deaths are not the law-abiding citizens with guns."

"True enough," Hartman allowed.

"Dad, look at it another way. There is a free world to protect. Our Constitutional system of freedom is not perfect, so maybe it can't be achieved in the most perfect of ways."

"Well, maybe I agree with you about international terrorists acting on our soil—they don't deserve our constitutional protections. But with Americans, I still want our own law enforcement to follow the letter of the law. As I intend to." Hartman reached out and patted Jeff's shoulder. "It's the right thing, Jeff. You'll see."

So that was that. They were going to let Nate run wild and potentially kill people. Great. Jeff didn't know what else to do. Miles had been quiet during the argument, and Jeff wondered if this would cause him to back out. He also wondered if Miles might put in a back door anyhow. Whatever he was thinking, he kept it to himself.

The rest of the meeting went on. They decided Hartman would begin acquiring the phones; Jeff and Miles would develop the software and a tiny integrated circuit which they would fit into the guts of the phones. All the software programming would be implemented on those chips, and if everything worked, any of the leaders could talk to another leader with an identically equipped phone and be certain that no one could intercept the conversation. The same would go for text messages. Jeff was also going to create a custom program to send encrypted email from computer to computer over the internet.

Miles said, "Okay Jeff. I'll meet you at the fort after dinner. We can get started clearing out the cobwebs. I'll bring my new Mac and we can run the internet cable, unless you think the wireless will work out to there."

Hartman said, "Thanks, Miles. But let me get some people I know to run some proper lines for you. I don't want anything visible or detectable around that barn. This is too important."

Miles and Hartman shared a look. Jeff couldn't decide if it was friendly. Jeff said, "Okay, fine, Dad. That will be great." He looked at his dad. "We done?"

Hartman said, "I think so."

"Cool," Jeff replied. He looked at Miles and said, "I have to get some cash. My bank is on the next block. If I go inside I don't have to pay a damn ATM fee. Pisses me off."

Hartman said, "Use the Arbor Bank ATM. They don't charge a fee." Hartman looked at his watch. "I'm late for my meeting with my banker."

Jeff was curious. "Meeting with your banker?"

"Investment advisor. He works with the bank. I meet him once a week. He handles all my investments."

The three men bussed their table and headed east on Washington Street and then north on Main toward Arbor Bank.

❧

HARTMAN HAD STUDIED COLONEL JEFF COOPER'S METHods and tactics of handgun combat, and he was one of the first students to complete all of the intensive handgun, rifle, and shotgun training courses at the now-famed Gunsite Training Center in Paulden, Arizona. One of Colonel Cooper's lasting contributions to close-quarters combat was the identification of four levels of threat awareness. The first level, white, denotes a complete lack of awareness of potential danger. People at this level often end up on the receiving end of a criminal's malicious deed. The next level, yellow, indicates a continuing awareness of one's surroundings—ever looking for the likely directions from which threats may come—and ever planning a response. Hartman had long since ingrained condition yellow into his mind. It is what had caused him to instinctively feel for his Glock 27 when Jeff had mentioned the strange sight of a man pulling a stocking over his head.

Hartman could only guess how many violent or threatening encounters he had avoided over the years as a result of his constant vigilance. Countless times, no doubt, he had avoided trouble by simply crossing over to the other side of a street. In this way, condition yellow had always served him well. It had kept him from slipping to Cooper's subsequent levels of threat awareness: condition orange, where hostile contact is likely, and condition black—the death battle.

Jeff had been exactly right as to what he thought he had seen. In fact, three men in sweat suits and wearing pantyhose over their heads were inside Arbor Bank and had just brandished semiautomatic pistols and demanded that everyone get on the floor. They had struck when they knew only two tellers, one manager, and one investment advisor would be working.

The robbers had done their homework and knew the tellers were the only persons within arm's reach of a silent alarm. Accordingly, the first thing they did upon entering the bank was to coolly shoot the tellers in the head. Next, the robbers split up and simultaneously entered the offices of the manager and the investment advisor, who had been talking with a walk-in customer since Hartman had not shown at the scheduled time. All three people—eyes wide with fear—were swiftly killed with head shots.

The intelligence source for the robbers had said Hartman was always on time. The source had provided a picture of him so they would make no mistake. The reality was, however, that killing Hartman was just a return favor to Leonard Williams for which they would get some guns and cash. None of the robbers had studied the picture. They had been asked to kill the man meeting with the investment advisor and they had complied. Task completed. The bank's money was what they were after. Two of the bandits covered the lobby while one jumped behind the counter and started filling his bag with cash.

Though it was Fall Art Fair Week, and the whole of downtown was mobbed, the bank was situated about two blocks off the path of the Art Fair travelers. In fact, being at an intersection situated away from most of the businesses, the bank got comparatively little walk-in traffic. Its location also provided a clean race north on Main Street to the M-14 expressway. It was a location just waiting to get hit.

Hartman had thought just that on several occasions. The location and absence of much walk-in traffic always made him a bit nervous.

When he wasn't meeting with his investment advisor he almost always used the outside money machine.

Jeff was a step ahead of Hartman and Miles as they crossed Huron Street and walked up to the bank door. Immediately, Hartman sensed that something was wrong. Out of the corner of his eye he could see through the glass facade into the bank. People were not milling about, and there seemed to be several people huddled together in one area. Jeff began to open the door and was just about to step in when Hartman grabbed him by the arm and pulled him back outside. Miles, who was right behind Jeff, was pushed sideways and stumbled, nearly falling to the pavement before he regained his balance and blurted "Hey! What the—"

Hartman's free hand slapped against Miles's shoulder even as he finished pulling Jeff out of the doorway.

"There is a problem inside. You two take off and get the police. *Now!*" Eyes wide with shock and confusion, Jeff and Miles ran off.

Hartman's mind was racing. *What's happening inside? Must be a robbery. How many of them? Are they armed? Have they killed anyone? Do they plan to kill more?* And the last question was most important. Hartman was not a police officer. Unless someone was in danger, he had no desire to insert himself into a confrontation with one or more armed men. Looking inside from the street, Hartman could see a masked gunman in a gray sweat suit beginning to line up people along the length of the tellers' counter. He was of average height but seemed quite stocky. The customers were facing toward the back of the bank. It looked as if they would be marched back, probably into the vault—probably to be executed.

Then Hartman saw something else that was troublesome. One of the gunmen had apparently been assigned to watch the front of the bank, and he was slowly approaching along the wall opposite the teller windows. Also masked, the approaching gunman wore blue sweat pants and a ratty blue sweatshirt, pulled tightly across his very ample stomach. There was a ragged hole at the belly button and it revealed a patch of white from underneath.

Hartman cursed himself for not thinking someone would be covering the door; what had the gunman already seen? What if he had seen Jeff and Miles take off? Hartman thought about running; just a few steps down the street and he could be out of any danger.

One of the hostages glanced toward the front of the bank, abject terror in her eyes.

That was enough. Hartman opened the bank door and strode in like nothing in the world was wrong.

"Get over there!" The fat gunman motioned violently with his pistol for Hartman to join the others lining up along the tellers' counter.

Hartman raised his hands above his head in submission. "No problem! Don't shoot me! I just came in to meet my banker!" It was his best rendition of a surprised and helpless customer. Fatty seemed to stare at him for a moment.

Hartman panicked, thinking they might frisk him for a weapon. He often felt his concealed Glock 27 was obvious to those around him. Fortunately, that is not the case in general, and it wasn't the case with these bank robbers. Fortune also smiled on Hartman insofar as the robbers did not understand Michigan's law on concealed carry. They assumed, incorrectly, that the law prohibited concealed pistols in a bank. They never even considered frisking customers for weapons.

Hartman could see a total of three gunmen. The third was taller than the other two, but he also wore a full gray sweat suit; he was behind the tellers' stations. As Hartman got in line with the other hostages, Fatty went back to his task, looking away from the interior of the bank, obviously scanning for threats from the outside. Hartman knew that he could pivot, draw from his inside-the-waistband holster, and take Fatty out.

The stocky gunman was going to be more difficult. He had his finger in the trigger guard of a 1911 style single-action semiautomatic, and he began to march everyone toward the back of the bank, weaving around desks and office partitions. The robbers were sure taking their time. Hartman thought about going for the stocky guy, but it would be difficult to get the drop on someone with his finger already on the trigger. Moreover, Fatty would surely respond before Hartman could pivot a full 180 degrees to engage him. No, that plan was a recipe for dying. And Hartman had no intention of that. Somehow, he had to localize at least two of the gunmen at the exact moment that the customers would be physically separated from the third. Hartman could then try to get the drop on the first two and take out the third before he got into a position to begin shooting innocents.

This was going to take a miracle.

The tall gunman behind the counter finished loading his bag with money and disappeared into a management office. He was probably looking for keys to open safe deposit boxes. The stocky gunman walked everyone past the open vault and lined them up against the back wall. Hartman, at the back of the line in the lobby, was now the closest person to the vault's entrance. A moment later, the tall gunman emerged from the management office and headed into the vault.

Only a few more moments passed and the tall gunman emerged from the vault wearing a smile that was big and twisted as it showed through the pantyhose. Immediately, he and the stocky gunman began to prod people into the vault with their guns. Both gunmen remained outside, one on either side of the huge vault door.

There were eight hostages, including Hartman, and as they filed in, Hartman realized he would be able to draw his Glock and probably turn to face one or the other of the gunmen without either of them noticing. It occurred to Hartman that the robbers might just lock the hostages inside and leave. That would be wonderful. They could just wait for the police to arrive and open the door.

Those hopes were dispelled by the distinct "click" that came from over Hartman's right shoulder—from the tall gunman who also carried a 1911 style single-action semiautomatic and appeared to carry it with a round in the chamber, safety on. The "click," therefore, was the disengagement of the gun's safety.

Hartman glanced over his left shoulder and saw the stocky gunman nod to the tall gunman.

They were about to be executed.

Hartman quickly stepped to his left and lunged forward, past the people in line and toward the stocky gunman, who was just turning his head back toward the prisoners. At the same time, Hartman reached behind his back with his right hand and drew his Glock. The tall gunman was not yet totally visible to Hartman, but from the tall gunman's side of the line there was a flash of light and a tremendous blast.

Everything went to slow motion.

Hartman's nostrils filled with the smell of burnt gunpowder and the sickening stench of exploding blood. As if on autopilot, Hartman put his front sight on the center mass of the stocky gunman and pulled the short-action trigger. Hartman's gun, loaded with Smith & Wesson .40 caliber, 135 grain Cor-Bon Hollow Points, jumped and then quickly came back to the target. Hartman pulled the trigger again. This time he saw the flash from his muzzle reflected in the gunman's wide-open eyes. Hartman became vaguely aware of screams from the hostages, who seemed to be diving helter-skelter for the floor.

The tall gunman had not prepared himself for the effect of firing his gun into a small and highly reflective space such as a vault. Even though he was standing just outside the door, the blast sufficiently stunned him that he paused to step back before firing again.

That had two effects. The first was to save another life as everyone in the vault had scattered, making a second shot more demanding. The second was to place the tall gunman more quickly in the sights of Hartman's Glock.

Hundreds of hours of training paid dividends. Hartman forced himself to think: front sight, press; front sight, press. He worked his Glock to eye level and put its front sight on the tall gunman's nose. While Hartman's focus was on his front sight, he had a vague image of the gunman's face. It was awkwardly twisted in apparent disbelief, staring back at Hartman, who was already pulling the trigger to send the first of two cranial shots on the way.

Both shots hit their mark. The tall gunman crumpled immediately and was most certainly dead before he hit the floor.

Hartman quickly pulled the tall gunman out of the arc of the vault door, and then put all of his weight into the door to close it. He spun the tumbler, locking everyone safely inside. He then moved to, and knelt behind, a waist-high partition that was only a few feet from the vault opening. Immediately, Hartman commenced a tactical reload. He reached with his left hand into his belt pouch and retrieved between his thumb and forefinger a fresh magazine; he raised that hand to the butt of the gun. His right hand fingered the magazine release on the Glock, and the partially depleted magazine dropped free.

And here is where theory ran smack into reality.

The idea is to use the left hand (already holding the fresh magazine between the thumb and forefinger) to catch the depleted (but not empty) magazine between the middle fingers. Then, by rotating the hand slightly, Hartman would insert the fresh magazine and use the butt of his palm to ram it home.

Unfortunately, in a death battle, Colonel Cooper's condition black, the body does not always do what the mind says—that is if, indeed, the mind functions well enough to say anything. So, instead of the left hand catching the rejected magazine, the hand fumbled and the partially depleted magazine hit the floor.

Hartman reflexively rammed home the full magazine. But, when he reached for the depleted magazine on the floor, his hand suddenly felt as though it had the dexterity of an overstuffed mitten. He succeeded in fumbling the magazine again, and this time it slid out of reach under a huge, immobile copy machine.

There was nothing to do. He would have to finish this battle with the nine rounds in the magazine and one still in the chamber.

Hartman crawled forward to the edge of the partition. He dared not look around it; he knew that Fatty was surely alerted to something gone wrong. If he were likewise stalking and watching the corner, Hartman's head popping into view would be an easy target.

Instead, Hartman got to his feet and, keeping as low as he could, backed away from the corner and put his gun out in front of him in a Weaver hold. Slowly, inch by inch, Hartman carved a semicircle around the corner, gradually bringing into view what was around the corner. Called "slicing the pie" at many training schools, it is the least dangerous way of conducting a search around a corner.

Sure enough. Hartman caught a glimpse of a shadow created by a light behind Fatty. Fatty was slowly moving toward the vault area. Hartman was sure Fatty had his gun leading the way. It would only be a moment or two before Fatty would be far enough toward the back of the bank that he would be able to see Hartman.

Hartman felt his muscles tense and he carefully aimed his Glock at a point where the fat man was most likely to appear. Hartman put his finger to the trigger. This was going to be a battle of speed, and he wanted to put lead into Fatty the instant he appeared from around the corner.

Hartman also knew that he would need an immediate stop if he hoped to avoid getting shot himself. If his first volley failed, the bad guy would certainly return fire. A solid cranial shot was the only way to achieve an immediate shutdown of the bad guy's nervous system.

Unfortunately, unlike the first two gunmen, who Hartman had surprised, Fatty was expecting trouble. Consequently, that perfect head shot was going to be difficult to attain. Hartman's stomach began to go sour. He did not like the situation.

Suddenly things went from slow motion back to full-speed and the gunman was suddenly in view.

Shit!

Fatty had been approaching with his gun in the low ready. That meant it was already aimed directly at the kneeling Hartman.

Hartman's hand surged in response to the surprise, his gun barked, and he saw a wall light explode behind the gunman.

No! He had jerked the first shot off target.

Hartman saw a flash of fire and immediately he felt an impact in his left arm and chest. Instinctively, Hartman pulled his aim down to center mass and fired twice. He adjusted his aim to the head and continued firing. In the meantime, however, he saw another flash, followed by another impact, this time in his stomach. Hartman's arm and chest began to scream with pain. His nostrils filled with the smell of spent gunpowder…

Hartman's second and third shots ripped into the fat man's heart, leaving it a quivering tangle of muscle. These wounds were not the cause of death, however; nor did they stop the fight, as a man can easily last 90 seconds or more beyond a stopped heart. Hartman's fourth shot grazed the side of Fatty's head and imbedded in the wall. Fortunately, Hartman's next two bullets found a wide open mouth—that must have opened in anguish or surprise, or both—and ripped through the back of Fatty's head, spewing blood, brain, bone, and scalp all over the place. Those shots ended the fight. Four rounds to spare.

Hartman blacked out a moment later. His last two thoughts were that he had failed in his great cause, and that his life had been stolen by a scumbag bank robber.

❧

NO MORE THAN A HALF MILE AWAY FROM THE FAILED BANK robbery, Bradley Fletcher sat at his desk at the University of Michigan Law School stewing over his recent interview on CNN with Senator Kennison, the new Director of the Bureau of Socially Correct Activities. He was second-guessing whether he should have responded to Kennison's tirade on guns killing people, children, blah, blah, blah. All losing arguments when subjected to the facts.

First off, the Supreme Court in *District of Columbia v. Heller* had been exactly right. It was absolutely clear, as the majority opinion had painstakingly detailed, that the framers of the Constitution intended *to preserve* the natural, inherent, inalienable right of the people to keep and bear arms for self-defense.

In St. George Tucker's version of Blackstone's Commentaries, recognized as the definitive treatise on English Law at the time of the founding of the United States, Tucker wrote that the right to keep and bear arms:

> ... may be considered as the true palladium of liberty .... The right to self-defence is the first law of nature: in most governments it has been the study of rulers to confine the right within the narrowest limits possible. Wherever standing armies are kept up, and the right of the people to keep and bear arms is, under any colour or pretext whatsoever, prohibited, liberty, if not already annihilated, is on the brink of destruction.

And Bradley had been exactly right about a case that had worked its way through the system and had been recently argued in front of the Supreme Court. *Jones v. Bouchard* could dramatically limit or even overturn *Heller*. In *Bouchard*, the Ninth Circuit had ruled that *Heller* applied only to a ban imposed by the federal government. "More importantly," the court had written, "we find it persuasive that the United Nations Department of Disarmament Affairs has proposed exactly this type of limitation on gun ownership."

A good friend, David Couples, a Professor at Stanford Law, had recently cracked Bradley up when he had been quoted as saying such thinking by the Ninth Circuit was "worthy of the Mad Hatter."

Problem was, the liberal majority on the Supreme Court, as oral argument had recently revealed, was impressed with the dissenting opinion of Justice Stevens and was about to throw the Second Amendment under the bus. And that had implications far beyond the courthouse. It would reach into homes all across America and seek to do the very thing the Second Amendment was designed to prevent.

But this was all a side-issue at the moment. The decision by the Ninth Circuit was controlling only in the Ninth Circuit, which covered most of the far western states. Importantly, it was not yet the law of the land. Oral argument had been pretty negative, but there was still a chance the Supreme Court would uphold *Heller*.

More pressing was his recent interview on CNN about the new Religious And Cultural Sensitivity Act (RCSA) and the federal agency, the Bureau of Socially Correct Activities (BSCA), that had been created to enforce these new "hate crime" laws.

Something was going on that didn't sit right. These laws were odious, to be sure. But there was something more... The thought was dangling around the periphery of his brain... He couldn't quite pull it in...

He navigated to one of his research folders and found it right away. Law Professor John Coffee had once explained:

> Although it is easy to identify distinguishing characteristics of the criminal law—e.g., the... role of intent... of incarceration as a sanction, and the... reliance on public enforcement—none of these is ultimately decisive.
>
> Rather the factor that most distinguishes the criminal law is its operation as a system of moral education and socialization. The criminal law is obeyed not simply because there is a legal threat underlying it, but because the public perceives its norms to be legitimate and deserving of compliance. Far more than tort law, the criminal law is a system for public communication of values.

Bradley's face flushed red with blood. He had read this several times before, but had just taken a meaning from it that he had never seen before. He muttered under his breath, "public perceives laws to be legitimate," and quickly pulled up the file containing the latest criminal acts as defined in the RCSA. He paged through the document until he found what he was looking for:

TITLE 18—CRIMES AND CRIMINAL PROCEDURE;

PART I—CRIMES; HATE SPEECH;

SECTION 241 (A)—DEFINITION OF HATE SPEECH;

> Any act, utterance, or publication of words, pictures, or drawings, or any other form of communication, that has the effect of affronting the dignity or religious esteem of a minority defined

in this section, as expressed to law enforcement personnel by such minority, shall constitute "Hate Speech."

Section 241(d)—Penalties;

Any person convicted of Hate Speech as defined in subsection (A) shall be fined under this title not more than $50,000 or imprisoned not more than seven years, or both.

Professor Coffee had been writing about utilizing the nation's laws to shape moral education and socialization. It had struck Bradley that the Religious And Cultural Sensitivity Act was part of a broad attempt by Saul Alinsky radicals who had come to power with Obama to "change" the character of the nation by changing— forcing, really, from the top down—a totally new set of norms that would be *perceived as legitimate.*

Bradley searched his drive for his material on Saul Alinsky. He found a collection of quotations from Alinsky:

> Remember we are talking about revolution, not revelation; Unlike other forms of more consensual "community building," community organizers generally assume that social change necessarily involves conflict and social struggle in order to generate collective power for the powerless.

This was fitting together in Bradley's mind. He recalled the demonstrations ACORN had organized against banks to pressure them into making sub-prime loans to "disadvantaged" neighborhoods where the home buyers did not qualify under normal mortgage guidelines. He recalled the cries of fraud made by Republicans when ACORN "found" hundreds of thousands of voters who were counted in the Census but who, on investigation by various conservative groups, could never be found at the addresses where they supposedly lived… and who went by names such as "B. Seainya," "B. Screwinya," and "MaMood Isbetta."

That, clearly, was the social struggle—the conflict—of which Alinsky wrote.

And so, it appeared, was the new RCSA. This time, however, it was the Muslims, more than the African Americans, who were using their community power to alter America.

Bradley continued reading:

> A revolutionary organizer must shake up the prevailing patterns of their lives—agitate, create disenchantment and discontent with the current values... the mass of our people... must feel so frustrated, so defeated, so lost, so futureless in the prevailing system that they are willing to let go the past and chance the future.

Bradley's stomach turned. He sat there looking at the words on his computer screen and couldn't believe it. Obama had promised change, but he had done so while playing a personal role in the destruction of America's capitalist system. The Stock Market crash, the unemployment, the loss in housing value and with it virtually all the equity Americans had built up over 80 years...

And then he had unleashed his legislative plans which were passed without debate, giving him virtual dictatorial power over the American economy. It was not a stretch to see the revolutionary plan: destroy the credit markets with billions in bad housing loans, and when the economy tanks, and companies are threatened with bankruptcy and millions are unemployed, print up money and give it away as "bail-outs" and unemployment benefits. Then, once everyone is hooked on the government's help, lower the boom. Take control of car companies, energy companies, financial institutions, student loans, and the health industry. Fire existing CEO's and entire boards of directors. Then:

> » Force bankruptcy or restructuring by going to current stock holders and telling them, essentially, "Guess what? The Government just took your stock and gave it to someone we like better."
>
> » Dictate the products you will make (tiny, electric cars, windmills, curlicue light bulbs, and solar panels).
>
> » Institute "cap and trade" and force the coal industry out of business while driving energy prices so high Americans will

be forced to buy and drive little egg beater cars the nationalized automobile companies are forced to make.

» Insure the perpetuation of the above by padding the rolls of
Democrat voters with millions of illegal immigrants reaping
the benefits of free money and health care.

Bradley started to get dizzy and put his head on his desk to relax.
Even if it had not all been a carefully orchestrated scheme, what
happened in fact followed the plan Alinsky had laid out—to the
letter.

Bradley looked up at his computer screen again and his eyes
focused on a lone quotation:

"This acceptance is the reformation essential to any revolution."

Well, the revolution had worked… and was *still* working. Bradley
felt as though a great weight was pressing on his head and he had
the sudden urge to lie down. His stomach was still threatening so he
again put his head on his desk and closed his eyes. He wondered if
this revolution could be stopped. Businesses had closed by the tens
of thousands since Obama had launched his "Change" with a capital "C" on the American people.

Someone had said the American electorate was a "hallucinating
mob," and Obama had certainly shown that to be true.

What Bradley wondered, now, was whether that mob might
eventually stop hallucinating…

After a few minutes of rest, Bradley picked his head up and swiveled around in his well-worn, brown leather chair. He gazed out
the only window in his rather smallish office. From the ninth floor,
he could just see the bright orange, rust, and red leaves that still
adorned the tips of the highest trees that surrounded the law school.
Ah, the fall colors. Bradley could feel his twisted stomach relax a bit.
This was Bradley's favorite time of the year. With a bit of surprise,
he noted that the sky was virtually cloudless—an unusual phenomenon for Michigan. He suddenly ached to be on the golf course.

Bradley swiveled his chair back around and made a conscious
decision to make himself feel better by taking a relaxed posture; he
put his scuffed brown oxfords up on his antique desk and wrapped

his hands behind his head. He glanced around his office and tried to take in the significance of some of the mementos. There were, of course, the numerous awards for his varied accomplishments; they covered nearly every open space on the walls. His prized Oxford Dictionaries were nestled in custom-built shelves that covered the north wall. On his desk was a signed picture from Arnold Palmer, whom he had met at a golf tournament given in memory of J.P. McCarthy, a famous Detroit radio personality.

Bradley's mind wandered and he thought back to his four years as an undergraduate at the University of Michigan. Those were carefree times. He could play around during the day and cram for a few hours in the evening, and still make it to the bars for a couple hours of dancing and collecting phone numbers from attractive coeds.

And that thought brought a twinge of remorse. All those phone numbers. All those good-looking women—whom he never got the courage to call. It was something he had never figured out. He could have called at least one of them, for heavens sake!

And he had wanted sex beyond belief. So, why hadn't he called?

He knew the answer, though it had taken years to figure it out. It was the game, the dishonesty. He just couldn't bring himself to act interested when all he wanted was a good lay. And maybe it was the always present sense that God did not want him screwing around.

Damn. Times like this he wished he could have put his concerns on the back burner and do it over again. Some of those coeds would have been a blast… Ah, but it was better this way, he rationalized. No misleading. No hurt feelings. No disappointed God. Plenty of time to excel at school and then his profession. And the award-covered walls made no mistake of his accomplishments.

The one thing he didn't display on his wall had come while he was an undergraduate. It was the letter of reprobation from the Dean of the University. He'd been caught playing Dungeons and Dragons in the university's maze of underground tunnels. It had been strictly prohibited, since someone had recently been hurt so trespassing. Now, thankfully, Bradley could smile at the memory. At the time, however, he had thought he was in so much trouble that he might not graduate. Fortunately, the powers-that-be took a typical Ann Arbor view of the "minor" deviations of their students.

The telephone rang and he instinctively reached for it, and then realized Beth was in the front office and would pick it up. He waited and tried to figure out who it was by Beth's reactions.

Beth Simmons was laughing. A petite brunette who rode her mountain bike to work every day, Beth was pushing middle age but still had a smile that could melt. She said, "I'll see if *The Great One* can spare a moment."

Bradley chuckled; it was a running joke Beth had with his brother that they refer to him as some type of nobility.

Bradley didn't wait for her to buzz him. "I've got it Beth. Thanks." He picked up the phone. "Bill?"

Bill Fletcher, JD, 46 years old, Special Agent in Charge (SAC) of the Detroit Field Office of the FBI, was calling from his cellular telephone as he steered his Lincoln west on I-94. He said, "Sir Bradley of Law, thank you for speaking with one of your loyal subjects." They both laughed. "Listen, I'm on my way into town and I'm starved. I wondered if we could meet at…uh…"

"Dominick's?"

"Yeah. That's it. Good thinking little brother."

"His Bradleyness to you."

Bill laughed again. "I just love that place. They still serve that Vietnamese dish… uh…"

"I'm surprised you can't remember since it's all you ever get. Bung Sao."

"Oh yeah. Must be this CRS disease."

"Can't remember stuff?"

"Shit, Bradley. Can't remember *shit*."

"Yeah, right. Anyhow, what time? I don't have a class until evening."

"Give me about 20 minutes. I'll come up to your office."

"No, it will take you 20 minutes to walk to the law school. This is Fall Art Fair Week."

"Nuts!"

"Yeah, I know. But we love it here in Ann Arbor." It was Bradley's best sarcastic tone.

"Okay, so I'll be there when I get there. See ya!" Bradley heard the line go dead. He knew his brother would have to park a mile away, and by the time he got here he would be ready to eat a horse. Bradley chuckled to himself. His brother cracked him up. He ate like a pig, never got fat, had a mind like a steel trap—but couldn't remember the name of one of his favorite dishes. Oh well...

Bradley loved Dominick's as much as his brother. It is one of those quaint college pub/restaurants that serves all of its drinks in Mason jars and has various types of inside and outside seating. Bill walked up to Bradley as he stood on the sidewalk waiting. They took a couple of seats on the long picnic table in the back courtyard. It was late afternoon, but the outside temperature was still comfortable for just shirt sleeves, so the place was packed with students enjoying their favorite beverages. Bill got his Bung Sao and began filling his face. Bradley wondered how Bill could stuff such huge bites into his mouth and not gag to death.

"Yeah..." Bill paused to take another bite, never looking up from his plate. He chewed it no more than twice, so far as Bradley could tell, and swallowed. "And I always forget how nice it is to sit out here in the open." His chopsticks dug in again.

"I don't see how you notice."

Bill glanced up quizzically and Bradley decided to leave him alone. The guy wasn't going to change now. He was a pig. And that was all there was to it. He decided to switch the subject. "A beautiful day like this makes me wish I could down a couple of brews. But I've got an evening class on search and seizure."

"Well, here's to you anyhow!" Bill raised his Mason jar of Coke. "To my famous brother!"

Bradley noticed a tinge of resentment in his brother's voice and he instantly felt uncomfortable. It was something of a sore spot with Bill. As long as Bradley could remember, Bill had done everything he could to tease or ridicule him. Bradley thought he understood the reason for Bill's repressed hostility—he had always one-upped whatever his brother had done before him. Bill made the honor roll in high school; Bradley made valedictorian. Bill went to Cornell Law School; Bradley went to Harvard. Bill failed to get a federal clerkship after law school and instead joined the FBI, where his career had recently begun to stagnate, despite his considerable investigative instincts; Bradley graduated with high honors and clerked for two years with the Second Circuit Court of Appeals and then for two years with Justice Stevens on the United States Supreme Court. After that, he was offered a position on the faculty at Yale Law School. With another six years of teaching and publishing, including two case books, one on search and seizure and the other on constitutional law, he found offers coming in from all the top law schools. Of those, he chose the University of Michigan Law School. He was 39 at the time.

Bill finished his Bung Sao and licked his chopsticks. "By the way, I saw your CNN interview with Senator Kennison. You made the guy look like a Neanderthal."

Bradley felt his hair on the back of his neck stiffen. He was still troubled about letting Kennison get in the only licks on the gun issue. "Do you think I should have responded on the gun stuff?"

Bill shook his head. "No. By not responding you made it look like the guy was blathering. You didn't give it the dignity of deserving a response."

"Did I come off arrogant?" Bradley flinched, waiting for Bill's answer.

"Well…" Bill looked into Bradley's eyes as if to say, "sorry."

Bradley cringed.

Bill said, "The real problem was that you needed a good tailor."

Bradley could see Bill was trying to hold back a smile. His brother played a lousy game of poker. Nevertheless, Bradley felt a flash of heat streak across his face. He said, "God, I hope I didn't look that bad!" He reached up and made sure his current bow tie was neat and even. It wasn't, and he fiddled with it. He could feel the red in his face. This was terrible. He had come off as arrogant *and* a slob.

"Relax, Brad, I'm just teasing you. I doubt anyone noticed."

No, only the 20 million viewers, Bradley thought. And this time Bill couldn't keep the smile off his face. Bill was really getting the better of him right now. The big jerk.

Bill continued, "Anyhow, the guy is a liar. Right out of the Obama mold. He reminded me of Baghdad Bob, when he was reporting that the American forces were nowhere near Baghdad but in the background you could see Abrams tanks rolling down the road.

"Were you teasing me about being a slob or arrogant, or both?" Bradley held his breath.

Bill smiled. "He knows that the RCSA is a bunch of crap. But we've got to enforce it, and between Obama and Wallmire we were told to hire over 100 Muslims as Special Agents because they figured a bunch of white attorneys wouldn't. And 19 of the 93 United States Attorneys are now Muslim, most of whom openly advocate for Sharia law."

Lord, Bradley thought, he had known these facts; but subconsciously, and most likely as a defense mechanism, he had tried not to pay them any attention. The United States Attorneys were the chief federal law enforcement officers in their respective jurisdictions and they prosecuted all criminal cases brought by the federal government. He was starting to feel woozy again.

Bill kept talking. "You know, if the anti-gun lobby gets its way and can swamp the gun industry and gun owners with even more federal regulations—man, that's what scares me. We thought we had a militia thing a few years back. Well, just wait." Bill grabbed his Mason jar and tossed down the last bit of cola. "I'm going to get another drink. Want one?" Bradley shook his head and Bill got up and headed to the order counter.

Bradley had to get his mind off the destruction of American's culture, its economic system, even its Second Amendment... He forced himself to glance around. The place was busy. Nearly every seat was taken at the picnic table. He turned his thoughts to his brother. Bill regretted his own career moves; that seemed clear by the way he liked to torment Bradley. The FBI was such a bureaucratic mess and had received so much ill publicity in the past dozen or so years. Almost on a monthly basis, this or that report surfaced about some investigation into a top FBI official accused of instituting a politically motivated investigation or one of a number of alleged coverups. It had to be a real emotional struggle to keep from getting jaded.

And then there had been an incident several years ago when Bill had been paired with another agent tasked on organized crime in the Detroit area. Bill never discussed it, so what Bradley knew, he had picked up from news articles. Bill's partner had been caught taking a bribe, and there had been some suspicion that Bill might have known about it, or possibly, that Bill might have been on the payroll, though no evidence to that effect ever came to light. The result, however, was that for several years Bill found himself tasked to small cases and always with a senior partner. It wasn't until fairly recently that some of the tarnish had finally rubbed off and he had been promoted to SAC of the Detroit office. It looked, however, as though this might be the last stop on Bill's ride to the top. Put simply, he wasn't Muslim or a "traditional" minority.

Yet, reaching the top of a profession brought its own problems. And for Bradley, most troublesome was the absence of a meaningful personal relationship. Hell, there was even a virtual lack of cheap, "Sex In The City" relationships, though maybe that was God's way of telling him to steer clear... Bradley was now 44 and was starting to regret his rather austere "state of affairs," as he jokingly quipped to his friends. Sure, he had found love while a student in law school. Julie McCracken was a beautiful red-head with firm breasts and a rear end that turned more heads than a tennis match at Center Court. Unfortunately, she decided that she hated the law and, even worse, that she would hate living with a man who loved it. The result was that now, except for an occasional date, Bradley lived a far too lonely existence.

His brother's personal life was quite the opposite. Wasn't that the way it went? You could have one or the other, but not both. Bill had found his wife in his first year of law school and was married that summer. They were still happily married, as far as Bradley could tell, though he wondered why they didn't have any kids. Probably it was Amanda's career as General Counsel for a very busy manufacturing firm. In any event, every time he saw them together, they appeared to be happy and mutually supportive. And from the tales his brother told him from the bedroom, there was no doubt that the svelte and muscular Amanda loved her husband.

Bill finally returned with his cola and sat down. "Ya know, I'm really concerned about this gun grab. In every state with shall-issue concealed carry permits, violent crime against individuals had dropped." Bradley blinked. His thoughts had run far afield of their previous conversation. His mind lingered on an image of Amanda digging her nails into Bill's back. It took a reluctant second for Bradley to shift gears. Bill went on, obviously upset. "There has been a virtual absence of accidents and heat-of-passion shootings that the liberals tried to scare everyone with. And yet, Wallmire forced states to rescind their "Shall Issue" CCW laws. He seems to think that limiting or banning lawfully owned and carried firearms is going to make us safer. Just the opposite is true. For crying out loud, banning guns hasn't worked in England, Canada, Australia, or any other country."

That was true, Bradley knew. Numerous studies had shown that violent crime had actually increased in countries that had instituted total bans on guns. He said, "But if the TV news says guns are bad, then they must be."

"Yeah. Ya know Bush's Patriot Act put the patriot types on guard. If we try to take their guns, look out. After all, it was the BATF going in to take the guns of the Branch Davidians that got this whole patriot thing started. Taking guns away from people is just a scary thing to do."

"True, but the patriots really scare you?"

"Damn right, brother. I'm the guy who has his life on the line. I'm the one they are going to ask to go disarm so-in-so."

Bradley didn't like the idea of his brother being in the line of fire for some liberal's false idea of how to make Utopia. But a socialist

Utopia, a Workers Paradise, was clearly where we were heading. It was strange that nearly the entire Democratic party thought it was a good idea to disarm one-hundred-million gun owners. A third of the population! That was a lot of people to piss off.

Bradley said, "Seems to me, with as many gun owners as we have, that guns are pretty mainstream American. And yet, you keep mentioning the patriots, the fringe radical right."

Bill's face got serious. "You don't have to be very radical to be pretty pissed about losing the Second Amendment."

"That's what I'm wondering. I've been giving a lot of thought to where Obama and Wallmire have been taking us. Our economy is trashed. Everyone is on food stamps, government health care… No one can, or is interested in, starting up a business given the regulations and confiscatory tax rates. I'm thinking, maybe the Tea Party and the patriots are more mainstream than the news media want us to believe."

Bill said, "You said it, really. The Tea Party, the militia, and America are upset about the same things. Ten years ago we thought the people tromping around the woods and preparing for who-knows-what were certifiable. But look at where we are now—nationalized health care, government ownership of auto companies, oppressive government regulation of virtually every industry, especially autos, energy, and pharmaceuticals… And no more Rush Limbaugh."

Bradley shook his head in disbelief of his own thoughts. Commonality between the patriots and Joe the Plumber was something MSNBC did not want anyone to grasp. "I guess it won't take much to push a sizable chunk of America right into the lap of the Tea Party and the patriots."

Bill nodded. "Black helicopters and implanted computer chips used to be a long way from mainstream America. And then Obama came along, and, well…"

Bradley rubbed his chin, "It occurs to me that the ACLU may try to make public singing of Christmas carols illegal."

Bill gave him a surprised look that turned contemplative. "Oh God."

"Will downtown Christmas decorations become…" Bradley couldn't even say it. The idea was so far beyond anything he had ever considered.

Bill's face was losing its color. He obviously knew where this was going, and what it would mean for everyone in federal law enforcement.

Just then a scruffy-looking college boy with huge bell bottom jeans and a face full of jewelry walked past their table carrying a stack of bumper stickers. He started handing them out, moving from one picnic table to the next. It was only a few moments before he was holding out a couple of bumper stickers for Bill and Bradley.

Bill took the bumper stickers and the young man said, "Cool, dude," and moved to the next table.

Bill set the bumper stickers on the table, stacked one on the other so presumably they were identical. Bradley had to read upside down, but it wasn't too hard. It read:

"GO TO BAAT FOR RIGHTS"

Bradley said, "You've got to be kidding. I can't take any more of this." He was going to have to see a psychiatrist pretty soon if this kept up. He tried to change the subject. "So, anyway, getting in any late season golf?"

Bill shook his head. "Been too busy. And Amanda has gotten me out running with her. She really wants me to lose a bit of weight."

Bradley was about to tell him that sounded pretty cool when he noticed someone standing at Dominick's back door with a tray in her hand. She was one of the best looking women he had ever seen. "Oh my," Bradley said, as she started walking toward them. He felt his heart skip as she made a beeline for the open spot on the bench right next to him. She was carrying a shoulder bag in one arm and in the other she was balancing a small plastic tray with her salad and drink. Apparently, she had been scanning the table for an open space.

"Well, little brother. Something to take your mind off all this crap." Obviously, Bill saw her, too. Just then, Bill's pager went off and he looked down to read it. "Bradley, I gotta go. Looks like we have a bank robbery in progress. Good timing for you. This way the young lady won't be enraptured by my presence and she can concentrate on you." They both chuckled and Bill jumped up and trotted away from the table. He yelled back, "Good luck!" It caused nearly everyone to glance toward them. Even the woman approaching turned to watch Bill go.

Bradley tried to melt into the seat. His face was flushed with embarrassment. He knew that everyone was looking at him. Bill most likely had intended just that. Bradley tried to force himself to remember that no one would really know the subject of Bill's comment. It just felt that way.

Bradley watched Bill dodge students as he made his way quickly out to the street. He felt a vague sense of jealousy for his brother. Rushing off to a bank robbery sounded almost romantic. On the other hand, getting shot at was definitely not his cup of tea. Maybe it wasn't Bill's either.

The young lady came closer and Bradley tried to turn away so as not to be obviously gawking. But the sight was gripping, and he didn't have the strength to look away. Her hair flowed softly, slowly, in the breeze. Skin tight Spandex showed off her long legs and toned muscles. A bright yellow top accented her youngish figure. She was a ballerina gracefully moving across the floor.

Then she was there—standing only inches away. She glanced at him as she set her tray on the table, just inches from his Mason jar of Coke. Strangely, her eyes seem to lack the vibrance that the rest of her body projected. Bradley willed himself to be nonchalant as she took her drink and salad off the tray and set them on the table. She set the now empty tray to the side and swung her legs, one by sensuous one, over the bench seat. Bradley fought off a terrible urge to reach up and check his bow tie. He prayed that it was straight.

Bradley was not the type to gawk at every good-looking woman on the street, but this woman reached into his chest and grabbed his heart. She commanded his attention, so much so that he became self-conscious of his gaze. With one great effort, he turned his head forward, but his eyes strained mightily to look at those legs.

Bradley tried to compose himself and evaluate the situation. Despite her fresh appearance, she was older. When she finally settled, she sat with slightly slumped shoulders. She even sighed and drooped her head. There was something strangely paradoxical about her presence.

Who in the heck was she? She didn't look like a student, and she wasn't dressed like a professor—unless she was done with classes. Yet she seemed educated.

He had to meet this woman.

He agonized over what he could say and not sound like an idiot or a pickup artist—not that there was any risk of that. His pulse quickened as he decided to make a move. He turned his head toward her and was just about to blurt out something when—

"Hi. My name is Anne Kreig." She smiled, reached out, and straightened his tie.

❧

CHAPTER 8

HARTMAN WAS HIGH ABOVE THE EARTH, RUNNING through the clouds as fast as he could. When he glanced back, he saw the hollow tip of a bullet racing after him. In the bullet's hollow was the face of Satan, sneering, laughing. The bullet came nearer… and nearer… Hartman started to panic. He tried to run faster, but instead his legs began to flail uselessly in the air and stopped moving forward altogether. The bullet raced toward him. Satan's face screamed hysterically—mouth open wide and unhinged at the jaw like a large snake or serpent. Inside the mouth, past the fangs and reddish brown throat, Satan's deep red tonsils waved violently.

Hartman blinked and suddenly the terror of Satan and the bullet were gone. But in their place was the bewilderment of tubes running into his mouth and nose, a rhythmic sound of something swishing, and a rapid, erratic beeping. His mind was just starting to sort things out when—

"Dad!"

Hartman tried to move his head, but couldn't; it must be held in place by the tubes down his throat and nose, he thought. Jeff's face appeared over the bed and Hartman realized he was alive! He gulped air into his lungs. The swishing and beeping surged.

Jeff said, "You are going to be fine. He got you in the left arm, and that bullet broke your arm and then lodged in your chest. But it was slowed and barely got your lung. The other shot got your stomach pretty good. It lodged in the large intestine. The doctors patched up everything. You got out of surgery a couple of hours ago. They tell me all the tubes will come out pretty soon. He was using nine millimeter hollow points, but neither expanded, though the one that hit your arm was pretty deformed. Anyway, the upshot, er, good news is, they say you should have a complete recovery."

Hartman smiled, or at least he tried; talking was useless with all these tubes. Events were coming back... slowly... as though coming through a dense fog... He had never been able to check the side offices at the bank. He tried, now, to picture them, but his mind's eye couldn't be dislodged from his last waking image... a fat man in blue sweat pants and a ratty blue sweatshirt, mouth open wide, with a mist of blood and head fragments blossoming out the back of his head. Hartman was so tired. Just thinking was an effort. He smiled (or tried to) again at Jeff, who seemed to understand—he smiled back. Hartman closed his eyes and was asleep in seconds. This time, there were no nightmares.

❧

BILL FLETCHER WAS WAITING OUTSIDE HARTMAN'S ROOM to speak again with Jeff. Something was nagging him about the shoot-out. His quick-response team had already reconstructed the deadly events. It was impressive, to say the least. Perhaps too impressive. Bill couldn't put his finger on what was bothering him, but Hartman seemed just too damned good with a gun. Bill knew that very few people, including the best in his own agency, possessed the tactical and marksmanship skills to take out those three armed and prepared gunmen. And so far as he could tell from the scene and interviews, Hartman had reacted only after the first hostage had been shot. That meant he had taken out all three gunmen after the first shot, but before they got off a second. Indeed, developing skills like that took more than extensive training; it took motivation. So, in addition to wanting to know where this very capable gunman had learned his trade, he wanted to know why.

Jeff stepped into the hospital corridor and looked right at him. Then, to Bill's surprise, Jeff briskly headed in the opposite direction.

Bill took a few quick steps after him. "Jeff Kreig! Could I have a minute with you? I've got a few questions."

Jeff stopped, turned around, and headed back. "Agent Fletcher. I'm sorry. Of course! My dad will be okay. You can probably talk to him tomorrow. Until then, I am at your service."

Bill was startled by the friendly and cooperative attitude. A slightly modified version of Shakespeare came to mind: *He doth protest too much, me thinks.* Bill said, "Your dad is obviously an excellent gunman. Know anything about where he acquired those skills?"

Jeff blinked. "Ah…well, I know he went to Gunsite a bunch of times." Jeff looked away, appearing to be interested in a nurse walking by.

Ah, Bill thought, *Gunsite explains things.* He knew a number of agents who owed their lives to Gunsite training. But he said nothing.

There was an uncomfortable pause. Jeff cast his glance all around the hospital corridor. "And he used to hunt a lot."

"You and your dad ever go shooting together at a range or anything like that?"

"No."

"Your dad ever compete in pistol competitions like IPSC, the International Shooting Confederation, or IDPA, International Defensive Pistol Association?"

"Not that I know of; but, say, wasn't my dad the good guy in this? Why all these questions?" Jeff's voice sounded strained.

"It's pretty clear your dad responded in defense of himself and other innocents. And his response was appropriate to the threat. Very appropriate, I might add. So, with the information we have, I'm sure no charges will be filed."

Jeff seemed to relax a little.

Bill said, "I don't have any more questions at this point. But I might after I have a chance to talk to your dad. Is that okay?"

Jeff nodded. "No problem. I'm happy to help you." He walked past Bill toward the elevators.

That was strange. A few moments ago, when Jeff had come out from Hartman's room, he had made a beeline *away* from the elevators.

❧

ANNE ROLLED OUT OF BED AND WALKED TO THE WINDOW. Her head was pounding with a splitting headache. She pushed back the curtain and squinted. The sun was already high and streaming into the southerly facing windows of her bedroom. As her eyes adjusted she could see the trees rustling gently. One of the last robins still in Michigan was perched proudly on a branch, happily chirping away, its bright-red chest blazing magnificently against the deep blue sky.

Anne groaned and jerked the curtains closed. She reached for a tissue to clear the sleep from her eyes and then stared at the clock, trying to focus on the hands in the now-darkened room. After a few seconds, she made them out and whispered, "Damn." Jeff would probably come home for lunch. She hated it when he came home before she was dressed. She threw on some black tights and a man's white dress shirt, and stumbled off to the kitchen to start the coffee. Maybe some caffeine and a couple of aspirin would ease her throbbing head.

The previous day had been a cataclysm of anxiety. Not surprisingly, she had slept horribly. The last time she recalled looking at the clock's luminous face was a quarter past five—A.M. The problem was in her head, she knew. Any traumatic event could cause her mind to run an endless loop, playing and replaying the trauma. And yesterday, there had been more than one trauma.

Now, slowly coming to, Anne started thinking again about Bradley Fletcher, the first of yesterday's traumas. Seated next to him at Dominick's, she had quickly recognized him from TV. Later, after a long conversation, he had asked her out and she had, against her tremendous desire, abruptly refused. The words had rushed out of her mouth before she could rein them in. And his disappointed eyes— Those eyes! She had come home completely torn up about it.

Then she saw TV images of her former husband being carried away on a stretcher, with orderlies alongside holding bags of plasma and blood.

And if that weren't enough, the next things splashed across the scene were close-ups of the attempted robbery's aftermath—pools of blood on the elegant, tiled floor and stunned bank customers/hostages who could barely speak.

Anne had gone into a state of near shock; an emergency call to her psychiatrist and a trip to an all-night pharmacy followed. After that, strong sedatives notwithstanding, she just couldn't stop thinking. And the thoughts came rapid-fire—the collection agency, anguished faces from the TV news, Hartman being loaded into the ambulance, the nasty lawyer on the phone. She thought of the things she had wanted to do with her life, of new love, of happiness... They were all out of reach, now. Then, in the midst of her anguish, she remembered the book she had picked up at the book store. Maybe. Just maybe. She'd retrieved it from her shoulder bag and read deep into the night—and morning.

The next day, Anne breathed a sigh of relief when Jeff walked into the kitchen—she was glad she had dressed—even if she was just retrieving her third cup of coffee. He might think this was her second or third *pot* of coffee. Jeff opened the Sub Zero and began snooping.

She said, "Did you stop at the hospital?"

Jeff nodded, though all Anne could see was the back of his head. "How is he?"

Head still inside the Sub Zero, he said, "Gonna be fine, Mom. He took a couple of hits, but nothing life-threatening, thank God."

A sense of relief rushed through Anne. "Thank God is right. Last night on the TV—"

"I know. Seemed pretty bad. But the crooks got the worst of it. Dad killed all three of them."

Anne felt light-headed at the thought. The crooks had killed innocent people and had tried to kill Hartman. They might even have tried to kill her son had Hartman not been alert—and armed. *Thank God for that, too.* Anne sighed. Still, they were humans, and it saddened her that death was necessary to halt their killing. Hartman was a big hero, thanks to several of the customer/hostages who had explained the amazing way Hartman responded. Anne glanced at Jeff, who was now rummaging through the cupboards. "How about a grilled cheese? I've got some of your favorite white cheddar and fresh challah bread from Zingerman's. Did you see the musk melon in the fridge? It's local and really good."

With his head still in a cupboard, Jeff said, "That'll be great, Mom. But you don't have to—"

"Nonsense," Anne cut him off. "I know you can make it yourself, but I want to do it."

Jeff turned around, regarding her for a moment. "Okay, Mom. If you want to." His eyes lingered on her.

"Okay, look, I've got this book and the guy says that most depression is from telling ourselves negative things. I know I constantly tell myself I'm a loser, messed up my life, ruined my marriage and all that. He says I'm saying those things to myself in an endless running dialogue, some of it subconsciously, and those statements are based on the erroneous belief that I'm no good."

"Makes sense, Mom."

Anne nodded. "Yes, I think it does. Anyway, the author makes a pretty good argument that, because God made us in his image, we really *are* works of art. And so he says if I can begin to accept *that* truth, and change my internal self-talk, well, maybe I can start to break this horrible cycle I'm in."

Jeff's eyes were bulging out of their sockets. "Mom! That's incredible! That sounds great!"

It did sound great, Anne had to admit. Maybe. Just maybe…

Jeff sat down at the kitchen table and grabbed the "Nation/State" and "Editorial" sections out of a pile of papers on the end of the table. *What odd choices,* Anne thought. He usually read the sports pages. Then she realized he was probably looking for something on the attempted bank robbery.

Anne set her coffee on the counter and opened a lower cabinet to pull out a frying pan. Suddenly she had a sense that he was walking toward her, and she turned around just as he reached her. He put his arms around her and held her head to his shoulder.

"I love you, Mom. And I know you still love Dad. He's going to be okay. Don't worry."

Anne's chest filled with pent-up emotion. Like a well striking oil and spurting a geyser, tears burst from her eyes. Her chest heaved with sobs. Jeff held her tightly. How did he know she needed this?

After minute or so, the tears slowed, then stopped. The heaving calmed. The knot in her chest loosened. Jeff released her—but it was a slow, deliberate release, where he held her shoulders as if communicating: I'm still right here. He sat at the breakfast bar. Anne couldn't think of anything to say, so she gave him a long look before turning away to work on the grilled cheese. Fortunately, the crying had alleviated her headache, or was it from that book…

Jeff tossed the papers back into the pile and punched the power button on the counter-top TV. The noon show was ending and the 12:30 news was about to begin.

Anne was peering under the skillet to adjust the flame when she heard the glass door just off the breakfast nook begin sliding open. She straightened up in time to see Jeff wave in Linda. Anne moaned. Why did everyone have to come over so damn early?

Linda stepped into the kitchen and stood there, as if expecting someone to speak first.

Jeff said, "My dad is fine. I saw him on my way home."

A wave of relief seemed to sweep across Linda's face; her knees buckled slightly and she reached out to the counter to steady herself. "Thank goodness," she said, and then, tentatively, softly, she asked, "Anne, you all right?"

Anne thought, *Thanks to my wonderful son.* She said, "Yes. I'm fine…" And she suddenly choked up with the realization that she had two people, right here, who really cared for her. Maybe God *was* working for her. Maybe He *was* on her side. Tears started to flow down her cheeks and splatter on her arm, the front edge of the Viking range, the tops of her shoes, and the floor.

This time Linda came over and hugged her from behind, resting the side of her face against the small of Anne's back. She could feel the warmth of Linda's face penetrate her blouse. Oh, God, it felt good. Her tears kept flowing, but they were beginning to feel like happy tears. After a minute or two, Linda released her and walked over to the kitchen table. She sat down, straightened her back, and asked,

"So, Anne, did you get down to the law school and pick up information on the LSAT?"

The question hit her like a punch in the face, and she stood there staring at the nearly finished grilled cheese, completely unable to speak. *My God*, law school was the *last* thing she wanted to think about. It was all too much; Hartman, Bradley Fletcher, the threatened suit, her own depression, and now law school. She turned to look at Linda and gave a barely audible, "Uh-huh."

Linda's eyes widened and she seemed ready to pounce.

Anne glanced at Jeff, who took the cue. He said, "Go easy on her, Linda."

Linda slumped down at the counter. She began fiddling with a pepper shaker then set it down with a thump. Her gaze lingered on it as she said, "I'm sorry to seem so callous." She lifted her head and glanced back and forth from Jeff to Anne, then lowered her head slightly. "It's just that I want so badly for you to get on your feet. Honestly, Anne—" She straightened her back, raised her chin, and became considerably more animated. "I'm so excited about you going to law school. I'm like a kid in a candy shop. I can't help it. Forgive me." Her eyes were a mix of sadness and excitement.

Anne walked over to Linda and touched her arm. Their eyes met and Anne felt her heart warm. The two people closest to her were reaching out and really trying to touch her. She could feel their love hanging in the air like a thick mist over a quiet stream.

Linda said, "Can you tell me what happened?"

Just then Anne noticed something on the counter-top television. Apparently it had caught Jeff's attention, too. She saw that it was an MSNBC Special Report. Linda was ignoring the TV and was obviously waiting for a response.

The throbbing returned to Anne's head, and she put her hands to the sides of her temples and squeezed to try to ease the pressure. Law school… She had let so much of her life get away. It was too late to fix. She would love to go back to school, but it was hard enough just to function every day. What would she do if she had to study and attend classes? No—it would be useless. She really didn't want to talk about this. She glanced at Jeff. "What's on the news?"

Jeff was grim. "You better see for yourself."

Anne stepped closer, as did Linda. The reporter's voice was strained and excited. Dark-colored helicopters could be seen flying in the background. The helicopters were firing missiles, and there were fantastic explosions occurring all around.

Always the same, Anne thought; *the United States attacking terrorists somewhere in the Arab world.* She had momentarily forgotten the grilled cheese and she hurried to the stove and grabbed the spatula. As she scooped up Jeff's sandwich, Bradley Fletcher jumped into her mind. Now, there was a man who screamed out for a woman's touch. On impulse, Anne said, "I got asked out."

Linda snapped her head away from the TV. "What? Who?"

Anne didn't know whether she should be offended by Linda's surprise. Defensively, Anne said, "Bradley Fletcher. He's a professor." She chose not to mention that he was a professor at the law school. "I met him at Dominick's and we had a nice talk. He asked about my music, dancing. I told him about my divorce. He told me a little about his family. His brother is the FBI agent who investigated the bank robbery."

An explosion occurred fairly close to the reporter, who was showered with dirt and dust. Linda turned back to the TV. The network cut to its studio for an "analysis."

Anne flipped the sandwich onto a plate and set it down in front of her son. "I'm sorry Jeff. I got it a little too dark on one side." *Typical me,* she thought. *Another screw-up.* He didn't respond. "Anyway, I said no. He is out of my league."

Linda turned back to Anne. "What?"

Linda was obviously torn between the TV and the conversation, and Anne hated it when Jeff did that. A bit of anger welled up. She snapped, "What the heck's so interesting? There is always some battle going on in the Middle East."

Jeff turned and looked Anne in the eye. His pained expression startled her. He said, "It's not the Middle East, Mom."

Exasperated, Anne said, "Okay, so it's in some other hot spot. What's the current one now?"

Deadpan, Jeff said, "Nevada."

Anne felt her heart skip a beat. She quickly moved back to the TV and turned up the sound.

The Special Report continued with an analysis of the conflict by George Kissinbho, MSNBC anchor, and Diya al Din Wasem, Director of the White House Military Office (WHMO).

Kissinbho said, "Mr. Wasem, it looks like we are seeing the fruit of the quick build-up of President Wallmire's Domestic Defense Force."

"Yes, George. That's exactly right. We have been looking for a good opportunity to show how well our United Nations' officers are working with the enlisted immigrants, and this is an excellent demonstration."

George Kissinbho raised an eyebrow and said, "You don't mean you were waiting, as though you wanted a conflict; you mean that Presidents Obama and Wallmire correctly realized that we needed a domestic force with the firepower—"

A look of fear and then relief flashed across Kissinbho's face as Wasem said, "Oh, yes—yes. Of course. That's exactly what I meant. It's terrible, really, that we need this type of military force operating against domestic terrorists. But this is a dangerous world."

"Now, in addition to overseeing the DDF, what else do you do as Director of the White House Military Office?"

"Well, George, thank you for asking. Under presidents prior to President Obama, the office pretty much just dealt with providing military support for White House functions. We took care of presidential transportation, his limo and Air Force One, Marine One. We also did medical support and emergency medical services."

"But now you do much more."

Wasem laughed. "Oh, yes. That we do. Now, with the support we have had from Presidents Obama and Wallmire, we have exclusive control over the DDF. Naturally, the president is the Commander in Chief of this force, but I command the DDF, sort of like his top general."

"Okay, Mr. Wasem, tell us about this operation."

"Yes, gladly. As you can see, and your reporter experienced, we have had a group called Unintended Consequences under investigation for quite a while. They directly seek to kill government officials, and they have been responsible for at least a dozen deaths of IRS agents and United States Attorneys just in the last two months. They believe all federal laws passed by the Obama and Wallmire administrations are invalid, and so they never turned in their assault rifles and cop-killer bullets as required by law."

"That's outrageous."

"Yes, I quite agree. And these people are led by a terrorist, a Len Rhyman, who heads up a paramilitary group we have had under FBI surveillance for some time in a small town in Nye County, Nevada. The town is built entirely upon Mr. Rhyman's property, so he has claimed that he and his people conduct no business with the outside world. They claim to have no telephones. They don't get any mail, food deliveries, or anything."

"Obviously, these people present a clear and present danger."

"Yes, George. No doubt about that. Anyhow, because of all this, they claim that the federal government has no jurisdiction under the Commerce Clause in the Constitution, and therefore he and his cult think we have no right to tell him what he can or can't do on his property."

George chuckled. "Well, they won't think that anymore, will they?"

"Indeed. President Obama was percipient when he laid the foundations for the Domestic Defense Force and funded it with enough money that we could acquire the same military hardware as the normal military. As you saw on TV, we deal decisively with terrorists. It's really quite a pleasure."

Kissinbho's face went ashen and he seemed to struggle for words. He said, "Ah, Mr. Wasem, you mean that it's a pleasure to have the defenses we have, given how heavily armed these terrorists were with assault rifles and illegal ammunition."

Wasem smiled broadly at Kissinbho. "Oh, right again, George. I get carried away, as you people say."

"Well, we want to thank you for coming in to give us—"

Jeff reached up and punched the off button. He said, "You hear that towel-head?"

"Jeff!" Anne blurted.

"Oh, Mom, come on. You heard him. He's happy to be killing Americans. We're infidels to him. And he said, 'as you people say.' What the hell is up with that? Is this guy even an American citizen?"

The reference to "you people" was odd, Anne had to agree. That Wasem guy seemed pretty happy to use all that firepower. And it was obvious to Anne that she had just seen, live via satellite, the violent deaths of scores of American citizens at the hands of what appeared to be a personal military force, to be used by the President of the United States against Americans. Something was not right.

Linda said, "My God. It's another Waco."

Anne was still in shock. "In Nevada? Why there?"

Jeff said, "You've been too depressed to notice much in the last year. This Rhyman guy has built an entire city on his personal property. And he's been claiming some sort of sovereignty or something."

Linda said what Anne was already thinking. "I read where Charlton Heston once said that the veneer of America is wearing thin. I think he was right. We are coming apart at the seams."

Anne said, "I agree. Not only have we lost our identity as a God-fearing nation, we've been special interested and politically corrected to death." She realized Jeff had already inhaled the sandwich, so she scooped up the plate in front of him and noticed that he was studying her very closely. Anne turned around and put her skillet and utensils in the dishwasher.

Jeff said, "That's what the patriots think."

Linda scoffed, half laughing as she spoke, "I didn't know anyone in the patriots had a brain."

Anne glanced at Jeff, and it was clear that Linda's comment did not sit well with him. Linda, however, was too busy chuckling to notice.

Anne's curiosity was piqued. She looked at Jeff. "I was just joking the other day, but now I wonder how much you really know about the patriots."

"Just that they aren't a bunch of crazies," Jeff responded, as he continued to glare at Linda, who seemed, finally, to sense that he had been offended. She abruptly stopped chuckling. He continued, "And their beliefs are not all that different from what most of us think. I mean, you agreed that we are falling apart at the seams. The patriots believe that, too. They are just taking a couple of precautionary steps in the event that things continue along this path. Wallmire's private military can attack citizens on private property, but what happens when a hundred million gun owners say enough is enough?"

Linda was leaning forward and seemed to be waiting for a chance to speak. As soon as Jeff paused, she jumped in. "Jeff, I'm sorry about what I said. I guess I don't know anything about them. I've just heard the typical stuff about black helicopters and things."

Jeff seemed to relax a bit. His expression softened. "That's okay. I know some people who are members, and they are not crazy or stupid. Just very concerned—" he pointed to the black screen, "—about what you just saw."

Before Anne had seen that "Special Report," she would have thought Jeff sounded a little alarmist. Now, she wasn't so sure. She glanced out to the living room to her gun case. She said, "I'm still trying to figure out what the people had done wrong to deserve getting attacked with missiles and bombs."

Jeff said, "You heard the guy. Supposedly they had big bad assault rifles—ah, hem, Mom, that you still have as well." Jeff broke into a big smile.

Anne's face flushed red. She hadn't thought of that. But Jeff was right. She had never received any notice about her Mini Ruger 14, but she had seen the reports on TV about the assault weapons ban, a bill that had a schedule for turning in all semiautomatic rifles with a caliber larger than the relatively new and very weak .17HMR, which was excellent for shooting squirrels and prairie dogs, but not much more. Her Ruger used the old 5.56 mm military cartridge, often called the .223, which was a serious man-killing round. That meant she was supposed to have turned in the gun several years ago.

For a brief moment she imagined military SWAT people shooting their way into her house.

Linda said, "Well, I don't see how it should be legal to own assault rifles. I mean, they kill lots of people and children."

Jeff raised his voice, "Come on, Linda, semi-auto rifles were rarely used in crimes to kill people or children. Constitutional Law expert David Couples showed that less than four percent of all homicides in the United States involved any type of rifle. And less than eight-tenths of one percent, that's point-eight percent, of homicides were perpetrated with rifles using military calibers."

Anne was taken aback with Jeff's detailed information. Where in the heck was he getting this? Linda seemed offended, and snapped, "Well, I heard on TV that lots of children are killed every day."

Anne watched Jeff roll his eyes. He said, "Linda, the facts simply don't support what you just said. And, by the way, since when did we start trusting TV for the truth?"

Linda's stare at Jeff was cold as ice, but she didn't say anything.

"And what if we ever have riots as they did back in 1968?"

Linda said, smugly, "I don't think it will ever get so bad that we have groups of looters roaming the streets—"

Jeff said, "You mean like in Los Angeles in '94?"

Linda's face blanched.

Anne had forgotten about that; so, apparently, had Linda. Reflexively, Anne came to her defense and said, "That's not likely to happen again." She couldn't remember the specifics of the riot, but she did recall that, lacking effective police protection, shop owners had stood on their roofs with the same kind of semiautomatic rifles—the Ruger Mini-14—she had in her gun safe, and which was now illegal. Still, she didn't think it would happen again, though, as she thought about it, nor could she think of a good reason why it wouldn't. She said, "I guess I can tell you this much: if everything does go to hell in a hand basket, I'd surely shoot anyone trying to break into the house." Anne nodded toward the living room and the gun safe that contained, in addition to her Cylinder & Slide 1911 and the Ruger Mini 14, a 12-gauge Remington 870 shotgun. In thinking about the possibility of needing their use, remote as it might be, she was glad Hartman had left those formidable weapons. She was also glad he had forced her to take lessons with both long guns as well as with her 1911. Sure as hell, if someone were to break in and threaten either deadly force, or such force as could inflict great bodily harm, the bastard was in for a moment or two of frightful, and profound, regret.

Linda piped up, "Listen, enough with all the doomsday stuff. You never answered me. What's this about someone asking you out for a date?"

Anne glanced at Linda, amazed at her tenacity. Oh, hell, there was no sense beating around the bush about who he was. "He's a law professor. We saw him on TV. Bradley Fletcher. I met him downtown. He seemed like a very nice man."

Both Jeff and Linda blurted simultaneously, "The professor on TV?"

After another moment, Jeff said, "Did I hear you say his brother is an FBI agent?"

◦

NATE SMITH WAS IN HIS KITCHEN AT HIS LODGE IN THE U.P. He was on the telephone with Leonard Williams, and he could hear the television in the living room drone on about the battle in Nevada. Right after the live report had ended, Nate had stormed out of the room, paced back and forth a few times in the kitchen, and flipped open his telephone. Outside his kitchen window there was an early snow and the flakes were big, heavy, and coming down hard. He was watching the ground turn a beautiful snowy white. Usually, the winter cheered him. Not tonight. "Leonard, my friend, this is the last straw. We can't let the feds do this! For God's sake this was against our brothers! Listen, I'm on my way to Ann Arbor in the morning. Let's meet first thing day after tomorrow, back here. No more screwing around. I'll talk to you then."

Nate had already been planing a visit to Ann Arbor when this latest attack by the government on American citizens had occurred. He had decided, what with Hartman out of commission, it was time to pay a little visit to his kid and that spook. If they were getting involved in the patriot's communication system, Nate wanted to know a little more about what they were doing. If they were up to something, their fate would be left to the will of God and Leonard Williams. As for this latest governmental malfeasance, something had to be done. He had to think. His followers would be looking to him. He began to pray. His mind focused on what he had just seen on television. Galatians 5:1 filled his mind:

> "It is for freedom that Christ has set us free. Stand firm, then, and do not let yourselves be burdened again by a yoke of slavery."

❧

CHAPTER 9

JEFF AND MILES WERE BUSY SETTING UP THEIR COMPUTERS and communications equipment. Hartman had called in favors with the patriot's connections in the electric and telephone utilities. As a result, power and communications lines were underground all the way to a small junction box just above the ground on an outside wall of the barn.

Jeff and Miles were both working in front of computer screens when Jeff's phone rang. It was Nate Smith. Jeff said, "Criminy! What the heck does he want?" He shot a glance at Miles. "Should I answer it?"

Miles shrugged his shoulders. "Maybe he wants to know what we want for Christmas."

Yeah, right, Jeff thought. But now it was too late; the call had gone to voice mail. A chill ran through his body. He'd known he would have to deal with Nate sooner or later. In a moment his phone buzzed, indicating the voice mail had come in. He punched it up and put it on speaker: "Ah, Jeff, this is Nate Smith. Call me back right away."

Miles said, "I suppose you better call him. He can't do much harm from the U.P. And he doesn't trust us already—so no need to add fuel to the fire."

Miles was right, so Jeff climbed out of the fort to get better reception. He'd been surprised that the call came in at all. Usually, the reception in the fort was zero. Standing in the barn he punched the "call back" button. Nate answered on the first ring. "Jeff, I'm near Ann Arbor and I want to see your set-up. Give me your address."

Jeff's heart leaped into his throat. This could not possibly be good.

Within 20 minutes Nate had parked his old Ford F-250 on a dirt road, at Jeff's direction, away from the route Anne would travel. In another 10 minutes he was coming down the ladder into the fort. Jeff recognized the checkered cocobolo grip of the handgun Nate had tucked into a behind-the-back concealment holster. As soon as his foot hit the floor, Nate turned to Jeff and said, "So why did you two get involved?"

This was what Jeff had feared. Nate didn't just want to see their equipment. He wanted to interrogate them. Jeff felt completely naked, as if Nate could see right through him. He was sure if he said anything, Nate would decipher the true meaning and realize he and Miles were there to conspire against him. They were dead.

Miles said, "We can help with the communications." Jeff snapped his head around in surprise. Thank God! At least Miles's brain wasn't locked up like a Windows computer.

Nate growled, "That wasn't my question." He kept his eyes trained on Jeff.

Shit, Jeff thought. *What could he tell him?* In a different time and place, with time to think, maybe he could come up with something. But Nate had surprised them, and his mere presence was tying Jeff's brain in knots. *Think!* He had to think. He wondered if he could claim that he and Miles had experienced the frustrations that led people to the patriots. They were a bit young for that, however, and they had no prior record of attending meetings that usually preceded full-fledged membership. His mind felt like the slush machine at the local Dairy Queen; it was working, but in very slow motion. He opened his mouth to try to say something—anything—to create a delay. But nothing came out. He just stood there, open-mouthed, feeling his heart pound like a jack hammer in his ears. He began to wonder if Nate could see the beads of perspiration forming around his forehead.

"Erich Fromm said that it was easier to talk about freedom than to live free." Miles said. Jeff snapped his head toward Miles in utter surprise. He'd never even heard Miles mention Erich Fromm—and who the hell was Erich Fromm anyway? Miles continued, "... by being responsible for one's self and by accepting the consequences of one's actions."

Nate's eyes widened and his mouth dropped open in surprise. For some reason Jeff got the funny idea that he looked as if he had swallowed a canary.

Miles continued, "In other words, the Great Society bull that the federal government sold my people has done as much harm as racial discrimination by whites. The fact is; nothing motivates like need. And if you take away the need, you take away motivation. The best way to subjugate an entire race is to put it on the dole. It kills motivation, fosters depression, breeds the wrong attitude."

Nate still had feathers in his mouth. Clearly, he hadn't expected Miles to be thoughtful, literary, and conservative. Miles was referring to some of the concepts in William Henry's book, *In Defense of Elitism*. Nate said nothing in reply.

Miles tightened his eyes and began waving his hands to punctuate his points. "The Left hates anything that is strong and successful in a competitive environment. White males, western civilization, rationality, elitism." Miles bored in on Nate. "Yet elitism and rationality form the basis of the advancement of humankind. By selecting the best, by promoting the best, and by rewarding the best, we encourage people to be their best. Even in its heyday, communism relied on elitism to field the most dominant Olympic teams the world has ever known." Miles softened his tone. "Don't you think it has been a mistake for the Left to identify so strongly with groups that have an image of being weak or repellent?"

Miles was playing it for all he was worth. And the thing of it was, it was working. Nate was totally taken in: he nodded his head when Miles nodded; he frowned when Miles frowned. In response to Miles's last question, Nate stood there with his mouth still partially open; his eyes were drawn tightly at the corners. Miles turned around and began working at the computer.

Thank God, Jeff thought, *that's over*. Miles had made his point, with serious punctuation. But more importantly, he had cleverly avoided answering Nate's question. Jeff wondered whether Nate would come back to it.

After a minute of standing there looking as if he were totally lost, Nate finally said, "So… What is this great plan you have?"

Miles said, "I doubt you would understand what we are doing here. How much do you know about C programming language, encryption algorithms, mud agents, chatter bots, stuff like that?" Miles shot Jeff a quick glance as if to say, let him chew on that.

"Nothing. Explain it in English," Nate replied.

Miles said, "Basically, we are going to generate customized software using the very best encryption algorithms and imbed that software into tiny electronic chips that we then install into the electronics of the iPhones."

Miles stopped and kept his gaze right at Nate.

Nate seems out of his element, and he must be coming to realize he knows nothing of this stuff. And we do, Jeff thought.

Then, as if to punctuate Jeff's thought, Miles continued, "The authorities can still do traffic analysis—watching the flow of encrypted messages. Our software will confuse that traffic analysis, in part by sending out bogus messages all over the place and in part by disguising the origin of the transmissions. Also, since every serious encryption algorithm has to be licensed by the feds, so they have the keys to break in, we are going to add an interface that will take the security of the PGP encryption up an order of magnitude. It will slow things down a little, especially our verbal communications, which will sound more like an overseas conversation, with delays, but the increase in security is worth it."

Nate's expression was blank; he stuffed the remainder of a 3 Musketeers bar into his mouth and tossed the wrapper at a trash can in the corner. The balled-up wrapper bounced off the rim, hit the wall behind, fell into the corner, and rolled around to the side of the trash. *No surprise there,* Jeff thought. *Looks dumb; eats junk; lousy shot.*

"What's that there?" Nate pointed to a table adjacent to the trash; on top of the table sat a box-shaped device with what looked like a small radio dish protruding out one side.

Jeff said, "Do you know anything about electromagnetic radiation?"

"Listen, punk, I asked you the question. By God don't give me any bull. What is it?"

Nate had obviously had it with the verbal games. Time to be direct. Jeff said, "It's a scanner, basically. We can use it to read the electromagnetic signals from a computer screen and/or the attached cables."

Nate's eyes flashed with intrigue. "Is that one of those TEMPEST things?"

Jeff was startled. "Yeah. Transient Electromagnetic Pulse Surveillance Technology. It's a classified project of the NSA and the Department of Defense." Jeff regarded the device with a bit of pride. "It's rumored they used a device like this—though I'm sure theirs was much more sophisticated—to break the Aldrich Ames case. What do you know about it?"

"Not much. Just heard about them. I wasn't sure one really existed. How does it work?"

Miles broke in, "In simple terms, your screen receives from the computer and then processes certain signals that tell LEDs to fire, and every time they fire they emit a measurable level of electromagnetic radiation. Our device has a phased array antenna that intercepts that radiation and, in real time, we get an exact image on our screen of what is appearing on the subject screen."

Nate's face lit up. "Praise the Lord."

"Jeff and I made it from mostly off-the-shelf parts. You just aim this end at the monitor you want to hack and plug this end into a port on any Mac with this software loaded." Miles held up a DVD that had been sitting in a disk organizer next to one of the computers. Nate's eyes followed Miles's hand as if it were holding the Holy

Grail. For a moment, Jeff wondered what the fuss was about. He and Miles had used the device to surreptitiously look at a few computer screens. Thrilling at first, it had quickly become terribly boring, watching people work on mundane letters, play games, or do their finances.

Nate said, "So where do you get the parts?"

Jeff replied, "We've got a few catalogues. Lots of places on line if you know what you are looking for."

Nate's eyes seemed to brighten and a slow smile spread across his face. Jeff felt a twinge of uneasiness. Nate said, "I think I could put that thing to good use. Mind if I borrow it for a while?" Nate snatched the disk out of Miles's hand, picked up the scanner, and said, "I've seen enough. Let me know when you get a little closer to being finished with your super duper computer crap. I'll be back." Nate turned and headed up the ladder.

Jeff and Miles looked at each other. Jeff couldn't believe Nate was leaving. They hadn't had to describe anything in any detail. It was almost as if Nate had forgotten why he had come there.

Jeff said, "Maybe it wasn't such a good idea to tell him about the scanner."

❧

BILL FLETCHER HAD ARRANGED TO MEET HARTMAN AT Hartman's home in the rural thumb area of Michigan, just north of the small town of Vassar. As he drove along the long, winding, dirt driveway to Hartman's home, he began to see why Hartman had wanted to meet elsewhere. Hartman had tried awfully hard to be "helpful" by offering to come to Detroit for the interview, but Bill's years as an investigator and student of armed combat were causing red flags to pop up everywhere.

For the entire length of the quarter-mile drive, there were expansive areas of lawn that stretched from the drive to fairly dense woods bursting with some of the most spectacular fall colors he had ever seen. The area approaching the driveway had been cleared of trees, shrubs, and anything else a person might use to hide. Apart from creating a nice-looking lawn, which is the only thing the untrained eye would note, the entire drive made for an excellent killing zone; the treeless lawn provided a clear field of fire from the cover and concealment of the surrounding woods.

Bill drove along with his windows open to catch the fragrance of grass and trees. He inhaled deeply and wondered how much more he could learn of the puzzle of Hartman Kreig—pieces of which were beginning to fit together.

Bill had waited for Hartman to heal up from his gunshots before interviewing him. There was no particular hurry. All the bad guys were dead, so the case was pretty much closed. Yet, Bill was interested in learning about Hartman's obvious skills with a handgun. That level of proficiency did not just happen. Bill's investigative instincts were also piqued by his prior conversation with Jeff Kreig. The younger Kreig was more than just nervous; he was hiding something. And that was the curious part. What the heck would he be hiding?

Hartman was standing at the front porch when Bill pulled up. It apparently hadn't rained in a while, and his car stirred up a large cloud of dust. Bill quickly raised the windows to prevent the dust from settling in his car. As he got out of the car he noticed that he had stirred up billows of dust all along the driveway.

The small house was sparsely furnished. A quick scan showed nothing out of the ordinary. It was a bachelor pad. A small TV sat on a table at one end of the living room. Next to it was a mini-stereo system sitting on an old chest. There was an Apple Computer in the opposite corner; it appeared to be off, or asleep. It was asleep, Bill decided. Several tiny green lights were glowing on the various pieces of equipment, which included what appeared to be an all-in-one scanner-printer-copier-fax machine, a router or some such, and likely a cable modem.

Hartman offered a beer or a pop. Bill took neither. The men sat at opposite ends of the small, rectangular kitchen table that extended well into the "living room." The place really was small.

As Bill expected by now, Hartman took the seat with a wall directly behind—probably a brick wall covered by drywall. It was the least obvious way to "bullet proof" your house.

One more piece of the puzzle, Bill thought as he watched Hartman fold his hands in front of him; his movements were so deliberate. His smile seemed relaxed. This was going to be interesting. "So how is our hero?" he asked as earnestly as he could.

Hartman's smile widened. "I'm no hero. I just did what a citizen with a permit to carry should do. But thanks for the compliment."

And he is modest, Bill thought. He had half-expected a bit of arrogance. "So how did the last guy nick you. You got the drop on the other two?"

"Screwed up."

And honest, Bill thought. "Okay. But how?" *So far,* Bill reminded himself. *Honest, so far.*

Hartman shook his head and glanced out the living room window which, Bill noticed for the first time, provided a clear view of approaching traffic on the driveway. "He came at me in the low ready. That put his muzzle on me without any effort to aim. It startled me and I jerked the first shot. A very basic mistake." Hartman rubbed his hand over his face. "I'm thirsty." He got up and headed toward the refrigerator. "You sure you don't want anything?"

Bill shook his head.

Hartman grabbed an exotic pale ale and came back to the table.

Bill said, "You're no beginner. Where did you learn to shoot like that?"

Hartman took a long swig and set the bottle down with a thud, causing the beer to foam up in the bottle. That made Bill thirsty. He glanced back up at Hartman and was startled to see that Hartman had been studying him while he had been fascinated by the foaming beer. This guy was good. He was very good.

Hartman stared into Bill's eyes as if to confirm what Bill already felt. Hartman said, "Gunsite. I've taken almost every combat course they offer: three on handguns, two on tactical rifle, combat shotgun,

edged weapons. I've done a few IPSC competitions, stuff like that."
He took another pull on his beer.

"Okay, that explains your expertise." Bill was well aware of the
skills imparted by Gunsite. It was generally accepted that completion of just the introductory week-long course on handguns was
equal, if not superior, to the training received by most police officers. What was troubling Bill was the strange way Hartman seemed
to be so relaxed and in control. Perhaps his next question would
change that. "Now a more personal question. Why?"

Hartman already had the beer up for another swig. He took his
time setting it down. "Why what?"

Time to push it—retake control with some pointed questions.
"Why such an interest in fighting skills? Surely that's not all necessary for self-defense. You have taken a lot of interest in learning how
to kill."

"I have?" Hartman smiled.

Bill was confused. Hartman had learned to kill; that was obvious.
So why deny it? Hartman was playing with him. And now it was getting irritating.

Hartman finished off his beer and went to the refrigerator for
another. He waved to the beer inside, and Bill again nodded "no."
Hartman sat back down, popped the cap, took a small sip and again
banged the bottle on the table. This time, Bill kept his eyes on
Hartman.

Hartman stared back, and for a tense moment neither said anything. Bill was about to break the silence by repeating the question
when Hartman said, "Which of those courses would you have suggested I not take? And if I followed your advice, would you guarantee the lives of the hostages I managed to save?"

Ouch. Bill grimaced inside. The guy was either pretty quick or
he had thought about this stuff for some time. Truth was, Bill knew
from FBI files, even a home defense scenario might necessitate any,
or all, of the weapons for which Hartman was evidently well trained.
But that merely begged the question Bill was most anxious to ask,
and which he felt Hartman would be least willing to answer.

"So, what sparked your personal interest in such training?"

Hartman paused before answering. He cast his eyes around the room, focused down at his hands, which he was rubbing together just above the table. *Interesting,* Bill thought, *the first signs of nervousness.* The question had hit home. Then, suddenly, a fire flared up in Hartman's gaze. It burst forth like a match flashing to life. Bill had the chilling thought that he was looking at the intense expression all three gunmen had probably taken to their graves.

Hartman pushed the beer to the side, nearly out of reach. He said, "30 years ago, police officers were respected and admired. Now they are pigs and regularly get sued by the criminals they arrest. Thirty years ago a woman could walk the streets in the evening. People left their doors unlocked so neighbors could drop by for coffee or even to grab something from your cupboard if you were not there to lend it. You would come home to see a thank-you note for the borrowed flour, or butter, or whatever. Criminals are so brazen now that they will break your car window, pull you out the door, shoot you as you lie in the street, and then calmly drive off in your car— all in the middle of a busy downtown intersection! Well, I decided long ago that no one was going to do that to me or my family, damn it!" Hartman slammed his fist on the table so hard the beer bottle jumped, rattled, and finally teetered over, splashing foamy beer across the table. Hartman quickly snapped it up, cursed, and mumbled something about the beer being too expensive to throw around.

Okay, Bill thought. *Probably a good idea to never cross this guy. Also probably a good idea to get out of Dodge before he really gets pissed off.* It was smart to avoid unnecessary danger. "Fine, Mr. Kreig. I personally agree with you. And I don't have any further questions at this point. Can I call you if I think of something else?" Of course, Bill knew—that Hartman knew—that Bill could call and continue his investigation. It just seemed like a good time to be extra polite.

"Sure. Fine." Hartman was swabbing up the beer with some paper towels. A fresh beer was already on the counter next to the refrigerator.

As Bill drove back to his office, he couldn't get the last few moments of his conversation with Hartman out of his mind. The guy had seemed so composed, actually in control of the interview. Several pieces of the puzzle had fallen into place. Then he got to talking about what things were like, what did he say, 30 years ago? And he got madder and madder as he spoke.

Then he just exploded…

❧

CHAPTER 10

NATE SMITH HEADED NORTH ON I-75 TO MEET WITH HIS best Communications, Command, Control and Intelligence (C3I) people. He hoped they could enhance Jeff and Miles's little device. With the grace of God, they would finally crack the security of the Energy Department.

Nate passed a large billboard advertisement by the ACLU seeking members. He rolled down his window and spat at the sign as he raced by at exactly 79 miles per hour. The ACLU would have government—no, United Nations' police—at every corner and in every home to make sure no one prayed or talked about creationism! And God forbid someone might want to put a Santa Claus on public property! Nate ran his hand through his hair and gritted his teeth. He came up on a slow-moving Toyota and swerved into the fast lane to pass. The driver was another oriental, sucking the country dry and buying Jap cars. Nate swerved back into the slow lane just a little too soon. The driver of the Toyota hit his brakes and flipped his middle finger at Nate, who returned the gesture.

Now he was really mad. Nate ran his hand through his hair and put the steering wheel in a death grip. This used to be a Christian nation—until the ACLU and the feds let every minority overrun the place. Now every self-proclaimed minority was trying to tell God-loving Americans what they could and couldn't do. It wasn't always like this…

Nate Smith had grown up on a small Nebraska farm. His parents were God-fearing and they regularly took Nate and his twin sister, Elizabeth, to church. Nate learned that the Heavenly Father rewarded those who lived a good life. Accordingly, Nate worked hard at everything he did. He earned good grades and was diligent in his physical conditioning program. In high school, he excelled as a halfback in football and he led his team to the state championship by scoring two touchdowns late in the fourth quarter, both on dramatic, long runs. He dreamed of one day playing for the Nebraska Cornhuskers.

Things quickly soured, however, when his family was in a terrible car accident while traveling home from the state championship football game. His father Caleb survived after a long stay in intensive care. His mother Louise and his sister Elizabeth died at the scene. Nate was stunned. How could God allow such a terrible thing? Neither his mom nor sister had committed any serious trespass. Nate's entire image of God was shattered. He dropped out of school and a short time later he fell away from the church for years, though he never completely stopped reading the Bible.

Nate's dad sold the farm and moved closer to his family in Omaha. For an entire year, Nate bummed around doing odd jobs at various farms. Finally, he decided that both his sister and his mom would have wanted him to get on with his life. He completed his high school degree and applied to the University of Nebraska.

The summer before his first semester at Nebraska, Nate walked on to the football team as a defensive halfback. Pretty quickly, however, he realized that something was wrong. He had changed and could no longer take the normal abuse football coaches dish out. In high school, he had always smiled and redoubled his efforts to do better. Now, however, his temper was on a short fuse, and he found himself snarling back at his coaches and teammates. Just before the opening game, Nate learned he had been demoted to third string and he promptly cussed out his coaches and quit.

Two semesters later, Nate quit college. He returned to his home town, took a job at the post office, and married his high-school sweetheart, Carena. Six months later, in a fit of rage against his boss, Nate stormed out of the post office and walked across the street and into the Navy recruiting station. He decided to try out for SEAL training and soon learned he had jumped from the frying pan into the fryer. For someone who couldn't handle authority, the military was not a great place in general, and the SEALS was arguably the worst place of all.

Yet, something was different this time. It wasn't a football game or a stupid job he had to suffer to keep. No, becoming one of the finest warriors in the world was the issue. And as hard as he had fought others before, now he fought himself to stay and endure. When the suffering was done, he was a United States Navy SEAL.

The following years of military life were bearable, however, only because he found his training and assignments so interesting and intensive. Life as a seal was more than busy, yet it still left plenty of time to contemplate the idiocy of the Navy brass.

Anger still brewed under the surface, and it finally boiled over when President Bush chickened out on finishing off Saddam Hussein. Nate's SEAL team had gone ashore off a submarine well north in Iraq. The men had risked their lives to locate Saddam and were preparing to eliminate him when the order came in to abort. Knowing it was a political decision merely intensified Nate's brewing frustration.

With the end of the Gulf War, Nate unhesitatingly left the military and took his wife and two-year old daughter Carrie to a farm near Prairie Creek, Idaho. It was a place, Nate had learned, that still had a one-room schoolhouse. The closest city with a population of over 100 was a two-hour drive in good weather. In winter, the roads were frequently impassible. When Carena expressed some concern about such an isolated locale, Nate assured his wife that they had all the modern conveniences. After all, Prairie Creek did receive mail twice a week.

Life slowed for Nate and, at first, he found the farm a welcome change from the military. Carena turned out to be a popular hostess, and Saturday evening card games became a regular community occurrence. Life was good.

Still, anger smoldered under the surface, and eventually it caused him to rail against authority. Anytime the Saturday evening confabulations turned to politics or government, Nate found himself venting enough hostility for the whole group. One evening, the topic of conversation centered on the unconstitutionality of the Federal Income Tax. One of the card-playing friends, Todd Sanders, explained he'd read somewhere that the Sixteenth Amendment was never legitimately ratified by the states. That meant the Federal Income Tax was invalid, and to enforce it was therefore unconstitutional. As a result, Todd, along with his wife Debbie, were going to become tax protesters and no longer pay any federal income tax.

Nate was impressed with the Sanders's courage and apparent knowledge of the tax law. That night, Nate made the decision to do some research on his own. If his friends were right, Nate was never again going to pay one red cent of income tax to the federal government.

When summer arrived, Nate headed into Grangeville, the closest city with a substantial library. With the help of an attractive young librarian, Nate gathered a number of materials and piled them into a secluded study carrel.

As luck, or fate, would have it, the librarian found Nate quite attractive, and she stopped by every few minutes to see if he needed anything else. In fact, Nate needed help getting through portions of the legal mumbo jumbo and the young lady was qualified, and willing. She also smelled terrific.

Nate returned a week later to continue his research. By now he had learned the librarian's first name, Emily, her age, 23, and that she was single and lived only a few blocks from the library. When he walked into the library her face lit up and she came out from behind the counter to meet him. Somewhat taken aback, but with his mind set on his research, Nate chitchatted for a few moments before excusing himself to his cubby full of books. For the first time, however, Nate noticed how good she looked, and when she turned away

PAGE 174 ◆ CAMERON REDDY

he found himself watching her rear, rounded and slender, shimmy back and forth in her skirt.

The day's research was extremely productive. Nate found a law text that explained how the United States Supreme Court held the Income Tax Act of 1894 to be unconstitutional since it placed a direct tax on income—without allocation among the states in proportion to population—as required by Article I of the United States Constitution. *Pollock v. Farmer's Loan & Trust Co.*, 157 U.S. 429 (1895), *affirmed on rehearing*, 158 U.S. 601 (1895). The court relied on the United States Constitution, Article I, Section 9, clause 4: "No Capitation, or other direct, Tax shall be laid, unless in Proportion to the Census…"

Interestingly, on rehearing, the court limited its ruling to income derived from real estate and invested property. As respected a general income tax, the court noted that *Springer v. United States*, 102 U.S. 586 (1880), had sustained the Civil War Income Tax under the guise of calling it a tax that would not be subject to the constitutional requirement of apportionment.

Nate wasn't sure what all that meant. He walked up to ask Emily. She was waiting for him.

As Nate approached, he noticed that Emily did not seem to be wearing a bra. *That's funny*, he thought. He hadn't noticed that when he came in.

Emily insisted on going back to the study carrel and she sat Nate in the chair and stood to his side, leaning across to read the text. When she finished reading, she pushed the book aside and sat on the desk, her pert breasts at Nate's eye level.

"It means the *Pollock* court was trying very hard to say that *Springer* stood on shaky ground. Who would object to an income tax during the war?" Nate was the one who started to feel as though he was on shaky ground. Emily's nipples seemed to beckon. She said, "I've got to lock up from noon to one o'clock. Can I make you a lunch?"

Nate felt an immediate surge in his loins as that part of his anatomy was fighting for decision-making authority. His conscience struck back hard with images of fire, brimstone, and his beautiful wife and child. But they were images. And Emily's breasts were right in front of him. And he knew that the rest of her was only a short walk away.

Nate stood and gave her a kiss. Still sitting on the desk directly in front of him, she quickly wrapped her legs around his waist and pulled him into her. He could feel his hardness press and grind into her and she gently worked her pelvic muscles. After a few moments, she released him, hopped down from the desk, reached out her hand and rubbed the bulge in his jeans. She told him to meet her at the back door. She would be there in just a second...

In several visits over the following weeks, Nate undressed more than the supposed constitutionality of the income tax.

On the issue of the income tax, Nate discovered that, with the decision in *Pollock* rejecting an income tax on income from real estate and invested property, and with the foundation of *Springer* called into question, the Sixteenth Amendment was clearly necessary to affirm the legality of the income tax:

> The Congress shall have power to lay and collect taxes on incomes, from whatever source derived, without apportionment among the several States, and without regard to any census or enumeration.

But therein was the rub: Incredibly, the Sixteenth Amendment had never been ratified by the requisite number of states. Emily dug up a copy of *The Law That Never Was—The Fraud of the 16th Amendment and Personal Income Tax,* by Martin J. "Red" Beckman and Bill Benson. Nate flipped open to a page that summarized the shocking irregularities in the ratification process:

» Several states voted on grammatically different versions of the Sixteenth Amendment.

» Some states failed to deliver certification of their vote.

» Some states, listed as ratifying the amendment, actually voted against ratification.

» In one case, nothing more than a telephone call from a governor was relied upon to conclude that his state had ratified the amendment.

Perhaps due to all of these irregularities, opined the authors Beckman and Benson, then Secretary of State Philander C. Knox obtained a legal memorandum from the Solicitor General on the issue of whether the amendment had passed.

That memorandum, even Nate could see, was fraught with unfounded assumptions and flawed logic. Moreover, in the process of concluding that the Sixteenth Amendment had been properly ratified, it acknowledged fatal irregularities in the ratification process!

It didn't take a rocket scientist to see the double-talk. The situation screamed fraud and conspiracy.

Nor, by the way, did it take a genius to see that Nate was getting deeper into trouble with Emily.

Nate forced himself to stay away from the library for a month. During that time he came to his senses and determined to call off the affair.

He also decided to stop paying federal taxes.

When he finally returned to the library, Emily had moved on to take a job on the West Coast. Nate stood looking at Emily's replacement, an elderly woman with a big head of white hair. She asked him whether anything was wrong, and he just turned and headed out the door and into the sunlight. Something *was* wrong: it had never occurred to Nate that Emily might have been using him more than he was using her! Nate walked briskly away.

Once away from the library, however, Nate's feelings shifted from anger to relief. He realized he had been given a new lease on life. A wave of humiliation swept over him, and he determined to be a more caring father and a more faithful husband.

Along with his renewed commitment to wife and child, Nate became a tireless worker and nearly doubled his farm's productivity. In addition, he found time to organize a tax protest group that nearly succeeded in electing to the United States Senate a staunch conservative who ran on a platform to abolish all federal income taxes.

Ultimately, of course, what Nate had really done by halting tax payments and heading up a congressional campaign was make himself a lightning rod for the Internal Revenue Service. Naturally, the IRS decided to draw a line in the sand.

The cute and clever policy in the IRS was to "lien first, ask questions later." Nate and Carena were actually fairly wealthy, largely because they had kept all of their money. As a result, they financed a legal battle that went all the way to the United States Court of Appeals.

Predictably, however, the Court of Appeals bowed to pragmatism. A ruling in favor of the tax protest would create the legal equivalent of an atomic explosion. It would unleash tax protesters all over the country, virtually wipe out the federal government's source of income and cause, thereby, government services to come to a screeching halt.

The Court of Appeals denied Nate's appeal without even requesting oral argument (an indication that the court found the issue easy to decide). And the IRS promptly confiscated and sold the Smiths' farm to pay off back taxes and the penalties which were, by then, astronomical.

Nate responded by taking his family even deeper into the mountains to live off the land and interact with as few people as possible. In fact, he and his wife were able to get along quite well hunting, fishing, and trading animal pelts for necessities they couldn't raise on their land. Once a month they would go into the tiny mountain town of Eagle Pass, Idaho, which sits nearly astride the Continental Divide, and trade pelts for flour, corn meal, and canned goods when they could not grow sufficient vegetables in their garden. They kept a cow for milk and butter, and a few chickens for eggs.

The fly in the ointment was that the IRS was not appeased.

Yes, the Smiths had paid their back taxes and penalties (with the proceeds from the confiscated farm). But the IRS didn't like the fact that Nate and Carena were able to barter and trade for all of the items they couldn't raise. In point of fact, the IRS loses millions in tax revenue each year to such "cash" transactions and other "trades" that never get reported. So the IRS, in cooperation with the BATF, which also was on the hunt for gun fanatics who seemed to flock to remote mountain regions, set up a sting operation.

Nate traded several fur pelts for some tools he needed and a used, Gunsite-customized Colt AR-15 Sporter equipped with a new laser sight that federal regulations had recently made illegal. To the glee of the IRS, the federal government once again had Nate in its sights.

The IRS and the BATF coordinated efforts and waited for the tax filing deadline. No return having been received from Nate and Carena, the two federal agencies carefully planned and timed the delivery of both the warrant to search the premises for illegal weapons and the IRS notice that Nate and Carena had under-reported their income due to bartering.

Three days later there was a drive-by shooting of an IRS office in nearby Missoula. Two IRS agents were cut by shattering glass. While there were no witnesses, Nate was the obvious suspect. The BATF and the FBI began planning their assault on the Smith's home.

☙

RECALLING THE SIMILARITIES WITH RANDY WEAVER AND the catastrophe at Ruby Ridge, where Randy Weaver's son and wife were killed, the BATF and FBI were careful to ensure that the shooting protocol was clearly defined. Unlike the order issued at Ruby Ridge, where FBI agents were given the authority to shoot on sight, in this instance an agent could shoot only if threatened, and only in defense.

The two agents assigned to watch the front and rear entrances of the Smiths' cabin were equipped with night-vision goggles. They had been watching since darkness fell, and it was very nearly dawn. So far, neither had seen anything: no lights in the cabin, no movement through the open windows. It had been a long night and both officers were struggling to stay awake. Al Morris, the 10-year veteran watching the rear entrance, had gotten bored and knew he was in danger of nodding off. To help stay awake, he began casting his gaze onto the mountain ridges surrounding the area. He had heard he might be able to spot an eagle or two. He was quickly moving his goggles from spot to spot, having the effect of shaking his head to stay awake. Then, after a few quick glances toward the ridges, he would turn back to focus on the cabin's rear door. He was certain he wouldn't miss anything. One or more lights would go on inside the cabin before someone headed out. Al was sure of it.

Al Morris, in fact, had the habit of getting up each morning and turning on every light in his bedroom (there were four) in order to see his way around. His wife Nancy was a restless sleeper and frequently woke from the flash of lights. However, since she did not work outside the home but took care of their two teenagers, she never complained to Al that he should use a little courtesy and keep the light show to a minimum.

Consequently, it never occurred to Al Morris that a man might go out of his way to guard his wife's sleep. As it was, on this morning, Nate intended to rise before Carena. He got up and in total darkness dressed and retrieved his fishing gear. He headed toward his back door, careful to not bump into anything that might make a noise and thus disturb his wife's sleep.

The sleepy agent Morris had just turned his gaze back to the ridge. He jerked his head to and fro a couple of times, thus checking several spots on the ridge, and quickly returned his watch to the rear door of the cabin. For a second, he thought he saw something in his peripheral view—something moving into the adjacent woods. Al felt his heart skip a beat as he scanned the darkness and wondered if he had just missed something. But, looking back to the cabin, he noted that no lights were on. He decided it must have been an animal, or perhaps just his imagination…

Forty minutes later, just as the sun was casting a halo around the edges of the ridge to the east, other agents saw a light go in the cabin. Within a few minutes they saw Carena come out the front door with her daughter in tow. They were apparently headed to the river, where it was known the Smiths washed their clothes. It wasn't realized, however, that the Smiths bathed themselves in the river.

It was the perfect opportunity to arrest Nate. With him alone in the cabin, or so they assumed, there would be no danger of collateral damage. Several FBI swat agents approached, each with his old Sig Sauer P226 held at low ready. Two agents headed toward the cabin and two headed toward the river. Two more agents, armed with Bennelli Super 90 semiautomatic shotguns, covered the agents approaching the cabin. Finally, two FBI snipers took up positions along a ridge that gave them a clear shot to the cabin. They were armed with Springfield M1A/M-21 Tactical sniper rifles. The agents who carried these guns were proud of their ability to hit a felon in the eye at 300+ yards. They were set up about 250 yards from the Smith's cabin. Everyone was clad in dark blue uniforms that had a bright yellow "FBI" insignia on the front and back.

Carena was standing on a rock that jutted into the water. She was naked from the waist up. Her hair was dripping water and she reached for a towel. Just beyond the towel lay Carena's Ruger Custom GP-100 with six-inch barrel, ported to tame the recoil of her 158 grain 357 Magnum +p cartridges. She was careful never to venture very far without her gun; teeth-bearing animals of various descriptions were a real danger to the unarmed. Carrie was sitting on an adjacent rock, waiting for her turn to wash up.

The morning sun was just coming over the canyon wall behind veteran FBI agents Hollings and Beckwith. They came around an outcropping of rocks and saw Carena about 40 yards away. They had holstered their sidearms—there being no immediate danger and assuredly not wanting to unduly startle Carena and her daughter.

Agent Beckwith announced, "Ma'am, FBI."

❧

CARENA HEARD SOMETHING AND LOOKED IN THE DIRECtion of the sound, which was, unfortunately, directly into the sun. She was unable to see details, and the rushing river was so loud.

All she could see was the silhouette of two men.

Carena was instantly and distinctly aware of her exposed breasts. She had heard of instances were women were accosted while bathing in the mountain rivers. It was rare, and usually dealt with quite sternly by the locals. But nevertheless, it had occurred on a couple of occasions.

Carena thought, *Well, these assholes are not going to rape my daughter!* Her pulse shot up and her eyes darted around her immediate surroundings. She knew the 357 was buried under some clothes.

Agents Hollings and Beckwith saw Carena lunge for some clothes on an adjacent rock. They assumed her modesty dictated that she put on a top.

In one smooth motion, Carena retrieved her weapon and thrust it forward in a rigid, Ayoob-inspired isosceles stance. Her fear had taken over and she was already experiencing the tunnel vision that comes when the fight-or-flight response is triggered. Further, her mind skipped over important parts of the training Nate had given her: against human threats, raise the gun to a low ready position, angled about 45 degrees away from the body and thus not directly at the threats, and place the index finger of the firing hand off the trigger and ramrod straight against the trigger guard.

Nate had stressed that she was not to raise the gun or place the finger on the trigger, or put her front sight on the threat, until she reasonably believed herself to be in immediate danger of grave, bodily harm.

◆

CARENA'S ACT OF POINTING THE 357 DIRECTLY AT THE agents caused both of them to respond exactly per *their* training. Both agents screamed, "Drop the gun" and dived sideways and away from each other—agent Beckwith to Carena's right and agent Hollings to her left. As they rolled on the ground each agent drew his sidearm. In a nearly perfectly choreographed motion, complete with dust flying, both agents came to a stop on their sides with their Sig Sauers trained. They both found their sights and, seeing that

Carena had not dropped her gun, they both started the long, first double action pull of the trigger…

❧

NOT ALL OF CARENA'S TRAINING HAD GONE OUT THE WINdow. She had hunted varmints with her 357 and was pretty good at hitting a moving target. The tactical problem, however, was new: she had never encountered multiple targets—let alone multiple targets pulling sidearms and aiming at her. The confusion caused Carena to pause a moment too long. She saw her front sight and a distant image of her first target. She pulled the long but smooth stroke of the revolver's trigger.

The muzzle of her gun jumped and spewed fire through the custom ports and out the front of the barrel.

Immediately, Carena pivoted to her left to engage the next target. Just as she found her front sight and began pulling the trigger, she felt a sharp impact in her chest. The impact caused her body to jerk and she pulled the trigger wildly in response. Instantly, she knew she had been shot and that she had missed the second target. She felt a second thump in the chest as she retrained her sights. This time, however, she gritted her teeth and ignored the searing, burning sensation. Again her gun jumped and spewed fire.

It was the last thing she saw.

❧

AGENT HOLLINGS WATCHED AS CARENA'S LEGS GAVE OUT and she crumpled to the ground. Through the screaming pain in his left shoulder, he knew that both of his shots had been center hits to her chest. He praised his training, which had bought the fractions of a second he had needed to get off a couple of shots before Carena had time to shoot his partner and pivot to engage him. Yet, he also cursed the puny 9 mm loads of his gun. The first shot to Carena's chest had most certainly pierced her heart, yet it had not shut down her nervous system quickly enough to spoil her ability to return fire.

From the blast Carena's gun had made, Hollings knew she had been firing a 357. He didn't have to look at his shoulder to know the effect of that famed round. Probably, he figured, his wound would not be fatal. On the other hand, he knew he'd played his last game of tennis.

Agent Hollings struggled to his feet and walked over to Beckwith. It was immediately clear that he was gone. Carena's first shot had been a direct cranial hit. Hollings walked over to Carena. She was sprawled over a rock only a foot or two from the swiftly running river. He glanced up at Carrie, who was trying to hide behind a couple of large boulders. He could see she was crying and suddenly he felt a lump in his throat. Only a moment ago he had shot a killer. Now, the sight of Carrie brought home the fact that he had also killed a mother. If only he could have the last 60 seconds back. The sound of the rushing water blotted out all other sounds and, para-doxically, filled his heart with agony. Tears began to roll down his cheeks.

❧

HEARING THE FIRST SHOTS, NATE HAD IMMEDIATELY TAKEN off in a full-speed sprint along the bank of the river—six-inch fishing knife in hand. Three times he had heard the dis-tinct report of his wife's 357. He had also heard two "pops" from what must have been small-bore semi-automatics. He was racing barefoot along the bank, scrambling over rocks and branches that littered the river. As he came around the outcropping of rocks that extended some 100 yards to the area Carena had been using to bathe, he saw someone standing over his half-naked wife. Nate raced the last 100 yards as swiftly as a leopard moving in for the kill.

❧

A GENT HOLLINGS WOULD HAVE BEEN BETTER OFF HAD HE died from Carena's gunshots. Instead, he felt himself thrown to the ground, whereupon Nate Smith jumped on him and brandished a huge knife. In stunned disbelief, Hollings watched as Nate plunged the fishing knife into his chest. In too much shock to respond, Hollings then watched as Nate viciously yanked down on the knife, rending open a huge cavity and exposing a heart that was still beating. The last thing Hollings saw was his own heart being ripped out of his body, with the arteries stretching and snapping and spurting blood everywhere.

☙

I T WAS ALL OVER BY THE TIME THE SEVERAL AGENTS WHO HAD unwittingly surrounded the cabin got down to the river. It looked like a cattle slaughter. Blood and internal body parts were everywhere; Nate had not stopped with tearing out Hollings's heart.

Nate was quietly sitting on a rock by the river. His daughter was next to him. They were both sobbing, and Nate was arrested without further incident.

Three months later Nate went to trial. The newly appointed federal prosecutor, the gray-haired and portly Ted Palmer, was a former plaintiff's attorney who knew precious little about criminal law. He also lacked a good sense of fairness, having had a typical career in private practice of getting a lot for a little.

With his policy-making authority, Mr. Palmer had created a new "no bargain" program and he charged Nate accordingly. In the river deaths, Nate was charged, under the "felony murder rule," with three counts of first-degree murder. In the drive-by shootings of the IRS agents, Nate was charged with two counts of attempted murder and two counts of felony firearm (the use or possession of a firearm in the course of committing a felony). Mr. Palmer steadfastly refused to offer lesser charges such as manslaughter in the river deaths, or reckless endangerment in the drive-by shootings.

On the defense was a court-appointed woman fresh from law school. Fortunately for Nate, however, Christy Daniels had excelled in a clinical law program and was keen-witted.

The trial saw the usual bevy of expert witnesses for both the prosecution and the defense. The prosecution's most damaging expert testimony regarded the ballistics. The young female FBI lab technician displayed blown-up pictures of the bullets fired into the IRS office and those fired at the agents. It was clear that the custom 357 left telltale marks on the bullets.

A fingerprint expert testified that the 357 contained Nate's fingerprints as well as Carena's. Circumstantially, it was also incriminating that the shots rang out within three days of Nate's receipt of the IRS notice and BATF search warrant.

The first defense witness was a psychiatrist, Dr. Edmund Beaumont. Dr. Beaumont testified that his examination of Nate showed that Nate had simply "lost it," and obviously had gone berserk. It was a clear case, Dr. Beaumont opined, of temporary insanity.

On cross examination, Prosecutor Palmer asked, "Dr. Beaumont, how far away from the deceased Agent Hollings was the defendant when the defendant first saw him?"

"As I said, the defendant was about 100 yards away from his wife and the agent when he first saw them."

"Dr. Beaumont, in your opinion, how long does it take for someone to form the criminal intent to kill?"

"It would vary based on intelligence."

"In the defendant's case?"

"It would also vary on the circumstances."

"Okay, then, in the circumstances in which the defendant found himself when he first saw Agent Hollings?"

"I would say that he could form the intent to kill within a few seconds. That would be a natural response to—"

"Yes. Thank you, Doctor. And how long did it take the defendant to cover the 100 or so yards to reach the agent?"

The doctor looked down in his lap and spoke in a barely audible tone. "About 12 seconds."

The judge interjected. "Please speak up, Doctor."

More loudly this time, the doctor said, "About 12 seconds."

Prosecutor Palmer said, "Thank you. Now, Doctor, isn't it possible, in fact likely, that the defendant saw his wife, formed the intent to kill, and carried out that intent, all in the time it took him to run that 100 yards?"

"It is possible. But—"

Prosecutor Palmer smiled at the doctor and turned his head toward the Judge. "Thank you, Doctor. No further questions, Your Honor."

Christy Daniels huffed, "I have a couple of follow-up questions for re-direct, Your Honor."

"Very well," said the judge.

Daniels jumped up from the defense table and strode confidently over to the witness stand.

"Dr. Beaumont, I have argued to the jury that the defendant lacked the necessary criminal intent, *the mens rea*, as it is referred to in the law. Upon seeing agent Hollings hovering over his bloodied and partially disrobed wife, he lapsed into an uncontrollable rage. I have argued that, at no specific point in time did Nate Smith stop and think, 'I am going to do x, y, and z, which will have the effect of killing Agent Hollings.' I have argued that there was no chance for premeditation—no malice aforethought. Everything happened as a single, reflexive, event... Now, Dr. Beaumont, do you still believe that I am right?"

"Yes."

"Doctor, when the defendant first saw Agent Hollings hovering over his wife, could he have known if his wife was in fact dead?"

"Objection!" boomed Ted Palmer. "The question requires the witness to speculate!"

"Counsel?" asked the judge, glaring skeptically at Ms. Daniels.

"Your Honor, the doctor is a medical doctor as well as a psychiatrist. I think he is qualified to opine on whether the physical condition, the state, if you will, of Ms. Smith, could have been ascertained by an untrained person some 100 yards away."

The judge quickly nodded. "Overruled. The witness may answer—"

The doctor continued, "No. He could not possibly have known she was dead, or even severely injured, until he was much closer. To know she was dead, or likely so, he would have had to be very close. The bullet wounds in her chest were very small. A nine millimeter bullet makes a very small hole."

Ms. Daniels asked, "So, the defendant would not have known the state of his wife until he was literally within reaching distance of Agent Hollings, who was still holding the gun he had used to kill Ms. Smith. Isn't that right?"

"Yes."

"Wouldn't you go berserk, Doctor, if that had been your wife?"

"Objection!"

"Sustained!"

"No further questions, Your Honor." Christy Daniels smiled at Nate Smith.

He smiled back.

Arrogant though he most decidedly was, Prosecutor Palmer was smart enough to recognize that he had been out-maneuvered. Further, he realized the jury would have trouble convicting a man whose wife had been killed while bathing by the river. Where he figured he had him, however, was with the two counts of attempted murder in the drive-by shooting.

The ballistics showed that the same gun used in the drive-by shooting had been used to kill Agent Beckwith and wound Agent Hollings.

Christy Daniels, he knew, was unable to refute the ballistics and hard science. Consequently, she did what any self-respecting defense lawyer does in these post, OJ Trial days—she pulled out a couple of mirrors and blew a few smoke screens. She pointed out that Nate had been run off from his land in Missoula and that the IRS had hounded him all the way to the back woods—all to get him for trading a few animal furs and owning a silly red dot sight—that had been legal only a few months before.

There was, however, one significant factual issue. Christy pointed out that there was a question as to whether the drive-by shooter might have been Carena—not Nate—since there was no eyewitness (Nate had testified that the Ruger 357 was Carena's, even though it was registered in his name).

The results of the jury deliberations were consistent with Max Weber's observations about modern states:

> They possess a monopoly on the Legitimate use of physical force, but to survive, that force must be seen as Legitimate by the Citizenry.

And so the jury felt that the IRS and the BATF had been way out of line in their pell-mell pursuit of Nate. After all, a woman on the jury later explained, "All of this was over a few pelts of furs that everyone in the county trades all the time. Why did the government single him out?"

It took 10 minutes to acquit on all counts.

❧

AFTER THE TRIAL, NATE DECIDED TO MOVE WITH HIS daughter Carrie to Detroit to see if he could "go legitimate" and latch on to one of those "high-paying, cake" union jobs (high-paying was now considered to be $17.00 per hour) at an auto facility. Nate packed what few belongings they had into an old Mustang a friend had rebuilt from a wreck and was willing to part with fairly cheaply.

Moving to the Detroit area, however, was another rude awakening—in more ways than one. The first awakening came as he drove around the city looking for an apartment. It never occurred to Nate that there were areas a white person was well advised to avoid, even in broad daylight. As Nate sat behind a car at a stop light, his gaze took in a grungy corner store with bars over plywood-filled windows. *Barred plywood.* Now that was a new one.

And then, out of the corner of his eye, Nate noticed that both rear doors of the car in front of him had swung open. Two African American men scrambled out. Nate snapped to attention but it was too late. Seemingly from out of nowhere came another African American—this one with a handgun he pointed at Nate's head. He wore blue sweats and a Detroit Tiger's baseball cap turned sideways.

This was obviously big trouble.

Nate's first thought was what to do with Carrie. She sat, wide eyed, beside him in the passenger seat.

The man—or boy—Nate realized, tapped the gun on the driver-side window. He yelled loudly to ensure that Nate could hear him through the window. Nate heard him well enough.

"Get the hell out or I'll shoot you and that pretty little girl in the fucking head."

There was nothing to do. Nate was unarmed and, in any event, this guy had the drop on him. Even had he been armed, Nate knew there was no way he could pull a gun and neutralize this punk before the punk could twitch his finger a couple of times and kill both of them where they sat.

With his path blocked in front, going backwards was the only way out. However, Nate also knew he could not put the car into reverse and step on the gas fast enough. That would take a full second or more, and this guy could probably fire two to three shots before the car would have a chance to respond to all of his manipulations. Even for a SEAL, there was nothing to do but obey. And pray for an opening. Nate quickly glanced around and saw no one who might offer aid or at least call the police.

Nate told Carrie they had to get out of the car and he reached over and unsnapped her seat belt. He took her by the hand and led her out the driver's side. He kept her close to his side as they exited the car.

Two men immediately jumped into the Mustang and revved the engine. Nate faced the boy with the gun. He was standing just far enough away that Nate would have to take a step or two to reach him; it was just too risky with his daughter at his side. The boy's eyes were large, round, and protruding slightly from their sockets. They seemed emotionless orbs that blinked once or twice as slowly and mechanically as a gate opening and closing. There was nothing human about them. They reminded Nate of a fish, head and all, that one sees displayed at a market. This boy's eyes were alive yet also dead. Nate felt his body shiver. He knew they were in grave trouble.

Nate pulled Carrie close just as the boy stepped forward and raised the gun toward Nate's face. Instinctively, Nate jerked his head away and blocked the boy's arm up and away, causing the gun to point far over their heads. The gun's trigger no sooner clicked when Nate thrust his palm into the boy's jaw and rammed bone into brain. The boy went limp and Nate let him drop to the ground.

The car squealed off just as a store owner came running out with a short-barrel shotgun. *Mother of God,* Nate thought. *That fast—and we were going to be dead.* Not being in a war zone, or so he had thought, Nate had let his training slip. It nearly had cost their lives.

These people were scary.

Nate examined the handgun. It was a nine millimeter Heckler & Koch P-7 that Nate could see was at least 10 years old. Its original blue treatment was barely evident. The serial number had been scratched off. Then Nate saw what had caused the malfunction. The unique squeeze-cocking gun, which has an excellent reputation for reliability, was so ill cared for that it was fouled to the point that the gun's slide had not returned to battery from the last time it was fired, which Nate guessed was probably not that long ago. And thankfully the dead boy, who couldn't be more than 16 years old, had never learned to "tap-rack" the slide of the gun which nearly always cures a failure to fire or, in this case, a failure to return to battery.

Nate released the magazine, racked the slide to remove the cartridge in the chamber, and put the gun in his back pocket. When the gun was new it went for a grand. Now, out of production, in top condition it was worth a small fortune. And cleaned up, it would still be an excellent self-defense weapon. As beat up as it was, it was probably still more valuable than the old Mustang. The store owner said nothing as he watched Nate clear the gun. Now he smiled at Nate and walked back toward his store. For the first time, Nate noticed that the store owner had donned a bullet-proof vest before coming out into the fray.

"Thanks," Nate said.

The store owner kept walking. Without turning back he said, "Nice gun. Keep it clean. I'll call the police in a half hour or so. God bless you and your little girl."

The next thing Nate did was to buy an old-model Honda Civic that he hoped would not be so attractive to car thieves. From there, he drove out to a rich-looking suburb where he stopped at a gas station to ask a few questions about places to live—*safe* places to live. He settled on an area called Shelby Township, which seemed benign enough with its relatively new strip-malls and multi-lane roads. It was the exact opposite of the mountains. Here, there were cars and traffic jams everywhere. Nate found a relatively inexpensive apartment complex that abutted the most congested mass of roads, businesses, cars, and people he had ever seen. The office manager of the apartment complex told him that the area was once just barren countryside until a millionaire developer put in a huge double-decker mall. Within 10 years, the manager explained, the farmland was gone and replaced helter-skelter by concrete, asphalt, buildings, cars, and people.

From his apartment window, Nate looked out over the expressway and the strip-malls, which stretched as far as he could see. He felt a lump form in his stomach. Working and living here would be, at best, a symbolic defeat of the agrarian life he really wanted; and at worst, it would be a dehumanizing and otherwise emotionally devastating experience. He glanced at Carrie, who had fallen asleep on the couch of their pre-furnished apartment. The lump in his stomach was replaced by a warm glow in his heart. At least his little girl could live and grow up in relative safety.

Nate and Carrie settled into their apartment and Nate wasted no time in hitting the pavement for one of those high-paying jobs. Every day, Nate would drop off Carrie at the day care center and set out on the job trail. Toward late afternoon, Nate would head to one of several local bars, not so much to drink as to pick up any scuttlebutt about who might be hiring. What he learned was not encouraging. Most of the people he talked to were of the opinion that employers associated with the Big Three auto companies were hiring mostly minorities. The joke on the street was, "If you are a minority, you can have a job. If you are a woman minority, you can have any job you want. If you are a woman minority and handicapped, just stay home and we'll pay you."

After a few weeks of fruitless attempts to land a job, Nate started to believe the scuttlebutt. And it turned out to be one of those things you don't really think is bothersome until you are at the short end. Nate had known, in a general way, that companies had affirmative action programs. It was no big deal—until he couldn't get a job.

Nate started to wonder what the hell had he done? Helping people seemed a fine enough goal. But why did it have to be at *his* expense? And that of his daughter's as well? God knew *she* hadn't done anything to deserve what she was getting. After several weeks of running around, Nate was even starting to resent their wasting his time with applications, physicals, and interviews, especially if they had no intention of hiring him.

The Michigan Employment Security Agency (MESC) had given him an introduction for an interview with TRW, a large parts supplier to the Big Three. Working for such a company was nearly as good as a job at the Big Three, so Nate figured there would be a good many applicants. He hoped, however, that the MESC hadn't handed out too many introduction cards. He needed a good job, and he needed it soon. The little savings he had been able to hold on to were nearly spent. He needed this job for his daughter. He was determined to put his best foot forward. It might be his best—and last—chance at a union job.

Nate had made special arrangements to drop off Carrie at day care before normal hours, since he wanted to be early and possibly the first person to be interviewed.

The sun was just breaking over the horizon when Nate pulled into the parking lot at TRW. To his initial dismay, there were already over 100 people in line. But as he got out of his car and headed to the line he noticed that most applicants sported sizable pot bellies, sloppy clothing, and stubbly faces. These people wouldn't stand a chance against his trim figure, clean clothes, and fresh shave. Plus, there were also only a few minorities in line. Maybe—just maybe—today would be the day. He picked up his pace to reach the line and began a slow trot to beat what was already a steady stream of cars pulling into the lot.

Nate's spirits really began to lift when the line started to move. He had heard from the MESC interviewer that there were over 50 jobs available. Surely this would be the day… The line kept moving and he stepped closer and closer to the door.

But then an odd thing began to happen.

First it was one car of four African Americans unloading near the front of the line and just stepping up to the door, cutting in front the people already standing in line. Then, a few minutes later, another car of three did the same. And a few minutes after that, two more cars with several more followed suit. And the real strange thing about it, Nate realized while standing there, was that he didn't see even one look of disapproval or objection from the others who were in line.

By the time Nate passed through the door into TRW, his hopes were dashed. So, this was as good a place as any to give someone a piece of his mind. He couldn't wait to get in front of the interviewer. Someone handed him an application that he just scribbled on as quickly as he could and turned it in. He was dying to tear into someone.

Nate never got the chance. As soon as he turned in his application, he was thanked by a kindly, middle-aged woman of obvious Scottish descent: "Now, we'll b callin' you in a wee bit if the applicants we've taken nor work out." Her huge smile was totally disarming. Depressed and defeated, Nate walked away, barely noticing the continuing stream of applicants hurriedly getting into line.

After leaving TRW, Nate picked up Carrie from the day care and stopped for a quick dinner at a small diner just down the street from their apartment. Carrie ordered her favorite: silver dollar pancakes. Nate watched her eat and tears filled his eyes. She was as innocent as could be, and yet the world was conspiring to harm her. He wiped his eyes with his shirtsleeve and checked his face in the reflection of the table-side jukebox.

She looked up, wide-eyed and worried. "Daddy, why aren't you eating?"

Nate broke from his thoughts and looked down at his batter-fried cod. He couldn't even remember having ordered it—or the waitress having served it.

"I guess I'm just not too hungry, darling."

Carrie smiled and seemed to take the answer, for she dived back into her pancakes, swirling them around in the maple syrup before bringing a large bite to her mouth. Nate watched with a lump in his throat. Somehow, despite all they had been through, she seemed to live with the grossly mistaken presumption that the world was a fair place.

Nate's mind wandered again, this time envisioning his little girl standing in line at a college admissions office, her heart set on attending. Out of nowhere comes a string of less qualified minorities who elbow past Carrie to the front of the line. Suddenly a faceless admissions officer steps to the door, waves all the minorities in, and then looks at Carrie and says, "I'm sorry, young lady, but you are not the right color." He then slams the door in her face. From behind the door Carrie hears laughter. She turns away in tears.

Nate's face was suddenly hot from anger. It was as if he had walked from an air conditioned building directly into the hot sun on a muggy day and been hit with a blast from a furnace. Before he could catch himself he said, "I've had enough of this shit."

"Daddy!"

Nate grimaced. He hated it when he swore in front of his child. He gritted his teeth. "I'm sorry, darling. Daddy didn't mean to say that."

Carrie paused, seeming to weigh whether to accept the apology. Then, without a word, she dug back into her pancakes.

After dinner Nate and Carrie headed back to the apartment and Carrie sat in front of a Disney special on TV. Nate had been putting off learning about computers and the internet. But he had heard that much could be learned about controversial topics by cruising web sites. Now, he finally felt the incentive to take up his neighbor's offer to let him try it out. Nate picked up the phone and within 20 minutes he was having a beer with Smitty, as the two of them sat side by side at the computer and surfed the net.

Nate had never said much to his neighbors, but he had often shared a beer with Smitty and talked about sports or hunting. Nate was surprised, therefore, to find that Smitty had bookmarked a number of sites that seemed to deal with issues that had plagued him: affirmative action, the federal government, and left-wing politics in general. As he jumped from site to site, he learned that there were a great many who shared his feelings.

Then Smitty jumped to a site that had a bunch of quotes from various leaders and revolutionaries. One really struck Nate. He asked Smitty to print it, as it seemed to explain why, in the face of so many minorities taking cuts in line at TRW, and literally elbowing others out of high-paying jobs, not one person had said a word. Nate pulled the paper out of the printer tray.

Alexis de Tocqueville had warned about a society beaten down by administrative despotism:

> It covers the surface of society with a network of small complicated rules, minute and uniform, through which the most original minds and the most energetic characters cannot penetrate, to rise above the crowd. The will of man is not shattered, but softened, bent, guided; men are seldom forced by it to act, but they are constantly restrained from acting: such a power does not destroy, but it prevents existence; it does not tyrannize, but it compresses, extinguishes, and stupefies a people, till each nation is reduced to be nothing better

than a flock of timid and industrious animals, of which the government is the Shepherd.

Nate read and re-read the passage, every time achieving a newer and deeper understanding. He took it to his apartment and studied it well into the night. When he woke the next morning he read it afresh and suddenly everything seemed crystal clear. Here was the root cause of America's decline. It was even hinted at in popular culture as the "dumbing-down" of America. But to be dumbed down was more than a cute play on words; it was more than, as implied, a general lowering of intelligence. Americans had become a stupefied flock of timid and industrious animals. Softened, bent, and guided, they had lost their spirit. Told by a government that their problems could be fixed by ever more government, Americans had lost not only the *will* to act but also the sense that they *should* act. Constantly restrained by an all-powerful, all-knowing government, Americans had lost their ability to think independently and their will to challenge proclamations from on high.

Nate rubbed his temples, which throbbed with each beat of his heart. He was on to something big, *or could be big,* he told himself. Fortunately, the one thing keeping a thread of the old American "can do" spirit alive was the federal government's penchant for getting too full of itself. It had started with President Roosevelt and had reached its apex with President Obama, but American government had made tyranny into an art form. And where there was full-blown tyranny, as there was now, there just had to be a will to resist…

So, with no good jobs available, Nate decided that was enough of the big city and its dispirited population. He had to find some like-minded people.

He loaded the car and took his daughter north. He was going to keep driving until the countryside met two criteria: it had to look more like Idaho—uncrowded, without so many damn telephone poles everywhere, and the population had to be way less tolerant of this affirmative action crap.

Nate didn't stop until he reached Ishpeming in the Upper Peninsula, the "U.P." of Michigan. There, he found a life more to his liking. The people, affectionately called "Yoopers," were hardy, self-sufficient, and talkative.

The only downside was that there were very few jobs—though he noted that his race and sex did not appear to be liabilities. A short time later he received an offer and took a job at what he thought must be the last full-service gas station on earth.

To his great delight, he quickly discovered that most Yoopers were upset with both the intrusiveness of the federal government and the pell-mell grab for "rights" by minorities.

What he didn't expect to discover was a wide-spread desire to actually secede from the state of Michigan. He recalled some talk about that sort of thing out west some years ago. But no one had seemed really serious about it, and Nate's thinking along those lines had not matured. He also recalled having considered the simple geography of the United States. Cutting out a portion of the western United States just seemed a strange thing to do.

With the U.P., however, there was a symmetry about its being a separate state, or even a sovereign nation. In fact, local opinions seemed pretty evenly split about which direction they should go. Many thought a new country could align with Canada, which was, it turns out, most desirous of obtaining the Upper Peninsula's vast natural resources unencumbered by the EPA and Michigan's Department of Natural Resources.

Nate discovered that the U.P. had several helter-skelter patriot groups that reflected widely divergent beliefs about what the patriots should do or be. Clearly, here was an opportunity to shape a formidable organization.

At the risk of losing his job, Nate printed up a short tract about opposing the ACLU and ACORN, and returning the country to its "Constitutional" origins. He passed it out to most gas customers and, before long, he was getting regular customers who wanted to talk. Within a year he was speaking to this or that group and expressing his views. Nate's boss at the gas station finally caught on to the tracts but apparently liked some of the ideas. It turned out that he ran an independent station and was happy to have the repeat customers. Before long, Nate began to take time off, with his boss's blessing, to travel and talk.

Nate met an attractive woman at one of the meetings and he was married within months to Catherine Hailer, the only child of the late Paul Hailer, former president of Northern Industries, Inc. Both of her parents died shortly after her marriage to Nate, and she promptly assumed control of her father's huge hunting estate.

Nate could hardly believe his good luck. His new wife just loved Carrie, and Nate could see that Carrie was warming to Catherine. Catherine's money and support enabled him to work full-time on his plans. And the hunting lodge served as the perfect meeting place for his growing patriot organization.

❧

NORTHERN POSSE

COMITATUS

Copper Harbor, Michigan

by Annikki Karvonen

Secession is all the rage. The Chicago Sentinel reports that four states are following our lead and have begun serious discussions on secession. Just last week, Imperial County California proposed to secede and form the new state of "Diego." "Our schools act more like nannies than educators and state and local taxes are in the stratosphere," said John Smith, spokesperson for the secession movement. "But the worst of it," he added, "is the unions. They control state government and we're done with it." Asked what the new state of Diego would do differently, Smith said, "We need to create an economic environment where people can start businesses, so the first thing we'll do

is cut regulations. Next, we will make damn sure budgets are balanced. But most important, if you ask us, we will protect the damn border."

Other states considering secession are Montana, Utah, Texas, and Arizona, which is putting a twist on the normal. In Arizona, liberal democrats—not Tea Party conservatives—want to form the state of "Freeforall." At times violently opposed to Arizona's conservative majority and its past efforts to protect its borders, Arizona liberals wish to encourage illegals to come across the border by presenting them with food stamps and "no-document" registration for both unemployment and health-care benefits.

Northern Posse Comitatus, Page 2

by Annikki Karvonen

Washington Times columnist James Robbins has previously reported on this growing phenomenon. He wondered what would be wrong with allowing liberals to secede in every state. "Think of it," he said, "if utopian liberal separatists want to implement economic policies in their states that will rocket them to a North Korean-style standard of living, who are we to stand in their way?"

We at the Comitatus couldn't agree more.

CHAPTER II

RAIN WAS FALLING IN THE COOL, EARLY-MORNING FOG. One of the former C3I officers, Jan Hunnington, had just finished her sixth cup of coffee and her bladder was about to burst. Good thing her partner, Tony Meyers, didn't drink coffee, because every 20 minutes Jan quietly tip-toed down the steps of the van and sneaked around the corner to a large bunch of heavy bushes. Fortunately, this early in the morning, the only activity in the well-to-do neighborhood was one BMW that came tearing out of a drive-way, undoubtedly to speed some bigwig to a burled walnut desk at least 20 floors up.

It was a stroke of luck that Ralph Martenass's home was secluded at the end of a cul-de-sac.

"Hand me that Thermos," Jan said. She could feel her head begin-ning to nod off, again.

"Sweetie, you better stop drinking so much caffeine. You know it's not good for your heart," Tony said.

"Oh, piss off. I just can't stand this early morning garbage. If I don't drink coffee I'll fall asleep for sure."

"Yeah, like it would make any difference. We ain't going to get anything anyhow. Either he isn't going to do anything serious or he's got a shielded system."

"Listen. I don't question orders. Nate—"

"Screw Nate—"

"I'd like to—"

"Yeah, keep your pants on. Catherine would rip your heart out."

"Hell, she could join us."

"Come on now, we don't ask, you don't tell." Tony smiled and Jan chuckled. She had never told anyone that was exactly why she had been discharged in the pre-Obama military. Now, she rued, acknowledging her bisexual interests would be a sure ticket to a general's star, or two.

Jan said, "Nate doesn't know crap. I keep telling him that the way to find out about shipments is to grease a few people. More likely that we'd get something than this."

"But Nate's a former SEAL and he loves this little electronic gizmo he scammed from Hartman's kid. And anyhow, didn't you make some modifications to it?"

"Yep. Nate asked me to increase its sensitivity and range. So I did and built it into the disk antenna on top." Jan pointed to the roof of the van. "But it still requires an idiot on the other end. And fat chance—wait, someone is just moving into the computer room."

Jan was keeping watch through an infrared scope that showed, even through the walls of a home, any movement of warm bodies. From the moving images in her scope, it appeared that Ralph Martenass had just walked into his den and was about to fire up his laptop.

❧

IT WAS 7:30 A.M. ONE OF THE BENEFITS OF WORKING AT HOME was that Ralph could get up, work for a few minutes, and head out to the golf course. It was just great. He didn't need to be dressed up, and he could even begin work while nursing, as he was this morning, his first cup of coffee. He settled down at a desk in front of his nice bay window and took another sip of his hot coffee. He set it on the desk and smiled as the steam rose in a wisp and disappeared. This home set-up was going to work out just fine, even if he couldn't make fun of that retard until Monday.

Ralph began reviewing several reports to determine optimal shipment schedules. He was smiling at how much faster this computer was than the one in his office. *And for a laptop,* he thought. It took a bit but he finally clicked "Transmit."

Satisfied, he got up and twisted to full open the semi-transparent vertical blinds. He caught a glimpse of a cable company van heading out of his cul-de-sac. *That's odd,* he thought. The van had a funny looking round disk on its roof. It looked vaguely familiar, though he couldn't place it. His stomach began to churn.

He went to freshen his coffee and get some Pepto Bismol. When he got to the kitchen a realization hit him and he belched up a stomach full of coffee and acid. Quickly he opened the cupboard and twisted the top off the Pepto Bismol and chugged a good portion down.

He had seen that van on a side street near his home the other day when he was out jogging. It might have been close enough to pick up sounds within his home. Good thing all his home communications were over the computer. He hadn't spoken anything about the warhead shipments. He had merely conducted the scheduling from his computer screen.

My computer screen, Ralph thought. "I wonder," he said to himself, vaguely recalling something from a security seminar. It took only a moment, however, and he concluded that nothing bad could have happened. After all, he rationalized, the DOD wouldn't have given him this laptop if it could be compromised. And, if the van was there to eavesdrop it required him to speak. That was obvious.

Department regulations called for altering the shipment schedule anytime there was a reasonable chance that there had been a security leak. That was the *last* thing that Ralph, wanted since it required filling out all sorts of reports that would not reflect well on his record. The personal razzing he would get would be unbearable.

And all this on the first day of telecommuting! He clenched his fists and cursed. Subconsciously, he also clenched his teeth to the point that they squeaked as they ground together.

After a few moments he came up with a cover story. He would report the van but he would do so in a few days—and on a day where he did not actually schedule any shipments from home. That was the safest way out.

❧

CHAPTER 12

BRADLEY FLETCHER SHOOK HIS HEAD IN DISGUST. HE tried to remain calm—but couldn't. Oddly, it was in these moments of intellectual anger that he did his best thinking and writing. His blood pressure shot through the roof every time he read Justice Stevens's dissenting opinion in *District of Columbia v. Heller*. And now that bit of legal propaganda was on its way to reversing *Heller* and, in the process, gutting the Second Amendment.

With a straight face, Justice Stevens had taken the position that the Second Amendment was never intended to apply to individuals. He'd talked in his dissent as if the founding fathers had never even *imagined* that anyone could possibly even think it *might* apply to individuals. Everyone knew, he claimed, that it is only applicable to a state militia.

It was an incredible display of hubris.

And it was incredibly wrong.

Bradley decided to take the major thrust of Steven's argument head on.

James Madison had been principal draftsman of the Second Amendment and had assembled the various proposals for amendments sent by the ratifying States. Adams had had, in fact, a wealth of material at his disposal, and Stevens had run with it. "With all of these sources upon which to draw," Stevens opined,

"[I]t is strikingly significant that Madison's first draft omitted any mention of nonmilitary use or possession of weapons. Rather, his original draft ... read:

> 'The right of the people to keep and bear arms shall not be infringed; a well armed, and well regulated militia being the best security of a free country; but no person religiously scrupulous of bearing arms, shall be compelled to render military service in person.'

Madison's decision to model the Second Amendment on the distinctly *military* Virginia proposal is therefore revealing, since it is clear that he *considered and rejected* formulations that would have unambiguously protected civilian uses of firearms. When Madison prepared his first draft, and when that draft was debated and modified, it is reasonable to assume that all participants in the drafting process were fully aware of the other formulations that would have protected civilian use and possession of weapons and that their choice to craft the Amendment as they did represented a rejection of those alternative formulations.

What a crock, Bradley thought. *The guy is either totally dishonest or an idiot.* He reached out to his keyboard and started to write. He hammered on the keys as fast as he could, skipping some citations that he would have to go back and insert:

> In point of fact, after the amendment was introduced by Madison and approved by the House, as noted by Professor David Couples, noted Second Amend scholar, the Senate, along with a couple other changes, specifically rejected a proposal to add the words "for the common defence" after "the right of the people to keep and bear arms."
>
> In rejecting the words "common defense," Professor Couples has noted, "the drafters made it clear that the Second Amendment right to arms was not solely for militia service." 1 Journal of the First Session of the Senate 71, 77 (1820).

That the right was not limited to militia service is also demonstrated by the writings of Tench Coxe, who was a close political ally of Madison and eventually served in Madison's sub-cabinet. During the ratification period he wrote a comprehensive, section-by-section exposition on the Bill of Rights. Regarding Madison's right to arms amendment, Coxe wrote: "As civil rulers … may attempt to tyrannize, and as the military forces … might pervert their power to the injury of their fellow-citizens, the people are confirmed … in their right to keep and bear their private arms." Federal Gazette, June 18, 1789, p. 2, (emphasis in original).

Moreover, as Justice Scalia amply demonstrated in the majority opinion, absolutely nothing in the history of the proposals for amendments indicated that the right to keep and bear arms was to be limited to a state militia.

So, concluding, as we must, that the proposal process showed only one thing—that formulations limiting the right to a militia were specifically rejected—we need to look outside that process to see if there is any significant support for the notion that the Second Amendment was thought to apply only to a militia.

The scholarly literature of the day reveals numerous examples of learned explanations of the Second Amendment. Overwhelmingly, they favor the individual rights view.

For example, one of the early treatises on constitutional law was written by Thomas Cooley in 1868. Regarding the Second Amendment, Cooley wrote, "The meaning of the provision undoubtedly is, that the people, from whom the militia must be taken, shall have the right to keep and bear arms; and they need no permission or regulation of law for the purpose."

Justice Stevens states that the preeminent Joseph Story issues "not so much as a whisper" that the Second Amendment redounds to individuals. Yet, in his famous 1833 Commentaries on the Constitution of the United States, Story states that the English Bill of Rights of 1688, though limited to protestants, which at the time comprised 95 percent of the population, is similar to the Second Amendment in that it gives individual citizens the right to "have arms for their defence suitable to their condition, and as allowed by law."

Yet another commentator, William Rawle, a prominent lawyer and a member of the Pennsylvania Assembly that ratified the Bill of Rights, published in 1825 a highly influential treatise analyzing the Second Amendment. He wrote, "The first [principle] is a declaration that a well regulated militia is necessary to the security of a free state; a proposition from which few will dissent... The corollary, from the first position is, that the right of the people to keep and bear arms shall not be infringed."

Among several other similar examples is perhaps the most authoritative of all. The most widely used legal treatise of the early Republic is the five-volume, 1803 American edition of William Blackstone's Commentaries on the Common Law of England, edited and annotated by St. George Tucker. In it, Tucker considered the "right of self defence" to be "the first law of nature," and the Second Amendment the "true palladium of liberty..."

Bradley wanted to go on writing. The examples were so many that it was inconceivable that Justice Stevens or anyone else could come to a contrary conclusion. Nevertheless, Bradley rued, anti-gun commentators and liberal professors were clamoring for *Heller* to be reversed on the absurd and manifestly incorrect conclusion that the Founding Fathers "considered and rejected formulations that would have unambiguously protected civilian uses of firearms." And, once it was reversed, Wallmire could seek a virtual ban of all firearms or, more circuitously, adopt, via treaty, the proposal of the United Nations Department of Disarmament Affairs, that no gun would be lawful if it 1) holds in its magazine or cylinder more than four cartridges or 2) can fire a bullet farther than 75 yards.

Fact was, Bradley had no ax to grind one way or the other on the whole issue of guns. He didn't really even like guns. The problem, however, was that Stevens had prostituted the United States Constitution and the Second Amendment. And that made Bradley mad as hell.

He gritted his teeth, pulled his laptop in close, and started again pounding the keyboard. The words flew from his mind onto the screen:

Moreover, the entire history of the Bill of Rights demonstrates that the Second Amendment's right to keep and bear arms is a personal right and is not dependent on a person's membership in a state-sanctioned militia.

To the point, every reference in the Bill of Rights to *"the people"* refers to individual citizens, to wit:

- the First Amendment … right of **the people** to peaceably assemble …

- the Second Amendment … right of **the people** to keep and bear Arms …

- the Fourth Amendment … right of **the people** to be secure … against unreasonable searches and seizures …

- the Ninth Amendment … enumeration in the Constitution, of certain rights shall not be construed to deny or disparage others retained by **the people** …

- the Tenth Amendment … powers not delegated to the United States by the Constitution … are reserved to the States … or to **the people**.

In every instance the United States Supreme Court has held that the words "the people" refer, amazingly enough, to the people.

Simply put, "the right of **the people** to keep and bear arms," tells us that **the people** have the right to keep and bear arms!

What's so damn hard to understand?

Bradley slammed the return key just as the phone rang. Of course, he wouldn't keep that last sentence in his article. But sometimes it just felt good to really let his hair down…

Bradley hated it when the phone rang while he was writing. He waited as long as he could… and picked up on the third ring. It was his brother, and his stomach turned. Their last meeting had ended badly. Bill had been in one of his moods where he seemed to resent Bradley's accomplishments.

Bill's career had stalled because of a question mark on his integrity—how could you ever prove that you hadn't taken bribes when your partner had? Yet, Bill never seemed to really understand how hard things were for Bradley at the law school. Truth was, Bradley was obsessed with obtaining tenure, without which his career would nosedive. He would be forced to leave the University of Michigan and accept a position at a lesser school. Bradley got chills every time he thought of it.

Bill said, "I never got a chance to ask you what happened to that woman at Dominick's? She was soooo good looking!"

Bradley's mood instantly crashed, but he tried to shake off his thoughts and concentrate on talking with his brother. Bradley said, "My usual luck." He paused for a second to remember her; she *was* very good looking, *and sexy*. The memory was enough to make his back teeth ache. Yet, it was more than the promise of good sex. She seemed to have depth—no, he corrected himself—she was as deep as the dark blue waters of a moon-lit ocean. The surface gave only a shimmering hint of what lay beneath. It would take a long, long time to navigate those depths.

And she had such presence! As a total stranger, she had reached out and straightened his tie. At first he was embarrassed by his own sloppiness. But the embarrassment quickly passed and was replaced by an awe for a woman who had the *je ne sais quoi* to smile just right and make it seem as though she was giving her best friend a touch-up. This was possibly the woman of his dreams.

Unfortunately, she had never called. Most likely, he considered, she took no special notice of him. As a result, she was just another frustrating memory.

Bradley said, "We talked, had a nice conversation. She is thinking of applying to law school. I offered to help her study and stuff, but like an idiot I didn't get her number, so I don't know whether I'll ever see her again. It's the…" Bradley paused to check his tongue, but he couldn't do it totally, "…freaking story of my life."

"Jeez, I can hear you smoldering from here. Don't be so angry, little brother. You never know. Maybe you'll meet her again. Listen, I'm on my way back to Detroit. I'll call you as soon as I'm back in town, and we can go to Dominick's. We'll find her."

Bradley thanked his brother for being a brother, and for a brief moment he felt better. But as soon as he hung up the phone he thought, *fat chance.* He would never see her again. And if he did, he'd blow it anyway. He put his Mac to sleep and headed out of the office, muttering, "I'm going to be single the rest of my life." He walked past Beth without saying good night. She frowned and stuck her tongue out but he didn't notice. He walked through the dark stacks to the elevator. A freaking miracle; the elevator was open and seemingly waiting for him. Bradley slammed the cracked and yellowed button marked "L-2" with his palm and waited for the old, lumbering elevator to descend to the second level, which was the ground floor. The damned thing never failed to piss him off. With every second he waited, the urge to get out of the building seemed to intensify. He felt like a Kentucky Derby race horse waiting for the gun, itching to explode out of the gate.

As the elevator inched its way down to the ground floor, Bradley felt as if the walls were closing in on him, snuffing out his life. Sure he was a successful professional. But law professors were no different from any others; it was publish or perish. At any time his writing might dry up and wither. He pictured Dean Wellington coming into his office and breaking it to him slowly, gently.

Yet that was only half the problem. Truth was, Bradley wanted a woman to love. He longed for someone to whom he could bring coffee in the morning, someone with whom he could go out to breakfast on a football Saturday. He imagined walking hand in hand along the tree-covered sidewalks surrounding his Burns Park home. He imagined the smell of the fall leaves scattered on the ground and the occasional wisp of her perfume. And it was beginning to look as if it wouldn't happen. He didn't know whether it was his job, or his personality, that kept him from a relationship. But in any event, he knew that, at *this* moment, he just had to get out of here!

Finally the doors began to open in intermittent jerks, and he squeezed himself through as soon as there was an opening large enough.

Of all things! He found his path blocked by a mob of giggling Asian visitors, probably high school students from their looks, crowding to get into the elevator. Bradley looked left and right to find a way off the elevator. The kids were pushing him back in! Frustrated now to the nth degree, he started to pry through the mob. He had to get away from these people!

He forced his way to the edge of the crowd, shoving past the last few chattering, smiling youngsters. He was just free of the mob and moving fast when a noise, perhaps someone dropping an arm full of thick law texts, took his attention for a second and he looked to the right…

❧

"CRAP. WRONG AGAIN. I GOT THESE ALL WRONG," ANNE said to no one, even though she had in fact gotten most of the questions right. *It's just not going to work*, Anne thought reflexively.

She was sitting at her breakfast bar taking a practice exam for the LSAT. Right next to the exam book sat her six-week guide on telling herself the truth, and next to that was a stack of index cards, each with a hand-written scripture she used to argue with herself whenever, as now, she began to tell herself she was useless. She looked at the card on top: Ephesians 2:10: *"For we are God's workmanship…"* And under the quote Anne had added a note: "Greek word for workmanship is 'work of art.'" Anne gritted her teeth and prayed, "God, if you made me in your image, and you did, and you call me a work of art, I am *not* useless, *dammit*! Amen."

It was turning out that taking practice exams was a blessing. They forced her mind to focus on something productive, and she liked the intellectual challenge. And, contrary to her still-too-frequent negative self-talk, she was doing quite well. Indeed, Linda believed Anne had a shot at getting into the University of Michigan, currently the second ranked law school in the nation.

Getting into Michigan was silly, Anne had protested, since it required an LSAT score pushing the 99th percentile. Anne was justifiably doubtful she would score that well. But it was worth trying, Linda had insisted.

So, down to the law school Anne and Linda had marched. Again, Anne was impressed with the erudite and highly cultured law school. It gave off an air of sophistication and exclusiveness that forewarned of the effort it would take to get in and, once there, to succeed.

Anne thought of that handsome, if a bit goofy, law professor, Bradley Fletcher. He had insisted she take his business card, which was still wedged into the corner of her dresser mirror. He wouldn't even remember her. Anne's stomach knotted. She would appease Linda and pick up the stupid application to the law school and go home. This was silly.

❧

LINDA WAS NOT GOING TO WASTE THIS OPPORTUNITY TO expose Anne to as much of the law school as she could. She had seen pictures of several Ivy League schools, and this place was at least as impressive. Walking across the lawn inside the quadrangle in silence, Anne seemed to be as awestruck as was Linda. This place really was inspiring. They reached the steps to the entrance and paused to read an inscription carved into the stone archway overhead: "Law Embodies the Wisdom of the Ages—Progress Comes Slowly." They looked at each other and shrugged their shoulders as if to say, "I have no idea." So the place was inspiring, *if a bit odd.*

Linda hoped she was reading Anne correctly and that Anne was equally impressed—though the carved inscription was rather pedestrian. Anne seemed to linger at the steps, apparently apprehensive about going in, so Linda smacked her on the behind and motioned forward. Anne shot her a hostile look, but obeyed and mounted the steps to the entrance. Linda followed as Anne opened the massive, ornately carved oak door into a vestibule and then into the main building itself. Immediately, they craned their necks to gape at the sheer space, height, and grandeur of the legal research building. This wasn't a multi-floor building, as Linda had initially thought. It was one huge, cavernous room. They stepped up to the main floor itself and stood, mouths agape. So this was the famous Reading Room. Linda had heard stories about it; how young coeds flocked to study here in hopes of snagging a brilliant young law student headed to a silk-stocking law firm or the board room of a Fortune 500 company. The first 10 to 15 feet of the walls were covered with beautifully detailed oak wainscoting. From there, the stained-glass windows rose at least 50 feet to a vaulted cathedral ceiling covered with ornately carved ceiling tiles. There was a strange hush to the building, and Linda realized they were standing on cork floors. The place was full of long, massive wood tables, each with a table-length, solid brass pharmacy-styled reading light. Over the tables hung huge chandeliers, each adorned with what had to be at least 50 small light bulbs. The wide, carved-wood chairs, each with a thick pad across the seat, provided seating for… Linda counted five chairs widely spaced, on each side of each table, and there had to be at least 30 rows of tables arrayed two across running the full length of the room. So, it looked like over 500 students could comfortably spread out their study materials without risk of encroaching upon their neighbors. *Amazing. The place is amazing,* Linda thought.

"Wow," Anne mumbled as she spied left and right, taking in the scene.

"Wow is right," Linda replied, pleased that Anne obviously was taken. Perhaps she wouldn't start nagging to hurry up and go home.

They started across the huge Reading Room. A large group of Asian students milled around an elevator entrance at the back of the room. On second thought, Linda decided, they must be visitors. There was something just too foreign about them. Real Asian *students* were more relaxed. These kids were giggling and gaping at the surroundings. Linda stopped at the periphery of the Asian visitors and asked a tall, red haired, freckled-faced young man about life as a law student. She acted as if she wanted to know for herself, but mostly she was trying to find out things Anne might want to know.

Anne appeared interested, but Linda suspected she was pushing Anne's patience.

Linda was facing the elevator and noticed, out of the corner of her eye, what looked to be a handsome professor get off the elevator. She would have paid him no further attention, but he seemed nervous, craning his head trying to find a path through the crowd of students pushing their way into the elevator. He clearly wanted off but was blocked. And that crooked bow tie seemed vaguely familiar. Then, as he began to weave his way through the students, one of them stumbled and fell backwards, held up by the students pressing forward. Linda couldn't tell whether the student had been pushed or just bumped and lost his balance of his own accord. But the perpetrator was clearly the professor, or whoever. Linda focused her attention and she could see, to her disgust, that he was damn near shoving his way through the students. Several of them were looking at him in surprise. He never so much as paused to acknowledge his impolite actions or to say "excuse me."

Linda flashed Anne a twisted face—a look they frequently shared and that signaled the presence of a jerk.

Linda continued to study the man as he made his way through the crowd. He was handsome, no doubt about that, even if his clothes seemed a little rumpled.

❧

ANNE KNEW LINDA WAS TRYING TO BE A GOOD FRIEND. BUT it was driving her crazy. Why, for heavens sake, would she stop and ask a bunch of kids about law school. As if Anne's experience, as an adult, would be the same. All Anne wanted to do was get to that damn admissions office, pick up the application, and take off. That would get Linda off her back.

They were heading across the Reading Room when Linda flashed her that funny, twisted-face look Linda saved for times when she had decided some guy was a loser.

Someone dropped a pile of books, some of them landing flat and making a muted smack on the cork floor.

Then a man ran smack dab into her; Anne stumbled backwards.

"Excuse me—" he blurted, as he lunged forward to catch her from falling.

"Bradley!" she shrieked, as he stopped her backward fall, and she wrapped her arms around him for support. For a moment they were nose to nose, and she even had to tilt her head backwards a bit to keep her face from pressing into his. She could smell his aftershave and her heart skipped a beat.

They separated and Bradley straightened his suit jacket. "Anne! Oh, my. I'm so sorry. I was looking the other way. My mind is so preoccupied. Are you—"

"Oh, fine. Just a little startled. Bradley, uh…" Her mind was catching up with events. The realization struck that the subject of Linda's twisted-face was Bradley Fletcher. *Oh God!* She barely got out the introduction, "… this… is Linda."

Bradley was still running his hands down the front of his jacket and shirt to iron out wrinkles from the crash. His voice was a little choppy as he appeared to struggle to regain his composure. He addressed Linda, "How do you do. It's a pleasure to meet you— though you must think I'm an absentminded professor—walking into people and such."

Linda's eyes narrowed. "No. That's not what I was thinking at all."

Bradley's face twisted in discomfort. Anne's face flushed with blood, and her stomach flipped. Clearly, he recognized Linda's sarcasm. Anne's heart began to pound in her ears and she started to panic. Bradley's face was still twisted in pain, and he and Linda were staring at each other like boxers before a title match.

Oh God! This is a nightmare. Her best friend—and the only man to come along in several years whom she liked—were faced off as if to battle.

Anne couldn't take it. She was *nothing*, had *nothing*, and was going *nowhere*. Then something happened that can only be attributed to Anne's past, her resulting emotional sensitivity, and her almost desperate desire to reorder her world and find value in her life. It was as though all past traumas rushed her at once. Anger, love, fear, and loneliness converged and clashed like armies of ancient warriors—swords, battle axes, and truncheons swinging, cleaving heads, arms, and entire bodies. The result was an involuntary reaction altogether out of proportion to reality but, when viewed in the context of the ferocious battle in her mind, was entirely rational: Anne suddenly felt an irresistible urge to escape the catastrophe that was playing out in her mind and before her eyes. A voice, shrill and pitched as fingernails across a blackboard, screamed inside her head: *Run!*

Linda's face confirmed the worst; she was braced for battle. Bradley's face was still screwed up in anguish.

"Great... *Just great*," Anne blurted out, her voice cracking. *I'll never find anyone,* she said to herself as she abruptly turned and bolted for the main exit. She wanted to run, but her feet seemed mired in glue. Panic overwhelmed, and she willed her feet to sludge through the sticky glue that held her. She tried to run faster... The door seemed so far away!

Suddenly the floor dropped away. Anne had the brief image of the exit door rushing at her, followed by the vague awareness of a tremendous impact.

Then there was nothing.

❖

BRADLEY STARTED AFTER HER IMMEDIATELY, BUT ANNE WAS quick. She broke into a dead run, and she had a several-step lead. Bradley knew the building, however, and he knew that the floor dropped several steps and formed a small landing in front of the exit doors. As soon as he saw Anne begin to fall forward, he knew she had not seen the drop-off, though it was marked by wide yellow tape (designed to protect against lawsuits more than to warn). He cringed and watched helplessly as she fell headfirst into one of the heavy wood doors.

❖

CHAPTER 13

HEAD WOUNDS BLEED BEYOND ALL RELATION TO THEIR gravity. So it was probably just as well that Anne did not regain consciousness before the paramedics carried her from the scene. She would have seen a frighteningly large pool of blood on the steps and landing leading into the Reading Room.

It was also a bit of good fortune that the door opened to the outside. The doctor said that might very well have saved her life. It also helped that a law student had just begun to open the door en route to an evening of study. At an angle, therefore, the solid-wood door did not act as a barrier so much as a deflector. Anne's head and right shoulder thus rammed the door simultaneously. The shoulder absorbed much of the force and helped push the door away from her head.

It was around midnight when Anne awoke, blinking her eyes. She was in a dense fog, and out of that she realized there was a man's face only a few inches away from her own—and it was no one she recognized.

Anne startled easily. Even in the familiar surroundings of her home, she might scream in fright at nothing more than Jeff walking into a room. Thus, it was natural that she would scream at the sight of this strange man in her face.

The doctor, startled by the scream, leapt back and grabbed his chest as if he were experiencing a heart attack. Terror in his eyes, he raced out of the room.

Bradley had dozed off in a chair in the corner. Still half-asleep, he lurched to his feet and immediately pitched to the side. He put his hand out to a table that couldn't hold his sideways-falling weight. It slid away with skittering jerks and tipped a vase full of flowers that went sprawling amid shattering glass and splashing water.

Anne recognized the skewed bow tie even before she recognized Bradley's face. The clamor helped to clear the fog in her head. Her heart was pounding from the initial alarm, but at least the world was coming into focus. Bradley was standing at the side of her bed, and Anne's first thought was that he looked like a puppy dog caught making a mess on the floor. Her heart went out to him.

Jeff walked into the room. "What the heck? I heard you scream from the bathroom down the hall."

Bradley said, "It seems that I become quite clumsy around attractive women."

Jeff glanced at the mess on the floor. "Well, Mom, Professor Fletcher, er—" Bradley raised his eyebrows and Jeff caught his meaning, "—Bradley, brought you some nice flowers, but he apparently changed his mind about giving them to you."

Bradley laughed and Anne chuckled. She said, "Jeff, would you mind picking them up so I can see what Bradley decided to not give me?"

Jeff and Bradley both bent down out of her sight and seemed to be fumbling about, piecing through glass and flowers.

Bradley held up a colorful bunch.

Anne squeaked, "Roses? Pink roses?" It wasn't a question as much as it was an expression of disbelief—she was hardly worth buying flowers for.

Bradley smiled and blushed. He reached out and took Anne's hand. She hungrily wrapped her fingers around his and was startled by his strength. His mild manners and handsome, yet accidental, habit of dress belied the warmth and strength of his body. She had forgotten what it was like to romantically hold hands. She caught a slight whiff of his aftershave and a tingling warmth flowed up her arm.

Bradley seemed to want to say something, but a nurse burst into the room with a broom, towels, a dust pan, and an ugly disposition. She elbowed Bradley and Jeff away, and they both stepped back from Anne's bed to give her room. Anne didn't let go of Bradley's hand, and his arm stretched out as he stepped away. The nurse gave Anne a nasty look and she released her grip.

Bradley stepped back.

Anne's heart skipped.

Bradley's movement triggered a sickening feeling that she could never have a relationship with him. He was at the pinnacle of success. She was on Prozac. Her blood immediately turned to ice, and her whole body shuddered as if exposed to an Arctic blast. She tried to swallow but couldn't.

The nurse finished and huffed out of the room. Bradley and Jeff approached the bed, and Bradley again reached out his hand. He was smiling.

Anne jerked her hand away from Bradley's grasp. "Don't," she gulped, as she tried to quickly turn her head away. She got her head only part way, however, when pain shot through her neck and she stopped. Instead, she stared at the ceiling—but out of the corner of her eye she could still see he was standing over her bed and hadn't withdrawn his hand. The smile was gone, however, and his mouth had dropped open.

Anne closed her eyes. If only she could put him out of her mind! She squeezed her eyelids closed as tightly as she could. After a moment she began to see stars and her head started to feel like it was spinning from drunkenness. She forced herself to keep her eyes closed, but she soon became nauseous and opened her eyes to keep from being sick. Her eyes darted around the room. Oddly, her panicky fears seemed to have subsided, and she half hoped to see Bradley. Jeff was standing at the foot of her bed. There was a blank expression on his face. Her heart began to sink.

"Bradley went home," Jeff said. "What the hell was that about?"

❧

Linda met Bradley at the hospital's elevator. She was about to step in; he was walking out. He had a troubled, disheveled look that was vaguely familiar. He wasn't watching where he was going—again. His eyes were pointed at the floor, and he was shaking his head. Linda had to step to the side to avoid him as he came off the elevator. She reached out with both hands and grabbed his arm as he passed. His forward momentum caused him to pitch forward and then swing around the axis formed by Linda and her outstretched arms.

"Whoa there! You do this all the time?"

Bradley said, "Oh my God." He stared at her and his mouth moved as if he were trying to speak, but no words would come forth. Obviously, he remembered her.

Linda was still holding his arm as the elevator doors began to close. She stepped into the elevator and yanked Bradley in.

They had the elevator to themselves.

As they ascended, she said, as sarcastically as she could, even pausing and dragging out the pronunciation of some of her words, "I see you have *a-lit-tle-prob-lem* with walking into people."

Bradley blushed crimson red. His face tightened up in anguish, as though someone had stuck a needle into his behind. He even appeared to be breaking out in a light sweat.

Linda regarded him for a second, mildly amused by his distress. "And I'm going to overlook your little problem because I know Anne was hoping we would hit it off. She needs us to be friends." Linda put on her best smile.

Bradley began to regain his composure. He said, "I can't tell you what a fool I feel like. And last night was... well... I was going to say that it was totally uncharacteristic of me. But..." Bradley shrugged his shoulders.

Linda smiled. He was recovering quickly.

Bradley said, "I was upset about something, and my mind was a million miles away. Which was also the case just a moment ago. I have been terribly rude and, frankly—" Bradley lowered his voice and looked away from her eyes. He scuffed his right shoe over the toe of his left shoe, and seemed to be struggling with what to say. He spoke partly to the side of the elevator and partly to the floor, "Frankly, I am horribly embarrassed."

Linda bent forward and to the side, thus lowering her head to Bradley's and catching his eyes. She said, "I didn't know lawyers could admit they were wrong. Isn't it a genetic thing?"

Bradley raised up and smiled. "I'm afraid you are more correct than either of us would like. But, I feel I owe you a slightly better explanation of what kind of person I try to be." He emphasized "try."

Linda waved her hand as if shooing him away. "Don't be silly. I've got you figured out. I just wouldn't want to be your insurance agent, since every time you get preoccupied with your thoughts—you run into stuff."

They both laughed.

Bradley said, "Anyway, running into things seems to be something Anne and I have in common."

They both laughed again. This guy was looking better all the time. That goofy bow tie was disarming, even cute, the way it seemed to be always askew. The elevator jerked, and then dropped slightly, leveling itself to the floor where Anne's room was located. Linda felt her stomach do a flip-flop at the sudden weightlessness. Before she could regain her stomach, the doors opened and she and Bradley stepped off. By unspoken mutual agreement, they lingered by the elevator to finish their conversation. The hallway was deserted. At one end, about 50 feet away, they could see a couple of nurses chatting over the counter at a nurses' station. One of the nurses turned and glanced at Linda and Bradley, but she quickly resumed her conversation with the other nurse.

Bradley said, "Anyhow, I feel a need to tell you a little something about myself. You and Anne are very good friends, and, well… you've got to think I'm *non compos mentis*."

Linda nodded. She didn't know the exact translation of Bradley's Latin, but she figured it meant something pretty close to crackbrained. This was beginning to get a little odd. Linda had hoped to convince Bradley that Anne wasn't nutty, and here he was trying to convince her that *he* wasn't.

He said, "Something bad…" Bradley cast his eyes downward, "… shameful… happened to my family when my brother and I were in grade school. And you know how mean kids can be—"

Linda nodded.

"Well, we both got ridiculed pretty badly for it." Bradley craned his head around to make sure no one else was in earshot.

"Anyway, because of what happened, my brother and I swore we would never do anything illegal or dishonest. It was too humiliating. In high school, we prided ourselves on being gentlemen." He raised his eyebrows. "You can imagine what kind of trouble that got us into with the cool kids."

Linda nodded, but she wondered what the heck prompted this life story.

"To make a long story short, we wanted always to do the right thing."

This guy was either lying through his teeth, or he was one of— no—he was the nicest guy she had ever met. She said, "I'm surprised you haven't been disbarred for your heretical beliefs."

Bradley laughed. "Anyhow, I hope you can see how disappointed I am in myself. Nearly knocking over students, pushing past them, and being so self-centered that I nearly did the same to you."

Ah, Linda thought. *Now the life story was making sense.* There was a sudden lowness to his voice—he was groveling! That cinched it. He was the real thing. She said, "Yes, I can see." This was definitely the man for her best friend. "Anne's lucky she met you."

Bradley's face turned solemn and downcast. "I'm afraid I may have already ruined the relationship—before we even had a chance to get it started."

That was funny. Linda was sure Anne liked him. She couldn't imagine what would have altered her feelings. "What do you mean?"

"It doesn't appear that Anne is interested in me anymore. It's kind of strange. One minute she seemed interested, the next she didn't. I have to admit that I am a bit confused—" Bradley's voice trailed off; he seemed to hope Linda would provide an explanation. What in the heck was going on? She had a suspicion, but wanted to talk with Anne before she said more. Bradley said, "Is there something the matter with her?"

That made Linda feel uneasy, and the sensation she had had on the elevator returned to her stomach. The last thing she wanted to do was dodge or mislead this man, given the things he had just spilled from his gut. But how could she explain Anne in a way that wouldn't scare him off? Anne was, apparently, already doing a good job of that. Moreover, it was really for Anne to tell about herself. Bradley was waiting for a response; Linda knew she had to say something. She cleared her throat. "Anne is a bit depressed."

"A bit?"

True enough, Linda thought. She said, "Running into a door might be a little much."

"Might? A little? You are quite diplomatic. Maybe you should consider law school."

Linda chuckled. She made a snap decision. Given his willingness to admit shortcomings, maybe it would be okay to tell him a bit about Anne. Prepare him a little. "Look, you might as well know. She has gone through a major depressive disorder. Still suffers from it. She can't handle stress well, obviously."

"I've read a fair amount about depression. I've often wondered if some form of it has been interfering with my life. But I still don't get the connection. I was rude to some students. Why would that cause Anne to take off and run headlong into a door?"

"Anne was hoping to see you again. I'm her best friend and she probably wanted me to meet you."

Bradley began to rub his chin, and his face seemed to light up. He said, "And we were at each other's throats right off the bat. Her depression probably means she desperately needs your approval of me." Bradley began to nod as if he were agreeing with himself. "She saw that wasn't going to happen, and it caused an overwhelming emotional reaction. It probably felt as if her world were collapsing. Though I'm not sure how to explain her change of heart today."

Linda found herself nodding along with Bradley. He really was impressively bright. She had to get Bradley and Anne together. She said, "She really is a wonderful woman. She's just been through a lot. I know she likes you. She *really* likes you."

Bradley's eyes softened. "I appreciate your talking with me. I was quite taken with her when we first met. Actually, I was hoping to, er, run into her again." He smiled.

Linda laughed. "Please do me a favor?"

"Sure."

She pulled out a piece of paper from her purse, scribbled a phone number, and handed it to Bradley. "Take Anne to lunch or something. Get to know her a little. I think you'll be impressed."

"I'll call her. Thanks." Bradley pressed the elevator button and the door opened. He stepped in and the doors closed.

Linda was pleasantly surprised that Bradley had not put on airs when talking to her—indeed, quite the opposite. He genuinely seemed appreciative of her. Well, maybe, just maybe…

❧

CHAPTER 14

ANNE WAS IN A COMPLETE FRENZY. SHE HAD ENLISTED both Jeff and Linda to help her decide what to wear. And nothing seemed right. She realized—too late to make a mad dash to the mall—that she had been depressed so long that she had not purchased a new dress in over a year. Jeff and Linda were seated in wicker chairs in Anne's bedroom. Anne kept going into her walk-in closet, trying an outfit, and emerging for evaluation. She tried one after another. Nothing looked good on her. Nothing ever *would* look good on her. Jeff began rapidly tapping his feet and Linda was staring off into space. Time was ticking away and before too much longer there was a risk that Bradley would arrive. Anne was starting to get panicky.

Jeff threw his vote for whatever she had on at the moment, and this moment, it was the black, high-neck dress that was sleeveless and clung to her slender figure as it curved down just past her knees, ending in a slightly sexy slit off to the side. Obviously, *he* never froze wearing stuff like that. Linda snapped out of her daze and became adamant about the cream little bombshell. Its length was mid-thigh, and it had a deep, scooped neck with full-length arms and bare shoulders. Obviously, *she* was warm-blooded. It was made entirely of very snug-fitting spandex that would show off every goose bump, among other things. The dress was way too sexy, and Anne was embarrassed that she owned it. She quickly slipped it on and looked in the mirror.

Anne could feel her face redden. This was definitely an "*ahem* me" dress. No way was she wearing it… tonight, anyhow.

Bradley had called Anne every day, and she had steadfastly refused to go out. Their conversations were short and awkward. But Anne had found the strength to open up just enough to let Bradley know she was happy that he was calling. In truth, she wanted to go out, but not until the red lump on her head stopped resembling freaking Mt. Everest.

Anne glanced out the window to make sure Bradley wasn't already there. It was windy and raining. She studied the rain for a moment and realized it was turning to sleet. That meant the temperature was dropping. Time to think of something a bit warmer to wear. She checked the wall clock. She had a full 20 minutes to find something with a bit more coverage. "I'm going to get a cup of coffee and sit down for a moment. I'm getting too worked up."

Linda said, "Bradley will like anything you wear."

Oh, *that* made her feel good. Bradley's ill-manner of dress hardly made him a critic. Yet, Linda was right. He was so affable he would probably like anything she did. And that was precisely what she needed. Anne nodded and headed to the kitchen for her coffee. As she walked through the house she felt nearly naked. She passed through the entryway with its expanses of glass, and the cooler temperature gave her a case of goose bumps. Thankfully, the kitchen was warmer. She ground some fresh beans and tossed them into the coffee maker. She watched the dark liquid drip into the decanter. A sweet aroma filled the air. Anne could already feel the coffee's heat warming her insides.

On the way back to the bedroom she stopped at the entry way. Almost immediately, her nipples began to harden and poke through the thin spandex. That was it. This outfit was just too much. Something sexy, but slightly more conservative, and warm, was in order. *Better get it off,* she thought, *before Bradley comes up the damn front walk.*

Anne glanced out the entry way glass that surrounded the front door and sipped her coffee. "Damn," she cursed under her breath.

The coffee was barely warm. The stupid coffee maker was so old she couldn't remember when she had bought it. This was the second time in the last few days that it didn't heat the coffee properly. Anne stood in the entry way for a moment, unable to decide what to do. To hell with it, she was cold and wanted some hot coffee. If Bradley showed up, well, he could wait. She headed back to the kitchen and popped the cup into the microwave. As soon as the coffee was hot, she started toward the bedroom, moving as quickly as she could without spilling.

Anne didn't see Bradley until he rang the doorbell—just as she was passing through the middle of the entryway. She stopped abruptly and coffee spilled over the rim of her cup. She swore as it burned her fingers. Bradley was looking at her through the narrow, full-height window just to the side of the door. He was carrying flowers. His smile suddenly changed to a look of concern.

A hot flash raced through Anne's body and she felt as if she were in a free fall. There was a sudden and strong impulse to run. She screamed inside her head, "Please God, not again!"

Then, oddly, she saw an image of herself, as though she were watching the scene from above. She could see herself grimace in pain—she imagined her body bent and twisted, in the throes of some sort of convulsion.

And she was stunned.

The image of this weak and fragile person was repulsive.

Anne found herself staring at Bradley who now seemed almost alarmed. After a few moments, she gritted her teeth, straightened her back, and smiled. She *could* do this… She stepped forward and opened the door. The words, "Come in, Bradley, so nice to see you," somehow came out of her mouth. She hoped they were not too sarcastic.

Bradley handed her the flowers. He was smiling again, though he also seemed to have one eye that was trying to peer into her thoughts… and the other was trying to peer under her Spandex.

Anne smiled and smelled the flowers. "Ah! They smell wonderful. Roses. Thank you. They're beautiful. I'll be back in a minute. Sit down." Anne turned abruptly and realized she couldn't do anything with the flowers, yet. She turned toward Bradley and handed them back. She smartly walked into the bedroom suite where Jeff and Linda lingered.

When Anne stepped into the bedroom Linda's eyes went wide. Anne thought, *What the heck?*

And at that moment the doorbell rang again. Jeff jumped up and headed out of the bedroom. As he passed, he, too, seemed to give Anne a long glance. He yelled ahead, "Come on in, Miles!"

Linda said, "Anne... you... you, look fantastic."

Yeah, right, She thought. "I look like a whore."

Linda cracked a smile but continued to regard her in a most peculiar way. "Nonsense. I bet Bradley likes it." Anne made a cross face. Linda said, "You sit here. I'll go entertain Bradley for a few minutes. You can't appear too anxious." Linda left.

Anne sat on the edge of the bed and closed her eyes. Bradley wouldn't like her. She would irritate him, or she'd say something stupid, or he'd think she was boring... And then suddenly she became aware of her reflexive thoughts. She stiffened her back. *No, dammit,* she said to herself. This would go well. She would succeed. She was a work of art.

A few minutes later she walked into the entryway. Miles, Bradley, and Jeff were talking. Bradley stopped mid-sentence and turned toward Anne. He flashed a warm smile—that lingered. "Are you ready?"

Oh, man, did Bradley have a great smile. It warmed her even in this sex-pot dress that was too late to change. She smiled back. "Yes, but finish your conversation. I'll get my coat, but you take your time." Anne headed to the closet, which was only a few feet away. She quickly retrieved her coat and draped it around her over-exposed body. She was going to beat this damn depression... *With God's help,* she reminded herself.

Bradley had turned back toward Miles. "It varies from semester to semester, but usually I teach within my specialties, which are constitutional law, criminal procedure, sometimes criminal law, always with an emphasis on search and seizure."

Miles said, "What do you think about the Religious and Cultural Sensitivities Act? From what I just read, they are talking about using it to silence opposition to the government. They've already shut down talk radio. They're arresting nuns. I mean, the Declaration of Independence says we have the right to throw off our form of government. Surely we still have the right to discuss the overthrow of our present government. I mean, we don't have fewer rights today than we did in 1776. Do we?"

Bradley seemed not to know what to say. But he nodded in agreement.

Jeff said, "Washington said: 'Government, like fire, is a dangerous servant and a fearful master.'" He reached into his wallet and pulled out a small card that looked to Anne like it had a quotation written on it. "And Abraham Lincoln said: 'This country, with its institutions, belongs to the people who inhabit. Whenever they shall grow weary of the existing government, they can exercise their constitutional right of amending it…'" Jeff paused and lowered his voice slightly, "'… or their revolutionary right to dismember or overthrow it.'"

Anne was taken aback. She was unaware that past presidents had said such things. Yet she was also surprised that it was Jeff who had quoted them. He had been a good student. But he had never memorized quotations—and he sure as heck never carried around in his pocket material he was trying to learn. This was really odd. Anne could see that Jeff's comments also took Bradley by surprise, who seemed to suddenly become more alert and animated.

Bradley said, "Actually, it's an interesting question. The limits of the right of the people to throw off their government have not been tested since the Civil War. We've had a lot of talk by states to affirm their sovereign powers under the Tenth Amendment. Texas was the first a few years back, and most recently I've seen some discussion in California and maybe a few others. But these have mostly been failed attempts to push back the reach of the federal government. They have not been very serious about seceding from the union."

Jeff eyes were wide with interest. He said, "Jefferson is the one who said: 'A little rebellion now and then is a good thing.'"

Bradley glanced at Anne and seemed to sense what she was thinking. "You two are surprisingly well versed." He turned to Anne and regarded her for a moment. "And you are stunning."

Anne felt her face begin to flush. She figured he was exaggerating, but she loved it anyway. Anne was beginning to feel good for the first time in a long, long while. She said, "Shall we go?"

Bradley quickly moved to open the door. Anne stepped into the cold night air. The wind, rain, and sleet had stopped, so she didn't grab an umbrella. They were a few miles down the road when a few rain drops appeared on the windshield and she regretted her decision. He was already on the main road and she didn't want him to turn back. Anne said, "Do you think it might keep raining?"

Bradley glanced at her and smiled. "It's in the forecast; but don't worry, I'm a big umbrella."

⬧

Big Sky News
Missoula, Montana

Heller Reversed
BY TOM BRIDGER

WASHINGTON, D.C.—In the most watched and most highly anticipated decision by the United States Supreme Court this year, the court today, in *Jones v. Bouchard*, overruled, 6-3, its 2008 decision in *District of Columbia v. Heller*, which found a ban on handgun possession in the home as well as storage requirements that rendered rifles and shotguns inoperable for immediate self-defense to be violations of the Second Amendment.

At issue in *Bouchard* were Washington's highly restrictive laws that effectively banned handguns by limiting the features of allowable guns to characteristics that either do not currently exist in the market or would render the gun ineffective for self-defense. Under Washington's law, no gun is lawful if it holds in its magazine or cylinder more than four cartridges or can fire a bullet farther than 75 yards. Today's ruling affirms the decision by United States Court of Appeals for the Ninth Circuit, which had held Washington's law a reasonable use of police power to guard against mass killings and to protect innocent bystanders from errant shots.

Associate Justice Najib Ahmed, writing for the majority that included Associate Justices Elena Kagan, Sonia Sotomayor, Elena Granholt, Ruth Bader Ginsburg, and Stephen Breyer, held that Heller misread the history of the Second Amendment and upset the well-understood ruling in United States v. Miller, that allowed regulation of the civilian use of firearms so long as the regulation would not interfere with the operation of a well-regulated militia. Contrary to Heller, the

Page 2, Big Sky News
Heller Reversed, Cont.

court today found no evidence that the Second Amendment was intended to protect private use or possession of weapons for activities like hunting or personal self-defense.

The Supreme Court also found it persuasive that the United Nations supported Washington's law. "We find it important," the court said, "that we have entered a new world order where our own constitutional principles should not stray too far from others in the world community. Thus, we take notice that other nations maintain strict control over ownership and use of firearms, and further that the United Nations Department of Disarmament Affairs has asked the United States to adopt exactly these types of limitations on gun use and ownership."

Chief Justice John Roberts, Jr., and Associate Justices Clarence Thomas and Samuel Alito voted in the minority.

<<<<>>>>

CHAPTER 15

NATE WAS IN THE KITCHEN AND HE PACED BACK AND forth, drinking coffee and watching the clock. Tonight would be his night. His four top lieutenants were with him, waiting for completion of an operation that would give them the power to pull three states from the blue column back to red.

It was well known that Obama's plan had worked to perfection. He first made millions of illegal immigrants legal. Then he opened the border to a deluge of millions more Arabs and Hispanics. This was probably sufficient to tilt several battleground states from red to blue in the last several elections. But Obama had taken another step. He had forced the United States Census Bureau to "partner" with ACORN and "estimate" hundreds of thousands more inner-city residents, whom no one could actually find, but who miraculously appeared to vote in the congressional and presidential elections.

Well, Nate and others had had enough of that crap. The very thing that allowed ACORN to perpetrate its fraud would be its undoing. Over 90 percent of Democrat votes came from the large, single, inner cities like Detroit in Michigan, Pittsburgh in Pennsylvania, and Chicago in Illinois. Obliterate these sources of fraud and power and a great stride would be taken in the long walk to returning America to its Christian and constitutional foundations.

The action taking place tonight would certainly give him the power to regain control of the patriots from Hartman. In just a couple of hours. He could taste it.

He looked at the cup of coffee he was holding and watched waves ripple across the top. As he pulled it to his lips, coffee spilled over the sides, burning his hand and making his hand jerk, causing nearly the whole cup to lap over the side. Nate let go rather than get burned again, and the cup shattered on the floor, spewing ceramic and black coffee everywhere.

One of his lieutenants, standing closest, cursed and tried, but failed, to jump away from the splashing coffee. It splattered from the knee down on his camouflage pants.

Nate blurted, "Mother of God, I've got to get this night over with!" He walked away from the mess and the stunned stares of the men around him. Hebrews 10:35-36 came to mind:

Therefore do not throw away your confidence, which has a great reward. For you have need of endurance, so that when you have done the will of God you may receive what is promised.

✦

JEFF AND MILES WERE FINALLY READY FOR THE DEMONSTRAtion. Jeff called everyone into the hall to crowd around the two computers. Jeff noted that Nate stood away, back behind everyone. He was rapidly opening and closing his knife with one hand as he paced about in a small circle. Nate's head was down, but he kept glancing up every moment or two. Hartman, Jeff saw, was also watching Nate.

Jeff and Miles had worked hard to devise secure cell and email networks. The solution was not particularly high tech or glamorous. It was, in fact, fairly mundane. Jeff had hoped to come up with something really spectacular and slick, but everything he and Miles looked at had more potential problems than what they chose— encryption of messages with a customized version of Pretty Good

Privacy (PGP) that would block usage of the backdoor keys PGP gave the government. Miles did most of the raw programing, and Jeff streamlined the user interface for speed of use while retaining just enough of the pretty icons and pop-up menus to make it easy for the computer illiterate.

When everyone was gathered around in a semi-circle, Jeff started his presentation, his voice cracking over the first few syllables. He was more nervous than he realized. "As a good number of you know—" Jeff coughed to feign something in his throat. His face was turning red. He just knew it. Damn, he hated looking like a wimp. Jeff hit his chest with his fist to confirm that something must have gotten caught in his throat; maybe they would think it was also making his face red. He continued, "Pretty Good Privacy or PGP has been widely available throughout the world. Beginning in 1994, the Massachusetts Institute of Technology became the official home of PGP. Anyone with a computer and a modem could log on to MIT's server, answer several questions, agree to federally mandated export restrictions, and download the program. This led a number of you to implement encryption in your computer communications. Partly for this reason—that a good number of you are already familiar with the basics—it's tailor-made for us. Also, it has been significantly improved over the years by Phil Zimmerman and his company and, best of all, it's free for noncommercial use, widely available, very easy to utilize, and Miles and I have added a few tricks to make it virtually impervious to government interference and code breakers." Jeff took a deep breath. He got that out pretty well. He tapped his chest again, just in case his face was still red.

Unfortunately, there were a few murmurs of disbelief. Probably, Jeff figured, it was the anti-computer types. These were the people he had to convince. And that was the hard part. Jeff knew, for example, explaining some of the mathematics behind the encryption would be useless. Even for the few who had college math under their belts, they had been too long away from textbooks to understand any of it. And for most, who had been some form of that whiny,

"Why do we have to know this?" bunch in high school, it would be completely unintelligible.

And then one of that whiny bunch spoke up. He had a long beard, a pony tail, a pot belly, and a tattered plaid shirt. Jeff doubted he had ever even touched a keyboard. The man said, "Doesn't going on line mean someone like the FBI can trace your every move? What's to stop them from screwing with my records to give me a criminal history, or, well, even a 4.0 grade average at Harvard?"

Someone from the group quipped, "Hey, Willie. Not much risk of anyone believing you went to Harvard!"

Everyone laughed, including Nate, who briefly craned his thick neck around to see who had made the comment then quickly returned his eyes to Jeff.

Jeff said, "You have been watching too many movies. Hollywood has always been long on drama but short on reality. Your birth records, for example, are likely not even on a computer." Jeff looked out among the patriot leaders crowding around. "How many of you were born before widespread computer use?"

Several people seemed to nod in understanding.

Jeff nodded back at them. "Right. In reality, such records are likely stuffed in file rooms in dark, dingy, hospital basements. Obviously, such records are virtually inaccessible to a computer hacker, FBI or otherwise."

Now feeling a bit more confident, Jeff raised his voice. "Creating a criminal record is an even more difficult task. I don't know this from experience, mind you—" Jeff smiled, "—but I remember a bit from my law class in college. Unless things have recently changed, virtually all criminal proceedings are documented in writing. Typically, there will be a written warrant—signed in ink by a judge. There will be a written police report—made out by hand by the arresting officer. There will be a typewritten court transcript documenting, verbatim, the charge or charges, the plea, bail issues, and other scheduling matters. The court transcript will be authenticated by the sworn and written statement of a court reporter. There will likely be an Appearance of Record, commonly mailed to the court as an enclosure to a written letter, on letterhead, that has been signed in ink by the defense attorney. And so on."

The same heckler of Willie quipped, "Well, Willie, so much for your Ph.D. in Sex Therapy!"

Everyone laughed, and Willie sat down. Jeff noted, with some pleasure, that Willie was now the one who was red-faced.

Jeff said, "This is a little confusing and it takes actually using the system to really understand it. But, basically, PGP is a combination of two encryption systems. As part of the program, you receive both a private key and a public key. The program takes care of the mechanics of using and obtaining the necessary keys. Both the new Quad DES algorithm and the Diffie-HellmanII algorithm, which are currently used by PGP, are considered to be unbreakable. It's estimated that a PGP-encrypted message cannot be broken by stringing together all of the computers in the world and running them for something like a thousand years." The murmurs of a moment ago were silenced. *Good*, Jeff thought, *at least that got everyone's attention.*

Jeff said, "When you get your phones and the software for the computer email, the PGP program will automatically start and generate your set of public and private keys. Then follow the program's instructions to post your public key on our server. Naturally, keep your private key secret. If anyone gets access to your computer they could obtain your private key and break into any of your messages. Here, gather around the computer and we'll show you how it works if you don't already know. Now, keep in mind this is a simplified example of what is happening automatically in your phones and with your email programs."

Several leaders began to crowd even closer around the computers.

Jeff turned to the keyboard to type a message that, he explained, would replicate both the cell transmissions and computer email. The message was being sent to the computer at which Miles was now sitting. "First," he said, "create your message and then click on the PGP icon. Select Encrypt and Sign. See how that brings up a list of Public Keys?"

Jeff looked over his shoulder to see if they were getting it. Several heads nodded and no one had a totally blank stare, so he figured so far, so good.

He continued, "Click on the Public Key of the person you are sending the message and you will be prompted to enter your passphrase. Now, this is important." Again Jeff looked around to make sure everyone was getting it. "PGP requires your Private Key to decrypt an incoming message or to sign an outgoing message. For that you must enter a passphrase which you must keep secret and not forget. So spend some time picking a combination of letters and numbers, or even symbols, that you can remember. Then, type it in and click Proceed. And watch this. Now, normally, this will not appear on your screen but I have it set up to give you just a feel for what is happening. This is called cipher text."

Everyone watched as Jeff typed: "All assets are in place. Plan is GO. God bless."

There were a couple of oohs and aahs with what came across the screen at the terminal at which Miles sat:

```
PGP//:
r93.msoep5;f,wgxi80n3%n(;,Y#s0#%
^boxu@_&n†åjdiwlw.mcjfp'Znvieoq]
q,irp-8503=fmzpA0EFMV/SL"o;/x
iewwq[vmvzu7t52kagfua[gkz/so8yfbf/
a0yif;s'ajwj4m,foinn^%BB*&%DGKLg
frb%^(3=+_-HJIY4%%&78##%80kgFE
```

Miles pushed the mouse here and there and clicked a couple of times as Jeff explained the process in reverse. After a brief pause, Miles's computer kicked out the message in English:

```
*** PGP Signature Status: good
*** Signer: Jeff Kreig <Jeff.jef-
fkreig@byforceofpatriots.com>
*** Signed: 06/30/2015 at 00:51
*** Verified: 06/30/2015 at 00:52
*** BEGIN PGP DECRYPTED/VERIFIED MES-
SAGE *** All assets are in place. Plan
is GO. God bless.
*** END PGP DECRYPTED/VERIFIED MESSAGE
***
```

The room was all smiles and Jeff was delighted. Nearly everyone appeared to grasp the power of the system—even if they had no idea how it worked. What mattered was that they could communicate in complex sentences, if necessary, and they could do so in secrecy and with speed. It was exactly what they wanted. Everyone seemed happy.

Everyone, that is, except Nate Smith. He seemed to have finally taken an interest and stopped his pacing at the back of the room. He stepped in from the back of the circle of people and faced Jeff. Nate scowled. "Since PGP is freely available, why did we need you two wizards to give us what some of us have already been using?"

A mixture of laughter and concerned-looking faces quickly spread around the room.

Jeff was ready for that. He glared back at Nate. "For your information, Miles and I have heavily customized the program to make the keys—that Obama required be given the government for all encryption programs—unusable on our cell and computer messages. Basically, we closed the backdoor PGP was required to write into the program to give the government access."

Nate glared, "Assuming that is true, how are we supposed to get cell reception where there are no towers within 50 miles?"

There was a murmur of concern.

"Oops, forget something?" Nate taunted.

"Glad you reminded me," Miles said, as he pulled from his duffel three small black objects. One was obviously an Apple iPhone, one looked like a large Hershey's Kiss, and the other was just a black box about the size of a couple of bundled cigarette packs.

There were a number of surprised faces as Miles pulled from the top of the iPhone an antenna that normal iPhones don't have. He then snapped the Hershey's Kiss thing on top of the antenna and the black box to the back of the iPhone.

Miles said, "Cellular telephones are often useless in the Upper Peninsula, gentlemen, because there are so few transmitting towers to pick up the signals from the puny transmitters that usually accompany these phones." Miles cleared his throat and turned the object in his hand as if it was a fine glass of wine. "You can think of it as a super digital cellular phone. This special battery pack, in combination with the enhancer on the custom installed antenna, increases the effective power over 200 times. This could exist in the civilian world, but the FCC would prohibit it because it creates way too much interference with other electrical devices. We, however, couldn't care less if we disrupt Aunt Millie's hearing aid for a few seconds while we transmit."

"As a result," Jeff chimed in, "you can speak much as you would with a two-way radio. You say what you want and you wait to get a response. You can't have a back and forth conversation like a normal phone, but that is because we are bundling the transmission of data in a different way. The chip we built into the phones sends out conversations in bursts, as opposed to a continuing data stream, as occurs with all other phones. This way, it's very hard to locate the data in the huge mass of data transmissions that run through cell towers and cell company equipment. Except for getting accustomed to speaking and then waiting for a response, it's seamless to you."

"But what if they jam us?" Nate asked. "How will the cellular transmission get through?" Jeff could see that Nate was agitated; he had probably begun to realize that the communications system would work just fine and Jeff and Miles were acquitting themselves well.

"They won't" Miles said flatly. "There is not a whole lot we can do if they try. But they won't cut the phone lines; and in the U.P. there are still a number of public phones scattered around. It's not very glamorous, but if necessary, the iPhones will have maps of locations of telephones; it won't be secure, but it's also not likely to be tapped."

Nate shot back, "Oh, right. Like we are going to stand at a telephone booth in broad daylight. What a stupid idea!" General laughter followed.

Jeff decided to let people get it out of their systems. Pausing for a moment was sure to increase their feelings of foolishness when they heard his retort. As the chuckling was dying down, Jeff said, "Remember the time of the year we're talking about…"

There were a few surprised faces in the crowd—and immediate silence.

Jeff said, "You needn't worry about looking conspicuous standing at a pay phone in military garb."

Oddly, Jeff noted, Nate still seemed quite nervous. He was quickly glancing to and fro, repeatedly looking at his watch. It was as though he were interested in something else. Then Jeff heard the faint sound of a telephone—perhaps a cell in someone's pocket. Immediately, Nate reached into his pocket and brought his phone to his ear, as he abruptly turned away from the group and rushed into an adjoining room. Jeff wondered what the hell that was about.

❧

CHAPTER 16

RAIN WAS COMING DOWN IN SHEETS AND IT WAS DOING its best to freeze as it hit the frosty windshield of the High-Mobility Multipurpose Wheeled Vehicle—a HMMWV. Leonard Williams and five former Navy SEALS were traveling in two stolen military HMMWVS that had been re-painted to civilian black. The two HMMWVS were accompanied by two cars driven by patriots. The cars were unremarkable American sedans. They were also stolen.

Leonard swore at his luck. If it were just rain, it wouldn't be a problem. But this was a big-ass mess. The defrosters and heavy-duty wipers were on full speed. Patches of slushy ice slowly migrated across the windshield, oblivious to all attempts at removal. Leonard was driving the lead vehicle and he needed to maintain his speed to make the target zone at the designated time. The conditions made him squint to see as far down the road as possible. To be late would be the biggest mistake of his life. Leonard touched his brakes to see if the expressway was getting slick from ice. He breathed a sigh of relief as the rubber grabbed without any hint of skidding. Their destination was a spot along Interstate 94 about 30 miles west of Detroit.

Leonard's HMMWV was a standard m1037 shelter carrier that carried troops and was frequently used by the United States Army as a quick and dirty command-and-control vehicle. Leonard's passenger, Lonny Webster, caressed his specially modified M4. Lonny, a lanky 30-year-old with nerves as calm as an early morning pond, had earned his seat across from Leonard by being the best marksman of the bunch. Leonard had no intention of dying for this operation.

Stu Smith was driving the other HMMWV, an M1026 retrofitted with two MK-19 40 mm grenade launchers that were presently hidden by a quick-remove canopy. Stu had two men to operate the grenade launchers and third person as backup. The grisly looking Stu was struggling with nodding off. The rain and ice weren't a significant bother; Stu cursed the constant spray being stirred up by Leonard's HMMWV in front. It left a muddy film the wipers couldn't seem to penetrate. And worse, the constant, rhythmic movement of the wipers was working as well as a couple of good belts of whiskey. Stu rubbed his large, calloused hand across his unshaven face and then slapped his cheek. "Got any of that coffee?"

Mark Guenther, the backup, was sitting in the front passenger's seat and he reached between his feet and pulled out a Thermos. Pouring steaming coffee into the lid/cup, he gently handed it to Stu, careful not to spill. "I'm still not so sure I trust Nate with these things." Mark was clean shaven and had a baby face that went along with his rap of being the weakest member of the crew.

Stu said nothing. Mark made Stu nervous.

Mark said, "I mean, how do we know he won't use them? I mean, there's supposed to be three of them in this shipment."

Stu said nothing.

Mark said, "Dammit." He shook his head and ran his hand through his blond, medium-length hair.

Stu knew he might have to shoot Mark. If he wavered, he was dead. And that would be a pity. Stu had met Mark's wife and two kids, both in high school. Nice family. Stu glanced in the rear-view mirror and got confirming nods from the two men in back. They were both single, their wives having divorced them shortly after they had returned from Afghanistan and begun to exhibit strange, and sometimes violent, psychological problems. Yup, it would really be a pity.

Like most of the Midwest's winter-and-speed-ravaged expressway system, I-94 was under construction for general maintenance purposes; and at this particular location, both east- and west-bound lanes narrowed to one lane for about a four-mile stretch. Near the east end of the construction zone there was a spot beneath a new overpass that was under construction, where I-94 narrowed even more and also undertook a series of severe lane shifts—to the point that drivers of the big wheelers had to keep a skilled hand on the steering wheel in order to avoid side-swiping the concrete lane barriers.

So bad, in fact, was this particular construction zone that during the past couple of weeks, traffic had backed up in both directions for miles. The resulting news coverage had brought it to Leonard Williams's attention. Up to that point, he had been stumped as to where to intercept the convoy, since it tended to travel on expressways whose wide, treeless swaths through the countryside made interdiction quite difficult. Secluded hiding places from which an ambush could be sprung were few and far between. It was no mistake by the Energy Department to travel expressways whenever possible.

Surveying the site beforehand, however, Leonard knew it was about as good as he could get. Even on an evening with little traffic, all vehicles slowed and some, such as the big trucks, slowed to a crawl. Moreover, at the partially constructed overpass, there were construction vehicles parked all around; Leonard knew the HMMWVS could easily hide among them. And for the short time he planned to be there, he figured there was little risk of being noticed by someone such as a patrolman who might get past his staged road blockage.

Leonard and his men finally arrived at the scene and Leonard checked his watch. Ten minutes before his calculations indicated the convoy would arrive. He had cut it a little close, but they had made it just the same. Leonard breathed a sigh of relief. He thought about Nate's meeting in the U.P. In a little while he would be able to telephone Nate with the good news. The rain and sleet finally began to ease. It was a good omen.

Even in the coolness of the HMMWV, with the engine off to avoid the risk of exhaust attracting attention, sweat began dripping from Leonard's forehead.

Calling it a convoy was perhaps an overstatement. The Energy Department shipped the warheads in a specially designed Fox NBC2 Reconnaissance Vehicle used in its basic form since Desert Storm to sniff for traces of chemical warfare agents. It had huge tires, three to a side, and was outfitted all around with light armor. Its good maneuverability, top speed of 65 miles per hour, and large cargo bay made it an excellent choice to carry live warheads.

Two armed guards rode in the cab of the Fox. They were protected by a special, small-arms-resistant windshield about the size of a normal automobile windshield. There were also similarly designed side windows, though somewhat smaller than you might find in an automobile. Nevertheless, visibility was quite good. Directly behind the driver and passenger hung two M4 rifles—though orders were to avoid, at all costs, a shoot-out. Avoidance and escape was the name of the game. Shooting it out was the job of the trailing vehicle.

Riding behind the Fox was a HMMWV configured into an M1026+ armament carrier. The "+" referred to the upgraded nature of the machine gun—from an M60 7.62 mm light machine gun—to a new gun based on the design of the Gatling seven-barrel cannon that made the United States Air Force A-10 "Warthog" so devastating.

The new machine gun, named the M6000, fired special armor-piercing, 20 mm high-impact rounds. Made with a top-secret metal alloy similar to that found in the armor of the M1A2 main battle tank, the rounds were so effective that the soldiers had been instructed to shoot, if at all possible, only in wide-open spaces.

Tests had shown that, used in a city, the rounds could rip through cars, steel, buildings, everything—like a hot knife through butter. In fact, if given time and aimed properly, it could actually rip apart and possibly topple a typical office building. Of course, it was designed to cut open an armored vehicle—considered a likely component of any terrorist attempt to steal a nuclear device.

The M1026+ was occupied by a driver, Danny Schulte, a fair skinned Midwesterner and veteran of Iraq and Afghanistan, two wiry, West Texas riflemen, Stan Claymore and Buddy Gist, from the Army's sharp-shooting squad, and the always smiling Senaud Redrick, former Pac-10 All American linebacker from Alabama, who gave up a professional football career to join this elite branch of the military that his father had founded. All were active duty in the United States Army's elite "SFA," a relatively new group, know as Special Forces, Antiterrorism.

Despite the apparent lack of force, the six men who guarded the warheads were as lethal as any 20 men in the world. They were also motivated.

Everyone understood the implications of a failed mission.

⋅⊛⋅

NUMEROUS REPORTS WERE SITTING ON THE DESK OF THE Director, Information Assurance, commonly referred to as the IAD (Information Assurance Directorate) for the National Security Agency. A red-headed Irishman whose parents had come through Ellis Island, Fred Macintire, was proud of his blood but thankful for his United States citizenship. He was both fiercely patriotic and exceedingly detail-oriented. It was not unusual to see him late at the office, as he was tonight.

Fred could delegate the task of reviewing all these reports, but he enjoyed the work. It was like putting together a huge puzzle. He was also very good at it. And presently he was looking at two unrelated reports of a gray van being sighted near the homes of various Defense Department officials. The last report had produced a license number and he was trying to figure out what was going on. He was waiting for the results of a check on the license when he noticed Ralph Martenass's reports.

"Hmmm." This was something. The third report of the van. And this one by the guy who schedules warhead shipments. He could feel the skin over his forehead begin to tighten and his palms begin to sweat. It was always this way when he knew he had stumbled onto something. It was an eerie feeling that rarely failed him. But now the game was much more serious than a friendly puzzle. He understood his job too well to see it merely as a game.

The phone rang and he got his report on the owner of the van. It was registered to Leonard Williams, who, the report indicated, was already on the Department of Homeland Security's watch list.

"Pick it up," Fred ordered. He slammed down the phone. *"Dammit!"*

Fred punched several commands into his computer and learned that a warhead shipment was currently underway. Quickly, he brought up a GPS map of the convoy's location. He needed to do two things immediately: contact the warhead convoy and order it to alter route until help could arrive, and ring both Selfridge and Kalamazoo air bases and request helicopter backup. He buzzed his secretary and got no answer.

He realized he was the only one still working.

He picked up the secure phone and started making the connections necessary to contact the convoy. He finally got a defense department operator to help. She agreed to let him know as soon as she got through to the convoy's commanding officer.

Fred dialed Ralph Martenass's office. He wanted to know more about this breach in security. There was no answer.

Fred sat and stewed.

Five minutes later the operator phoned with the convoy's commanding officer on the line. "This is Fred Macintire, Director, Information Assurance Directorate for the National Security Agency, and I need to advise you that the secrecy of your shipment may have been compromised. You should immediately alter planned course and coordinate with Selfridge and Kalamazoo ANG (Air National Guard) bases for air backup. I've alerted both bases but you need to take it from there. They are on I-94, just west of

Detroit…" He finished by giving the officer details on pulling up the GPS tracking map.

Two Apache AH-64D Longbow attack helicopters were ordered to take off from Selfridge Air National Guard Base, northeast of Detroit. Unfortunately, one had developed a bearing problem on its main rotor and had been grounded for over two months. Defense cuts had allocated only two aircraft to the base, and commanders had to fill out reams of paperwork and wait months to obtain spare parts.

Still, the one operational bird was ready to fly just 15 minutes from the time Fred Macintire had called. It headed toward the west side of Detroit, expecting to receive an exact location in flight. Able to fly at speeds well in excess of 200 miles per hour, it would take less than 20 minutes to get to the general area, and then another couple to get close enough to provide fire assistance.

In addition to the M230, 30 MM chain gun located under the nose, which could fire over 600 armor-piercing rounds per minute, the Apache had been quickly armed for close support with 16 Hellfire missiles on four, four-rail launchers, and four air-to-air missiles. The aging Apache was designed for night operations and contained Lockheed Martin's newest Arrowhead/VNsight system of long-wave infrared and enhanced visible light/near infrared sensor capabilities. Mounted at the chin of the aircraft on turrets that slewed left, right, up, and down in sync with the helmets of the pilot and co-pilot, the Arrowhead/VNsight system projected images and targeting information in the pilot's and co-pilot's visors that allowed greatly enhanced vision and targeting through rain, fog, smoke, and the brownout of blinding sand and dust. In short, the Arrowhead/VNsight system, in combination with the computer-controlled firing systems, made the AH-64D Longbow one of the world's most fearsome weapons.

❖

THE CONSTRUCTION ZONE FORCED THE CONVOY TO SLOW TO about 10 miles per hour. Colin James, the skinny and

pimple-faced driver of the Fox, saw the lane shifts ahead and determined that it would be a tight fit. Lieutenant Manuel Chavez, sitting
in the passenger seat, had just finished speaking to his commanding
officer and was beginning to radio back the appropriate warnings
and instructions to the M1026+ HMMWV.

Ahead, Chavez could see the array of construction equipment
that was common to bridge building. A crane, a couple of bulldozers and, just over the top of the bulldozers, he could make out the
profile of the top of an M1037 HMMWV.

What the hell? An M1037 HMMWV?

Chavez's pulse hit the stratosphere. He knew a firefight was
imminent. Chavez grabbed the radio hand set. "Contact! Contact!
Ahead 100 yards. Likely armed Hum-V on right. Look for others!
This is no fucking joke!" Chavez had always wondered what battle
was like. He had heard all the tales and knew that he should be filled
with paralyzing terror. Yet, so far, he wasn't. His mind was still functioning, calculating. He prayed it would continue thus.

Colin James didn't need to be told what to do. With hostiles
identified in front, Chavez knew he would move to the side to allow
the armed M1026+ to go past and meet the enemy. On both sides,
however, the heavy concrete lane barriers trapped them in. James
wouldn't likely risk going over them, getting hung up, and then not
be able to go anywhere.

Colin yelled, "I can't pull to the side!"

Chavez barked, "Stop. Make them come to us!"

Colin stood on the brakes so abruptly that the M1026+ rammed
them from behind and, unknown to Chavez and James, knocked its
forward passenger unconscious as his head hit the A-pillar.

❧

LEONARD WILLIAMS DIDN'T KNOW IT, BUT PARKING HIS
HMMWVs behind construction equipment was his only mistake
in planning. He neglected to realize that the men in the Fox would
have a much higher vantage point than he had in his HMMWV. He
hadn't envisioned that they could see the canopy of his M1037

HMMWV behind the bulldozers.

Leonard had been watching and counting down the seconds to the attack. When he saw the Fox stop, he knew that, somehow, they had become aware of the ambush.

"Go! Go! Go!" he screamed into the radio. He couldn't call it off now—and he might as well preserve as much surprise as possible. He reasoned that if the convoy had not been at least partially surprised, it would not have gotten even this close.

The two cars that had followed the patriot's HMMWVs had been sitting just outside the construction zone for both east- and westbound lanes. They immediately drove into the construction zone about two hundred yards and pulled up lengthwise, perpendicular to the lane, effectively blocking any cars or trucks from entering. To this point they had also served as lookouts, ready to notify Leonard in the event that a police vehicle had fortuitously entered the construction zone. Now, however, with their cars in place and the tires slashed, they simply walked away, toward a predetermined pickup location.

Leonard gunned the 150 hp General Motors diesel engine and pulled out onto the expressway, headed directly at the Fox. His passenger, Lonny Webster, opened fire into its front cab. He was firing rounds stolen from the United States Army's classified inventory of armor-piercing ordinance. The bullets were based on the technology behind the wildly successful "Silver Bullet" of the 1991 Persian Gulf War. The "Silver Bullet" was actually a 120-mm tank round known as a High-Velocity, Armor-Piercing, Fin-Stabilized, Discarding-Sabot (HVAPFSDS) projectile. It featured a depleted-uranium penetrator that would strike with such force concentrated on its tip that it caused the defending armor to literally melt and flow out of the way. The United States Army had been working on a small caliber version for use by the infantry in a beefed-up version of its standard assault rifle, the M4. Several of the beefed-up guns, along with thousands of test rounds, were known to have been stolen in the last year. Needless to say, the small-arms-resistant windshield of the Fox didn't stand a chance against the quasi-HVAPFSDS rounds.

Simultaneously, the second HMMWV came out from behind the partially constructed overpass support and headed up the open space between the east- and west-bound lanes. "Shaky" Buck Jones and Mike Ballantine were manning the grenade launchers. They were fingering the triggers, ready to fire into the Army HMMWV the second it came into view.

Out of the corner of his eye, Leonard saw his second HMMWV flash past and his first feeling was of exhilaration. Leonard knew that Shaky and Mike had waited a long time to extract vengeance on the military establishment that had so destroyed their lives. This was their sweet revenge. Leonard blazed with pride. Things were going well; the front cab of the Fox was already shredded.

It was looking to be a rout.

❧

"TAKING FIRE! TAKING FIRE! I-94 TWO MILES WEST OF Michigan Avenue. In construction zone! Hostiles in at least two military Hum-Vs. One directly in front of us, one flanking. Out!" Chavez was crouched under the dash of the Fox. Colin James was slumped over the steering wheel. His face was covered with blood that was dripping down the steering column, down his leg, and pooling on the floor. James's eyes were wide open.

Chavez's immediate concern was what to do. He knew he was being converged upon and he knew his fire support was behind him, right where the enemy had obviously planned. His only weapon was an M4 that he had grabbed from a rack behind the front seat just before the fusillade of bullets ripped into the cab. He guessed that he would be fired upon if he showed his face above the dash. It seemed his only chance was to run for it. Surely, if he stayed in the cab, they would soon be around to the side and could, with the advanced ordinance they obviously had, shoot him through the lightly armored door. Fortunately, he was presently protected by the Fox's huge diesel engine and thick fire wall.

A HMMWV can cover 100 yards in a matter of seconds. Chavez knew he had to act quickly. He turned himself around under the dash, put the M4 on the bench seat and reached up to the door handle with his left hand. He heard the hostile HMMWV begin to slow as it approached. He pulled the interior handle of the Fox's passenger door, pushed it open with a tremendous thrust, and jumped as far as he could.

❧

LEONARD, STILL IN THE DRIVER'S SEAT OF HIS HMMWV, SAW the passenger door of the Fox open and someone scramble out and disappear behind the concrete lane barriers. Suddenly Leonard was annoyed that the very feature that trapped his prey (the lane barriers) now provided an escape route or worse—a hiding place from which *he* could be shot. Leonard cursed his bad luck in losing the element of total surprise. His plans had called for shooting the two in the Fox and blowing up the following HMMWV before anyone knew they were even under attack. Now he had a problem. That lucky bastard who had just jumped out of the Fox was going to spoil his day unless he was found quickly and killed.

As Leonard leaped from the HMMWV armed with his M16A2, he began to sense another problem. He had expected to hear at least one explosion, and hopefully two, from the grenades to be fired from his other HMMWV. Instead, he heard racing engines that were getting farther away. His stomach began to turn. What was going on?

❧

DANNY SCHULTE HAD BEEN A TANK DRIVER IN IRAQ, AND HE knew that moving objects stayed alive and sitting ones didn't. As soon as he realized that the Fox was under fire, he threw his HMMWV into reverse and put his foot to the floor. He had not moved backwards more than 50 yards when a hostile HMMWV he recognized as a M1026 grenade launcher came into view.

Danny was under no illusions about being able to outrace, going backwards, the oncoming grenade launcher. And he also knew that its gunners would only take a few seconds to get a fix on him and fire. But the few precious seconds gave his own gunner, Senaud Redrick, a chance to unsheathe the Gatling gun and take aim.

It was not a matter of who could shoot first but who, by choice of weapon, had to be more careful to shoot accurately. The patriots had not bargained on trying to hit a rapidly moving target. They had been sure of surprise and of finding a stopped or slowly moving (toward them) HMMWV. Thus, their grenade launchers were the weapons of choice. Moreover, only one had to hit home to kill everyone in the HMMWV.

The problem they now faced was decidedly unsettling. They would get off two shots, that was almost certain. But hitting a moving target from a moving and jostling platform, without nice computer-controlled systems, was a bit of an art. Consequently, it took a fair amount of skill to gauge speeds, directions, and lead firing distance. Thankfully, "Shaky" Buck Jones and Mike Ballantine were both good, and they needed just a couple more seconds…

The man behind the Gatling gun, Senaud Redrick, had no intention of allowing those precious seconds. With over 4000 rounds loaded, he had no need to hit his target with the first shot. As a result, as soon as the approaching HMMWV was even close to his front sight, he pulled the trigger. He did not care if he hit them. He knew the first rule of combat—incoming fire has the right of way. He also knew that incoming fire had a most unsettling effect on those trying to aim their own weapons.

❧

"What the—" MIKE BALLANTINE SAW A HUGE STREAK OF fire shoot out from the military HMMWV. He knew that normal machine guns didn't breathe *that* much fire. Reflexively, both "Shaky" Jones and Mike Ballantine pulled their respective triggers.

The rounds from the M6000 Gatling gun ripped the patriot's HMMWV right down the middle and nearly sliced the vehicle in two. None of the patriots was hit, but the portions of the vehicle on which "Shaky" Jones and Mike Ballantine were standing, and to which the grenade launchers were attached, began to split—a millisecond before the grenades launched. The slight movement threw off their aim by just enough and the grenades exploded, one behind and one in front of the army HMMWV. The patriot's HMMWV, on the other hand, collapsed down the middle, dug into the earth, and immediately flipped and twisted in midair, landing with the screech of ripping metal. An immense cloud of mud and dirt flew up into the wind, which blew most of it back onto the twisted wreckage and its four occupants, all of whom had smashed bodies and broken necks.

Leonard got out of his HMMWV and was momentarily surprised by the stinging to his face. The wind had whipped up and the sleet felt like hundreds of needles pricking at him. He grunted and hurried over to check the driver of the Fox. He was still alive, but probably not for long. Then he heard the explosions of the grenades and he looked down the expressway. The sleet was coming at him nearly horizontal to the ground. He put his hand to his face to shield his eyes. He was rewarded with the view of his compatriots flipping and twisting through the air.

And he knew it was over.

The warheads were within his grasp, but he couldn't touch them.

As he half expected, the next sound he heard was the Army HMMWV changing direction and beginning to race forward through the wet slush that covered the expressway.

His only choice was to escape.

Taking a quick look at the approaching HMMWV, as if to give his mind one last chance to figure out how to save the mission, Leonard slammed his hand into the side of the Fox. Lonny Webster was shooting at the approaching HMMWV but it kept coming. Suddenly fire shot out and tore up the ground just in front of them but well off to the side of the Fox.

"Forget it," Leonard shouted, and the two of them rushed back to their HMMWV. The Fox stood between them and the approaching HMMWV. They wheeled their own HMMWV around and made a hasty escape up the side of the embankment. They disappeared into the darkness on the opposite side of the half-constructed bridge.

The escaping HMMWV was spotted by the Apache helicopter as it raced to the scene. With two Apaches, one could have followed the escaping HMMWV. With only one, however, security of the warheads was paramount. Chasing bad guys would have to be left to the police.

Thirty minutes later Leonard and his three survivors had changed to another vehicle, leaving the HMMWV in a field. In another 30 minutes Leonard was far enough north that he felt safe in using his phone. It was a call he did not want to make.

Nate had told him to take more men and more firepower on the mission, and Leonard had assured him he had plenty of both. Further, Leonard knew that Nate had planned to announce he was in control of three nuclear warheads that would be used to take out the inner cities of three states that the bogus census and ACORN voter fraud had made blue. It would certainly have catapulted him back into command of the American Patriots.

Leonard cringed and felt his stomach turn. No. This was not going to make Nate happy at all.

Leonard listened to the phone ringing on the other end. He hoped Nate was in a good mood.

❧

NATE THREW HIS CELL PHONE AGAINST THE WALL AND watched it shatter into dozens of pieces. His heart pounded. He screamed, *"He fucked it up! Mother of God he fucked it up! I don't have the warheads! God damn him! I'll kill that fucker! GOD DAMN him!"*

Nate shook his head and ran his hands slowly and heavily over his face and then through his hair, pulling the roots and sending a shiver down his spine. He looked to the ceiling and prayed, "Forgive me God for taking your name in vain. I have sinned. Wash my blood, oh Lord, for You are great and mighty, King of Kings, Lord of Lords, the Alpha and Omega. And forgive them, Lord, for they—I—have failed."

Nate paused a moment and closed his eyes. "I shall accept this as Your will-be-done, Lord. I can see now that You have other plans and that I let my selfishness get in the way. Show me the way, my Lord, and Thy will be done."

Nate opened his eyes. He still yearned to lash out in violence and he knew his anger was a sign of God's will. "Thank you," he said, and his mind went blank—except for focusing on the anger and pounding inside his chest. Suddenly Nate felt his lower jaw jerk to the left and he heard a simultaneous "crack/screech." It broke the trance. He stuck his right forefinger into his mouth and he felt a gaping crack in a tooth on the side of his mouth.

Then, miraculously, he was filled with the joy he knew could come only from being a vessel of God's will.

⤥

CHAPTER 17

THE GRAY VAN WAS PARKED AT A LITTLE GREASY SPOON along one of the many back roads of Upstate New York. The local troopers had been advised that the occupants were probably armed and extremely dangerous. The troopers were lucky, however, and found all four patriots laughing and joking as they exited the little diner. They were apprehended without incident, and the vehicle was quickly impounded and inventoried.

For reasons of national security, the New York State Police had not been fully advised as to the nature of the crimes committed by their detainees. The investigation would be run, at least initially, by the FBI's Joint Terrorism Task Force (JTTF) in Washington D.C.

The FBI had the van and its contents transferred to its crime lab. After x-raying everything for booby traps, a bright lab technician began to examine the electronic components that made up the van's surveillance system. A tall woman, 32 years old, with black hair and a Dartmouth, Ph.D., in physics, Maureen Silver had never seen anything like it before. Nevertheless, she knew instantly what it was.

Maureen believed the scanner had been designed and assembled in stages. The initial receiver appeared to be homemade; it was elegantly simple and constructed from inexpensive components, many of which were identified by part numbers. Maureen guessed they might be available at any electronics store. It would be interesting to see whether the part numbers could be traced to a manufacturer, wholesaler, and/or retail outlet. That might give them a starting point for determining who had made this thing.

The rest of the system looked as if it had been assembled by professionals. It was a bit more technically sophisticated and constructed of expensive components, none of which had any telltale sign of origin. Whoever finished this thing, she concluded, had some bucks and was the muscle behind the operation.

Maureen's next step was to examine the software in the laptop computer that apparently formed the brains of the system. She was not an expert programmer but she knew enough to be dangerous. She was not surprised to see that the software had the same look to it as did the scanner. A concise program that had been embellished with more cumbersome code to take advantage of the mechanical enhancements. She had no doubt it could efficiently read an unprotected computer screen from up to 100 yards away.

Maureen's report was sent "upstairs" to Lynn Roberts, the Deputy Director of the FBI. Forty-eight years old, Lynn had a full head of wavy blond hair sitting atop one of the agency's most brilliant minds. A summa cum laude graduate of the University of Chicago Law School, Lynn was known for his quick, acerbic wit, as well as a blistering serve on the tennis court.

Lynn immediately requested teams of agents in each of the 50-plus FBI field offices across the nation to begin running through the long, tedious, process of contacting every electronic parts manufacturer, supplier, wholesaler, and retailer. Eventually, Lynn was sure, one or more of the teams would find some matches with the part numbers used in the scanner.

Bill Fletcher, as the Special Agent In Charge (SAC) for the Detroit office, received the request from Lynn Roberts. Within the hour, Bill had assigned the job to two of his best agents, Tim Bannister and Cindy Cooper. Tim was considered bright even among a group of highly intelligent agents. He was unquestionably one of the finest shooters in the ranks of the FBI. Tim's young partner, Cindy Cooper, was also a top prospect. She had a masters in electrical engineering from Michigan State University and was a recent graduate of the FBI Academy in Quantico, where she had received the latest in surveillance and firearms training. She had also taken, on her own time, advanced tactical courses at Gunsite and Thunder Ranch.

Tim and Cindy worked long into the night, pouring through business and manufacturing registers, trade publications, telephone books, and the internet. By 11 the next morning, they had assembled a long list of companies that dealt, in one way or another, with small electrical components of the type used to assemble the scanner. Next, they began the process of contacting each of the companies to determine if they would voluntarily open up their records. Tim and Cindy knew this phase of the investigation would take several days, if not a week or two. Then, once a list was compiled of the companies that refused or failed to cooperate, FBI lawyers would begin the process of preparing, filing, and serving subpoenas.

◆

A BEAUTIFUL LIGHT SNOW WAS FALLING AND COATING Nate's lodge in pure white. There was a very slight breeze making the dry snowflakes swirl gracefully around the corners of the various buildings. Nate Smith was sitting in his old Ford F-250 parked in his driveway (the purchase of a truck now required a permit issued by a federal Gas Compliance Official—and very few were given out). Nate loved watching it snow here, so deep in the woods, where God's beauty was all around. He rolled down the driver's side window and spat out a long line of brown, tobacco-laced saliva. The stringy gob stretched out as it flew and formed into a serpentine shape before it hit the ground with the hiss of melting snow. A mist of snow blew into the cab before Nate could get the window back up. He shivered and raised the collar of his parka. "We've got to take him out."

"Hartman?"

Nate glared at Leonard Williams. *How dumb could this guy be?* Nate turned the key in the ignition.

Leonard said, "Good idea, but what's your plan?"

Nate wanted, at the moment, to kill Leonard.

Nate had tried to capture power by obtaining the means to obliterate millions of Democrats in key inner cities. That had failed. He had tried to have Hartman killed. And that had failed.

Nate said, "Since your screw-ups, it's not going to be easy." Nate put the truck in gear and headed out the snow-covered dirt road that led away from his lodge. Nate was not one to drive slowly, especially when mad, and the truck fishtailed violently in the snow. He burped and the acid in his stomach seemed to come all the way up his throat. Nate reached into his pocket and fumbled for his Tums. He tore at the wrapper and quickly popped two into his mouth, welcoming the chalky taste.

A big bump, followed by the rear end of the truck fishtailing around a curve and spewing snow and gravel as it went, brought up more acid. Nate moaned as the burning sensation completely overwhelmed the two Tums. He ripped off the wrapper to the rest of the Tums and threw them all into his mouth. He spoke as he chewed the mass of chalk. "We are going to use the increased surveillance... since your warhead FUBAR." Nate gulped down the mass and wiped his mouth with the back of his hand. "What I need you to do is pick out three or four of our people who have some bomb-making ability and who we can afford to lose. And then locate the three or four best we have. I have *other plans* for them."

"What do you mean, 'afford to lose'?"

"*For God's sake,* do I have to write *everything* in crayon? Just get me a couple of people we can live without. We will set up two facilities; one genuine, one patsy. They should think they are safe. That's all you need to know right now."

Nate burped up a stomach full of acid.

❧

Big Sky News
Missoula, Montana

Calls for Confiscation of Firearms
New UnAmerican Act
BY TOM BRIDGER

WASHINGTON, D.C.—Senators Harriet Blead, (D—Nevada), Dianne Flamsteal, (D—California), and Lancy Pilltakesie (D—California) today called for confiscation of all firearms. "The only people who want to own guns are racists, and that alone should make guns illegal," Flamsteal told a packed room of reporters from the advocacy networks. She added, "But with *Heller* now shown to be bad law, we need to move forward and make America safe again. The Wild West days are over."

In a related development, BSN has learned from inside sources that Democrat lawmakers have begun work on what is known as the Omnibus Un-American Act. Calls to numerous congressional offices were met with outright denials or "no comment." Nevertheless, BSN has learned

that the act will enable prosecution of "enemies of the state," who are defined as those voicing opinions that are anti-gay, anti-open borders, pro-life, pro-gun, pro-military or any other position deemed to be contrary to the advancement of "social justice." Other provisions of the act will require everyone prosecuted under the act, as well as all returning military veterans, to undergo "political rehabilitation" by the BSCA to ferret out anti-collectivist, right-wing sentiments. Our source indicates that the act will be announced in the near future and will accompany television ads ridiculing unbridled freedom of speech.

<<<<>>>>

WASHINGTON, D.C.—Also announced today by Nicholas Ruslennin, the White House Czar on Democratic Centralism, is an

Establishment of Official Networks
by Tom Bridger

Executive Order signed by the president that establishes official "advocacy" networks that will be given exclusive access to the president. Networks must submit applications to Ruslennin, who said he will carefully examine submitted video of broadcasts and the texts of published articles.

"As our dear President Obama demonstrated brilliantly, the press must be not only a collective propagandist and a collective agitator, but it must be a collective organizer of the masses. Those who talk about freedom of the press go backwards and halt the inevitable course toward social justice. We must curtail misunderstood, exaggerated, and outdated so-called 'constitutional rights.' It is the proper thing to do." Ruslennin said.

<<<<>>>>

THE NEW YORK-DUBAI TIMES

MONTANA, TEXAS, & ALASKA ASSERT
SOVEREIGNTY OVER GUN RIGHTS

HELENA, Mont. (AP)—In a shockingly bold assertion of sovereignty, the secession-minded states of Montana, Utah, Texas, and Arizona last week declared that their state constitutions, granting the right to individual citizens to keep and bear arms, preempt the Un-American Act which they say is unconstitutional. Further, all four states have asserted plenary power over the intrastate manufacture and sale of firearms, ammunition, and accessories.

The states assert that guns, ammunition, and accessories manufactured in state, and sold only in state to people who sign affidavits that they will keep their purchases in state, are exempt from federal rules because no state lines are crossed and therefore the Commerce Clause of the Constitution, which gives the federal government power to regulate commerce between the states, is not apposite. The states have taken the position that the federal government has grossly overstepped the confines of the Constitution in regulating activity which occurs exclusively within a state's boundaries. The bills are waiting for signatures of the respective state governors.

The law in Montana was written by Republican Rep. Carry Texman, who said, "The founding fathers intended the federal government to have only the powers enumerated in the United States Constitution. Specifically, the Ninth and Tenth Amendments of the Constitution indicate that the states, and only the states, have responsibility for regulating intrastate commerce. The federal government has no power in this area whatsoever. Moreover, since the federal government has no authority to control intrastate commerce, it has no authority to tell us that we cannot make arms. And if we can make them, we can keep them and bear them according to our state constitutions and according to the United States Constitution.

Page 2, New York-Dubai Times
Sovereignty over gun rights, Cont.

The Second Amendment hasn't been repealed, yet!"

The Wallmire administration has warned that the president may order legislators arrested and tried for felony violations of the Un-American Act. Apparently undaunted, these ruggedly independent states have decided to send a clear message to the president. Moreover, the legislatures have provided for their state militias and attorneys general to defend anyone threatened with arrest or prosecution by the federal government.

Rep. Texman said he expected these bills to spark desperately needed economic development in their respective states. Governor Logan James, R-Mont., says he will sign his state's bill, and added, "We're talking about gun manufacturers, gun accessory manufacturers, ammunition, and ammunition reloaders. With the federal government's success in destroying the firearms industry in the last 20 years, we have been approached by dozens of small, independent operators, begging us to enact this law

and to protect them from federal persecution and prosecution."

"I applaud Carry Texman's effort to put the federal government in its place," said Governor Kristi Kalin, R-Arizona. "Americans have been conditioned for decades to accept Washington's intrusion into their lives. We have grown far too submissive and, dog-gone-it, Washington has gotten used to doing whatever it wants."

Janet Milford, a spokeswoman for the federal Bureau of Alcohol, Tobacco, Firearms and Explosives, said that "guns are easily transported across state lines and that gives us authority under the Interstate Commerce Clause to regulate all aspects of their manufacture, sale, and use." President Wallmire, when asked about the situation in his weekly press conference, said his administration is studying all options. Asked whether options include using the DDF or other enforcement agencies to force compliance with federal law, President Wallmire said, "Naturally."

CHAPTER 18

I T WAS A BEAUTIFUL, SUNNY DAY IN ANN ARBOR, WITH THE
temperature in the mid-thirties. Professor Bradley Fletcher,
who loved the cool fresh air, had the windows cracked open to
his office on the seventh floor of the law school's research "stacks,"
as they were called. Actually, this part of the law school resembled,
at least from the inside, a series of dark dungeons filled with narrow
aisles, each with dim-flickering florescent lights that barely illuminated the thousands upon thousands of books, leaflets, and other
variously bound papers seemingly "stacked" on shelf after shelf, rising from the floor to the ceiling.

Professor Fletcher's office was not much more than a large cubi-
cle built into one end of the stacks. In front of his office was an even
smaller room that served as the secretarial station. Behind Bradley's
office was a door that led to a little-used stairwell, largely forgotten,
since everyone used the elevator at the opposite end of the stacks.
Long ago, professors had used the "private" stairwell to move from
floor to floor of the library with little bother from students.

Bradley had just pulled out his Mac and his screen flashed with
the title of his present article:

Jones v. Bouchard: THE UNITED NATIONS OF AMERICA.

Bradley looked at his title and shook his head. In a way, he
couldn't believe what was happening. The Supreme Court had
actually considered the opinion of the United Nations in deciding
what the founding fathers intended when they penned the Second

Amendment. This was beyond anything he had ever seen—though he had seen a lot in the last several years as the nation had been turned upside down since the Obama presidency. Justice Ahmed had written in the majority opinion that the founding fathers intended the United States Constitution to be an evolving document, and since the world had evolved to embrace the principles of the United Nations, so America had to evolve to embrace the idea that some of its outdated rights must give way to the new world order.

The New World Order…

Fifteen years ago the simple mention of the idea got you branded a whack-job militia nut.

Now it was a foundational principle upon which American jurisprudence was based.

It made Bradley's head spin.

And it was only the beginning.

The United Nations had just gone on record claiming "the United States discriminates against the rest of the world since the Bill of Rights applies only to Americans." None of Bradley's prodigious analytical skills could untangle what that meant.

It had taken Congress only a matter of hours to debate and pass, in both houses, the Omnibus Un-American Act, and it had been signed into law the same day by president Wallmire. The following day, yesterday, the United Nations had offered to send in "neutral" troops to perform the task of confiscating all privately owned firearms. It was believed that Wallmire was going to use his 1,250,000 strong Domestic Defense Force, complete with Hellfire-armed attack helicopters.

Bradley was scared. Charlton Heston had famously quipped that the government would only get his gun from "my cold, dead hands." Bradley wondered how many Americans shared that view.

"Bradley, I'm freezing my you-know-what off. Would you please close the window? And your brother is on the line," yelled Bradley's secretary, Beth Simmons.

"Thanks. Sorry about the cold. Close the office door if you want, but I'll close the window anyhow. And don't wait so long to yell at me if you are cold. Okay?" Beth stepped in from her desk and closed the window before Bradley had a chance. She smiled as she headed back to her desk. "Thanks, Beth." Bradley turned his attention to the call. "Hi, Bill. Told you so."

"Yeah, yeah, little brother."

Bradley rolled his eyes to the ceiling. He didn't really hate being called "little brother," but he could never come to like it, especially since it was one of Bill's ways to jab him.

Bill said, "You were right—as usual. Do you really think the president will have the United Nations come in and confiscate guns?"

"Why, when he has his personal Domestic Defense Force that's staffed with United Nations officers?"

"Christ," Bill said, "it will start a riot, and we'll be the ones to have to solve it."

"Not a riot, Bill, a revolution. This is the most scary stuff I've ever seen. And the anti-gun left is on every newscast pleading: 'if it will save just one life!' God, Bill, we're going down the tubes." Bradley wanted to say what he really thought, but Beth hadn't closed the door between their offices. Bradley made a mental note to thank her; he knew she kept the door open because he disliked using the intercom, though she frequently got chilled from his open window.

"But how will all this start a revolution if Kennison, Flamsteal, Pilltakesie, and Blead are being so effective? Doesn't their effectiveness rule out any widespread opposition? I mean, they are getting the public to buy into it. Right?"

Bradley shifted the phone to his other ear. "The majority that watches TV, yes. The advocacy channels have over 40 million viewers at any given time, compared to three million for Fox. Michael Savage has already been jailed for hate speech. And they are currently investigating Rush, Levin, Hannity, and Coulter. With talk radio off the air, there is simply no conservative answer. The public's ability to think critically went out with the remote control. Still, the 76 million who voted against Wallmire are still out there somewhere. They can still think. Most of them are armed. And their backs are up against the wall."

"Oh, God, this is too depressing."

"Maddening, more like it." Bradley was finding it increasingly difficult to restrain his mouth. A blood vessel began throbbing in his temple. It was time to change the subject. "Have you done any skiing yet? I understand Lovell's Corners has opened a new trail this year—Broken Wrist, or some funny name like that. Something to do with a famous lawyer crashing in a bike race—I didn't get the whole story. Anyhow, the trail is supposed to be pretty good."

"Was up there last weekend. Amanda and I did 60 k. And I've lost 10 pounds. She still skis circles around me. I just can't get the hang of skate skiing."

"We'll have to get together. Maybe we can plan a weekend up north; or, if you come into town, I can give you a lesson here in Ann Arbor if there is enough snow."

"That would be great. We've been working on a string of bank robberies that seem to be working their way out towards you. It looks like the bad guys might be from around Ann Arbor, so I'll be there a lot."

"Excellent. It will be good to see you more often. I've got someone I want you to meet."

⬦

What a hunk, ANNE KREIG THOUGHT, AS SHE GAZED INTO Bradley's eyes, her chin propped up by her hand with her elbow on the white cotton tablecloth of the Gandy Dancer restaurant. A candle twinkled in a wine bottle that was covered in the multi-colored wax drippings of what must have been hundreds of candles. The wine bottle itself was snuggled in a wicker basket.

The Leelanau Cellars Fall Medley wine was delicious and it was causing her head to sway, ever so slightly, on her supporting arm. She knew she was tipsy and she felt damn good about it—even if dinner hadn't yet been served!

Anne and Bradley were sitting in the most secluded seat in the former-train-station-turned-restaurant. It was a little nook off to the side of a small dining room. Bradley told her that the maître' d informed him that it had once housed the ticket booth that served customers much like a modern fast food drive-through. Whatever it once was, right now it was the most romantic place in the world.

Anne made a mental note to slow down on the vino until she got something in her stomach. Her nervousness had kept her from eating all day, and the wine was clearly going right to her head. The last thing in the world she wanted was to fail to impress Bradley Fletcher.

Their first date had been a smashing success. He had taken her to the re-opened Bird of Paradise, where Diana Krall was making her triumphant return. Diana was a star now, but the Bird had been her first real gig. Anne was thrilled. Diana sang all the songs Anne had sung way back when. And Diana did it with such style! After the first show Bradley even paid a large tip to the doorman (who was also wearing a bow tie) so that they could get into the second show which was standing-room-only. Afterwards, back home and standing on her porch, "you-know-what me" dress notwithstanding, he had been the perfect gentleman and said goodbye with a quick kiss on the lips.

Presently, he was gazing into her eyes, and it was rekindling all sorts of feelings that she had not experienced in a long while. Everything about this man was appealing to her. His education. His looks—handsome but needing the refinement that a woman could provide. The cute dimple on his right cheek when he smiled. His courteousness!

She couldn't remember the last time a man had walked around to the passenger side of a car not only to let her in but also to let her out. He had given her his arm when they crossed the uneven red bricks that made up the road and sidewalk surrounding the restaurant. He had even shooed away the host and pulled out the dining chair himself.

She was already thinking he was her knight in shining armor when he insisted upon ordering one of the items upon which she couldn't decide: broiled scrod. His express intention was to give it up if she did not like her blackened tuna.

Yet, there was something about him that left a lingering doubt. She couldn't put her finger on it, and the wine wasn't helping. But there *was* something. Perhaps it was his cute appearance. She would have preferred a little roughness. Perhaps it was his rather clear devotion to his career and the law.

There also seemed a stiffness—was that the right word?—to his personality. She had the sense that he needed to relax, to begin noticing that his tie was crooked, that his belt was worn, that his shoes were scuffed. His mind was just so preoccupied with intellectual thoughts. It made her wonder. He spoke slowly and in near-perfect sentences. He was the kind to come to a complete stop at a stop sign—even with visibility in all directions and not a person or car in sight.

"You have the prettiest smile, Anne." He was still gazing into her eyes.

But, oh, she could get used to this…

Dinner was over before she knew it, and he was leading her out over the rough bricks to the passenger side of his car. She got in and knew immediately that she wanted him. She was being led into temptation… and for the moment, didn't care!

"Anne, so what do you think?" She almost laughed out loud, and barely concealed her amusement at the timeliness of his question. *Boy, wouldn't he like to know!*

"What's so funny?" Bradley asked. With a grin, he put the Volvo in gear and pulled out onto the road.

"Oh, nothing, really, I was just thinking about how much of this town I've been missing, and how nice it has been to meet you." *The rascal knows what I'm thinking!* That smile of his seemed to telegraph that he knew *exactly*.

Bradley took his eyes from the road and cast a long glance at her. It melted her heart. He said, "You know, I've been thinking the same thing." He quickly scanned the road ahead and looked back to Anne. "I'm so worried about my classes and publishing that I rarely get outside the four walls of the Law Quad, except to walk home." Bradley returned his gaze to the road and seemed to be thinking. When he pulled into Anne's driveway, he jumped out and opened the door for her. They walked toward her front porch and he held out his hand for her when they reached the steps. They walked up the steps, hand in hand.

Anne couldn't decide what to do. She wanted to ravish him. But she was terrified of being too fast. He was, after all, a law professor. She couldn't imagine him doing anything that wasn't thought out in a very intellectual manner. She had a funny thought that maybe she should file a motion to get him into bed, and it made her smile. But then the smile faded; there was a small voice telling her "no." But it was a small voice.

Bradley tilted his head as a puppy will do when trying to decipher something its master has said. He was also smiling. Anne knew it was the moment of truth. Her heart was racing a hundred miles an hour. Still, she couldn't decide!

Bradley made the decision for her. He leaned down and kissed her. Anne waited to feel his arms wrap around her and pull her close; she knew she would immediately respond by reaching behind her and opening the door and pulling him in.

But Bradley's arms didn't wrap around her. Instead, she felt his hands move to her arms, just below her shoulders. He tightened his grip as he gently, but briefly, kissed her. Then he held her at arm's length and looked into her eyes.

"I had a great time. I'll give you a call very soon." Bradley turned and took the porch steps two at a time, and he appeared to almost run to his car. He looked back to her and waved just before he ducked into the car. Anne stood on the porch, watching the tail lights disappear around the bend in the drive.

Her legs began to shake.

❧

Chicago, Illinois

ITWAS AN AGENT IN CHICAGO THAT FIRST WALKED INTO A Radio Shack and discovered matching part numbers for the scanner. On further inquiry of the store clerk, the near-breathless agent learned that the same parts were sold throughout Radio Shack's national chain of electronics stores. The agent was already heading out the door to report his findings when the clerk stopped him.

"You know, we take the name and address of everyone who purchases something. It's all right here in the computer." The clerk patted the top of the point of sale computer.

✦

CHAPTER 19

THE PRESIDENT SMILED INTO THE CAMERAS. "LET THE world know that this administration, and this president, today have formed a crucible for justice. Today the free world of democracy strikes back against the terrors of anarchy and lawlessness. Today, as President of these United States, I have signed into law the Un-American Act, a most potent weapon—a weapon with which law enforcement officers can batter the walls of divisiveness and despotism…"

"Look at that communist jerk," Anne Kreig said as she reached for the remote sitting on the coffee table. She hit the "off" button and glanced out the picture window. It was beginning to snow. Linda had come over to watch a movie, but Anne had had the television on when the president's face appeared with a special announcement.

Linda said, "He and Obama have really changed our world, that's for sure. And did you see, he didn't say who would be knocking at our doors."

Anne changed her mind and thought that maybe she should hear what her president was saying. She hit the select button and the president's face reappeared.

"What are you—"

"Shhh. I think we should listen to what he has to say."

"Come on, let's watch the movie and start a fire. And anyway, since when have you been interested in politics—"

"Since I've met a law professor and decided to go to law school. Shhh. Listen!"

"… unlawful for terrorists to plot the destruction of our democratic ideals, unlawful for subversives to arm themselves and form private enclaves within which they believe the laws of this nation can be suspended. From this day forward, only those who can demonstrate compelling need shall be granted a permit to purchase or to own a firearm. After July 4, the Domestic Defense Force will be going door to door to collect all weapons of war and death from the public. I urge your support for this most noble cause." The president paused for the applause to subside.

"And to encourage those who currently own banned weapons of any kind to turn them in to the DDF, a part of this directive creates a federal commission to establish the amount of compensation that will be given for each weapon collected."

"Holy crap," whispered Anne as she watched the president pause again for applause which, she noted, was deafening.

"To ensure fairness, the commission's price will not be less than the purchase price that a citizen can prove was paid. Where there is no longer any evidence of the purchase price, the commission will establish a fair market price." Again there was a pause, and this time the television camera panned over the huge crowd gathered on the White House lawn.

The camera focused on Sandy Jones, whom the president had introduced earlier, whose husband and son had been killed by an intruder to their home. The intruder had commandeered the family's handgun.

The camera did a closeup and focused on the tears streaming down her plump, rounded cheeks.

❧

HARTMAN HIT THE POWER BUTTON AND WATCHED HIS screen go blank. He was sitting in front of his television with a growler of Wolverine Pale Ale he had brought home from his last trip to Ann Arbor. He was in his favorite brown leather chair, with deep cushions and wide, heavily padded arms. Outside, an early fall snow was driving horizontally across his front window. He had a small fire going in the corner fireplace.

Drinking his favorite beer, sitting in his favorite chair, watching the near blizzard conditions outside his window, Hartman knew he should feel pretty good. As it was, his stomach felt like he had swallowed a burning piece of coal. He had watched the president's little show and was calculating its effects.

Hartman knew the president's announcement had been watched, in angry disbelief, all across the nation. It was a clever bit of law-making. The Second Amendment was not violated, the president had insisted. Indeed, just as Al Gore had proclaimed that the debate was over regarding global warming (despite the fact that the earth had actually begun to cool since he made that ridiculous proclamation), so the debate about the meaning of the Second Amendment was declared over, settled, and of no further interest. The amendment did not apply to the people; it applied only to the states' rights to maintain an armed militia. Period.

Further, the president stated, his law did not outlaw all firearms. Those demonstrating a "compelling need" could still own a gun that met the conditions of the United Nations Department of Disarmament Affairs. What a joke that was! A gun that couldn't shoot 75 yards was a gun that would do nothing to stop a bad guy. There were no such guns on the market because there was no more purpose in having a gun that didn't kill than there was in having a knife that wouldn't cut.

No question about it; this was the last straw. Opposition—even violent opposition—would not be limited to "Tea Party racists." It would reach deep into a society that had, according to some estimates, over one hundred million gun owners, many of whom considered owning a firearm the essence of Americanism. The right to keep and bear arms was not simply infringed by this law; it was extinguished.

The ban on virtually all guns would snatch from living-room gun cases millions of prized hunting rifles, exquisite custom-made side-by-side and over-and-under sporting shotguns, as well as several million relics such as the German Mausers, British Lee-Enfields, and American M1 Garands brought back from two world wars. The Ruger Mini 14 was no longer legal—the gun that had been brandished to such effect on the porches and rooftops during the LA riots. Guns which had once stood between frightened citizens and lawless predators: the Brownings, the Remington Speedmasters, the Ruger 10/22, the Colt Match Target, and various models made by Marlin and Springfield, just to name a few, were now illegal. This would obviously destroy the entire firearms industry.

Another interesting characteristic of the president's little game was the ploy of calling the patriots "subversive" and "terrorist." The same had occurred through out U.S. history. In the early days of the U.S. labor movement, strikers were called subversive and communist and attacked, at times, by the U.S. military. The anti-Vietnam and Civil Rights movements were the next to be called subversive to justify FBI counterintelligence programs that were rampant from 1956 through the early 1970s. These programs were designed to expose, disrupt, misdirect, discredit, or otherwise neutralize dissident individuals and political organizations.

Oddly enough, the difference now was that federal power wasn't being used to secure the type of country the founding fathers had envisioned. It was no longer "One Nation Under God." It was a nation that kowtowed to every sensitivity, to every minority that made it, legally or illegally, to its shores. Street signs were being posted in neighborhoods in Arabic, Spanish, Chinese, or Korean, and sometimes all of the above. Schools were being forced by the federal government to teach gay lifestyles and the history, culture, and traditions of Islam, including the wondrous benefits of Sharia law (with no objection, of course, from the ACLU). And not only was Sharia law being enforced by courts all over the country, other ethnic groups were following suit and demanding quasi-autonomous regions where they could live and govern themselves as they saw fit. Arabs, African Americans, and hispanics had even begun demanding a designated portion of state and federal budgets. Only

American Indians held themselves apart from the insanity. As the true "Americans," they somehow intrinsically understood that their America had been sucker-punched by liberals and Islam and was reeling. And it pissed them off.

These minorities, really nations within a nation, clearly did not want respect alone. Like the Arab minority in Israel and the Quebeçois in Canada back in 1995, they wanted substantive attributes of statehood. And the closer they were getting to achieving their goal, the more Americans were feeling a loss of their own national character.

Hartman knew that on-line services were about to be deluged with inquiries about the web sites of patriot organizations. Encrypted transmissions as well as old fashioned, face-to-face conversations over coffee and across backyard hedges—were about to increase by an order of magnitude, or two.

Hartman got up from his comfy chair and walked to the computer. His heart was heavy, and his stomach still felt like it was on fire. He started typing the commands that would take the country back—by force of patriots.

❧

THE NEW YORK-DUBAI TIMES

CRIME & POLICE
GOVERNMENT CRACKS PATRIOT TERROR CELLS; METES OUT NECESSARY JUSTICE

WASHINGTON D.C. (AP)—Diya al Din Wasem, Director of the White House Military Office and commander of the Domestic Defense Force (DDF), and Qadir Abdullah, Director of the FBI, jointly announced a coordinated effort between the agencies which today resulted in the arrests of 82 alleged members of Unintended Consequences, a group that seeks to overthrow the government with targeted assassinations. The arrests are part of an ongoing investigation and follow grand jury indictments in Nevada, Montana, Georgia, Missouri, Ohio, and Kansas. Members of Unintended Consequences believe all federal laws passed by the Obama and Wallmire administrations are invalid.

The arrests were made during predawn raids conducted by hundreds of FBI agents, supported by dozens of DDF and FBI Anti-terror SWAT teams, backed up by over 60 Hellfire-armed Apache Helicopters. Director of the FBI, Qadir Abdullah, confirmed that eight terrorists could not be arrested as they died in their homes destroyed by Hellfire missiles. "Six co-conspirator wives and nine hate-filled children were also killed," Abdullah said.

"These were all terrorists who plotted to overthrow the government, spewed hate speech at public meetings, and expressed their intention to keep their weapons past the July 4 deadline for turning in all firearms as required by the Omnibus Un-American Act," Abdullah said.

A minor disturbance occurred when Thomas Bridger, a reporter for the unapproved newspaper, *Big Sky News*, asked why "white Christians" were being so aggressively pursued. Mr. Abdullah attempted to reply and the reporter cut him off and demanded: "What crime have

THE NEW YORK-DUBAI TIMES

PAGE 2, THE NEW YORK-DUBI TIMES; GOVERNMENT CRACKS TERROR CELLS, CONTINUED.

these children committed?" Understandably angered by such impertinence, Abdullah replied, "We can't afford to wait until they do something serious. The RCSA and the Un-American Act give us enough to go in and stop these terrorists before they can do serious harm. That was the whole point to those laws."

Mr. Bridger was subdued and quickly escorted from the area. Sources from law enforcement agencies, who asked to remain anonymous because they were not authorized to discuss the case, indicated that Mr. Bridger has been arrested and will be charged with felony hate speech, as an Arab in attendance complained that Bridger's questions were offensive.

In a related development, a man who would only describe himself as "George Washington" contacted the *Times* and declared that the men will be ready the next time. "They better come in shooting, cause we ain't giving up our guns, no way, no how," the otherwise unidentified caller said.

When contacted about the statements of the man calling himself "George Washington," Abdullah said he hoped it was a crank caller. "If he represents the remaining members of Unintended Consequences, we will have a full scale battle in front of us. You can tell your readers not to worry, however, because we will strike when they least expect it, and we will strike with overwhelming force."

THE NEW YORK-DUBAI TIMES

CRIME & POLICE
TENS OF THOUSANDS ARRESTED FOR VIOLATIONS OF THE RCSA

WASHINGTON D.C. (AP)— Agents from the FBI and the Bureau of Socially Correct Activities (BSCA) arrested 86,274 people last week in a nationwide crack down on violations of the RCSA. Director of the BSCA, Elmer Kennison, indicated that all but 12 of the arrests were of white terrorists for actions "contrary to the well-being of the United States." "Of course," Kennison said, "there were also a number of violations for comments that demonstrated anti-gay, pro-life, and pro-gun ideas." Asked if all such comments were publicly made, Kennison replied, "Of course not. Sometimes the most dangerous conversations are made in private. And we have very sophisticated ways to learn about these things."

CHAPTER 20

COLONEL JOHN RIGGINS, UNITED STATES ARMY, commanded the Army's Opposing Force Regiment (OPFOR) at the Army's National Training Center (NTC) at Fort Irwin in the desert of Nevada. His OPFOR played the role of the "enemy" in training exercises and war games. Riggins stood an even six feet and was 190 pounds of unquestionable piss and vinegar, with the reddish-brown hair and handsome features of his father, and the generous smile and blue eyes of his mother.

Riggins was crouched on a parched hilltop with the stocky, gray-haired brigadier general, Carlan Bragg. With high-powered binoculars, they were peering through sun-bathed clouds of dust being thrown up by the movements of a force-on-force exercise. Bragg's visiting battalion from the 3rd Armored Cavalry Regiment (ACR) out of Fort Bliss, Texas, called the "Blue Force," was attacking a dug-in OPFOR. The general was none too pleased.

"Who are these guys, Colonel? Your OPFOR is one-fifth the size of my attacking Blue. This should have been sufficient superiority against a dug-in defensive force. But against your troops, I don't think ten-to-one would be enough."

"Must be the best performance of their lives, General, Sir." Riggins tried to sound surprised.

"Goddamn hope so, John, your guys are cleaning my clock. Jesus they are good. Where the hell did you get such good troops?" The general kept his eyes on the battle.

The stalwart and supremely confident Riggins was momentarily startled. He felt an uncharacteristic shiver run down his spine. Thankfully, no one had ever asked that question. Riggins settled himself and contemplated the question for a moment. The general didn't really want to know. He was too engrossed in watching his troops get thumped. Riggins decided that giving a fairly vague answer posed less risk than avoiding the question. His gut instincts were invariably right. "Mostly Michigan, Sir."

"What?"

Riggins jaw tensed. He tried to quickly evaluate if it was too late to change the story. Had the general missed what he said, or was he expressing surprise? If it was the former, there was still time to change the story. But if it was the latter, undue suspicion would be aroused. He decided to stick with his original gut feeling. "Michigan. Out of some coincidence most are Scandinavian and Finnish. Very tough and very clever. Independent thinkers."

"Humph," Bragg snorted. He glanced at Riggins and went back to watching the battle through the binoculars.

Riggins breathed a sigh of relief. He had just dodged a bullet. If this general had the suspicious mind of the former Soviet KGB, the gig would be up. Indeed, a little careful research into the personnel records would reveal a number of irregularities that, together, had conspired to put all these "Yoopers" under his command. But that had been the easy part. The more difficult part was finding the right people to get into the army in the first place. Riggins let his mind wander back in time…

Since Oklahoma City, it had been thought by those in government that the military served as fertile recruiting ground for various patriot groups. Indeed, since the Obama administration, ex-military had been routinely watched by the various federal law enforcement agencies, and over 2,000 had been arrested in the past several years on suspicion of planning terrorist attacks. Much to the chagrin of the government, however, none of those arrested had been convicted, since local juries refused to put heroes away for nothing more than disagreeing with the Obama and Wallmire administrations.

Riggins had simply turned the idea around; *he brought militant minds into the military.* And since the Obama presidency, there had been no shortage of militant minds.

John Riggins, or "Johnny" as he was called as a boy, had grown up in Houghton–Hancock, two small towns in Michigan's Upper Peninsula that are separated by Lake Linden and its waterway which, in combination, span the length of the Keweenaw Peninsula. His family had settled in the U.P. when his grandfather sought work in one of the state's bustling copper mines. Even before the California Gold Rush, the U.P. was a land of immense opportunity, blessed, as it was, with the most pure copper in the world, vast forests, and rich resources of iron ore.

Yet, the U.P. was a land for the strong and hardy; over 200 inches of snow fell during winters—easily as harsh as those of Anchorage, Alaska.

Interestingly, all the harshness attracted thousands of Scandinavians, who flocked to a land that was reminiscent of their home. Self-made, self-reliant, and furiously independent, these people came to make their fortunes in, or related to, the mining industry. And without a doubt—many fortunes were made. In fact, so wealthy were mining communities that the small town of Calumet became the home of what is, even today, one of the finest and most elaborate opera halls in the world.

As copper mining was the lifeblood of the Upper Peninsula, so was it also important to the young nation. That importance was underscored by the formation of the line forming the break between the eastern and central time zones. Boston capitalists, who invested heavily in Michigan's copper mines, wanted the mines in the same time zone as the Boston Stock Exchange. As a result, to capture the scattered mines, the time zone follows a fairly straight path to the north through the United States until it enters the southern-most portion of the Upper Peninsula. There, at a point just south of Escanaba, Michigan, the time zone repeatedly zigzags north, then west, then north, then west. At one point it even moves south!

The copper in Michigan lies deep beneath the surface, in veins that run through solid rock. Often found in large chunks weighing as much as several hundred tons, the task of extracting it was, and is, extremely difficult. Sometimes the miners could get enough explosive powder around the boulder of copper to dislodge it from the rock, whereupon it would be hauled to the surface. Sometimes no amount of explosives could loosen the raw material, and sometimes what was freed was simply too large and heavy to hoist to the surface. Consequently, miners would be forced to literally chisel it into thousands and thousands of pieces about the size of a quarter. The "chips" would then be hauled out.

Soon, however, copper began to be mined in other parts of the world and in the western United States In these locales, the copper frequently could be strip-mined, and this proved far less expensive. Soon, the purer Michigan copper lost out and, one by one, the copper mines closed. Today, not one mine is operational and ghost towns dot the western side of the Upper Peninsula. With the loss of its copper mines, the Upper Peninsula died.

And with its death, came the birth of a people who felt abandoned by Michigan's lower peninsula and, to a large degree, the rest of the nation. It was the birth of a people to whom big, intrusive government was anathema. Many years ago Yoopers began to call for secession from Michigan and the establishment of their peninsula as the state of Superior; now the call was to secede from the *union*.

With this social and political backdrop, Colonel Riggins took every chance he could get to go home and meet with disgruntled youths who might be willing to subvert authority for a greater cause. He would encourage those to enlist in the Army and he saw to it that they were ultimately sent to him at the NTC in Nevada. Thus, virtually everyone in OPFOR had been drawn from the Upper Peninsula.

It took a number of years to accomplish, but ultimately Riggins had about two hundred supremely loyal troops, and another three hundred who could be counted on to defend, but perhaps not attack.

And Riggins hoped that an attack would not be necessary. Indeed, he hoped beyond hope that bloodshed could be avoided entirely. Riggins had too much military blood in him. The stars and stripes were a deep part of his heritage.

As a child, Johnny used to listen to his father, Lieutenant Colonel William "Red" Riggins, talk for hours about the battles he had fought in Patton's Third Army as it marched toward Paris. Red was a man who clearly loved his country, and he had a Purple Heart and the Congressional Medal of Honor to prove it. That story was Johnny's favorite and involved the Third Army nearing Paris. Against withering machine-gunfire, Red had made his way on his belly, inch by inch, to the front of a pillbox that was decimating his troops. Twice, his right leg was hit by enemy fire as he crawled. Losing blood and consciousness, he finally reached the pillbox and sat up underneath the wide but very short opening through which the machine gun was firing. Red pulled the pin on the grenade and raised his hand to toss it into the slit. As his hand reached up, however, it ran into a stream of machine-gunfire that nearly ripped his hand from his wrist. The live grenade dropped back in his lap, and only the grace of God, as Red described it, allowed him to grab the grenade with his left hand and quickly toss it into the pillbox.

Like father like son, and Red's love of the military and of country rubbed off on Johnny, who determined at an early age to enter West Point and someday become a national hero, leading his country into victorious battle. As Johnny aged, however, he began to notice disturbing signs of a country falling apart—or "going to Hell," as he came to call it. In West Point during the 1970s, John watched in horror as anti-American signs and slogans went up all over. "Down with USA" was a popular slogan that stuck in his mind, and he began to hate the liberal pukes, socialists, and communists who were behind it.

As John grew, however, so did his disillusionment with the political and legal forces that were wrecking the country—even when the liberal pukes, socialists, and communists could not. The country was going to hell, but it wasn't the commies who were causing it—at least until Obama had come to power. The damn politicians in Washington were so concerned with their personal well-being that not one of them could make his or her self-interest secondary to doing something good for the country. Consequently, virtually every government agency had lost touch with its original purposes, was horribly run, and was developing a mind and purpose all its own. These agencies simultaneously ravaged the country with their regulations and savaged the country with their payroll—now well over three *trillion* dollars a year.

The list of federal agencies was growing almost monthly. The sheer number of agencies was difficult to fathom unless you looked at the actual list, which had grown into the hundreds:

(Author's note: just page through this list of over 400 to see what I'm talking about. Only a couple are fictional.)

A

9-11 and 8-24 Commissions (National Commissions on Man-Caused Disasters Upon the United States)

Administration on Aging (AOA)

Administration for Children and Families (ACF)

Administrative Committee of the Federal Register

Advisory Council on Historic Preservation

African Development Foundation

Agency for Advancement for Affirmative Action (AAAA)

Agency for Healthcare Research and Quality (AHRQ)

Agency for International Development

Agency for Toxic Substances and Disease Registry

Agricultural Marketing Service

Agricultural Research Service

Agriculture Department (USDA)

Alcohol and Tobacco Tax and Trade Bureau (Treasury)

Alcohol, Tobacco, Firearms and Explosives Bureau (BATF)

American Battle Monuments Commission

American Samoa

AMTRAK (National Railroad Passenger Corporation)

Animal and Plant Health Inspection Service
Appalachian Regional Commission
Architect of the Capitol
Architectural and Transportation Barriers Compliance Board (Access
  Board)
Arctic Research Commission
Armed Forces Retirement Home
Arms Control and International Security
Arthritis and Musculoskeletal Interagency Coordinating Committee
B
Barry M. Goldwater Scholarship and Excellence in Education
  Foundation
Bilingual Education and Minority Languages Affairs Office
Botanic Garden
Broadcasting Board of Governors (Voice of America, Radio/TV Marti
  and more)
Bureau of Alcohol and Tobacco Tax and Trade (Treasury)
Bureau of Alcohol, Tobacco, Firearms, and Explosives (Justice)
Bureau of the Census
Bureau of Economic Analysis (BEA)
Bureau of Engraving and Printing
Bureau of Indian Affairs (BIA)
Bureau of Industry and Security (formerly the Bureau of Export
  Administration)
Bureau of International Labor Affairs
Bureau of Justice Statistics
Bureau of Labor Statistics
Bureau of Land Management (BLM)
Bureau of Prisons
Bureau of Public Debt
Bureau of Reclamation
Bureau of Socially Correct Activities (BSCA)
Bureau of Transportation Statistics
C
Census Bureau
Center for Nutrition Policy and Promotion
Centers for Disease Control and Prevention (CDC)
Centers for Medicare & Medicaid Services (formerly the Health Care
  Financing Administration)
Central Intelligence Agency (CIA)
Chemical Safety and Hazard Investigations Board

Chief Financial Officers Council
Chief Information Officers Council
Citizens' Stamp Advisory Committee
Citizenship and Immigration Services Bureau (formerly Immigration and Naturalization Service)
Civilian Radioactive Waste Management
Coalition Provisional Authority (in Iraq)
Coalition Provisional Authority Inspector General
Commerce Department
Commission of Fine Arts
Commission on Civil Rights
Commission on the Intelligence Capabilities of the United States Regarding Weapons of Mass Destruction
Commission on International Religious Freedom
Committee for the Implementation of Textile Agreements
Committee for Purchase from People Who Are Blind or Severely Disabled
Commodity Futures Trading Commission
Community Development Office (Agriculture Department)
Community Oriented Policing Services (COPS)
Community Planning and Development
Comptroller of the Currency Office
Congressional Budget Office (CBO)
Constitution Center
Consumer Product Safety Commission (CPSC)
Cooperative State Research, Education and Extension Service
Coordinating Council on Juvenile Justice and Delinquency Prevention
Corporation for National and Community Service
Council of Economic Advisers
Council on Environmental Quality
Court of International Trade
Customs and Border Protection
D
Defense Advanced Research Projects Agency (DARPA)
Defense Commissary Agency
Defense Contract Audit Agency
Defense Contract Management Agency
Defense Field Activities
Defense Finance and Accounting Service (DFAS)
Defense Information Systems Agency (DISA)

Defense Intelligence Agency
Defense Legal Services Agency
Defense Logistics Agency (DLA)
Defense Nuclear Facilities Safety Board
Defense Security Cooperation Agency
Defense Security Service
Defense Threat Reduction Agency
Delaware River Basin Commission
Denali Commission
Department of Agriculture (USDA)
Department of Commerce (DOC)
Department of Defense (DOD)
Department of Defense Cyber Crime Center (DC3)
Department of Defense Inspector General
Department of Education (ED)
Department of Energy (DOE)
Department of Health and Human Services (HHS)
Department of Homeland Security (DHS)
Department of Housing and Urban Development (HUD)
Department of the Interior (DOI)
Department of Justice (DOJ)
Department of Labor (DOL)
Department of State (DOS)
Department of Transportation (DOT)
Department of the Treasury
Department of Veterans Affairs (VA)
Disability Employment Policy Office
Domestic Policy Council
Drug Enforcement Administration (DEA)
E
Economic Analysis, Bureau of
Economic, Business and Agricultural Affairs (State Department)
Economic and Statistics Administration
Economic Development Administration
Economic Research Service
Education Department (ED)
Election Assistance Commission
Elementary and Secondary Education
Employee Benefits Security Administration (formerly the Pension
    and Welfare Benefits Administration)
Employment and Training Administration (Labor Department)

Employment Standards Administration
Endangered Species Committee
Energy Department (DOE)
Energy Efficiency and Renewable Energy
Energy Information Administration
Enforcement (Treasury Department)
Engraving and Printing, Bureau of
Environment, Safety and Health
Environmental Management (Energy Department)
Environmental Protection Agency (EPA)
Equal Employment Opportunity Commission (EEOC)
Executive Office for Immigration Review
Export Administration (now the Bureau of Industry and Security)
Export-Import Bank of the United States
F
Fair Housing and Equal Opportunity
Faith-Based and Community Initiatives Office
Farm Credit Administration
Farm Service Agency
Federal Accounting Standards Advisory Board
Federal Aviation Administration (FAA)
Federal Bureau of Investigation (FBI)
Federal Bureau of Prisons
Federal Communications Commission (FCC)
Federal Citizen Information Center (FCIC)
Federal Consulting Group
Federal Deposit Insurance Corporation (FDIC)
Federal Election Commission
Federal Emergency Management Agency (FEMA)
Federal Energy Regulatory Commission
Federal Executive Boards
Federal Financial Institutions Examination Council
Federal Financing Bank
Federal Highway Administration
Federal Housing Enterprise Oversight
Federal Housing Finance Board
Federal Interagency Committee for the Management of Noxious and
    Exotic Weeds
Federal Interagency Council on Statistical Policy
Federal Judicial Center
Federal Labor Relations Authority

Labor Statistics, Bureau of
Land Management, Bureau of
Lead Hazard Control (Housing and Urban Development
      Department)
Legal Services Corporation
Library of Congress
M
Marine Mammal Commission
Maritime Administration
Marketing and Regulatory Programs (Agriculture Department)
Marshall Islands
Marshals Service
Medicare Payment Advisory Commission (formerly the Physician
      Payment Review Commission and the Prospective Payment
      Assessment Commission)
Merit Systems Protection Board
Migratory Bird Conservation Commission
Mine Safety and Health Administration
Mineral Management Service
Minority Business Development Agency
Mint
Missile Defense Agency
Mississippi River Commission
Morris K. Udall Foundation: Scholarship and Excellence in National
      Environmental Policy
Multifamily Housing Office
N
National Aeronautics and Space Administration (NASA)
National Agricultural Statistics Service
National AIDS Policy Office
National Archives and Records Administration (NARA)
National Bipartisan Commission on the Future of Medicare
National Capital Planning Commission
National Cemetery Administration (Veterans Affairs Department)
National Commission on Libraries and Information Science
National Communications System (Homeland Security)
National Constitution Center
National Council on Disability
National Credit Union Administration
National Defense University
National Drug Intelligence Center

National Economic Council
National Endowment for the Arts
National Endowment for the Humanities
National Gallery of Art
National Highway Traffic Safety Administration
National Imagery and Mapping Agency
National Indian Gaming Commission
National Institute of Justice
National Institute of Standards and Technology (NIST)
National Institutes of Health (NIH)
National Interagency Fire Center
National Labor Relations Board
National Laboratories (Energy Department)
National Marine Fisheries
National Mediation Board
National Nuclear Security Administration
National Ocean Service
National Oceanic and Atmospheric Administration (NOAA)
National Park Foundation
National Park Service
National Railroad Passenger Corporation (AMTRAK)
National Reconnaissance Organization
National Science Foundation
National Security Agency/Central Security Service
National Security Council
National Technical Information Service
National Telecommunications and Information Administration
National Transportation Safety Board
National Weather Service
Natural Resources Conservation Service
Navajo and Hopi Relocation Commission
Northern Mariana Islands
Northwest Power Planning Council
Nuclear Energy, Science and Technology
Nuclear Regulatory Commission
Nuclear Waste Technical Review Board
O
Occupational Safety & Health Administration (OSHA)
Occupational Safety and Health Review Commission
Office of Compliance
Office of Federal Housing Enterprise Oversight

Office of Gas Compliance (OGC)
Office of Government Ethics
Office of Information and Regulatory Affairs (OIRA)
Office of Management and Budget (OMB)
Office of National Drug Control Policy (ONDCP)
Office of Personnel Management
Office of Science and Technology Policy
Office of Scientific and Technical Information
Office of Special Counsel
Office of Thrift Supervision
Overseas Private Investment Corporation
P
Pardon Attorney Office
Parole Commission (Justice Department)
Patent and Trademark Office
Peace Corps
Pension and Welfare Benefits Administration (now the Employee
    Benefits Security Administration)
Pension Benefit Guaranty Corporation
Policy Development and Research (Housing and Urban Development
    Department)
Political Affairs (State Department)
Postal Rate Commission
Postal Service (USPS)
Postsecondary Education
Power Administrations
President's Commission on Moon, Mars and Beyond
Presidents Commission on the U.S. Postal Service
President's Council on Integrity and Efficiency
President's Foreign Intelligence Advisory Board
Presidio Trust
Public Debt, Bureau of
Public Diplomacy and Public Affairs (State Department)
Public Health Preparedness Office
Public and Indian Housing
R
Radio and TV Marti (Espaol)
Radio Free Asia (RFA)
Radio Free Europe/Radio Liberty (RFE/RL)
Railroad Retirement Board
Reclamation, Bureau of

U
U.S. Border Patrol (now Customs and Border Protection)
U.S. Centennial of Flight Commission
U.S. Citizenship and Immigration Services
U.S. Customs and Border Protection
U.S. Immigration and Customs Enforcement
U.S. International Trade Commission
U.S. Mission to the United Nations
U.S. National Central Bureau - Interpol (Justice Department)
U.S. Postal Service
U.S. Sentencing Commission
Uniformed Services University of the Health Sciences
V
Veterans Affairs Department (VA)
Veterans Benefits Administration
Veterans Day National Committee
Veterans' Employment and Training Service
Veterans Health Administration
Vietnam Educational Foundation
Vocational and Adult Education
Voice of America (VOA)
W
White House Commission on Presidential Scholars
White House Commission on the National Moment of Remembrance
White House Office of Administration
Women's Bureau (Labor Department)
Woodrow Wilson International Center for Scholars
Worldnet Television

The list of agencies, commissions, committees, bureaus, offices, and centers clearly demonstrated a government gone mad. A government that had lost sight of the fact that it serves the people—not the other way around. Ruby Ridge, Waco, and Nye County had been three of the most glaring examples. But there were others, many of which never made the national news but were well publicized in an effective, if disjointed, network of underground news leaflets, faxes, shortwave radio, email, and secret computer discussion groups.

"Colonel!" Bragg shouted for the third time.

"Uh, sorry, General, I must have been daydreaming."

Bragg frowned and Riggins instantly saw that such a comment was an insult to the General's forces.

"I didn't mean anything, General. It's just—"

"Never mind, John. I imagine this does get boring. Next time, I promise you, my troops will be ready. It will be my personal goal to see that you don't daydream in the middle of getting your butt kicked!"

They both smiled.

"I accept the challenge, General."

"Now, if you will excuse me, I am going to rip off a few heads. I'll see you in an hour when we do post-game analysis." Bragg headed off the hilltop, jogging toward his battle commander's tank.

Riggins watched him go, but his mind soon drifted again. He began wondering how the engineers were doing with designing the appropriate modifications to the Russian missile system so that it would operate on the USAF's A-10 "Warthog." The blueprints for the plane had been surprisingly easy to get, since membership in the patriots included people from every socioeconomic group and every industry in the nation, including the aeronautics industry and the maker of the A-10.

When finished, the missiles and related components would be shipped in pieces, spread out over several weeks. Actual attachment to the A-10s would not, of course, be accomplished until the aircraft and pilots went AWOL. This meant that there would be no possibility of testing the systems and little time to overcome unforeseen problems.

And that bugged Riggins. If warfare had taught him anything, it was that one needed to allocate time and resources for FUBARS. He would have no extra time. Everything had to literally drop into place: missiles, aft-weapons radar, weapons controls, wiring, transmitters, receivers. It was, to be sure, the trickiest part of the deal.

❖

SENATOR DIANNE FLAMSTEAL CAST AN ACCUSING GLANCE around the Oval Office, hoping it would add to the theatrics of her presentation. She needed to deflect the blame. Present were President Wallmire; General Leighton, Chairman, Joint Chiefs of Staff; Secretary of Defense, William Turner; Todd Barnstorm, the president's National Security Advisor; and two secret service agents, who stood opposite each other with their backs to the wall.

Flamsteal, as Chairman of the Senate's Committee on National Security Affairs, had been part of a huge miscalculation, and it was imperative that blame get directed elsewhere. She said, "Mr. President, it was a widely held misconception, going all the way back to Desert Storm, that Soviet weaponry was demonstrably inferior. As you know, following annihilation of Iraq in Desert Storm, Soviet weapons were so devalued that reduced sales hastened the collapse of the Soviet Union."

The president nodded.

"Well," Flamsteal continued, "the Pentagon tells me, *now*, that the Soviets traditionally produced two versions of most of their military hardware. A front-line version, with all the bells and whistles, for its own troops, and a… uh." The Senator's face reddened. "This was their term, Mr. President, not mine. Their stripped-down stuff was called their 'monkey version.'"

"Monkey?" the president squawked in a high-pitched voice.

Todd Barnstorm, the president's National Security Advisor, jumped in. "Uh, Mr. President, I've had quite enough of the senator belittling defense and making racist comments."

"I have done no such thing!" Flamsteal shot back. She was angry now. How dare this hack upbraid the esteemed Senator Flamsteal! She ran her finger under her gold necklace. It was getting very warm in the Oval Office.

Secretary of Defense William Turner said, "Mr. President, that's the Soviet's own term, sir. Shows that others are quite capable of being asses." He looked directly at Flamsteal.

That got a chuckle out of everyone but Flamsteal, who thought the heat in the Oval Office was getting oppressive. She had been a big part of Obama gutting the American military. Unfortunately, what had come to light was embarrassing, and demonstrated that the headlong rush to eliminate high tech weapons had been a mistake.

The president frowned. "You're telling me the Soviets actually had superior weapons yet lost the image as a producer of high technology arms?"

General Leighton, Chairman, Joint Chiefs of Staff, said, "It seems the Soviets were terrified of letting their allies use the best equipment. The monkey versions, stripped of technological advancements, were provided to the likes of Iraq."

The president's face tightened. "So what's your point? That we defeated the Soviet's second string?" His words had a definite edge. Flamsteal smiled.

General Leighton was apparently unperturbed. *Probably,* Flamsteal thought, *the guy is too dumb to know when the president is pulling his chain.* Flamsteal was beginning to feel better. The general said, "In a word, Mr. President, that's right. In fact, we have learned in the last few months that some of their top designs, top concepts, were—are—far superior to anything we have."

The president's eyes widened. "Our intelligence finally gives us some useful information?" The president looked to Flamsteal.

This was humiliating. Beads of sweat formed around Flamsteal's face. The CIA had not discovered this information, thanks to Flamsteal's relentless efforts to cut the CIA's budget to a tenth of what it had been during the Bush-43 years. Flamsteal forced herself to tell the president how they had discovered Russia's technological advancements. She half mumbled: "The Russians are selling front-line hardware on the world market—"

The president cut her off. Clearly irritated, he barked, "You telling me we found out by attending a weapons bazaar?"

Flamsteal looked around to see whether anyone would help her out. She got nothing but blank stares. The blood vessels in her temples started to pound. She looked at the president and was suddenly dizzy. Good thing she was sitting or she felt sure she would have pitched over. She tried to articulate her explanation, but the muscles in her face and jaw were getting harder and harder to move. She mumbled, "The Russians are frequent vendors at trade shows across the world. We have learned that they have been selling two air-to-air missiles: the R-73 and R-77 from the Vympel design bureau—"

The president interrupted, still with an edge in his voice, "The what?"

Todd Barnstorm interjected and Flamsteal breathed a huge sigh of relief. He said, "It's their top design group." The president nodded.

General Leighton added, "The R-77 is a Russian knockoff of our AIM-120—uh, our Advanced Medium-Range Air-to-Air Missile."

"I know what it is!" The president's face was red with anger. Flamsteal could barely contain her pleasure. This time he was mad at someone else.

"Uh, sorry, sir." The general stared squarely into the president's eyes. The general had eyes of steel, Flamsteal knew from experience. Flamsteal could see he was using them now on the president, who visibly calmed.

The general continued, "Anyhow, the AIM-120 is the bread and butter of our pilots since it can be fired before visual. Once fired, it has an active seeker, so the pilot can disengage before the victim knows he is under attack. The AIM-120 has worked superbly and our pilots rely on it, big time."

The president said, "I lost you. What's the problem?"

"The R-77 is better than the AIM-120 in two crucial respects. It is significantly longer range and it has a unique innovation: a trellis-like tail surface and shorter, low-drag wings, making the missile far more maneuverable. So, our pilots can be fired upon by the enemy before the enemy is in range of our weapons—and it appears that we will play hell avoiding being hit."

"Okay. I don't like it. Go on."

"Even more worrisome, Mr. President, is the R-73, which is without equal. It is a short-range air-to-air missile used within visual. It has 22 aerodynamic surfaces and control devices. This missile

accomplishes what, for our designers, has been the impossible."
General Leighton paused for effect.

"The R-73 can be fired aft."

The president's face was blank.

General Leighton said, "Uh, Mr. President... That's significant. We are not talking about a ballistic projectile such as a bullet."
General Leighton noticed one of the secret service agents snap to
attention and place a hand inside his suit coat. "This *flies* to a target
it selects."

The president's face was still blank. It was clear that physics was
not his strong suit. *What a dipstick,* Flamsteal thought.

William Turner piped up, "It's no small feat, Mr. President, when
you consider, when dropped from the aircraft, the missile is traveling backward at 600 miles per hour."

That got the president's attention. *This was like educating
a schoolboy,* Flamsteal thought, all too happy to be out of the
conversation.

Turner said, "Then, as the missile accelerates, its air speed drops
to zero before it attains positive airspeed." Turner paused to let that
sink in. "This creates two interesting problems. Fast computers
solve the first problem: at negative air speed, moving a rudder—say
to the left—causes the opposite effect compared to when the missile
has attained positive air speed. Thus, the guidance system has to be
programmed to quickly reverse everything."

The president nodded. "Well, duh," Flamsteal said under her
breath.

Turner said, "The second problem is more troublesome. At, and
near, zero air speed, the missile's aerodynamic surfaces become
useless. The missile can become unstable and may begin to tumble.
Definitely not a good thing."

The president grimaced and everyone breathed a sigh of relief;
he seemingly understood.

Turner said, "The R-73 overcomes this problem by a method
called thrust vectoring. At the nozzle of the jet engine are two
tabs that act like your thumb over a water hose. As you move your

thumb around, the water sprays in different directions. The tabs thus direct the jet exhaust in such a manner that the missile maintains its course through its non-aerodynamic stage."

General Leighton interjected, "This capability, alone, transforms air-to-air combat. Traditional BFM—"

The president interrupted, "Basic Flight Maneuvers." *Well,* Flamsteal thought, *the school boy earns a ribbon.*

"Uh… yes, BFM calls for the attacker to fire in a head-on position and escape before being fired at or, if forced into visual range, to maneuver behind the target and shoot like hell. Now, when our pilot begins to maneuver to the traditional six o'clock position to fire sidewinders or his machine gun, the bogey can shoot his R-73. It appears certain that the R-73 will get our pilot before he is in position to fire his own weapons—"

The president held up his hand as if to tell the general to stop. He said, "And you're telling me that these missiles are currently in production?"

"Yes."

The president appeared to think about that for a second. He said, "Okay, so what's the big deal. We aren't at war with Russia, and it's unlikely we will be."

Flamsteal was finally ready to get back into the conversation and claim her position. She said, "The problem is that Russia is starved for money and I believe they have struck a deal on a number of these proprietary missiles."

The president's face became drawn again. "With whom?"

❧

CHAPTER 21

"YOU ARE CRAZY, BRAD. I'M NOT GOING TO USE THAT thing! Stop it!"

"Oh, Bill, relax. Trust me. I'm your brother. This is a proven technique. You've nothing to be embarrassed about. Most people do it."

A couple of retirees who were within earshot, but on the other side of a stand of palm trees, couldn't contain their curiosity. They put their clubs down and walked over to the tree-line and peered through. Bradley was blowing up a multicolored beach ball. It was odd, to be sure, but not as exciting as they had hoped. They walked back to the tee shaking their heads.

Bill said, "I should never have offered my frequent flyer tickets to come down here for a weekend."

"Oh shut up. Where else could we golf but here in sunny Florida?"

"Maybe you teach skiing better?"

Bradley glared. "Here, just put this between your knees and take a normal practice swing. I got this technique right out of an article by David Leadbetter, probably the most successful golf instructor in the world. It will cure your slice."

Bill placed the ball between his knees and addressed the imaginary golf ball. He took a swing and looked a little like a hen trying to golf while squatting to lay an egg. "I feel like an idiot! How is this beach ball going to help my swing?"

Bradley wanted to fall over laughing, but he restrained himself with every fiber in his body. In as natural a voice as he could muster, he said, "It forces your legs into proper position…"

Bill's eyes went wide. "Proper position?"

"… and the legs control your torso's position, which is the primary influence on your arms and the swing. Just try it. Here, I'll tee up a ball. Your practice swing looked a hundred percent better." Bill raised his eyebrows. "Okay. So I lied about your practice swing. Just do it again." Bradley gave him a big, fake smile.

Bill took another swing, except this time he looked a little less like a squatting hen and a little more like the big, coordinated man he was. And he even hit the ball. Bill watched in apparent disbelief as the ball took off high, seemed to hang in the sky, and then drew left as it headed back to earth. It finally landed some 220 yards out. There was a small splash as the ball hit some standing water on the fairway; it had rained heavily earlier in the morning.

"Holy Toledo! I've never hit a drive like that in my life! Yes!"

"See, I told you, big brother. Now the trick is to swing like that without the beach ball. It does sort of stand out." Bill swaggered back to his bag and sheathed his driver. He stood facing Bradley, but to the side of the tee, his legs bowed slightly, thumbs in his waist band, chest puffed out. Bradley teed up and unceremoniously screamed a 280 yard drive down the middle of the fairway.

Bill grunted. "You've always got to be just a little better." He turned away abruptly and headed down the fairway without further comment.

Bradley was taken aback. Where had that come from? He stood on the tee for a moment and then hurried to catch up.

Bill spoke as soon as Bradley was along side him. "So, anyhow, what's up with you little brother?"

There was that "little brother" again. What in the heck was wrong? He decided to let it be. Maybe it was the stress of Bill's job.

As naturally as he could, he said, "You won't believe who I just had lunch with."

"Dean Wellington. You're getting tenure." There was a barely perceptible bite to his words.

"Well, no. Though that would be pretty great too. I had lunch with that woman from Dominick's—"

Someone yelled, "Fore!" Bill and Bradley reflexively ducked their heads.

"—Anne Kreig."

The warning was for someone on the adjacent fairway and Bill was already walking again. What in the heck was eating him? Now Bradley was getting irritated. "Dominick's, THE WOMAN AT DOMINICK'S!"

Bill stopped and turned. His surly mood was suddenly gone. "I'm sorry Brad. You're talking about that good-looking gal?"

Bradley nodded, suddenly disarmed. "And guess what? She is going to take the LSAT."

"Good for her." They walked along side by side.

"I'm going to help her study."

Bill stopped and faced Bradley. "Can you do that?"

"There's no conflict of interest or ethical violation. It's not like I'm giving her inside tips on how to apply to Michigan Law."

"What if she tries?"

"Come on, Bill. She is smart, but she has been away from school too long to do well on all the complex algebra, trigonometry, geometry, reading comprehension. And to get into Michigan, nowadays, she would have to score in the high ninetieth percentile."

"But what if she did? Could you still see her?"

"Uh, good question. I'd have to reread the regulations. Probably not."

"Could you live with that?"

"It's not a realistic concern. I'd put a hundred bucks on her getting into Wayne State and being happy as a lark."

A couple of holes later, Bill said, "You know that attempt on the warheads?" Without waiting for Bradley to answer, Bill continued,

"Director Abdullah himself just transferred the desk to me."
"Transferring the desk" meant he was being put in charge of the investigation.

"That's great!"

"Yeah. He called me and said he liked the work I did last year on the Mob heavies."

Bill and Bradley were waiting for a foursome still on the green. They swung their short irons to keep loose. It was a short par four, and with Bill's drive, his approach was only a firm eight iron.

Bill continued, "I know you disagree with it, but from my perspective, I'm damn glad the president signed the Un-American Act. We need the ability to go after the anti-government types. I guess I'm a little concerned with the gun confiscation stuff, but I'm sure the president will return all the guns when this dies down."

Bradley studied Bill for a moment. He could hardly believe what he had just heard. He had never imagined his brother would go along with something that clearly violated *both* the First and the Second Amendments. And the president would give back all the guns? What Kool-Aid had Bill been drinking? The green cleared and Bradley nodded for Bill to swing away. Bradley watched his brother address the ball and begin his ritual of fidgeting the club head around the ball, shifting his weight from foot to foot, looking to the target, back to the ball, back to the target, and on and on. Bradley was losing patience when Bill finally started his back swing. Bradley's expert eye instantly identified several problems. It was going to be ugly…

The club head drove into the ground about three inches behind the ball. Mud, grass, and water flew everywhere. The ball flipped airborne and landed about 20 feet down the fairway.

Bill groaned. "I invoke my Official GAMS Winter Rules."
"What?"

Bill smiled. "The Official, Gentlemen's, Augmented, Modified, Supplemental, Winter Rules of Golf, applicable year round."

Bradley faked a light laugh. He was having trouble digesting the idea that his brother was serious about law enforcement activities that so clearly violated the United States Constitution.

Bill continued, "And rule 17, entitled 'Divot In Flight Further Than Ball In Play,' states: 'When any portion of player's divot has traveled to a location closer to the pin than his ball, the attendant embarrassment is punishment enough, and the player shall forthwith advance his ball to said location and the player may further invoke any other rule, or combination of rules, as may be necessary to secure an advantageous lie.'"

Bradley laughed despite himself. That *was* pretty funny. He said, "I like your rules, not your politics."

Bill appeared to ignore the comment and moved up to his ball; he switched clubs to what Bradley assumed was a nine iron. Bill started his setup process anew with nearly the same result. Dirt and grass advanced almost as far as the ball. Bill slumped his shoulders and shook his head. He and Bradley moved up again. Bill said, "I can't mention specifics, other than what you have seen in the news, but we've seen a big increase in chatter from NRA and patriot types. They are using encrypted cell phones that have an unauthorized encryption algorithm. Pretty clever, actually, since they are able to mask the encrypted packets of data in burst transmissions, so we pick up only a small fraction of what we think is going on. And we haven't been able to crack the algorithm yet. So something is being planned. And it scares me."

"Well," Bradley said, "what evidence do you have that they are planning something illegal? Are they are threatening to keep their guns? And if so, what kind of threat is that? And we use military helicopters and Hellfire missiles to kill them? I mean, really. It's insanity, Bill. So tell me, what evidence do you have that they plan something actually illegal?" Bradley had worked himself into a lather and he knew that his brother would be reluctant to disclose specifics about evidence supporting a finding of probable cause, but he was taken aback by Bill's characterization of NRA and patriot members being *per se* involved in illegal activity. Before the Un-American Act it wasn't illegal to discuss things such as gun rights, returning to constitutional foundations, or even advocating for a change in government.

Bradley pulled out his sand wedge. His swing was picture perfect and the ball arched high and hung majestically in the air. It hit just to the right of the pin, about 10 yards past, dug into the wet green, skipped once, and then pulled all the way back—to leave about a six-foot putt for birdie.

Bill improved his lie pursuant, apparently, to the aforesaid rule 17. He muttered something that Bradley couldn't hear, and set up for his approach with a look of determination. This time, Bill addressed the ball and quickly started his back swing. It looked to be much better… And it was. Bill clipped the back side of the ball on a nice descending stroke and sent it high and straight.

"Nice shot. You're on the green!"

"Thanks. Even a broken clock is right twice a day." Bill wiped his club on his towel. They both headed toward the green. "Anyhow, I shouldn't say this, but we don't have any probable cause according to what we used to consider probable cause. Things are different now."

Bradley's face flushed with blood. "Did you just say what I think you said?"

Bill gave him a blank look.

"Come on, Bill, you can't tell me you agree with that."

Bill lined up his putt and quickly stroked it about halfway to the hole. Still away, he quickly addressed the ball and knocked it 15 feet past. He walked past Bradley to the other side of the hole and again lined up. This time he fidgeted and fidgeted, and then stood still as a rock. Finally, he stroked the putt and it caught the edge of the hole, rimmed three quarters around, and dropped.

Thank God, Bradley thought. It was painful to watch. Bradley had already scanned the subtle breaks in the green. He stepped up and knocked it down. He popped the ball out of the cup with a flick of his Ping Answer putter.

Bill replaced the pin and mumbled, "Nice putt."

Bradley said thanks and headed to the next tee. They walked in silence. Bradley knew his brother had heard him; Bill was choosing to remain silent. Bradley decided to push it. "Bill. I'm serious. Are you telling me you agree with this?"

Bill stopped and set his bag down. "Look, Brad, I don't want to get into a fight… but, yes. I do. Just as I agreed with President Bush, I agree with Wallmire. We need to protect the country."

"But don't you think there is a difference targeting, profiling, the people who attacked us and who tried but failed again and again throughout the Bush presidency, yet under Obama killed a million in San Francisco?"

"Well, that's part of my point. As soon as we stopped profiling Muslims they set off a nuclear bomb."

"Bill. Those were Islamists. Not Americans who risked their lives fighting for our country. Not Americans who have purchased guns to protect themselves from Islamists!"

"But Americans just tried to hijack three nuclear warheads."

"That's true. But we don't know what they were going to do with them. And it still doesn't justify profiling all former military. Except for a handful of guys, literally millions of ex-military people have done nothing but put their lives on the line for us. On the other hand, how many Muslims are in the NRA? How many have served in the military? The answer is, not *that* many. And the point is, Muslims have committed, worldwide, over 20,000 deadly attacks since 9/11. It's Muslims that we have caught—on our soil—*over a hundred times* trying to commit terrorism. And it's Muslims we've been fighting in several wars over the past 20 years. We haven't been fighting American gun owners. Citizens who own firearms— and certainly the ones who actually have permits to carry concealed—are some of the most law abiding people in the world. We needed, and still need, to watch Arabs precisely because 90 percent of them are Muslim. And a central tenant of their religion is to enslave or kill infidels—and that's us."

"That's racist, Brad."

"Oh bull crap. It's reality. How is it racist to point out the truth?"

They had just reached the tee but Bill did an about face and headed toward the clubhouse, leaving Bradley standing alone on the tee.

☙

Big Sky News
Missoula, Montana

Arizona Sheriff Investigated for Discrimination Against Illegal aliens
BY JACK MARLEY, BSN STAFF WRITER

SIERRA VISTA, ARIZONA – The Bureau of Socially Correct Activities (BSCA) has launched an investigation into the Cochise County Sheriff's Office following allegations by the ACLU and ACORN that Sheriff Ned Clifford and dozens of his deputies have violated the civil rights of illegal aliens.

Elmer Kennison, the Director of the BSCA, indicated that Clifford and his department are being investigated for discriminatory police practices, unconstitutional searches and seizures, discrimination based on national origin, and failure to provide meaningful access to services for Limited English Proficient individuals. Kennison further indicated that the investigation was undertaken pursuant to provisions of the Religious And Cultural Sensitivities Act."

Sheriff Clifford told Big Sky News that he has done nothing more than uphold the laws of Arizona, and that he will not back down or be intimidated by "federal big shots."

"We've arrested over two thousand illegals for forgery, kidnapping, assault, robbery, murder, drunk driving, all manner of drug crimes including smuggling and distribution. And that's in just six months," Clifford indicated. "Additionally, we have discovered that we have over 20,000 illegal aliens in our state prisons. And do you think the federal government will deport them? We've been told, 'no way.' And what's worse, they tell me we've violated federal law for just checking on their status. I mean, how can that be? We've arrested and tried them in court. And they have been sentenced. And it's illegal for us to find out if they are citizens? Ever since Obama, the nation has been upside down," Clifford said.

CHAPTER 22

ANNE'S ALARM WENT OFF AT 5:00 A.M. SHE ROLLED OVER, reached out from under the toasty-warm down comforter and hit the snooze. Ten minutes later she hit the snooze again. Ten minutes later she hit the snooze again. Ten minutes later she hit the off button and dragged herself out of bed into the comparatively cold bedroom air. She shivered and wrapped her arms around herself in a vain effort to recapture the wonderful warmth of that thick comforter. The flannel pajamas needed reinforcement and she headed to the closet for a robe.

What in the hell was she doing getting up in the middle of the night? This was madness. She hadn't been able to fall asleep until, what was it? Two-thirty A.M. was the last she recalled seeing on the alarm clock. *For cripes sake.* How in the hell was she going to take the LSAT on less than three hours of sleep? Well, it didn't really matter, did it? She would do it. She was a work of art and that was that. If she failed, so be it. At least it wouldn't be for not trying—or for not getting out of bed.

Anne dizzily stumbled to the kitchen and stabbed at the switch on the coffee maker, missing it twice before it clicked to on. She slumped her upper body onto the counter and set her head against the cool tile. After a moment, she raised her head and glanced out the kitchen window. As often happens in Michigan, a cool fall morning had put a light dusting of snow on everything; the landscape was covered with a pretty white blanket.

Anne groaned. The snow meant the roads would be slow and she and Linda, who had offered to drive her to the exam, had guessed right in giving themselves a little extra time. But it also meant they could not waste any time. Anne grabbed the coffee pot, which had filled only to the one-cup line. She needed the strong stuff. Anne again cursed her poor luck. She had been informed by the LSDAS that her first choice of test location, the University of Michigan, had been denied; she had been bumped to her second choice: Michigan State University, some sixty miles northwest of Ann Arbor.

Anne had purchased every LSAT practice book she could find. Hour after hour, Anne raced through multiple-choice questions, scribbled calculations in the margins of the test books, and hurriedly marked her answers by darkening in the little circles on the computer-graded answer sheets. Small piles of erasure stubble and the shaved wood from her 50-cent pencil sharpener covered her desk in the den. She had finished eight practice exams and, in the process, discovered that she actually enjoyed working on logic and math questions. The only problem was that she read slowly and struggled to finish all the questions in time. Still, the questions she answered she mostly got right.

Linda knocked on Anne's front door at exactly 6:15. They had to be to the test by 8:15. Linda drove west on I-94. It was snowing lightly. They got only about five miles out of town, however, when the navigation system told them of a backup just ahead. They decided to exit at Fletcher and take the back roads. As they drove through the sleepy little towns of Chelsea, Stockbridge, and Dansville, they were surprised to see as many as 50 cars parked around each of the various towns' VFW and American Legion halls.

Anne said, "What on earth could they be meeting about so early in the morning? And in all these little burgs?"

"Oh, who knows? Probably something to do with hunting or fishing. That's all people seem to do in these little towns."

"Come on. You're not serious."

"Yes, I am. I grew up in a little town and that's all anyone ever got uppity about. Hunting and fishing rights and licenses and such."

Anne couldn't believe her ears. Linda was usually more sophisticated than that. But it wasn't worth arguing over. She was beginning to get nervous. Really nervous. Her stomach was doing flip-flops and she was starting to feel sick. It was smarter to sit quietly and hope the queasiness would go away. Then suddenly the tension got to Anne and she blurted out, "Oh, I'll be glad when this exam is over!" Linda nodded and rolled her eyes. They drove the rest of the way in silence—except for Anne's stomach—which made threatening noises and gestures at every turn, curve, and dip in the road.

By the time they got to the test room—a huge classroom that looked more like an auditorium that could seat a million students—Anne's stomach was in knots and she felt as if she would throw up at any minute. It was all she could do to register, collect the test materials, including two pencils, and find an open seat. She flopped herself into the seat and tried to relax. After a moment she noticed that the LSAT proctor appeared to begin giving out instructions and talking into a microphone. Stupid thing wasn't on, however, and he was just blithely talking away. It was a good thing she had taken so many practice tests and didn't need the instructions.

Linda waved from the doorway into the classroom, presumably wishing her good luck—

Suddenly the proctor's microphone blared out at full volume and Anne jumped six feet into the air, or so it seemed. She dropped her test booklet, computer-scored answer sheet, and both pencils—each of which began to roll down the sloped floor of the jam-packed classroom. She scooped up her papers and then jumped up to chase the pencils, but found that she couldn't squeeze between the seats in front of her. She watched as the pencils kept rolling down the sloped floor.

At that moment, the proctor said, "Start!" Anne blinked and then stared at the proctor in disbelief. This wasn't happening. It *couldn't* be happening. They had to stop the test and wait. She wasn't ready. *Oh my God!*

Anne then discovered she had been feeling nauseous for good reason, and she caught herself just in time. She covered her mouth with both hands and was barely able to keep the vomit from spewing out. Frantically, she looked around and saw that people were beginning to look at her. She began to search for a path through the cramped seating. Her body was screaming, revolting. Her leg muscles began twitching to run—like a dog might lurch and stop, lurch and stop, when anticipating the toss of a stick.

Something kept her feet planted. A portion of scripture flashed before her eyes. She could see it as though she was looking at the page in her Bible.

Consider it pure joy, my brothers, whenever you face trials of many kinds, because you know that the testing of your faith develops perseverance. Perseverance must finish its work so that you may be mature and complete, not lacking anything.

There was only one thing to do. There was only one thing she *could* do.

She swallowed the vomit.

Then something good happened.

A young man had noticed the pencils rolling under his chair and he had picked them up and had begun a pass-back to Anne. Presently, a young Oriental woman was smiling at her and holding out the pencils. Anne reached out and took them as though they were a heavenly gift—which of course they were.

She made her way back to her seat. Her mouth had a horribly nasty taste in it, and her throat was burning from the stomach acid and bile. She realized that she must smell like vomit, but if she did, the students around her were ignoring it. The clock on the wall indicated that she had lost only four minutes. She still had 36 to finish the section. She took a deep breath, exhaled slowly, opened the test booklet, and started reading essay number one.

Four hours later, Anne closed her booklet and passed it toward the aisle, where the proctor was collecting them. She let out a sigh of relief and realized for the first time that her breath really did smell like vomit.

Linda made her way to Anne's row. Nearly everyone was gathering up coats and heading towards the exits at the front and back of the huge classroom. A procession of people trying to get out made Anne and Linda squeeze up against the seats. When the last one was past, Linda said, "Well, that was some show you put on at the start. I thought you were going to walk out."

"You don't know the half of it. But anyhow, it's over. Thanks for all the help."

"Well, how do you think you did?" Linda's face was full of hope.

"I failed. I didn't finish any of my sections and I was forced to guess on the last five or six in each area."

Linda frowned. "Well, don't dwell on it. It's over. And you never know." She pulled Anne's arm. "Come on, let's get out of here."

The drive home was uneventful. They decided to take the same scenic route home that they had used to get to East Lansing. Bright sunlight reflected off the fresh snow. The roads were dry.

Linda said, "Gosh, it's a beautiful day."

Anne was trying hard to feel cheerful, but was losing the battle. The test had taken it out of her. She didn't feel sick any longer, just totally spent. She propped her head against the window, closed her eyes, and tried to nap. After several minutes of her head bumping against the window, she abandoned her attempt at napping. Instead, she just stared out the window, squinting into the bright snow.

Linda said, "Look at that. There are still a bunch of cars at that American Legion hall." They drove through the next small town and saw the same thing, 20 to 50 cars parked around a VFW hall.

Anne said, "They must be planning something big."

The scene repeated itself in each town they passed. When they finally arrived back in Ann Arbor, the only thing Anne could think about was sleeping—and washing her mouth out with Scope. *God*, she felt awful. Anne walked in her front door and made a beeline for the bathroom; from there she headed directly to the couch. In the back of her mind, she knew it was somewhere around two P.M. She flopped onto the couch, scrunched a polar-fleece throw into a pillow, and was asleep within seconds.

Someone rapped on the door at 7:30 P.M.

Anne jerked her head up from her pillow and, for a second, wondered where in the hell she was. It suddenly dawned on her—as her head swayed from dizziness—she had slept through the afternoon and that was probably Bradley at the door. She had promised Bradley they would go out on the town to celebrate taking the LSAT. Now, that was the *last* thing she felt like doing. "Oh God. Not tonight," she mumbled as she sat up on the couch and dropped her feet to the floor.

The door rattled again, this time a bit harder. It was making her head pound.

"I'm coming!" God, she wanted to strangle whoever was making so much noise! Oh, her head hurt! She stood on her feet and started to waver. Quickly she put her hand out to the coffee table to steady herself. This time the pounding on the door was hard enough to make the inlaid glass rattle. It had to be Bradley. "Just a minute!" Anne put her hand to her head in an attempt to ease the throbbing. "I am going to strangle him!"

Anne stumbled to the door as fast as she could. She was in the same clothes she had worn when she took the LSAT; now, however, they were rumpled and askew. Her hair was snarled and the side of her face still had a big red mark from sleeping on her left hand. She could still taste Scope and vomit. And, to add insult to injury, she had developed a nasty case of heartburn. The corners of her eyes were drawn tight with anger. Her jaw was set. Anne got to the door and whipped it open.

She immediately groaned.

Bradley was holding a dozen roses and sported a mile-wide smile. His hair was groomed with a perfect part on the side. It was as though he had just come from the stylist. His casual shirt and slacks were freshly pressed. His bow tie was crooked.

Bradley bubbled, "Hi Anne! Congratulations! How did you do? Don't answer—I'm sure you did great! I've gotten reservations at your favorite restaurant!" Bradley gazed at Anne with admiring eyes. His hand started toward his tie and he restrained it. He said, apparently in total seriousness, "Are you ready to go?"

The man is a meathead, Anne thought. But what could she do? He was like a puppy to whom you have just come home from a long absence. "Come in and wait in the living room." Anne turned her back to Bradley and headed directly to the bedroom. She was nearly out of earshot when she said, "This may take a while."

Bradley seemed unaffected by the slight. He yelled out to her as she disappeared around the corner, "No problem! I'll call to change the reservations."

"Fine!" she said as she closed her bedroom door. She couldn't believe he was still making so much damn noise.

❧

B RADLEY WAS CERTAIN ANNE WOULD START TO FEEL BET- ter as soon as she got something to eat. When she climbed into the car she had immediately reclined the seat and closed her eyes. She mumbled something about an Olympic headache. Thus far, the drive had been in total silence. Traffic was light on west-bound I-94. The early-morning accident had made the news—something about a double trailer jackknifing and blocking both west-bound lanes. At least it was clear now. Bradley couldn't tell whether Anne was sleeping, and he didn't want to disturb her if she was. He was taking her to her favorite restaurant, the Common Grill in Chelsea, a small town about 20 miles west of Ann Arbor.

They pulled into the parking lot of the restaurant and Bradley decided to leave the car running for heat and just sit for a while. With the Volvo quietly idling, he could see Anne's relaxed breathing that signaled sleep. She looked so precious. The heck with the reservation. She was wiped out. He would let her sleep. He could wait to ask her about Jeff's possible patriot involvement. Truth was, he was terrified of poisoning their relationship. He was already harboring feelings he was afraid would scare her off.

An hour passed and Bradley was gazing at the soft contours of Anne's face when her eyes blinked open. Anne jerked up her head, scanned her surroundings, looked wide-eyed at Bradley and blinked.

"I let you sleep, Anne. You must be so whipped from taking the LSAT. Perhaps I should have let you sleep at home instead of dragging you out here to dinner?"

"I'm sorry—I fell asleep." Her tone of voice was softer; it no longer had the edge it had demonstrated before her nap. Gone was the strain in the corners of her eyes.

"Don't be silly; you must be really spent."

"I've never done that—"

"Anne, relax. I'm happy just to be with you. It makes me feel good that you felt comfortable enough with me to nap. I enjoyed letting you sleep. I was foolish, and forgot what an ordeal taking the LSAT is. We should have planned this for tomorrow night. You need a day to recover."

Anne stared at Bradley. It seemed that her breathing was suddenly constricted, yet she was trying to speak. He mouth moved but nothing came out. Then she became still, and her eyes bored in on Bradley's. It was as though she were trying to make a decision. After a moment, she leaned forward. Bradley felt a hand on his right thigh. She moved her head toward his and he was engulfed by the sweet smell of her skin. His heart began to pound. Her incredibly soft, warm lips were suddenly against his. The feeling was intoxicating. His heart began to pound even faster. He wanted her close to him—as close as possible. He wanted to feel himself enveloped around her entire body. He wrapped his left hand around her waist and pulled her toward him. She responded by opening her mouth wider and deepening her kisses. She unsnapped both of their seat belts and pulled slowly on one of the strands of his bow tie. He felt it fall apart and a moment later her right hand returned to his leg. This time, she did not contain herself to his thigh.

Bradley moaned slightly as her hand brushed over the bulge in his pants. Apparently, she took the sound to be one of approval, and the next thing he felt was a tug on his zipper…

Bradley watched a middle-aged couple park their car at the other end of the lot and walk into the Common Grill's back door. He was never so glad that he always parked far away from other cars.

Suddenly he clenched his teeth and let out a deep growl. He started to feel light-headed and he laid his head back on the car headrest. He closed his eyes and was sure he could fall asleep. Anne began to neatly put things away. He felt a playful bite through his pants.

Bradley raised Anne's head and caressed her face with his hands. There seemed to be some form of torment in her eyes; she seemed to be fighting back tears. Bradley leaned forward and pressed his lips to hers. He pulled her head gently with his hands and could feel her neck and back muscles stiffen for a moment and then relax and give in. She slipped her body into his, like a puzzle piece that slides effortlessly into place.

Should he tell her he loved her? Would she take him to be over-zealous? Insincere? Yet he felt so much. The urge to tell her was almost irresistible… But, what if he couldn't maintain his feelings? The last thing he wanted was to raise her expectations and hopes, only to change his own mind.

That would destroy her.

He remembered all too well seeing her bolt across the law library and fall headlong into the door. And that was simply because he and Linda had started off on the wrong foot. No, this was a woman who needed him to be consistent. And that meant going slowly. But *she* had moved quickly. And he hadn't tried to stop her. Well, truth be told, he had wanted sex just as badly (apparently anyhow) as did she. And that reminded him … She probably didn't want him to get gymnastic in the car. He would take care of her after dinner in the comfort of his place. He would take care of her. Big time.

"Bradley," Anne murmured, "let's forget the fancy dinner and go to your place and order pizza and split a bottle of wine."

Bradley threw the transmission into drive and stomped on the accelerator.

❧

CHAPTER 23

THE DOMINO'S DELIVERY PERSON RANG THE DOORBELL at 11:00 P.M. and Anne watched Bradley hurriedly rummage through a pile of clothes at the foot of his bed. He found his wrinkled pants and quickly slipped them on. He didn't find his underpants.

Just as well, Anne thought.

She found his shirt and put it on. Initially, she had struggled with getting intimate—knowing, as she did, where she wanted it to lead. Yet her conscience bothered her. She had been studying her book about changing her internal monologue and telling herself the truth, and she'd been reading all of the scripture on which it was based. She knew that Paul, in Romans, talked about always doing the very thing he didn't want to do while not doing the good things he wanted to do. Her mind flashed back to a highlighted page in her Bible:

> *As it is, it is no longer I myself who do it, but it is sin living in me. ... For what I do is not the good I want to do; no, the evil I do not want to do— this I keep on doing. Now if I do what I do not want to do, it is no longer I who do it, but it is sin living in me that does it.*

And, *oh my,* did the sin living in her want more of Bradley…

Sitting on Bradley's bed, all the covers strewed about on the floor, they devoured the large pepperoni pizza with gusto. Bradley tossed the empty pizza box onto the floor and reclined on his side.

He grinned and beckoned her by extending his hand, palm up, and slowly, repeatedly, curling his index finger toward him.

Men, Anne thought. *Food, sex, and sports.* She gazed into his eyes and then nodded toward the growing bulge just below his waist. Tossing her better judgment to the wind, she said, "I better do something about that…"

⌾

IT WAS A SUNNY MORNING, THE KIND THAT LOOKS LIKE IT'S warmer than it really is. Anne studied the distance to her mailbox and decided to run for it without bundling up. Her long pajamas were pretty warm. But halfway there she knew it had been a mistake. It was freezing and the cold pierced the cotton like a knife. By the time she got back inside she was shaking and had goose bumps everywhere. Standing in the entryway, she shuffled through the usual junk mail. A couple of bills… And there, inconspicuously stuck between her water and telephone bills, was a computer slip—a perforated, tear-open envelope, with the initials "LSDAS." She knew that meant the Law School Data Assembly Service.

This was her LSAT score.

Anne's heart pushed itself up between her ears, or so it seemed. All she could hear was a pounding in her head. She weaved toward the kitchen, twice dropping the other mail. She fell into a chair at the kitchen table and held the computer envelope with both hands.

She stared at the envelope. The damn thing trembled in her hands.

She was terrified to open it—and at the same time she wanted to open it so badly she thought the anticipation might kill her.

The sunlight was streaming into the kitchen and she held the envelope up so the light could illuminate the writing inside. As soon as she began to make out some of the words she jerked the envelope down, out of the light. She set the envelope down on the table. Her heart was still pounding in her ears.

Should she call Linda first? Or Bradley? Or Jeff? Her mind began to race and she lost track of things. After a moment she said, "What am I doing?"

She knew the answer. She was stalling. And as that thought came to her she felt a shiver of anger at her own weakness. "Work of art. Work of art. I'm a work of art," she repeated as she grabbed the envelope. "You are not going to defeat me!" She ripped off one end and yanked out the thin piece of paper that held her score.

She couldn't figure it out.

She looked up in the top left corner and saw her name and address. *Okay,* she thought, *that's me.* The top right corner contained a bunch of numbers she didn't recognize. The two bottom corners contained no information at all. She scanned from corner to corner until, finally, she started to concentrate on the numbers on the top right. But *those* numbers didn't make any sense. They *couldn't* be her score. She looked back at the left corner. Yep, it still said Anne Kreig.

She looked at the top right corner…

The LSDAS had just changed the scoring system, *again.* Of course, it had explained the new system in literature, but Anne had not been interested at the time and she had never read it. As a result, Anne couldn't figure out how well she had done from her numerical score. The numbers *following* her score told the story, however. The first number indicated the percentile rank of her score compared to all scores over the last five years, and the second number gave the percentile rank for this particular sitting.

The numbers were 99 and 98.

The phone rang.

When Anne reached the phone, the caller ID indicated it was Linda. Anne picked up the phone and screamed at the top of her lungs.

After several nearly unintelligible exchanges between the women, Linda, so excited she was sucking in air with each breath, said, "So… where do… you want… to go to… school. With that score… you can write your… ticket!"

Anne paused to catch her own breath. There was no doubt in her mind. "Here. I want to go to U of M." She didn't say that she also wanted to be near Bradley.

"Thank heavens. I was afraid you might relocate. I want to be with you."

Anne was touched and a little bit ashamed. She hadn't thought of Linda—the person most responsible for this opportunity. Anne swallowed hard and told herself she had to be more considerate. Well, she could start right now. "You know, Linda, I can't believe it. You and Jeff and Bradley have helped so much. And now I have the chance to turn my life in a new direction." Linda mumbled something to the effect that it was nothing and that God had a hand in it, but Anne didn't respond. Her mind had been overrun by a horrifying thought—Bradley was a professor at U of M.

Time stood still.

After a moment, Anne's head started to spin and she felt dizzy. Linda was talking but Anne didn't hear a word. "I suddenly feel woozy, Linda. I'd better lie down for a minute. I'll call you back a little later. Okay?"

"No problem. Oh, what are you going to say to Bradley? He'll die."

I don't know about him, but I might, she thought.

The next day Anne was standing in front of the only window in Bradley's office. Frost had accumulated on the inside corners of the window and on the molding. She was watching students come and go from the law school and was trying to imagine herself in their shoes. It was a cold winter's day and there was a blanket of new snow from the night before. It covered the piles of dirty snow and grime along all the roads and in parking lots where plows churned up all manner of debris. She noticed that some of the students seemed at ease, laughing with others and occasionally picking up a handful of snow and forming a snowball and tossing it harmlessly at a street post. Others seemed distinctly uptight, pacing and looking straight ahead as if they were hurrying to something important, ignoring the winter beauty. She wondered which she would be, at ease or uptight—if she went.

Ironically, the issue was in doubt precisely because she had scored so well on the LSAT. She was terrified of asking Bradley about school or university regulations concerning dating students. Yet this was law school, for heaven's sake. She tried to convince herself that the rules would be different for grown students. Law students were adults, after all.

But, what if… what if it was prohibited? What was more important to her? Bradley or a law degree? Love or an intellectual challenge? Companionship or an absorbing, fascinating career?

Bradley was massaging the finishing touches on some kind of memo he was writing at his—what was it? Well, it was his computer that he didn't like to call a computer. Apparently, all Apple users (addicts is probably a better name) called their computers by personalized names. Anne recalled Jeff and Miles did the same, but felt a little sheepish that she couldn't remember what any of these guys called their computers. Men. They also seemed to always have a name for their… *thing.* And it was always "Big this-or-that," or some such. Bradley's was "The Magic Wand." Well, she certainly couldn't argue with that. He claimed to have picked up the name from a friend in law school. Men were so funny. They shared the damnedest things.

Bradley was also funny about his writing. He liked to refer to his work as something alive that needed nourishment, exercise, fresh air, massage. Presently, Bradley was so deeply involved in his memo or whatever that he probably didn't remember she was in the room.

In addition to being torn up over the university regulations, which she was just sure would prevent her from dating Bradley, Anne's stomach was churning and growling, and her mind kept imagining a big plate of pasta marinara for lunch. She turned away from the window. Bradley had such an intense look on his face. He must have been one of those serious-type students. He was pounding the keys.

Bradley's phone rang and it made Anne jump. The phone kept ringing and it looked like Bradley wasn't going to answer it.

"Bradley, your secretary is at lunch."

"Oh!" Bradley snapped his head up from his screen and stared at Anne for a moment as if he was in a daze. Then, he seemed to come back to earth and he picked up the phone. "Hello… Bill? What's up? … Really? Sure. Is it something you can fax? Okay. Good. I'll call you as soon as I've had a chance to review it… You just caught me—I'm going to lunch with her… Goof. You can't ever remember names. Anne Kreig… Bill? You there? Oh, I thought I lost you. Yes, Anne Kreig. She is his former wife. Okay. See you."

Bradley turned to Anne. "That was funny."

"Your brother?"

"Yeah. He seemed startled that you are related to Hartman."

"He knows my ex?"

"Sure. FBI. Remember?"

"Bank robberies. Okay. Makes sense. So I'm related…"

"That's what I thought was funny. Why would that be significant?"

"Probably just a surprise."

"Yeah. Prob… ab… ly." That last word seemed to slowly roll off Bradley's tongue as if he was in some deep thought. Then, suddenly, he came out of it. "Anyhow, he says they have begun to unravel some militia thing. He's going to fax me something."

"Sounds kind of spooky. I thought we were through with that." Anne was a little bothered by what seemed to be odd behavior, first by Bill on the other end of the line when Bradley mentioned her name, and then a few moments later by Bradley. She didn't know what to think of it.

"Not a chance. Beliefs run way too deep. And frankly, I have nothing against people who argue for this or that. For crying out loud, I'm a professor of the First Amendment. But I sure don't like blowing up federal buildings to make a point—even if someone thinks it's an artistic form of expression."

The fax machine started beeping. They both walked over and read the incoming fax:

A DRAFT OUTLINE ON HOW TO FORM A MORE PERFECT UNION·

Reaffirm the U.S. Constitution, the Bill Of Rights, and further establish that the Supreme Court shall have the power to declare acts of the Legislative and Executive branches to be in violation of the U.S. Constitution only where the act would infringe upon something actually written in the Constitution or upon a judicial function.

Several examples illustrate how the Supreme Court shall decide cases in the future.

1. The court will not rule that the president must answer a civil suit during the pendency of his term. His or her refusal to do so would not infringe upon anything written in the Constitution or upon a judicial function. It would merely infringe upon the plaintiff's desire to haul the Commander In Chief into court. The issue, being thus clearly political, would be left for the president to work out with his constituents and the legislature, which could, if it desired, speak on the issue by passage of an appropriate act.

2. The court will overrule cases where it has created substantive rights, such as the right to an abortion. The right to an abortion, being a religious, political, and social issue, is something that will have to be debated and enacted into law by state legislatures (the power to affect such issues does not inhere in the federal Congress). Nine old crotchety justices, trained to analyze the correctness of legal decisions based on precedent, are uniquely unsuited to determine, out of thin air whether, and to what extent, a woman should have such a right. The court will make no such pronouncements. It is for the states to decide.

3. The court will overrule Wickard v. Filburn and its progeny. Congress has the power to regulate Commerce among the several States. It does not have the power to regulate life itself. Accordingly, all regulatory agencies shall be dissolved and all regulations shall be immediately revoked. All of them. The power

to regulate anything other than commerce among the states is reserved to the states, which can regulate to their hearts' desires.

The federal Congress shall study the issue of what regulatory powers directly impact the efficient functioning of commerce among the states. Protection of the environment as well as wage and employment laws are an examples of things that are within the exclusive power of the states. Of course, it is within the power of the states to work together and enact similar laws (called "uniform acts") so that consistency among the states can be achieved.

To the extent that the federal Congress desires to regulate commerce among the states, it shall enact one regulation at a time (with full debate on the actual language of the regulation). No regulations shall be issued by any agency within the executive branch. Further, all federal regulations shall have a sunset of no more than five years from the date enacted and must therefore be debated and renewed, if at all, on the floor of Congress.

4. The court shall only step in and rule on a legislative act that appears to be beyond the power of the federal government or, if within such power, if there is evidence that the elected representatives failed in their jobs—to properly represent.

Thus, if the legislature decrees for or against an affirmative action program to promote minorities to positions they would not obtain on their own, the Supreme Court will review only whether the legislators gave due consideration to all constituents, including the minorities vis-à-vis the majority (or pluralities).

In other words, the inquiry will be of the process by which the law came to be; the inquiry will not be concerned with the outcome of that process. If evidence comes to light that one group, be it minority or otherwise, exerted improper influence (threats, gifts, or anything other than promises of votes or no votes) on one or more representatives, the court will rule the law unconstitutional. If it desires, the legislature could then reconsider the law and seek to pass it again—this time without the constitutional infirmity.

Bradley said, "This is sort of a melding of conservatism and the concepts out of *Democracy and Distrust.*" He was shaking his head.

Anne said, "I've heard of that somewhere." She was getting another eerie feeling.

Bradley gave Anne a funny look. "Really? It's kind of a scholarly type book that you would have to seek out; it's not well known out of the circle of constitutional scholars. Actually, however, it's one of the most impressive books to come out in many years on the theory of proper constitutional decision-making. It's been criticized by some, but the guy was right-on."

Anne was almost afraid to ask who the author was. Something told her she would know him. Now that she thought about it, Jeff and Miles had talked constitutional this or that on more than one occasion. She had thought it was odd.

"John Hart Ely. Great thinker."

Anne froze. She remembered Jeff's mentioning that name. This was unnerving. She stared at Bradley and had a vague sensation that he could read her thoughts. She quickly turned and walked to the window.

"Anne, you okay?"

Anne's head felt numb and her mouth was dry. This was an entirely different dilemma. It was beginning to appear that her son was involved in the patriot movement. And that was illegal, wasn't it? Damn, she couldn't remember the details of what was and wasn't illegal membership in a group. Surely he would be nothing more than a member. Anyhow, the questions were: What would happen if Bradley found out? Would he tell his brother? A heat flash coursed through her body.

And regrettably, her other dilemma—the one she had had when she came to see Bradley—remained. If she attended Michigan, she knew... well, she hoped... he would feel a pressure to sneak around and jeopardize his career. However, it would be unfair to put him in that position. She just couldn't do it. *God, this was getting complicated.*

Anne slowly turned and walked over to Bradley. She knew her cheeks were red from the flush of heat that had rushed to her face. How could she get out of this mess? She had to find a way he wouldn't be able to ruin his career and be able to send her son to prison.

Suddenly, Anne had a tremendous urge to press her body against Bradley's. She gulped and thought: *one last time.* Oh how she wanted to avoid sin. And oh how she wanted him…

Impulsively, she said, "We're alone."

Bradley stepped to her and she snuggled close—pressing herself, hard, against him.

Bradley seemed to have to tear himself away. He walked to his office door and closed it. He moved so smoothly, gracefully. It conjured the image of a tiger powerfully making his way to mate. He would not be denied. Her heart started to pound. He turned the lock and walked back. She already had her blouse unbuttoned and her bra undone by the time their lips met in a fierce, desperate kiss. Bradley lifted her and set her on the edge of his desk. He let go of her just long enough to let her pull up her skirt and wrap her legs around his waist. She felt him struggling with his pants and then heard his buckle hit the floor…

Tears spilled out of the corners of her eyes.

⇥

JEFF COULDN'T BELIEVE HOW MANY PAMPHLETS AND POLITIcal tracts were necessary to support the patriots' educational and recruitment efforts. The fort underneath the barn had proven convenient not only for the secure computer networking of the patriot leaders. For both economy and security, Hartman had pulled in all the patriots' desktop publishing.

Recruitment was becoming easier in direct proportion to the federal government's tightening and abusive grip on America, its economy, and its people. Jeff glanced at a motto he had framed on the wall:

> *Power tends to corrupt, and absolute power corrupts absolutely.*
>
> *Lord Acton*

Once the facts were studied, it was easy to see that most of the laws imposed on the citizens and businesses of the nation were created, not by elected legislators, but by employees of the EPA, FDA, HUD, IRS, DHS, HHS, FTC, FCC, FAA, EEOC, DOE, DOC, DOJ, DOS, USDA, RCSA, BSCA, AAAA, BATF, OSHA and many, many others, beholden to no one except their employer. One of Jeff's favorite anecdotes consisted of a tee shirt that was popular around Ann Arbor, a site of a large EPA facility. The tee shirt proudly boasted:

EPA—WE REGULATE THE CRAP OUT OF AMERICA'S AIR.

A rebuttal tee shirt was subsequently created by some enterprising folks:

EPA REGULATES THE CRAP OUT OF AMERICA'S AIR...
NO WONDER IT'S FULL OF SHIT!

Membership was increasing everywhere—but in the U.P. it was skyrocketing. Town meetings, secret and public, were occurring at an unprecedented level. Already, 70 percent of the adult citizens in the Upper Peninsula were bona fide members of the American Patriots.

◆

BILL FLETCHER WAS SITTING IN HIS STUFFY, FLORESCENT-lit Detroit office in the Robert McNamara Building. There was only one window to the outside and it didn't open. The ventilation system had not been updated since the building was constructed in the early 70's, or was it earlier? In any event, it sure as heck was before all the hub-hub about sick office buildings and the need to circulate fresh air.

Bill had a corner office on the top of the three floors occupied by the FBI. Despite his standing as the top agent in Detroit, Bill's office was just big enough to fit a bank of file cabinets that housed seemingly thousands of case histories, his steel desk and credenza, his matching leather executive chair, and two gray, bent-steel and vinyl-covered visitor's chairs. All in all, except for the stale air, it wasn't too shabby. But what the hell did it matter? Bill didn't persevere through his FBI career for the office perks. He had joined to satisfy his desire to do what was right—at least that's what he had been telling himself lately. Just last year he had put the biggest feather in his cap with the successful prosecution of three crime bosses in Detroit. He had hoped that it would turn his career around, erase the big question mark on his record. But the word was, he wasn't going anywhere at anytime in the foreseeable future. And not a day went by when he didn't think about his idiot partner taking bribe money. And all the while, his charmed little brother continued to rise higher and higher.

Bill reached over to his "in" basket and picked up a memo about some Russian missiles that were suspected of being shipped to Michigan by way of the Great Lakes. Wonderful. His early years with the Agency had been in Kansas and Iowa. He knew nothing of shipping and would have to learn fast. He made a mental note to ask his secretary to find someone from the East or West Coast who could help.

The next item in the basket was the report generated by Tim and Cindy. They and the two teams of agents reporting to them were halfway through the Radio Shack records and expected to be done within the week. It turned out that, for several years, the chain had operated a unique marketing scheme whereby the store clerks routinely entered into the point-of-sale computers all purchasers' names, addresses and telephone numbers. That data was then automatically linked to the items purchased. Most items were identified by part numbers. There was one problem, however. Upon a cross-check of the records, it appeared that over a dozen stores had not supplied records.

Bill picked up the phone and called Tim. What he learned gave him an instant case of heartburn. The stores which had not provided records had all had some type of computer malfunction. In several cases, the computers were reported to have crashed and the information was wiped out. Apparently no one even knew whether they could find all the broken computers. They hadn't been in use for so long it was feared they were unobtainable.

◆

CHAPTER 24

I T WAS MID-AFTERNOON AND THE SUN WAS BRIGHT RED AS it drooped toward the horizon. Bradley was speeding in his Volvo sedan west along the country road to Anne's house. He fought the sun's glare, twisting his head at various angles to take advantage of the visor. There were also slick spots that occasionally caused his knuckles to turn white. He would talk to Anne and get to the bottom of things once and for all.

After their last love-making in his office, Anne had suddenly gotten sick and abruptly left. Since then, she had not called nor had she answered her telephone. Damn caller ID. He had even tried to block his ID, but when he did, her telephone rejected the call and gave him a very curt message.

So the only alternative was to drive out and stand on her porch. He was wearing a pretty heavy jacket so he figured he could ring her doorbell for a long time.

It took 20 minutes.

Anne finally opened the door and let him in. Bradley suspected that what had caused his plan to work was the fact that her two Miniature Schnauzers had been barking nonstop.

Bradley stepped into the entryway. Anne didn't offer to take his coat. She stood with her arms crossed as if she were on a mission herself.

He wanted to go to her. "What in the heck did I do, Anne?"

"You're a professor."

"Yes, and hoping for tenure. But what does that—" It dawned on him. "How did you do on the LSAT?"

"Ninety-ninth percentile."

Anne looked away, but not before Bradley caught a glimpse of a tear running down her cheek.

She said, her face to the wall, "I'm not going to go to law school." She wiped a tear away with the back of her hand.

"What?" It was an automatic question. He had heard her perfectly well, but was stalling for time to digest the information. She had done well enough to get accepted to Michigan Law, but had decided to forego law school all together. She must be concerned that ethics rules would prohibit their relationship.

He wondered whether he could ask her to go to a lesser school, such as Wayne State. The general rule was to attend the best school to which one was accepted, and Michigan Law was one of the great prizes. From Anne's practice tests it had seemed she would place herself into a good regional school—not one of the top two or three in the nation.

Attending Michigan would mean they couldn't continue their relationship. And Anne appeared to have decided to go to Michigan. That explained cutting off the relationship. But it didn't explain why she wouldn't go to *any* law school.

He was still missing something.

"Why not go to Wayne State? It's not a bad school. Or, with that score, you can probably go anywhere: Berkeley, Chicago, maybe Stanford or Yale. Harvard?" He knew he was fishing.

She looked him in the eye. "Wayne State is just not practical. From my house on the west side of Ann Arbor, it's over an hour drive. And I'm just not going to drive into the heart of Detroit every day. It's way too dangerous. And there's no way I'd move."

Bradley knew he couldn't argue with the danger presented with driving to and from Detroit. The place had degenerated into a virtual kill zone for white people crazy enough to go there. The situation was making his stomach start to knot. "But when you took the LSAT, you didn't really think you would be able to get into U of M, so hadn't you considered driving to one of the Detroit schools, or to Michigan State in Lansing?"

"Not really." Anne reached for a tissue on a nearby table and blew her nose.

So that meant she had to go to Michigan. She couldn't miss the opportunity of a lifetime. But if she goes… That opened up a can of worms. It would be a risk to his career if he continued to see her. Yet he wanted her. He needed her. And, he sensed, she needed him. He wondered if she would allow him to take such a risk… Finally, he understood.

She didn't want him to take the risk—so she had tried to cut off the relationship. It must have ripped her heart out. Well nuts to that. This was the love of a lifetime. It was worth the risk. He stepped closer. "I want you to go to law school here at Michigan."

Anne put both of her hands to the sides of her face. Tears still rolled down her cheeks. Her eyes were bloodshot. "But what about us? It's too dangerous for you."

"Look, Anne, you must take advantage of the opportunity you have. You owe that to yourself, regardless of me. As for the "us" part of it, somehow I will manage it. I have to. For you—and for me."

Anne blinked and turned her face away. "I can't let you. It's not just about us."

Bradley squinted. "What?"

Again facing the wall, she said, "I can't tell you. But there is something." Anne started crying in heaves. "Please, Bradley. Go. I can't see you!" She ran out of the entryway and was quickly out of sight.

Bradley heard the bedroom door close and he could just make out the muffled sounds of crying.

He had no intention of leaving. He walked to the bedroom and slowly opened the door. She was sitting on the bed, trying to stop crying and wiping her eyes with the backs of her hands. He walked over and sat on the edge of the bed. "Please, whatever it is, we can work it out." He put his arm around her, and she leaned into him and put her head on his shoulder. He raised her head to his and kissed her tear-stained lips. They tasted salty. She smelled of perfume and warm skin. He kissed her deeply. She seemed to melt into his arms. "Anne, I think I am falling in love with you." He reclined onto the bed, pulling her with him…

⟶

ANNE WAS IN THE KITCHEN WAITING FOR JEFF TO COME home from work. She had just flipped on the table-top TV and caught the tail end of a report about a winter storm warning. She walked over to the window and noted, in the receding light of dusk, that the skies were clear for as far as the eye could see.

There was already some snow cover, but it was just enough to frustrate the snow lovers. She was just thinking that she must have missed the part of the weather report that said the storm wasn't due until the next day when Jeff walked in. She was ready and had planned on wasting no time in getting to the point.

"All right, Buster Brown, what's going on with you and the patriots?" Jeff did a double take and set his Coleman lunch box on the kitchen table. He sighed and slumped down on one of the bar stools.

"You don't want to know."

"Wanna bet?"

"Mom," Jeff glanced up with a smile, "if I tell you, then I'll have to kill you." He appeared to be struggling to keep his smile.

"Not going to work. I want to know what is going on in my house. You may be putting me at risk. You may be putting Bradley Fletcher at risk… that is, if you haven't already."

Jeff's face seemed to lose some of its color and took on a pained expression. The corners of his eyes wrinkled and he ran his hand over his face. He looked down at his feet and then into Anne's face.

"Mom, I'm sorry. Truth is, Miles and I swore to secrecy. And quite literally, our lives could be at risk if I tell you too much. So you will just have to trust me."

Anne nodded and put one hand on the bar stool just in case Jeff really blew her away.

"Okay. We're careful to do nothing illegal, but we work out of the fort in the garage…"

When he was done, Anne was glad she had grabbed the bar stool. The world was falling apart, figuratively and literally. And it was being orchestrated from her barn! By her son! By her ex-husband! By the son of her best friend! All on top of her dilemma with Bradley. It was just too much. *Way* too much. Her head felt like a pressure cooker whistling and bulging and ready to blow. It was hot, overstressed, and screaming for release.

But what in the hell should she do? What *could* she do?

"Mom, you okay?"

Anne could feel her legs begin to shake and wobble. She thought of running out the back door and across the fields. She wouldn't stop. Ever…

Instead, she turned herself around, still holding the bar stool for support, and peered into the living room. There, against the back wall, partially obscured by the big, comfy leather couch, was the liquor cabinet. It had cut crystal doors and Anne could see the image, all shimmery through the crystal, of a tall bottle of vodka. She lifted her hand from the stool and stood for a moment, making sure she still had enough balance to make the trip. Unsteadily, she put one foot in front of the other until she was at the liquor cabinet. She slowly opened the crystal door and pulled out the bottle of Belvedere.

"Mom, what are you doing?" Jeff had followed her into the living room.

Anne paused, her back to Jeff, and she put both hands on the cabinet.

"Mom, don't."

Anne reached into the cabinet and pulled out a double old fashioned glass in her favorite, exquisitely cut Waterford crystal. She set it on the cabinet with a loud clank. With both hands she gripped the Belvedere Polish Vodka and twisted the cap, breaking the seal.

"Mom, I can't let you do this."

Anne turned to face Jeff. She glared at him and he seemed to get the message. She turned back around, grabbed the glass with her left hand, the bottle with her right, and brought them together. She poured the glass full and set both the bottle and tumbler on the cabinet. She stared at her drink for a moment, mesmerized by the reflections in the multifaceted cuts in the fine crystal. Otherwise, her mind was blank. There was no feeling. No anger. Just emptiness.

She reached out with both hands, grabbed the crystal and slowly, solemnly, brought it to her lips.

Anne stayed in bed for most of three days. Polishing off half a bottle of the Belvedere vodka had ensured a titanic hangover. And to go with the hangover, she had a flaming case of heartburn. Most of the time she tossed and turned in that ugly middle ground, unable to sleep or to wake up. Way too many thoughts were raging through her mind; Jeff would take center stage, and she imagined him in full military dress, only to be quickly gunned down by Bradley, or Hartman, or by the police storming her house.

On the third day of wretchedness, she found in her mail box a large envelope from the University of Michigan Law School. Of course, she had expected to gain admission, given the published profiles of past entering classes, but it was still a shock to receive what she assumed to be the letter of acceptance.

Without opening it she flicked it like a Frisbee. She watched it spin into a corner of her bedroom, smack against one wall and then the other, and fall ingloriously to the floor.

Anne slumped back in bed and, for the first time in three days, finally slept soundly.

She woke at five the next morning. But it was not the usual way of slowly coming to, needing several cups of coffee to even hold a simple conversation. This was more like being ejected from a fitful dream—a dream which she couldn't remember, but which heaved her out of bed at once fully awake, aware.

And angry.

She sat up in bed. It took a moment to figure out the object of her anger. She ran down the list: Jeff, Bradley, Hartman. But none of them seemed to be it. Something made her glance at the floor in the corner of the bedroom where she saw envelope from the law school. She got up to get it.

There was a nice letter congratulating her for such brilliant academic and non-academic achievements, along with other admission materials. Anne read and reread every word of the admissions packet as she puttered around the house. She studied the pictures in the Law School Bulletin, which was apparently the school's primary promotional piece. The students looked so smart.

So thoughtful. So thoroughly qualified. And the professors seemed, well, they just looked so much like professors.

Anne glanced at the vodka bottle, half-empty, on her night stand. She had a sudden and uncontrollable gag response. Fortunately, there was nothing in her stomach to come up.

The object of her anger began to dawn on her. It wasn't pretty. But there was no one else. She was angry with herself. The letter from the University of Michigan Law School made that clear—or, rather, the bottle of Belvedere and the letter.

The contrast was bewildering.

In the acceptance letter, she saw herself battling through the difficulties of studying for, and then taking, the LSAT; she saw herself fulfilling, in some way, her life's ambition to excel in the arts; she saw a woman recovered from the ravages of poor decisions, lousy luck, and an opportunistic society.

In the bottle of booze she saw the ease and comfort of her life slipping away—giving way to the forces that pushed her to this brink. In that scene, however, she saw a disappointed son, a distraught best friend, a lost love… But most of all she saw a woman totally, utterly, and irrevocably destroyed.

Despite the events whirling around her, one thing was clear: she had to attend Michigan Law School. Attending Michigan meant fixing what was broken. That was the first priority. The rest she would take one at a time. She would talk more with Jeff about what he was really doing, she would avoid Bradley until she felt stronger, and she would end their relationship.

She wouldn't let Bradley change her mind. But to resist him, well, she knew it would take a little time before she was strong enough.

❧

CHAPTER 25

BILL FLETCHER HAD ORDERED BACKGROUND CHECKS ON a 1,000-plus names that were linked with one or more of the parts used in the scanner, and he had ordered immediate surveillance on several people who were linked to the purchase of all major component parts. The problem was that a dozen stores, including the Ann Arbor Radio Shack, had lost or somehow garbled their records. It took weeks to find all of the broken-down computers, many of which had been buried deep in spare rooms or even sold to parts dealers.

All but two of the computers were eventually tracked down and sent to the FBI's National Cyber Investigative Joint Task Force in Washington, D.C. One of those computers, however, had met a particularly cruel fate. Having been pulled off the line at Radio Shack for hard drive failure, it had sat in a corner and then on a loading dock, where a hi-lo driver had skewered it with the long metal forks of his lift. And it had been a bullseye. The outer case of drive itself had been partially folded, and it looked more like a boomerang than a computer hard drive. The technicians at the FBI could see this was a situation that called for the heavies, and the boomerang drive was sent off to the Defense Computer Forensics Laboratory inside the Department of Defense's Cyber Crime Center, known affectionately as "DC3."

In the old days, DC3 conducted hard drive repair and recovery in what are known as "clean boxes," which resemble a neonatal intensive care unit, where doctors can reach in and touch extremely premature babies without subjecting them to germs in the environment. With the increase in cyber crime and cyber terrorism, the Department of Defense installed a state-of-the-art clean room, located deep within the DC3 facility. Visitors and employees were required to don an outfit that resembled an astronaut's space suit. Once past the thumb-print recognition security gate, an air shower that blew gale force winds over every square inch of one's body, and air-lock doors that made a swishing sound when they opened and closed, newcomers were usually struck by the omnipresent drone created by the multimillion dollar air filtration equipment.

The room was, in fact, an electronics laboratory configured like a small war room. Large monitors were set in a semi-circle along one wall, and facing the monitors were several rows of desks with all manner of computers and electronic testing equipment.

Such was the workplace for Special Agent Holly Nesterbrant. Holly, at 29, was one of the bright computer experts working for the Department of Defense. She was just a bit shorter than a full six feet tall and had long blond hair. A bombshell she was, a dummy she wasn't. Her Masters in Computer Science from MIT, earned magna cum laude, made it apparent that she was at home, and comfortable, in the cyberworld of bits and bytes.

The space-age setup was a function more of the need for cleanliness than of any need for security or technological sophistication. Indeed, the Department of Defense had learned the same lesson computer component manufacturers had learned; even ordinary dust particles have electrical charges that tend to wreak havoc on the highly sensitive media used to manufacture memory components.

In this case, Holly had disassembled the boomerang hard drive and had mounted the fractured pieces of the disk onto the DC3's latest toy: a Magnetic Force Microscope that looked more like Doc Emmett's Flux Capacitor in *Back To The Future* than a microscope.

Jennifer Polaski, a rather plain looking but also quite bright summer intern from Georgetown University, had just come into the clean room and was watching intently, trying to learn. She said, "Holly, this all still amazes me. You know? It's like electricity. I can't see it, so I don't believe it really works."

"Yeah, I know what you mean," Holly gave a tired laugh—she had already put in a full day's work.

"But really, Holly, as much as I know about circuits and stuff, I really don't understand anything about computer media storage. It was one of the classes I got bumped out of last semester. What exactly are you doing? What is it you are looking for?"

Holly sighed. "Good questions. A fact not well understood, Jenn, is that all information a computer receives, processes, and then kicks out is contained in a series of ones and zeros. On a computer's hard disk, for example, there are concentric rings, or tracks, sort of like the tracks on an old phonograph record, except the disk is coated with a material that can hold magnetic charges in those tracks. The tracks are subdivided into very small blocks of disk space. When the hard drive's head passes over the individual blocks, a current runs through the head and that current magnetizes a small area, causing the magnetic particles on the disk to be rearranged. If the current in the head flows in one direction, the particles are arranged to face north, if the current flows in the opposite direction, the particles face south. An area with north-oriented particles represents a one and an area with south-oriented particles represents a zero."

"A binary system."

"Exactly. Think of Morse Code; it communicates by sequences of dots and dashes. A computer works basically the same way, and is able to make out numerals, letters, and, ultimately, quite complex commands, by stringing together ones and zeros, referred to as bits, in specific orders. There are eight bits to a byte. A simple keyboard stroke of the letter "A" might be transmitted to the computer's CPU as 11011000, which is a byte."

"So, the hard drive's head then passes over the platter's sectors and alternates its current to orient the particles, say, north, north, south, north, north, and so on, eight times to constitute a byte."

"Yup."

Jennifer leaned a little closer to the screen to see what Holly was looking at. Holly continued, "The first computers didn't have anything like this hard disk I'm working on. They had to store the ones and zeros in a monstrous sequence of 'on' or 'off' valves. Computers occupied entire city blocks. And now look at it."

Holly leaned away from the monitor so Jennifer could get a closer look. Holly was mapping the individual magnetic grains which had been oriented north or south when the platter had been intact and installed in a Radio Shack computer. Each magnetic field was about 10 nanometers in size.

Jennifer said, "It looks like a million little ridges all lined up in perfect symmetry and all in concentric circles. There are millions of them! Billions!"

Holly nodded. "Ten nanometers, Jen. A piece of paper is about 180,000 nanometers thick. So, there are about 18,000 little hash marks, each one representing a one or a zero, in space the thickness of a piece of paper—on every one of those rings."

"And there must be a thousand rings!" Jennifer blurted and shook her head. "Unbelievable. So how does this Magnetic Force Microscope work?"

"Well, it has an incredibly tiny head that is very slightly magnetized, and it sits on the end of a very flexible and cantilevered arm. And the arm is indexed by a laser beam. So, when the arm moves over the little nanometer-sized fields, it moves up or down an infinitesimally small amount depending on the polarity of the field on the disk. And the laser recognizes the movement and records a one or a zero. The problem, obviously, is we have to do this manually because the platter is busted into three pieces so it won't spin. If we could spin it we could do this in a hot second."

Jennifer stepped back from the monitor to look at the disk pieces in the middle of the machine. It resembled a plate full of lasagna that she had recently seen in the bottom of a picnic bag that had been dropped. The lasagna had kept the pieces of the plate pretty much in orientation to each other. But busted to hell it was. "So what happens when the ones and zeros span one of the cracks in the disk?"

Holly smiled. The youngster was catching on fast. "That's the hard part. In the space of the crack and the fragmented edges we could possibly lose an entire Tom Clancy novel." She looked at Jennifer. "Let's hope that's not where the important stuff is."

❧

SHOPPING FOR HER FIRST SEMESTER TEXTBOOKS WAS AS fascinating as it was unnerving. Linda had offered to come along, but Anne was beginning to wonder if it was just to make sure she was really going through with this law school thing. She and Linda had shouldered their way through the crowded entrance into Ulrich's, one of the local college bookstores. Initially, Anne was taken by the piles and piles of books stacked anywhere and everywhere they would fit. There must have been tens of thousands of books. Some of the stacks were higher than she could reach. Next to each stack, or sometimes stuck between books in the stack, was a small card with scrawled handwriting that identified the title and the class for which that book had been requested by the professor. There was everything from huge medical texts to tiny Penguin Classic paperbacks. There was even a whole wall dedicated to Cliff Notes and similar publications. It appeared that one could purchase "summaries" or "outlines" for virtually every major text and for most classes offered by the university.

Finally, Linda and Anne made it to the legal section. There, things turned from fascinating to unnerving. The legal texts were enormous. They were completely unwieldy. And they were expensive! Several books pushed over the $200 mark. Anne had wondered why there was a row of shopping carts just past the entrance; it should have been a warning. Each book seemed to be bigger and thicker than the previous: Criminal Law, Torts, Constitutional Law, Contracts, Property.

Plus, any book printed more than a few months ago required a supplement that was usually at least half as thick as the original.

Anne thought wryly that she might need a second mortgage on her home to pay for everything.

Anne picked up the text on torts. "What the heck is a tort? Sounds like something to bake."

"Miles says it's a cookbook on how to destroy America."

"Clever pun. Did he mean it?"

"Sometimes he has these half-baked ideas." Linda rolled her eyes, smiled coyly, and hunched her shoulders. Anne rarely saw Linda make a pun, but when she did, she always acted like it was something she couldn't help. Anne made an exaggerated frown and both women laughed.

But inside Anne screamed.

She hadn't told Linda anything about their sons' involvement in the patriots. She was terrified of what Linda might do. Would she turn them in? Just Miles? And if just Miles, would that inevitably implicate Jeff? Yet, Linda was her best friend and she had never had secrets. Linda knew her life story, and Anne knew Linda's. Anne tried to keep her mind on her shopping. She picked up, *American Constitutional Law: Cases and Comments,* and studied the cover. It was written by Bradley. Linda glanced over Anne's shoulder to see what she was looking at. Anne said, "The Supreme Court is in the news almost daily. I keep seeing ACORN ads for turning the AAAA pay-equalization supplement into a constitutional amendment."

"That the Agency for Advancement of Affirmative Action?" asked Linda.

Anne glanced at her and nodded.

Linda said, "Miles says the Supreme Court has run wild granting rights to everyone. He says the patriots have it right; they believe it should be strictly—"

Anne suddenly felt dizzy and bumped into a stack of books at the end of the aisle, sending 20 or so books crashing to the floor. Anne knew she had to sit down before she toppled head-long into something. "Look at clumsy me," she said, hoping to cover her unstable condition. A book store worker rushed over and began stacking the fallen books. He gave Anne an indignant look and she glared back. The nerve of him. It was an accident.

Linda said, "Oh, anyhow, it's all a bunch of nonsense. Somebody is always complaining about something. Let's get to the register." They headed to the front of the store and Anne began to unload her books onto the counter. Linda chuckled, "Actually, now that I'm thinking about it, maybe Miles is a closet militia type."

The woman behind the register gave a wide-eyed glance at Linda. Anne was glad Linda was standing behind her and couldn't see her face, because she was sure it was white as a ghost. Anne knew she had to do something to feign humor at what Linda obviously believed were outrageous and unthinkable assertions about her son. Without glancing back, Anne did her best to sound light and airy: "Yeah, right. A regular Mark from Michigan."

‹ə›

CHAPTER 26

FIVE PAGES INTO THE FIRST CHAPTER OF *American Constitutional Law: Cases and Comments*, and Anne was intrigued. She was sitting at her kitchen table, *Black's Law Dictionary* at her side, reading the decision by the United States Supreme Court in the case of *Marbury v. Madison*. It wasn't anything like she had imagined. The case reflected a battle that was waged at the highest levels of the young republic's government. *Marbury* was, the text explained, the most epochal case in the history of the United States Supreme Court. To the litigants, it was a matter of personal wealth, accomplishment, fame, and national security.

On February 27, 1801, the holdover Federalist Congress passed the Circuit Court Act that authorized lame-duck President Adams to pack the court with 42 justices. President Adams quickly appointed staunch Federalists, and they were confirmed by the Senate on March 3. John Marshall, Adams's Secretary of State, attempted to deliver the commissions that evening—since the next day the Republicans and Thomas Jefferson were to take office.

Upon taking office the following morning, the Republicans were delighted to discover that some of the sealed commissions had not been delivered. President Jefferson, through his Secretary of State, James Madison, refused to deliver the remaining commissions.

William Marbury was one of the justices who had not received his commission. With his legal career thus threatened, he filed suit in the United States Supreme Court against Secretary of State, James Madison, seeking a writ of mandamus to compel Madison to deliver the commission.

The trouble, according to the Supreme Court, came from the fact that plaintiff Marbury's status was not such as to give the court jurisdiction to hear his claim. The court's jurisdiction was established by the United States Constitution. Anne flipped to the Appendix and read the text of Article Three. She found the pertinent part:

> In all cases affecting ambassadors, other public ministers and consuls, ... the Supreme Court shall have original jurisdiction. In all other cases ... the Supreme Court shall have appellate jurisdiction.

> *U.S. Constitution, Article Three, Section Two.*

Nowhere was original jurisdiction provided for an aggrieved judge. However, Marbury claimed that the court's original jurisdiction had recently been expanded by the Judiciary Act of 1789, and therefore the court could hear his suit.

Chief Justice John Marshall who, interestingly, as President Adams's Secretary of State, was the person who had failed to deliver Marbury's commission, wrote the opinion of the court. It seemed easy enough to understand. Marshall made two primary points:

» The Supreme Court was the final arbiter of the Constitution, and

» The Supreme Court had power to disallow acts of Congress or the president that violated the Constitution.

Thus, to the extent that the Judiciary Act purported to expand the court's jurisdiction as set forth in the Constitution, it was in violation of the Constitution to try to increase that jurisdiction. Accordingly, the court could not act on Plaintiff Marbury's request.

That made sense. The Supreme Court frequently overruled federal laws.

Anne read the case again just to make sure she understood it. This time, however, something made her wonder about the

Supreme Court's assertion of its authority to disallow acts of
Congress or the president. She didn't recall anything like that from
her reading of Article Three of the United States Constitution. She
flipped back to the Appendix and, sure enough, *the court's power to
overrule Congress or the president was not in the text of the Constitution.*

How could this be? How could the Supreme Court claim for itself
such a power?

Anne put the book down, walked to the counter, and started
brewing a pot of coffee. As she watched it drip into the decanter,
she recalled Linda's comments about Miles's anger over the way
federal and state courts have granted rights that, apparently, they
had no authority to grant... *That must be what the patriots are angry
about—one of the things, anyhow. Interesting...* The *Marbury* court did
its own version of granting rights it had no legal authority to grant;
it seized for itself the power to overrule the other branches of government.
Could the unabated proliferation of "rights" go all the way back to
Marbury?

When the coffee was finished brewing, Anne poured a cup and
headed back to the kitchen table. She opened the text to the table
of contents and scanned it. There was a section titled, "Substantive
Due Process: Constitutional Rights in Modern Society." She opened
to the section and read a case that sounded familiar: *Roe v. Wade...*

Okay, so in *Roe v. Wade* the Supreme Court invalidated state
laws that prohibited abortions. What was the big deal? The court
granted a limited right to an abortion based on the right to privacy in the Constitution. It certainly made sense; it seemed the
right thing to do. Women should have a right to the privacy of their
bodies.

Out of curiosity, Anne picked up the casebook and flipped back
again to the Constitution. This time she read it from start to finish...

There was *nothing* about a right to privacy, and nothing at all
about abortions.

She reread *Roe v. Wade*. Now how in the heck did the court grant
a right and claim it was from the Constitution, when it was not

BY FORCE OF PATRIOTS   •   PAGE 353

listed or even mentioned in the Constitution? What was going on here? Maybe she was missing something…

The next morning, Anne's heart was fluttering with excitement as she stood at the base of the steps heading up into the University of Michigan Law School. It was approaching eight A.M. and already she could tell it was going to be a sunny day. She had parked her car about a quarter mile away. The walk was invigorating and the air fragrant with the smells of late spring. To her left there were several cherry trees on the lawn of the law school and they were in full bloom. The grass had just been cut and smelled of watermelons; at least that's what she always thought fresh-cut grass smelled like.

Anne wanted the moment to last and she inhaled deeply. She shifted her leather briefcase for the umpteenth time; it held her books for her three morning classes, and the things were so heavy the leather strap kept digging into her shoulder. No wonder so many law students carried those big, ugly, hiker's back packs with thick, padded straps.

Students were bustling past her up the deeply worn steps. Anne wondered how many thousands of students had walked here. And they seemed in such a hurry! For a brief moment, she had a panicky feeling that maybe she had miscalculated and was late. A quick glance at her watch made the panic go away. She had time—almost 10 minutes. She intended to loiter her way to the classroom, savoring the sensation of life anew.

Anne stepped into her first law class and was immediately breathless and overcome with an awe for, well… everything. There was the strikingly alert and youthful appearance of her classmates. She hadn't really noticed their faces as they bustled helter-skelter outside and then in the corridors of the law school. But now things were different, more immediate and real. Everyone looked so smart—stunningly smart, actually.

And then there was the classroom. It had an antique and stately sheen that conjured thoughts of brilliant minds debating lofty legal principles. Anne stood just inside the door to the large classroom and gaped at the 20 or so rows of dark-stained wood tables, spanning continuously from one side of the room to the other, set off in concentric semi-circles emanating from the front podium to the back wall of the room. The chairs were evenly spaced behind all of the curved rows, which were flanked on both sides by stairs that led upwards, as in a typical auditorium, toward the back of the room. Along the entire length of the outside wall were cathedral-like windows that rose majestically to the high ceiling covered with ornate carvings. The windows had bottom panes that opened with brass metal latches so darkened with age and use that their original shine and color were barely perceptible.

And there, right in front of her, taking seats and spreading out their note pads and law texts, were the people against whom… Anne's reverence turned abruptly to competitiveness. Awed she was; naive she wasn't. This was one of the most competitive schools in the nation, or so she had read. These were students who would guard their opinions prior to a class so that you could not steal their thunder in front of a professor. They would protest that they were confused, behind in assignments, and barely studying when, in fact, they were enlightened, probably two cases ahead, and studying voraciously. These were people who would feign a willingness to help, yet actually hope for you to fail.

So there was going to be an ugly side to law school. Oh well. Wasn't it always the case? She tried to shake it off and search for a friendly face; that's where she would sit. There, in the first row of students (the third row of seats), was a smiling young man with a boyish face that reminded her of Jeff. She made a beeline for the open seat to his right and sat down. He didn't look at her and she wondered if the friendly face was a sham. God, she hoped it wasn't starting already! There would be plenty of time to be competitive. And when that time came, damn it, she was going to be as good as any of these kids. Anne glanced at the clock at the front of the room. It was 8:00. She sat up straight and opened her constitutional law text to *Marbury v. Madison*. She was ready.

Bradley rushed into the classroom about a minute late, at least according to the clock on the wall, and quickly stepped up behind the lectern. He set his text down and reached into several pockets before pulling his reading glasses out of the left, inside pocket of his sport coat. He placed the glasses on the text and looked out over the class; he did a double take when he saw Anne in the first row of students. He seemed agitated, even flustered, and she hoped it wasn't over her. Then she reproved herself for such an arrogant thought. Sure, she had not called him since their last meeting—*when was it? Must have been a month ago. Was it two?* And no doubt, he had been initially angry, probably distraught. After all, he had claimed that he loved her. She thought, *Imagine that. And so soon.* Well, anyhow, she was sure it was over, as it needed to be.

She had gone over it a million times. Not to put too fine a point on it, but Bradley was simply too dangerous to her son. Moreover, Bradley's life hardly seemed big enough to accommodate her. He was so centered on his career and his drive to attain tenure. She couldn't ask him to risk it all by violating some university prohibition against dating students. No. It was best to just cut it off before it became impossible to do so.

Bradley was still looking out over the class when he flipped opened his text. His reading glasses, sitting on the cover of the text, were flung high into the air, landed on the floor, and skidded to a stop against the adjacent wall. Abruptly, Bradley turned to retrieve his glasses and his shoulder caught the side of the lectern and sent it teetering; he hurriedly turned back and steadied it. Unfortunately, he didn't move fast enough and his text slid off and flopped to the floor. It landed open, with its pages facing down and awkwardly bent.

Bradley glanced up at the class, smartly straightened his bow tie with both hands, and said, "I sure hope everyone has read the assignment." It broke the class up that had been, to that point, in a state of shock. As the class continued to laugh, Bradley collected his glasses, his text, and himself.

He asked, "Assume the following: the year is 1803 and you are the president of the United States, which has criminal procedure developed to current standards; your Marines have been battling Islamic

pirates in Tripoli, and a number of pirates have been captured
and interrogated; the Supreme Court has just ruled that you must
release your prisoners because you failed to issue Miranda warnings
before they were interrogated. Would you comply?"

A young man three seats to the side of Anne raised his hand. He
must be one of the "gunners" she had heard about. They were the
ones who most wanted to impress. Bradley pointed to him.

"Yes. *Marbury v. Madison* held that the Supreme Court was the
final arbiter of the Constitution and that the court could command
both the executive and legislative branches."

"Okay, that's a good start."

Anne noticed that the young man looked perplexed, apparently
thinking he had nailed the answer. A couple more hands went up
and Bradley pointed to another young man. This one, Anne thought,
was a throwback to the '60s, complete with tie-dyed tee shirt, long
scraggly hair, and sandals.

"Dude, he has to. In *The Federalist Papers*, Hamilton explained
that the court should act as a check on the legislature and executive.
It's part of the checks and balances, man."

Anne thought his tone was a little condescending, as if he
regarded the question as too easy. Apparently, Bradley got the same
impression. He shot back, "What authority is that on the president?
The Federalist Papers are interesting to read, and give us insights
into what the founding fathers were thinking, but they are not law."

Out of the corner of her eye, Anne could see Mr. "Dude" flush
red in embarrassment. Her own stomach began to turn slightly as
she realized how emotionally charged everyone seemed to be. This
was looking to be serious.

Then, to her total amazement, she was raising *her* hand. As it
hung in the air, she thought of pulling it down, since Bradley apparently did not see it right away. Something kept it there, however,
and she felt a lump in her throat as Bradley turned his head toward
her. *Oh God*, she thought, glancing around. He couldn't avoid her.
She was the only one with a raised hand!

Bradley seemed determined to avoid her, however, as he paused and looked around the room to see whether anyone else had a hand in the air. Anne looked around again. Nope. She was the only one. Bradley pointed to her.

Anne's voice quivered slightly, "In 1803, I think the president would have told the Supreme Court to go fly a kite."

As soon as the words were out of her mouth, Anne noticed Bradley's face balloon out. He immediately exclaimed in a booming voice that startled everyone, "Five years! Five years!" He thrust out his right hand with five fingers out.

Anne was sure her heart stopped. From the corner of her eye she could see that everyone was looking at her. Mouths were wide open. Eyes were bugged out. Oh, God. How could she be so stupid! She had made a fool of herself. She glanced at the door and thought of making a run for it. She would never return... How could she have been so stupid as to think she could go to law school? She was a music major for Heaven's sake. Then, strangely, Anne became aware of Bradley talking again. His words started to filter back into her consciousness.

"... been asking that question for five years... For five years. And that's the first time anyone has ever gotten it right!"

What did he say? She looked around and noticed that the other students weren't looking at her in horror. It was more of a look of... envy? No. Couldn't be.

"In fact," Bradley said, "the Constitution, in Article Three, gives the judiciary power over all cases, in Law and Equity, arising under this Constitution, the Laws of the United States, and Treaties, etc. Article Six tells us that the Constitution is the supreme law of the land. But nowhere in the Constitution does it say that the judicial branch has authority over the executive or the legislative. And neither does it give the executive branch or the legislature authority over the judiciary. Thus, there is absolutely no reason to believe that a president would think the court could order him around. Not in 1803. But, Ms.—"

"Kreig," Anne interjected, smiling inwardly at his clever way of feigning that he didn't know her.

"What do you think would be the outcome today?"

"Well, up until Obama ignored several court orders to reinstitute drilling in the Gulf of Mexico, and when he ignored the Supreme Court's ruling that Obamacare was unconstitutional, which was shortly reversed when Justices Kennedy and Scalia were killed and subsequently replaced by Obama. Anyhow, previous to all that, absolutely. Presidents always followed the Supreme Court without even raising the question. Clinton did."

"Yes. Now let's get to the question of why for so long was there such a deference accorded a ruling of the Supreme Court."

Bradley pointed to the back of the class and Anne had to twist her head around to see. The woman looked to be somewhat older than the other classmates. Her clothes looked to be out of Cosmopolitan. Her accent was clearly European: "Marshall's assertion of the court's superior authority over the legislature and the executive was never seriously challenged because it favored the Republicans who took power. Moreover, the ruling did not confront either the legislative or executive branches; its great trick is that it did not require enforcement. The court merely declined to act on Marbury's request. Nobody, as you Americans say, beefed. Since then, federal courts have embarked on a course of statesmanship. Judges have felt it within their authority to perceive a natural or fundamental law and apply it to the facts of a case. Any time there is a gap in the law, such as occurred in the case of abortions, where something is not clearly set forth in your constitution and your Congress has not spoken, the court steps in and makes policy. It makes the law. In England, we have learned, this is a singularly unique component of your jurisprudence. It accounts, in part, for the fact that the United States Constitution is the shortest constitution of any nation in the world. Your federal courts just keep adding addenda in the form of opinions."

Wow, Anne thought. *She sure knows her stuff.* Apparently, Bradley was similarly impressed.

"Very good, Ms.—"

"Peacock. Karen Peacock."

"Well, Ms. Peacock, you impress with your knowledge."

"Thank you, Professor Fletcher. I was a political science major with an emphasis on American constitutional law. So you see, some of this is not particularly new to me. I trust I'm not out of line."

"Not at all, Ms. Peacock. But I'm interested in knowing whether your studies brought to light some of the more intriguing facts of the case. For example, Marshall never cited the language of the Judiciary Act that he felt unconstitutionally broadened the court's original jurisdiction. That's the only time that has ever happened. No other Supreme Court opinion has failed to cite the language on which it has ruled. Doesn't it strike some of you as odd?" Bradley glanced around the room.

He continued. "In fact, reread the material and I challenge any of you to come up with a solid defense of Marshall's textual argument, and tell me whether you think that he authorized later courts to read the Constitution expansively and engage in policy-making from the bench." Bradley paused to let everyone take notes.

"Further, consider whether it was unethical for Marshall to be involved in the decision, let alone write the opinion, when he was the very person who failed to deliver Marbury's commission."

Anne was mildly surprised at what Bradley was suggesting: that the Chief Justice of the Supreme Court had acted improperly.

Bradley walked to the other side of the room. "The majority of the members of the First Congress who passed the Judiciary Act had been delegates to the Constitutional Convention. They knew the limits they, themselves, had placed in the Constitution regarding the court's jurisdiction. Does anyone think it odd that they would shortly thereafter draft an Act in contravention, as Marshall claimed, of the Constitution they wrote?" Bradley glanced at the clock on the wall. Class was almost over. He said, "I want everyone to read the handout that has the text of the Religious and Cultural Sensitivities Act, as well as the so-called Un-American Act. That's the new federal law banning weapons and public discourse that is anti-gay, anti-open borders, pro-life, pro-gun; basically it bans discussion of conservative ideas. It's likely to be challenged, but so far no one has had the courage to be excoriated by the advocacy networks. Query whether someone would be prosecuted by the current administration for having the impertinence to challenge the law in court."

Bradley scanned the class and asked, "Any questions?"

There were none, or at least everyone was already afraid of speaking.

"Okay... I'll see everyone Wednesday. Sit where you want for the rest of the semester, since I will pass around a seating chart so that I can get to know your names."

And with that, Bradley walked out of the room. Anne was slightly miffed that he didn't even try to catch her eye as he left.

On the way home from classes, Anne thought about Bradley's class. She was still glowing from having correctly answered the Big Question, but she was troubled by the spin Bradley had put on the end of his lecture. She had understood his drift—that the Supreme Court will defy ethics and logic to arrive at the decision it wants. Yet it conflicted with her initial impression of the law and the courts as being above political riffraff. On the other hand, it certainly fit with the experience she and Hartman had undergone with the lawsuit against their printing business. In theory, the law was honorable; in practice, it was contemptuous.

And he had seemed so aloof... so... well, she could hardly blame him. She had been the one to cut things off. He must be hurt, and avoiding eye contact or any hint of familiarity was his way of coping. Anne tightened her jaw. If that was it, so be it.

So why couldn't she get him out of her mind? She chuckled to herself, recalling how he had tossed his glasses off the lectern, and then nearly upset the whole thing. And he had been so quick to recover, cracking a joke as he did. He really was good with the students. That was clear. They seemed to take to him.

As did she.

This was going to be a problem. She would be close to him several times a week, possibly several more times in chance crossings as they went their separate ways around the law school. It seemed that he could deal with it. But could she?

She wanted him. *By God*, she wanted him!

When Anne got home she immediately sat down on the couch in the living room and played with her puppies—she still liked to think of them as puppies even though they were mature adults. With tail wagging like crazy, Roni brought her toy-of-the-week and pushed it repeatedly into Anne's leg until Anne finally grabbed it away and tossed it across the room. Roni raced after it and brought it back, and immediately began pressing it into her leg. Meanwhile, Cara jumped up on the couch and wanted to get in Anne's face and lick it off. Inasmuch as Cara was generally successful in this endeavor, it made simultaneous play with Roni difficult, which, Anne presumed, was exactly Cara's intent. Suddenly Cara abbreviated her licking onslaught to snatch away Roni's toy and shake it violently back and forth as if it were a rodent her instincts had trained her to kill. When she appeared satisfied that Roni could no longer use it to gain Anne's attention, she abandoned it and returned her efforts to licking. Anne got up from the couch to get away from the reach of her demanding, but loving, puppies.

Anne landed at the finely polished mahogany table with ornately carved legs that sat in the middle of the small library. She pulled out her constitutional law material and started to read the Un-American Act.

Jeff walked in from a softball game. He was covered with dust, and his pants showed blood at the back of his left thigh.

She said, "Rough game?"

"No. We won. But it took me sliding in at the plate for the winning run. How was your first day of classes?"

"Just fantastic. It's really exciting. I've never been around so many very bright people. It is invigorating—and challenging." Jeff's eyes seemed to linger on her, and she wondered if she had a smudge or something on her face. And what if it had been there all day!

Quickly, she ran her hand over her face to check for the offending substance. She grabbed her purse and pulled out a mirror...
Nothing there.

Jeff said, "What are you doing? There's nothing on your face. I
was just noticing how good you look. In fact, you look great. I'm so
glad you enrolled in law school. And just think, soon I won't have to
worry about speeding tickets anymore."

Anne smiled. "Yeah, fat chance, Buster. I'm not going to law
school to bail your butt out of anything!" They both laughed and
grinned like kids. Jeff headed toward the kitchen. He was such
a wonderful son. Sure, he was into this patriot stuff. But he had
shown her some of the documents they published that cited past
Supreme Court decisions on the First Amendment that demonstrated their positions were clearly legal as the Constitution had
been interpreted for over 200 years. And as long as they didn't violate the Constitution, why shouldn't he be in an organization he
believed in? His patriot organization wanted to fix a lot of what
was wrong with the country. What was wrong with that? He had
even told her of their hope to peaceably establish a separate state
and possibly a sovereign nation composed of several other states
that wanted to secede. Well, she knew that the U.P. had wanted
separate statehood for a long time. And how realistic was that? In
the final analysis, Anne decided her son's patriot organization had
good intentions but was hopelessly underpowered to do anything
significant.

Anne yelled toward the kitchen, "Hey, Jeff!" He was probably
going to break out a beer. A moment later, Jeff walked back into
the library with a frosty bottle of Bell's Pale Ale in his hand. It was
already half-gone.

He burped, barely covering it with his hand, and said, "Yeah?"

"Have you heard anything about this new law President Wallmire
signed that bans guns as well as groups that advocate conservative
views?"

"Are you kidding? The Un-American Act sponsored by
Flamsteal? I'm just waiting for the DDF to come over to collect our

guns. Guns? What guns? I don't know anyone who owns any guns. Do you?"

"Aren't they registered? Can't the government just look up the records?"

"Oh, those guns! I have no idea where they went. Haven't seen a gun around here in—gosh, can't remember when."

"That won't fly, Jeff."

"They are going to have to prosecute most of the people in the country. No one I have talked to intends to turn over their guns. No way, no how. And what about your Mini Ruger 14 that was supposed to be turned in when the latest assault weapons ban went into effect? Hmmm?"

She kept forgetting about that gun. It was a semiautomatic rifle with a caliber larger than the .17HMR. So, technically, she was committing a crime by keeping it. And what about everyone else in the country, as Jeff said? Would they be willing to give up guns like her Remington 870 shotgun, the quintessential home-defense weapon? And her beloved custom .45? She'd have to give that up as well.

Nationwide confiscation would be a problem. Anne wasn't sure she would give up her .45 even if they came to the door looking for it. Jeff was right. People *were* going to resist giving up guns that protected them, that had been used to thwart violent attacks, and that offered a level of security no police force could. According to the news, the president was going to wait a bit after July 4 to allow voluntary compliance before he planned to send out the DDF. Apparently he knew there would be trouble. The question was, would people get violent over it? She wondered how this could happen in the United States of America? The Second Amendment was dead. The First Amendment was being ripped to shreds by the liberals. Her image of the law was being attacked, again. She'd been too depressed the last few years to pay much attention to Obama's, and then Wallmire's, revolutionary changes to America. Now, however, she was waking up—perhaps in the same way much of the nation was waking up—or more accurately, being roused out of bed by someone ripping off your covers, grabbing your pajamas, and throwing you out your own front door.

That hallowed image of the law and her law school—which only hours before had filled her mind—burst apart like the now virtually extinct incandescent light bulb caught between asphalt and a steam roller.

Jeff seemed to read her mind: "Messes up the concept of judicial review, doesn't it? Elections have consequences, don't they? A far left Supreme Court has allowed the Marxists to really advance their remake of the country. But, truth is, Mom, we were in serious trouble before Obama. We had allowed liberals to dominate our schools, inculcating their ideas of entitlements and wealth redistribution. We let them set the dialogue. They told us what we can say, what we're permitted to think."

"Inculcating?" That word seemed out of place coming from her blue-collar son.

"Hey, I've been reading a lot lately."

"Apparently you have. I'm impressed that you know stuff about judicial review. It's not something you encounter outside of fairly serious discussions of constitutional law. We are studying it in my con law class. I guess the patriots are more sophisticated than I thought. I just never pictured the Supreme Court as a political entity. It's supposed to be about insuring that no laws are passed by the federal government or the states that violate the Constitution. Seems to me you can read the Constitution, read the suspect law, and say yes or no, based on the language in the documents. What did the founding fathers write? What did they mean? What does the suspect law say? Does its operation trench on rights protected by or established in the Constitution? These seem to be fairly straight-forward questions. Politics shouldn't be a part of it. Sure, it takes a monster intellect to make some of the fine distinctions and analyze what is going on, and then elucidate it. But that is precisely why we should employ the brightest judges who will stick to the actual language of the Constitution. If they go beyond the Constitution, they must necessarily invoke their personal view of what should or shouldn't be. Like *Roe v. Wade*. There is NOTHING in the Constitution about a right of privacy in someone's body. That's hogwash. I like the *results* of the decision—I think it's a fair solution to an issue fraught with theological, religious, personal, and political beliefs. But it is *not* a solution that should have been created by nine old farts in Washington D.C. The solution should have been debated and found in the various states."

"But Mom, politics was part of it right from the start. President Adams, on his last day as president, tried to pack the court with 42 staunchly Federalist justices the day before the Republican Thomas Jefferson was to take office. That's how it got started. Marbury didn't get the papers—I guess they called it a 'commission,' that would have established his judgeship, and he sued to have the commission delivered. The Supreme Court said the Judicial Act that allowed President Adams to appoint the judges was a violation of the Constitution, when really it wasn't. After all, the same people who wrote the Judicial Act wrote the Constitution."

"Now how in the heck do you know about *Marbury v Madison*? We just covered it today in my con law class."

Jeff smiled. "We're not a bunch of dummies, Mom."

You could say that again, Anne thought. She put her hand to her forehead. She could feel a splitting headache coming on. "I'm going to lie down for a bit. This is just too much for one day." She got all the way to the bedroom and thought of one more question she just had to ask Jeff. She walked back out to the living room where he was sitting with his second Pale Ale and both puppies.

"What do you think would happen if the government started to crack down on your people?" She was terming everything in the abstract "your" people, because it made things less threatening.

"They already have. The FBI has arrested a number of people. Fortunately, they have been going after the real radicals. That's not us; we have a far superior communication system. And we have been very careful to limit what gets out in the public. Everything is very benign."

Anne relaxed a bit. "Well thank God for that. Just don't get radical on me."

"Oh, no problem, Mom. But remember: 'resistance to tyrants is obedience to God.'"

The smile was gone from Jeff's face. His tone was suddenly serious. Anne felt the hair on the back of her neck begin to tingle. "Where did you get that crazy idea?"

Jeff seemed to have something on the tip of his tongue, but he didn't answer.

Anne said, "I mean, that sounds like something some Islamist would say. Jeff, you're scaring me. I don't want you caught up in anything serious. I mean, screw this Un-American crap. I can see you ignoring that, as long as you are careful. But don't get into anything serious." She could feel her heart begin to pound. Jeff looked directly into her eyes. A chill raced across her skin.

Jeff turned and headed toward the bathroom. He disappeared around the corner and then, a moment later, reappeared.

He said, "That's a direct quote of Benjamin Franklin."

❧

The New York-Dubai Times

The Law & Courts
Poll: Most think Constitution calls for Supreme Court to Create Rights and Entitlements

NEW YORK—While a vast majority (92%) of Americans say the Supreme Court should adhere to the requirements set forth in the Constitution, most (68%) believe the Supreme Court should be free to establish rights that seem appropriate given current social and political realities. When asked whether the text of the Constitution identified a right to privacy in one's body, which right formed the basis for the court's ruling in *Roe v. Wade*, 78% of those polled said "yes."

This year's poll shows a significant increase in the public's awareness of constitutional issues. Indeed, a full 64% reported they had read at least a portion of the text of the Constitution in the last six months. That number compares with 54% from a year ago, and only 9% when the survey was first conducted in 2008.

Asked to discuss the results of the poll, constitutional expert Bradley Fletcher, Professor of Law at the University of Michigan, expressed surprise at the increase in readership of the Constitution, stating that, in years past, "Very few of my students have read the full text of the Constitution before they take my introductory class."

On the other hand, Professor Fletcher explained, he was not surprised at the public's erroneous view of the role of the Supreme Court. He said, "The court has been performing legislative functions for so long that the public has become accustomed to its activist role in society. So it's no wonder the general public is confused about the distinctions between social and political decisions that the Constitution leaves to the legislative branch, verses the scope of

PAGE 2, NEW YORK-DUBAI TIMES
MOST THINK COURTS SHOULD CREATE RIGHTS, CONT.

judicial review to be performed by the judiciary."

Professor Fletcher elaborated by noting that the issue decided in *Roe v. Wade* is a political and social matter best left for the legislative branches of the various states which, he said, "are singularly qualified to address the competing points of view."

The Constitution, Professor Fletcher noted, "is purposefully silent on social and political issues." The role of the United States Supreme Court, he said, "is to ensure that the legislature fairly considers all points of view, and makes its decision balancing such consideration with the expressed wishes of its constituents."

"When legislators leave the hard decisions to the Supreme Court," Professor Fletcher explained, "they are disregarding their constitutional responsibilities."

CHAPTER 27

ANNE AWOKE EARLY WITH A TERRIBLE HEADACHE. SHE had tossed and turned all night. Her mind was awash with thoughts of Bradley—could she risk a relationship? And if so, would he?; law school—the workload was oppressive, with time-consuming assignments in all five of her classes; Jeff—could he be getting himself in serious trouble?; the patriots—disconcerting as it was, it was beginning to appear that they had legitimate complaints; Benjamin Franklin—"Resistance to tyrants is obedience to God"; and the coming gun confiscation—news agencies were atwitter about people swearing that the only way the United Nations was getting their guns was to come in shooting. Her head was swirling.

She tossed her covers off, sat up, and grabbed the aspirin bottle from the nightstand. She needed instant relief and didn't want to take the time to get up and walk to the bathroom for water. She put four aspirin in her mouth, chewed, and nearly threw up.

After a moment of just sitting there, Anne stood and made her way to the bathroom. She glanced at herself in the mirror and was startled by what she saw. Splitting headache, chalky aspirin, and disheveled hair notwithstanding, her eyes seemed to have a fire behind them. There was an intensity she hadn't seen in years.

The front door of the house slammed shut and Anne jumped. Jeff was leaving for work. Did he have to be so loud? Maybe some coffee would help. She headed to the kitchen.

After three cups of coffee and about 30 minutes of staring off into space, Anne decided to get something done. She had a couple of hours before her first class so she walked into the living room, sat in her leather reading chair, and pulled her constitutional law case book out of her briefcase. She turned slightly to look outside and was surprised to see that it wasn't raining—for once. When she turned back, the book tilted on her lap and flipped open to the Appendix and the reprints of the Constitution and the Bill of Rights. She scanned here and there:

In Order to form a more perfect Union…

no warrants shall issue,

but upon probable cause…

The powers not delegated to the United

States…

are reserved to the States…

or to the people.

Suddenly, Anne recalled walking through the dimly lit halls and archways of the law school, feeling the coolness from the stone floor and walls, knowing that some of the nation's greatest legal minds had walked the same halls, breathed the same air, studied the same words. The words which had made the United States the greatest republic the earth has ever known.

Maybe the patriots have their points—but to throw the whole thing away?

Maybe things just needed to be kept in perspective.

❧

BRADLEY SAW ANNE COMING DOWN THE HALL AND decided to duck into the classroom to avoid meeting her at the door. It didn't work, totally anyhow, and their eyes made contact. Immediately he had the urge to go to her, to scoop her up in his arms—she looked so good. Her eyes bored in on him like laser beams—her chin raised prominently. Somehow, she just looked, well, intense. Put together. Attractive. Then he recalled that she was the one who had cut him off. His back stiffened. No. He wouldn't give in. Anne paused and seemed to study him, then she continued into the classroom.

From behind the lectern, Bradley watched the students file in and study the room for the best place to sit. Whatever spot they picked, that would be it for the semester. No one, save the gunners, wanted to get very close. And even the gunners would try to stay back just a little—to feign nonchalance. This was always interesting to watch. Bradley allowed himself to smile at Anne. She smiled back, but it seemed forced. Once everyone was seated, Bradley passed around the seating chart and started his lecture.

"What does *Marbury* tell us about how the court will decide a First or Second Amendment challenge to the Un-American Act?"

Anne's hand shot up. Bradley waited a moment, hoping someone else would raise a hand. No one did. *Crap*. He didn't want to get into a dialogue with Anne so soon. He needed time to let his hurt, his longing, settle to the back of his mind. Reluctantly, he pointed at Anne, careful not to say her name, since the seating chart had not made it back to him.

Anne sat straight up. "Actually, I'm confused about the matter. I just don't know what's going on with our legal system." A number of students broke out laughing; a few snickered. Bradley noticed the 1960s hippy rolling his eyes. Bradley gritted his teeth. They were jerks. It had always been something that upset Bradley; getting into Michigan Law said absolutely nothing about one's personal integrity or proclivity towards kindness and courtesy.

Anne continued, "On one hand, when I read things like the Declaration of Independence and the Constitution, I get a sense of awe and majesty—a sense that the law's exacting procedures and principles give it a quality…" Anne held out one hand and rubbed her thumb and fingers together as if judging the quality of a piece of cloth. "… a substance… I think it was Joseph Addison who said of education what I'm trying to say about the law. He said, as I recall, 'it chastens vice, guides virtue, and gives, at once, grace and government to genius.'" Anne paused and Bradley noted that the jerks had cut their demeaning actions. "On the other hand, a case like *Marbury* tells me that the actual text of the law may have little to do with the outcome when it interferes with the personal senti-ments—activist goals—of the justices, or the president."

Bradley was stunned. And so, it seemed, from the absolute silence that had blanketed the room, were the rest of the students. This line of thought was something he might expect from a very thoughtful lawyer who had been in practice for 20 years. It was way beyond the juvenile concepts held by most of his first-year students. Truth was, he didn't even know what to say in response. And there sat Anne, bright eyed, leaning forward in her seat.

All his doubts about Anne Kreig flew out the window. This woman needed to be his wife. She was a jewel—a diamond. He was going to rethink the matters of dating a student and Jeff's involve-ment in the patriots. From her words he knew she would not pos-sibly get involved in anything illegal. She was too thoughtful, too aware of right and wrong. Indeed, she put most of the legal profes-sion to absolute shame. Bradley felt an immense pride in having her as a student, as a friend, and hopefully…

He had to get back to his class. A few students were starting to look at him a little funny. Now, however, he was far less concerned with things turning into a dialogue with Anne. The seating chart was finally passed back, and he noticed a hand raised in the back of the class. He quickly looked at the chart and called out her name.

"Ms. Jones?"

Ms. Jones said, "It seems that the court is willing to go beyond the four corners of the Constitution—that is, to look outside the Constitution for guidance—as there was nothing in the Constitution that required Marshall's ruling. One of the notes a page or two after the case talked about Professor Lawrence Tribe. According to him, when the judges look beyond the Constitution's four corners, what they see will be colored by their own eyes—by their own personal view of fundamental rights."

Ms. Peacock was waving her hand. Bradley pointed to her. "Yes?"

"I've read a bit of Tribe and find him quite off the mark. In fact, he gets into it with another American law professor, John Hart Ely, who, I believe, is, or was, a dean somewhere... Anyway, they get into it in a way that fits nicely into the sticky wicket you have with your Un-American Act. For example, Tribe says that a distinction between laws burdening homosexuals, such as prohibiting gay marriage, and laws sending pickpockets to jail, depends, necessarily, on a substantive theory of which group is exercising a fundamental right and which group is not. He says a law against gay marriage should be ruled unconstitutional because of the desire to protect the fundamental value of personhood, of freely exploring one's sexual identity. On the other hand, a law putting burglars in prison offends no notion of fundamental law."

Ms. Peacock paused and reached into her purse for a tissue and blew her nose. Bradley wondered where in the heck he got these students. They were already so versed in constitutional issues. And thoughtful. This was really strange. He recalled the interview he had done for the New York Times poll indicating a vastly increased interest in constitutional issues. Clearly, more people had been reading the Constitution than in the past. What was happening in society to cause this? Something made him think of Jeff and his friend. They, too, had been surprisingly versed. Bradley shook his head and tuned back into Ms. Peacock's dissertation.

"People like Tribe believe that the courts should be employed when a group fails to get what it wants from the political process. Look what happened in California a while back. The citizens banned same sex marriage by putting it right in their constitution. Then the California Supreme Court comes along and says that it's unconstitutional. I mean, how is that? The citizens put it *in their constitution* and the court says its *un*constitutional. Seems a bit upside down. Anyway, the liberal thought process is that judicial intervention will be in sync with the particular direction of society—with society's evolving view of what is, and isn't, a fundamental right. Thus, in the case of the Un-American Act, or even the Religious and Cultural Sensitivities Act, liberals will say that justices should put their noses to the wind and observe the direction of change in America. Judges should be willing to curtail rights of an oppressive majority in view of more important goals of not offending a minority such as Muslims."

Bradley said, "So on balance, we should give up the First Amendment to avoid offending minorities."

"I didn't say that's the decision I would make. Personally, I think you folks have gotten everything backwards."

"Fair enough," Bradley said. "You said that you found Tribe 'off the mark.' Explain."

"It's easy. First off, if you have a supreme court that snoops around looking for the direction of change in society, how in heaven's name are they to know when they have found it? How does the court recognize a dead-end in the political process? I should have thought a properly amended state constitution would not represent a dead-end, but rather the *appropriate end* to the political process. How does the court tell the difference? How does it really know the direction of change in society at any moment or, even if it knows, how does it contribute to that change in a way that doesn't accelerate it too much or too little? And of course, this all begs the larger question of why nine old fogies—"

There was a murmur of laughter and chuckles and Ms. Peacock paused, smiled, and continued, "—feel they are better suited, as judges, to entertain political questions that your Constitution unambiguously leaves to the other branches of government."

Amazing, Bradley thought. *Simply amazing.* This was going to be the most fun constitutional law class he had ever had. He said, "All right then, how would *you* rule on the Un-American Act?"

"That's easy, too. John Hart Ely, and this would also be my preference, would have a look at the legislative process that generated the bill. He—I, would determine if the legislative decision classifies groups in a way that leaves us suspicious of the propriety or accuracy of the classification. Thus, I would closely examine laws against homosexuals, but not burglars, precisely because I have no doubt about the accuracy of the legislative perceptions about burglars, whereas, regarding homosexuals, I may doubt legislators' ability to accurately define the contours of the group or, not being homosexuals, they may fail to recognize the importance to a homosexual of the right to practice and display sexual identity. The Un-American Act targets persons who threaten the security of the United States, so they are like the burglars, and we have no doubt about the accuracy of legislative perceptions. Therefore, the court, if it follows a process-based inquiry, per Ely, would uphold the law. On the other hand, if the court uses a fundamental rights view, it's possible that it would invalidate the law because it trenches so closely on long-established First and Second Amendment rights."

Bradley said, "I liked your analysis until the end. I think there is a very good question whether Congress accurately apprehended the nature of the people most affected by the law. That is, these two laws are really attacks by Democrats against Tea Party conservatives who Democrats class as racist, potential terrorists, and weapons fanatics. And I've seen nuns arrested for passing out Bibles, and reporters arrested for asking questions that challenge the current administration. I think this *might be* a case where Ely would say there has been a misapprehension of the group regulated. On the other hand, conservatives lost the political process and elections have consequences. Obama told everyone that. And it's certainly unseemly to have political parties running to the Supreme Court every time they get beaten."

Anne had her hand up. Bradley pointed to her.

"Aren't we getting off track on this? Seems to me the Un-American Act, as well as the RCSA, violate other provisions of the Constitution—like the First Amendment right of free speech and the Second Amendment right to keep and bear arms. And let's look at the political process that started with Obama. He bullied private companies, threatened private citizens, ignored property rights, and basically moved us toward a socialist country. And he did it by refusing to enforce our immigration law that let millions of illegals into the country who now vote. He should have been impeached!" Anne thumped on her textbook with the knuckles of her hand, which she had curled into a fist. "The Bill of Rights clearly establishes my right to bear arms—to speak my mind—regardless of who dislikes my guns or my words."

Bradley said, "That's a good point." Anne's hand shot up again and he almost called out her name but caught himself. He had stepped away from the lectern so he walked back and glanced at the chart. "Ms. Kreig. Do you have something else to add?"

"Seems to me the law is like a rock sitting in a stream. It has a pretty side that is seen by the casual observer. But reach into the current and pull it up. Underneath, you will find a slimy surface, mud, and leeches." She raised her textbook to eye level and then tilted it so she could see its underside. "Judges are beholden to the political leanings of the president who appointed them. Presidents nominate this conservative or that liberal, and the senate confirmation hearings are more concerned with the political or social views of the judge. No one cares that he or she possesses the necessary analytical abilities." Anne suddenly released her textbook and let it fall from eye level. It dropped toward her desk, pages fluttering as the cover flew open. The book landed with a double thump, the first as the binding hit on end and the second as the book settled flat and the cover slammed closed. "It's a crock!"

Bradley blinked at the noise. He was excited by Anne's theatrics and conviction, which seemed contagious. Several other students were nodding and smiling. One, sitting behind Anne, even stood and leaned over the curved table and patted her on the back. She turned and smiled at him. Bradley recalled that she had been a professional singer—a performer. Well, her ability to manipulate an audience was evident. This was all amazing, and terribly exciting. He had never seen or heard of such an informed, interested, and involved group of students. It was as if the public was obsessed with something and looking to the Constitution to figure it out.

❧

ANNE WATCHED BRADLEY WALK ACROSS THE ROOM. HE seemed to be suddenly taken away by his own thoughts. She looked around and the class seemed to have noticed it, too; but no one was saying anything. They seemed content to wait out the last minutes of class.

Anne thought about how Obama had started the process that unraveled the country and the world. The riots in Europe, in Africa, and here in the United States. The killing of two conservative Supreme Court justices by leftists so that Obama and Wallmire could appoint liberals and overturn decisions like *Heller*. The way Obama had twisted bankruptcy law and had given the United Auto Workers so much stock in General Motors. The way Obama had ignored federal judges, usurped Congress by his hundreds and hundreds of Executive Orders as well as appointment of more and more regulators and czars. The law had become a joke. The world was upside down. How, after all, could nuns get arrested for handing out Bibles? Yet it had happened.

For over two hundred years American law had established and maintained order in this highly complex society. Anne thought back to her initial class discussions on property law and how the concept of private property ordered society. In her class on contracts she could see how every transaction in the business world, and even daily events like going to the grocery store, are governed by law. The law of torts seemed to be all about legally enforcing the assertion, "You can't do that to me, I've got my rights!" And even that had grown out of a regard for the well-being and property rights of others. We had accomplished so much as a nation…

Despite its misuse by both sides of the political isle, Anne reminded herself, the law *still* defined what it meant to be an American. It structured, governed, and guided American society as nowhere else in the world. The United States of America had become the embodiment of law in practice. Incompetence, malfeasance, envy, and hate notwithstanding, American law had become the world's finest expression of justice, of fairness, and of man's benevolent treatment of fellow man.

❧

CHAPTER 28

Sitting in his Detroit office, Bill Fletcher reached into his burled-walnut "in" box. It was so exquisitely finished that the wood reflected images on its polished surfaces. He had a matching "out" box sitting—no, it was *displayed* next to it. They were gifts from Bradley, who had found them at one of Ann Arbor's famous Summer Art Fairs. Bill smiled at the boxes, and a pang of guilt ran through his body. Why did Bradley have to be so damn nice to him?

Bill picked up the report from the FBI's National Cyber Investigative Joint Task Force. It was full of technical computer jargon that he mostly, but grudgingly, understood. He grunted. His agents were always speaking in the lingo of gigabytes and megahertz, bus speed and bus width, high memory and video memory, etcetera, etcetera. It drove him crazy. He glanced at his new high-tech telephone that had functions the purposes for which were a total mystery. For some odd reason he suddenly pictured his wife's bread maker. She loved the damn thing, and he had to admit it made some really great bread. But he had no idea how she operated its array of computerized buttons. He shook his head. He could apprehend the world's most wanted and despicable criminals, yet he couldn't make a loaf of bread, he thought, ah, "wryly."

Bill flipped to the last page which contained just a list of names. There were hundreds. He scanned down the list and stopped reading as soon as he saw the name Jeff Kreig.

"Interesting."

Until now, his investigation of Jeff and Hartman had raised suspicions that there was more going on than they had allowed. And his brother's mention of Anne Kreig had been a weird coincidence. Even though she was related, it was no big deal to be related to people who had not committed any crimes. But this could, if it panned out the way his gut said it would, make things very different. He tried to recall what Bradley had last told him about his relationship with Anne. The relationship had seemed, at first, to be going along well. Bradley had helped her to good effect on the LSAT. But there had been some kind of problem, and he seemed to recall that Bradley hadn't dated her in several weeks. Oh! He probably couldn't date a student! Of course. That must be it. Good thing, too. Because if he were still seeing her, and Jeff turned out to be the architect of the scanner used on the attempt on the warheads... Ugh. He didn't even want to think of it.

But he thought of it anyhow. The implications ran in good and bad directions. On one hand, it was a break that could repair his career, erase the question mark from the bribe scandal... On the other hand, it was also a catastrophe that could ruin his brother. And if he tried to cover for his brother, or if it even looked as if he had tried...

Bill belched up acid. His office suddenly felt stuffier than usual. He made a mental note to check the thermostat in the lobby.

Thus far in his career, making decisions had been a matter of clarity. Do the best job possible, be meticulous in searching for and collecting evidence, investigate all leads to the extent, and with such expediency, as warranted by the circumstances. Go after bad guys. Leave good guys alone.

But the matters never involved his brother—his flesh and blood. Bill knew his brother couldn't possibly be involved in anything having to do with the patriots. But if his name came up in the investigation... possibly as a recent lover of Anne Kreig, a frequent guest at her house... a friend of Jeff's. The publicity, still assuming he was innocent, would be crushing. Bill's investigative mind was in overdrive, however, and he could even see the possibility that his brother had knowledge of what was happening.

He also saw what would happen if he didn't implicate his brother. Some would question whether there had been favoritism, a willingness to look the other way. It would be a rerun of the nightmare he had endured with his former partner.

It would be the end of his career.

Tim Bannister and Cindy Cooper appeared at the door to Bill's office. Tim said, "What's up, boss? You look a little ill."

"Oh, it's just the office. It's too stuffy in here for me. It's nothing. I'm fine, really. It's just the office. I'm fine—"

"Okay, okay. We got the point." Tim raised his eyebrows, and that made Bill even more uncomfortable. It had been obvious that he was overplaying something. For God's sake, he had to settle down. He wiped his shirtsleeve across his forehead and tried to regain his composure. He said, "I think we just got our first real break on the warhead case. It may be that our man is related to the shooter in the Ann Arbor bank attempt. His son is on this list anyhow, and my gut tells me something is rotten." Bill's mind drifted. He wondered if he should assign more agents to the case. There had been a disturbing rash of bank robberies in and around Detroit to which he assigned considerable manpower in an effort to keep the peace with Detroit's new "anti-crime" mayor. Wasn't that a joke. Disbarred, disgraced, ex-convict Kwame Kilpatrick had shown a long time ago that the words "anti-crime mayor" and "Detroit" didn't even belong in the same language.

Tim said, "That's interesting."

"What?"

"I said, that's interesting." Tim's eyes tightened down on Bill, and then he glanced at Cindy. She shrugged.

Bill had the sense that Tim was wondering if he'd been told everything. Cindy, if she suspected the same, was hiding it well. Bill could feel his office walls closing in. No one else knew about Bradley and Anne Kreig. Cindy said something about bank jobs quieting down, but Bill knew he had missed most of it. He said, "I'm sorry, Cindy. My mind drifted."

"I said the bank jobs have quieted down, so we came down here to see if you needed any help with anything." Bill nodded. Her willingness to work should have made him feel good.

Tim said, "So there may be quite a bit more to this Kreig fellow. I understand he was quite a shooter."

Bill's mind froze. He knew he had to say something, but feared that everything he could say would lead in a direction his heart did not want to take. He tried something innocuous: "When I interviewed him, I knew something... Self-defense-minded civilians don't just happen to be *that* good at gun-fighting."

Tim said, "From what I've heard, whoever put the surveillance device together was patriot-involved, or at least conspired with the patriots. So, if his kid did the scanner, it's likely that Hartman also has a link."

Cindy cut in, "Think he's the one behind the bomb plant?"

Bill had thought of that. Working on an anonymous tip, agents had discovered a small, run-down tool shop that had a back room being used to process the components to make a fertilizer bomb. Since its discovery several weeks ago, Bill had had a team watching and listening. He was sure it was the patriots, and he was hoping that it would lead to some big fish. And now it was... But too much was happening. He had to get a handle on things, brother or not. He was in control of the investigation. His agents would do exactly as they were told. There was no need for them to go after Anne for the time being. After all, there was absolutely no indication that she had anything to do with the patriots.

But it was his career at stake.

He said, "My bet is that one or the both of them are involved in the plant."

Tim and Cindy both smiled. Tim said, "What a coup. We could watch them both. What about a bug on their telephones and cars?"

Bill shuddered. He wanted to move forward. His agents were making the right assumptions. He got up and walked to his office window. Outside, on rain-drenched streets, cars were plodding along with wipers going full tilt; people were bundled up in raincoats, holding umbrellas, and wearing all manner of boots and galoshes. People picked their way to avoid puddles or runoff from buildings and held their faces away from the wind-driven rain. "Great drive home," Bill cursed under his breath. A trucker was unloading a pallet of... it looked like cans of chili, for the Coney Island next door. Bill said, "We need to do this the old fashioned way. The patriots have some agents of their own and they may have hacked our DCSNet (with a mouse click the FBI can use this system to perform instant wire-taps on almost any communications device in the country). I've got a memo on my desk, somewhere in that pile—" Without taking his eyes off the trucker, Bill waved back at his desk in the manner that you would use to signal for someone to go away, "—that says we've blown several investigations when the targets learned we were on to them. Seems we are under surveillance on our own fancy surveillance system. So, anyhow, we have to use extra caution until the situation can be evaluated."

Tim said, "Wow. So we have to go on site? That's risky business. Takes a lot longer."

"Tell me." FBI agents preferred their DCSNet point and click system which allowed them to link directly into the telecom equip-ment— land line and cellular—and which also enabled them to turn on microphones of most cell phones even when the phones appeared, to their owners, to be "off." On-site bugs, on the other hand, were fraught with risks, some of which involved big dogs with very sharp teeth.

Cindy said, "Another problem, gentlemen. And this involves phys-ical taps. The patriots have become pretty sophisticated at TDR."

Bill turned away from the window and screwed up his face. "What?" He had frequently thought that the young recruits were too full of school books.

"Time Domain Reflectometry. It's the analysis of a conductor, whether wire, cable, or fiber optic, by sending a signal down line. Sort of like radar. You look at the signal's reflection. The delay between the initial pulse and the reflected pulse indicates the location of the end of the wire—or a bug, basically."

Bill's eyebrows raised at the same time as his jaw dropped. Cindy smiled; she seemed to have peered inside Bill's head and knew his bias against some of the newest techniques. She shrugged her shoulders and poured it on. "You divide the time of the delay by the speed of light, multiply by the velocity of propagation for that particular conduit, and then divide the result by two. TDR analysis will not detect capacitively isolated devices or inductive taps. You need a high frequency crosstalk evaluation. Fortunately, they are not likely to have that equipment or expertise, yet."

Bill rolled his eyes and groaned. He knew, that she knew, that she had just blown him away. He said, "Well, if they do all that we're screwed. We'll just have to risk it. Can you do it?"

"Yep." Cindy made one big nod of her head. Then she smiled playfully and said, with just enough sunny confidence to really rub it in, "No prob-lem-ah."

Tim laughed and said, "She's right, you know. I've even seen ads in some magazines and on web sites for tap detectors. Must be that TDR stuff. If either the kid or the old man is important, they are likely careful enough to have something like that."

For crying out loud, Bill thought. He was going to have to do something to keep up with technology. He had thought he was doing great with his cell phone. Oh well. "Okay. You're on it. You know the drills. And for Heaven's sake, be careful. I want solid intelligence." Bill watched his best team share a series of nonverbal cues as they headed out of his office. He had to admit, they worked well together—and the reason was obvious; they respected each other. Tim was not threatened by Cindy's expertise, young though she was. And that spoke nearly as well for him as it did for Cindy's training. Truth was, they knew each other as well as, or better than, they knew their respective spouses. From personal experience, Bill knew that it was something not entirely appreciated by spouses. Work relationships tended to mature in the life-and-death moments that had the ugly habit of punctuating FBI careers.

Bill was still watching Cindy and Tim walk down the hall when Bradley appeared. They passed each other with polite, nonverbal acknowledgments. It made Bill feel even creepier—and guilty as hell. Bradley bumping into these two investigators was ominous.

"What in the heck are you doing here in Detroit? I thought all Ann Arborites got nosebleeds east of U.S. 23?"

Bradley laughed. "I don't have any classes until late afternoon. I was at a morning seminar at Wayne State. I thought I would stop by. Maybe go to lunch?"

Bradley was the last person with whom he wanted to go to lunch.

"Um… I'm kind of busy."

"I'm buying. Come on. I don't get to see you that often."

Oh God, Bill thought. He said, "Let's go." He headed to the lobby and Bradley followed a half step behind.

Bill could hear his brother's footsteps, sense his presence, and picture his face. How could he sacrifice his brother for his own career? The guilt was overwhelming and he felt as if he were burning up in his suit. When they got to the lobby, Bill said, "There is something I've got to talk to you about."

Bradley suddenly seemed apprehensive, and said, "Is this about Jeff Kreig?"

The question hit Bill between the eyes. He had wanted to move slowly toward the subject; Bradley had just eliminated any room to be subtle. Now Bill had no choice but to tell his brother to avoid contact with Anne Kreig; she was poison. Yet, he had to be careful…

Bill stared at his brother for a moment. He didn't know what to say, and then he just started talking: "Actually, I was going to tell you about Jeff. And you are not going to like it. We have obtained evidence that might link Jeff to the attack on the warheads."

Bradley's face went white.

❧

IT WAS A LONG DRIVE BACK TO ANN ARBOR. BRADLEY CAREfully steered his Volvo along the rain-slicked expressway. He was having a hard time concentrating on driving. So Jeff was a suspect in the warhead attack. Bradley had thought he might have a heart attack right there in the lobby of the FBI. After that, Bill had insisted they go to the most expensive restaurant, and he wouldn't hear of Bradley even paying the tip.

Yet, more was going on than Bill was acknowledging…

The revelation about Jeff was enough by itself. But Bradley couldn't get over that he had just bared his heart to Anne; he had even offered to risk his career to continue their relationship. All these events had placed Bradley's head in a vice, and his brother had just tightened it down a few turns. And for extra fun, lunch was putting him to sleep. He kept shaking his head to stay awake.

Anne had spurned him and it had broken his heart. He saw her in class and around the school, and except for their intensive and highly intellectual discussions in class, they never spoke beyond informal pleasantries. She hadn't called and had never returned his calls. Worse, she'd never told him why.

But now he knew, didn't he? This had to be it. Jeff's involvement wasn't just speculation by the FBI. Bradley had suspected it himself. And Anne surely knew. How could she not know? She was no dummy.

Anne had to know she could subject him to devastating publicity, if not criminal prosecution. The thought struck that she might have rejected him to protect him. Bradley's chest tightened with a mixture of longing and fear. Being linked to the attempt on the warheads would absolutely destroy his reputation. The drive-by media, and that jerk Director of the BSCA Kennison, would tear him apart. *Too bad*, he thought wryly, that he hadn't organized a domestic terrorist organization and actually blown up dozens of buildings, including a portion of the U.S. Capitol Building. If he had, like William Ayers before him, Bradley would be offered immediate tenure.

But there was one question that begged for an answer: why hadn't Anne said anything? If she loved him, why wouldn't she confide in him?

Why?

")

OUTSIDE THE KREIG HOME, TIM BANNISTER AND CINDY Cooper were driving slowly past the house in the third unmarked car they had used that day. They were taking notes and pictures that would be used to set up surveillance. Anne's two schnauzers were sitting on the back of her couch in the family room, watching the car move slowly past. Roni started to growl.

Cindy and Tim had driven past the house and were turning around to make another pass when Anne walked into the room with her constitutional law text. Roni again started to growl and Anne passed by her leather reading chair and went to the window. She pulled a blind to the side and glanced out. It had started to rain, but that was all she saw. She chastised Roni for growling and turned away. Roni, with ears back, jumped off the couch and sulked out of the room. Anne made herself comfortable in her reading chair and opened her text.

Cara, still sitting on the back of the couch, watched quietly as the car made its second pass. Cindy aimed a large camera lens at the house.

❧

Big Sky News
Missoula, Montana

ACORN MOBILIZES AGAINST MEMBERS OF CONGRESS
BY JACK MARLEY, BSN STAFF WRITER

WE at BSN have scoured the advocacy networks for news of several incidents that have been reported to us though individual eye witnesses. Internet reports from conservative web sites have apparently been blocked by the government. Accordingly, reports are sketchy and of course subject to verification, but it appears that ACORN has organized protests at the homes of members of Congress who have indicated that they will seek to repeal the Un-American Act.

It further appears that in at least a dozen separate incidents rocks have been thrown through front windows, tires have been slashed, homes have been set ablaze, and ACORN human blockades have prevented timely access by paramedics and fire departments. Several people have only just escaped their burning homes and have sustained second and third-degree burns.

In the most egregious case reported so far, a car in a garage has exploded underneath a bedroom. An infant girl sleeping in her crib in a bedroom above the garage dropped through the disintegrating floor into the raging flames. She was pronounced dead at the scene, according to the eye witness report we received. Unfortunately, the eye witness became involved in a struggle for her cell phone and moments later the line went dead. We have been unable to regain contact.

<<<<>>>>

CHAPTER 29

BILL FLETCHER WAS SITTING ON THE EDGE OF HIS leather chair, elbows on his calendar desk pad, reading and rereading some material on TDR. It was raining again. It rained every damn day. And Detroit drivers were apparently rendered incompetent by water. All this meant that the homeward rush hour, which was really more like two-and-a-half hours, would be a serious headache.

Bill's secretary stepped in and handed him Tim and Cindy's report from the initial canvassing of the Kreig home. Acid again rose up from his stomach. He was going to have to see the doctor; this heartburn was getting too regular. The report indicated that surveillance to establish routines would be difficult. There was minimal traffic on the road and there were no homes or buildings nearby that could hide agents and equipment. This would slow things down, which part of him wanted and part of him did not. Moving slowly would certainly make it less likely that his brother's name would surface.

But on that point, Bill was having second thoughts; had he done the right thing in telling Bradley that Jeff was a suspect in an FBI investigation? What if Bradley mentioned something to Anne, who might say something to Jeff? This was turning into a nightmare.

A solution popped into his mind, but his heart tried, and failed, to reject it. *Catch Bradley conjugating with the Kreigs...*

But that raised a problem. Bradley was smart; he would have figured out to stay away. Yet, a relationship couldn't be cut off cold turkey. It would probably take Bradley time to turn it off. Could his agents do the surveillance quickly enough? He could not send in agents to bug the home until they knew the habits of its occupants. And Anne had two dogs. That complicated things. He would bet a hundred bucks she left them to roam freely in the house when she went away. He would have to figure out some way to get around them. That would take more time. Bill reached into his top right desk drawer and pulled out a pack of Tums. He tore the wrapper and popped two into his mouth.

⥿

THE OUTGOING STUDENTS THREW OPEN THE CLASSROOM doors. Bradley saw his brother in the hallway and groaned. What the heck did he want? Bradley wanted to talk with Anne. This was the worst time for Bill to show up. As the classroom emptied, Bradley noted that Anne was lingering toward the back of the classroom to talk to students. With Bill here, that was just as well. Until he had a chance to talk to Anne about Jeff, he didn't want Anne meeting Bill. *Mother meets fbi investigator trying to send son to prison.* It gave Bradley chills. Too much could happen, and all of it was bad.

Bradley stepped out of the classroom and immediately headed away, forcing Bill to hustle to catch up.

"Brad, how are classes going? Getting into the swing of the new year?"

"Yeah. It's always an adjustment. So what's up?"

"Nothing, really. I was just nearby and thought I would stop in to see you. It's great to be working so much in Ann Arbor. Have you had lunch yet? I'll buy."

That fast, Bradley felt like a jerk for wishing his brother hadn't come by. Bradley smiled and put his hand on Bill's shoulder. "Let me drop this stuff off in my office and we can walk down to the Red Hawk. I know you like Dominick's, but I want to get farther away from the Quad. Okay?" Bill nodded but avoided Bradley's glance.

Out on the street, heading to the Red Hawk, Bill said, "Actually, I didn't just happen by." Bradley cringed; he really didn't want to hear what Bill was to say. "All that stuff I told you about our investigation. Jeff Kreig and all… uh, I guess I just wanted to make sure you didn't say—accidentally of course—anything to Anne Kreig. I mean, she lives with Jeff. She may even… Well, you understand. Right?"

Bradley understood, all right; perhaps too well. He was irritated with Bill for implying that he would jeopardize the investigation by disclosing something to Anne or to Jeff. And he was hurt that Bill was here principally to protect his own hide—and right after he had scolded himself for not being happy to see his brother.

But on the other hand… He *had* intended to tell Anne *something*. She was innocent. He had to warn her, didn't he? He had to tell her to make sure Jeff wasn't involved with the warhead. Knowing Anne, as he did, it had to be a mistake. Yet, saying even the slightest thing could jeopardize the FBI investigation. It would violate his brother's trust, not to mention ruin him. And saying anything might well be illegal.

But he wanted Anne to be his wife.

Bill and Bradley reached the Red Hawk and were quickly seated at a table along the front window, facing State Street. Bradley immediately ordered a double Scotch, straight.

Bill said, "Make that two."

Bradley did a double take and his gaze lingered on his brother. Bradley had never known him to drink during working hours. Something was clearly bothering him. Bill was watching someone at the bar and his jaw muscles were set as though he was biting on a nail.

Bradley wanted to know the details of the investigation. Was Bill already aware of things that would implicate Anne? Surveillance bugs… Shit! He hadn't thought of that. He wondered, *does Bill already have any bugs or taps, or… uh, wiretaps, or whatever the heck they're called?* If so, Bradley couldn't even risk calling Anne, except under some pretext relating to law school. And even that would be suspect. Bradley turned to face the window. A couple in their middle-ages walked by holding hands and smiling. It made his heart ache. God, he wanted to be with Anne.

❧

CHAPTER 30

BRADLEY'S ALARM CLOCK WENT OFF AND HE JERKED upright. He was sweating. He'd had a horrible nightmare, the kind you can't remember—except for the terror. Bradley ran his hands over his stubbly face and wiped the crustiness out of his eyes.

As Bradley's mind journeyed from sleep to wakefulness, he sensed, vaguely at first, and then more concretely as the journey continued, that something was wrong. After a few moments, he was sufficiently awake to recognize that his nightmare had trickled into these, his first waking moments. His pulse increased and he felt a sense of panic. Something terrifying was still chasing him... He couldn't see it or identify it, but he could *feel* it.

He shivered, threw the covers off, and hurried to the bathroom. He had to get ready as fast as he could. The more distance he could put between this state of sleepy wakefulness the better chance he had of escaping whatever it was that pursued him.

Bradley skipped his usual oatmeal breakfast and instead grabbed a Zingerman's brioche. He planned to eat it while he walked to work. Since he lived in the upscale Burns Park neighborhood, the law school was only a 15 to 20 minute walk away. Usually, he enjoyed strolling along the old, tree-lined sidewalks with their cracked and pockmarked surfaces, the occasional rise of one section as a result of a tree root, and the several badly worn but visible "WPA" imprints from the WWII-era Works Project Association. This morning, however, Bradley didn't notice the sidewalk or several of his elderly neighbors who waved to him from their front porches. From the minute his foot stepped outside his house, he literally ran all the way to the law school and then up the back stairs to his office on the seventh floor. By the time he got to his leather chair, he was out of breath and sweating profusely. His briefcase was in one hand, the brioche in the other. And he had figured out the nightmare.

It was Anne.

The urge to talk with her and straighten some of this out was overwhelming. Was she involved in the patriots? Did she know Jeff was? Should he tell her that the FBI suspected Jeff?

Bradley stared at his office phone. He could just pick it up, press a few buttons and be talking with her. Just like that. Assuming she would answer his call, that is.

He shoved both hands into his pants pockets.

He had to resist. Calling was way too risky. Bill probably already had the phones tapped. Bradley shivered under his sweat-drenched clothes. His mind involuntarily ran though a scenario where he made such a call that was recorded. He pictured his brother shaking his head and beginning to frown, the reel-to-reel tape rolling (of course it would be digitally recorded, but in his mind he saw the image of the tape reels slowing turning).

No matter what he did, he would violate the trust of someone—his brother, Anne, the law, his students, his administration. Was there anyone who would not condemn him? A suffocating oppressiveness closed in. The coolness of the room penetrated his wet clothes, and he began shivering.

❖

BILL FLETCHER HAD BEEN SITTING IN HIS DETROIT OFFICE, staring at the file in front of him for several minutes. He closed his eyes and wished that new, more helpful information would materialize within the file's manila leaves. He had learned that Jeff left for work early—about 5:30 A.M.—and returned about nine hours later. And he knew that Jeff was always around the house or barn until the next morning. He'd discovered the African American fella, one Miles Larson, who often came over and went into the barn with Jeff, where they stayed usually for several hours. Two or three times a week Jeff had visitors who drove up in big pickup trucks emblazoned with patriotic bumper stickers. They often carted off a box or two of what seemed to be printouts. Bill had gotten a couple of long-range camera shots that showed the visitors examining the contents of a box and sometimes holding up a patriot promotional document. Bill had put tails on all visitors, but so far nothing of significance had turned up.

Bill had also learned that Anne never left the home before eight in the morning. She always had books in her hand, a backpack, or a briefcase. And she was at the law school for four to six hours, five days a week.

Weekends, Bill had learned, were helter-skelter, with the Kreig home more and more appearing to be a hub of patriot activity.

And then there had been Anne's summer-term final exams. A perfect time to get agents in to plant bugs... Or so Bill had thought. Bill knew from his brother that final law exams last four hours—plenty of time for his agents—until Anne came pealing back down the road just 40 minutes after she had left. Bill's team was nearly caught with its pants down. Bill hadn't known about take-home exams! That near catastrophe had spooked the spooks, and Bill didn't want to risk blowing the surveillance until he had a rock-solid idea she would be gone for a while. Now, with fall classes under way, she was back to a regular schedule.

Bill really would have preferred to obtain information from off-site devices. He had tried activating the microphones in Jeff's and Anne's cell phones, but Jeff had apparently installed some defensive software. He had carefully considered using a long-range sound crew. But the only location where they could set up a long-range microphone with a direct shot at the house was in a field across from the Kreig home. Unfortunately, since the field was fallow, the crew had to remain about 500 yards back from the road, hidden in a swale. The Kreig house was a full 100 yards back from its side of the road. That was simply too far away for even the FBI's newest gear. There were woods some 100 yards to the back of the house, but with the barn and other stands of trees and rows of dense shrubs, there was no way to get a sound print from a window or even to properly observe people coming and going.

The upshot was that Bill had no choice but to go inside and plant a couple of bugs.

⌐∂

NORMALLY, WHEN ANNE STUDIED, SHE DIDN'T HEAD TO THE comfy leather reading chair in the living room until later in the evening, sort of as a reward for having worked so hard. She could also concentrate better sitting upright on the hard kitchen chairs, beautifully constructed of quarter sawn red oak. The kitchen was also nice because the coffee pot—needed for grinding through hour after hour of judicial opinions—was close by.

The previous evening, Anne had fallen asleep while reading her property text. It had been well past 11 P.M. when she had zonked out. She'd been sitting in her reading chair and awoke with a start sometime in the middle of the night. In a haze, she'd set her book off to the side of the chair and stumbled off to bed.

The alarm clock buzzed and Anne commenced her normal morning procedure of drinking several cups of coffee, taking a nice hot shower, downing a couple pieces of Zingerman's bread (toasted and buttered with Zingerman's amazingly sweet homemade butter) and taking a quick glance at the previous afternoon's *Ann Arbor News*.

This morning she had lingered a little too long with her coffee and then she spilled a cup all over the kitchen floor. By the time she had cleaned up the mess and showered, she didn't have time for breakfast. She rushed out of the house, grabbing her new heavy-duty trail pack where she had set it off to the side of the kitchen table.

⌐∂

PRECISELY ONE HOUR AFTER ANNE HAD HEADED DOWN THE dusty road to her first class of the morning, Cindy Cooper and Tim Bannister moved toward the back door of the Kreig home. They had waited because, on several occasions in the past, Anne apparently had forgotten something and had come racing back to the house, only to rush in, presumably find what she had left behind, and leave again. In response, Bill Fletcher had put a team at the law school to confirm when she had gone into class. Once she was in her first class, she was always gone for at least four hours. They would have plenty of time. Tim was carrying a duffel bag and a small cage and Cindy had a briefcase.

Cindy and Tim were being directed over a secure radio by two agents in an FBI surveillance van parked down the road in the direction from which Anne and Jeff almost always headed to and from the house. The van was disguised with the logo and markings of a local cable company.

Tim picked the lock and opened the back door. They both walked in and listened. Suddenly the two dogs came running toward the back door, barking like hell. Tim quickly set the cage on the floor and opened its door. He then drew two huge rawhide bones out of his duffel. One of the benefits of their surveillance had been to see, on several occasions, Anne or Jeff bring in a couple of new rawhides and play keep away with their dogs. It never failed that both dogs would chase whoever had the rawhide. Tim held the rawhides out toward the dogs as they approached.

Both Cara and Roni stopped short of the agents and started their symbolic routine of snapping, growling, and barking. After a few moments, however, the dogs calmed and approached warily. Tim put the rawhides in the cage and he and Cindy backed away.

It worked.

Both dogs entered the cage. Tim quickly closed the door. It seemed the dogs hardly noticed, so enthralled they were with their new chews. Tim and Cindy shared a smile and quickly went to work. Bugs were successfully placed in the bedrooms, kitchen, library, and living room. For good measure, they also decided to bug both land line telephones.

At the law school, classes had started and the halls had cleared of other students. The young FBI agents, Karen Davenport and Rick Smith, were just out of college so they blended in with the law students. Problem was, once Anne had gone into class, and the halls cleared, the agents felt too conspicuous hanging around an empty hallway. Thus, Rick and Karen usually waited outside the school building and watched Anne enter and exit. Observing her entering was no issue, as they always got a handoff from the team trailing her from home and so they knew from what direction she would approach the school. (It changed often, as Anne, like most students with cars, always had to hunt for an open parking spot, which sometimes could only be found several blocks from where she had parked the day before.)

Today, Karen had underdressed and she was freezing. Walking around briskly wasn't helping, so Rick had told her to go back to their car and get another layer to put under her light coat. While she was gone, however, Rick had developed an urgent need to take a pee. He looked at his watch… It was between hours, so Anne was less likely to emerge from the school, and Dominick's with a bathroom was just a block down the street. He would be on the wrong side of the school to see her come out if she exited the same door she had used to enter, but peeing in his pants was simply not an option.

↫

ANNE FINISHED TALKING WITH A FRIEND IN CON LAW, AGAIN avoiding Bradley, who lingered at the front of the room talking with students. After Bradley finished with the students, he headed off. Anne was the last person to leave the room, and she left to prepare for her property class. She had an hour between classes, so she decided to work in the austere atmosphere of the Reading Room. It was already her favorite place in the law school; it had served her well during her summer semester finals, where she had garnered two As, one B+, and two Bs. When she reached the reading room and found a seat she liked, she rummaged through her humongous backpack. At that point she realized why it had felt so light. She must have forgotten to put the property text back in when she had had it out last night.

Anne glanced at her watch. She *had to have the book* if she hoped to participate in class. She realized if she hurried, she could just make it back just in time. She quickly packed up and rushed out the Reading

Room doors. Today, as luck had had it, she'd searched and searched and *finally* found a spot in front of a parking meter on the west side of the school, right on State Street.

⭓

BACK IN THE FBI SURVEILLANCE VAN, TIM AND CINDY BEGAN to test their bugs. All the transmitters were working and then, unexpectedly, one cut out.

"Damn!" Cindy said. "Looks like I've got infant mortality on the living room phone. It worked when I tested it in the house. Damn!"

"You and your engineering-speak. Infant mortality," Tim chuckled and then glanced at his watch and shrugged. "We've got plenty of time."

Cindy frowned. She was always getting teased for her book knowledge. "Okay. I don't have any choice—after the big fuss I made to Bill about these high-tech bugs and my supreme ability to install them." She screwed her face up in mock anguish. They both laughed, grabbed their stuff, and headed back to the Kreig house.

The living room phone was one of the new, secure-channel models, and the case was a bugger to open. Cindy had had some trouble the first time, and she was struggling with it again. She finally got it open and had just placed the bug when her earpiece started screaming.

"Lawbooks (their code name for Anne) is approaching in her car. She is pulling into the drive. Get out! Get out!"

"I can't stop! I've got the phone half apart!"

Tim, who had been baby-sitting the dogs in the cage, came running into the living room. "Can I do anything?"

"Pray." Cindy's hands were working furiously. Little screws were rolling all over the end table. Beads of perspiration began to form on her head.

Outside, Anne got out of the car and walked to the street to get her mail and the paper. She glanced at the mail, put the several pieces under her arm, and headed up the walk.

Cindy was calling on every nerve she had. The last screw was giving her fits, and she had to apply quite a bit of pressure to get it to thread into the base of the phone. She was afraid it was stripping, but she didn't have time to pull it out and start over. It had to go in. Out of the corner of her eye, she saw Anne's shadow through the front blinds which, *thank God*, were closed. She heard the key scratch around the keyhole and finally find its mark. The locks tumblers matched up with a click and the door began to squeak open.

Tim had already gone to the dog cage and was waiting to snatch the dogs out and steal back the rawhides. He hoped the little schnauzers would again be good sports.

Got it! Cindy said to herself as the last screw suddenly pushed into place. She set the phone down and rushed to the back door. Tim gave her a blank stare and she immediately understood the problem. If they went out the back door, the dogs would likely bark…

And then they got lucky. As if on cue, both dogs heard noises at the front door and raced to the front of the house, barking up a storm. Tim and Cindy quietly opened the back door and slipped out.

❧

BY THE END OF THE DAY, ANNE WAS WIPED OUT. WHAT WITH having to rush home to retrieve her property text, rush back to school—barely making it in time for class—study after classes in the Reading Room, drive home in the cold rain. She *hated* cold rain. The dirt road they lived off always turned into a sea of mud. And she *hated* always having to take her car to the wash. And she *hated* wet clothes. And she *hated*—Oh, man, this was getting stressful.

The law was interesting, but it was also compressing her life. Study, sleep, eat, go to class; study, sleep, eat, go to class. There wasn't even time to use the bathroom, or so it seemed. Some of her classmates had even joked about the need to arrest all bodily functions. School was making her nervous, irritable, tired… and totally exhilarated!

Anne hung up her coat and headed to the kitchen. It was getting close to dinner time and she wondered where Jeff was. A moment later he came in the door and sat at the kitchen table.

He gave her an easy smile. "How were classes today?"

"Fine. They are really interesting. But I have to be careful about getting too stressed out. I feel like I'm moving my life forward, but it certainly costs."

Jeff smiled and nodded. "I don't feel like cooking anything. I'm sure you don't. How about we order a pizza?"

Anne sighed. She had been stressed about just that: making something for the two of them for dinner. Jeff had made a huge salad a couple of days ago, full of various dark greens, onions, red and green peppers, and garlic croutons. They had finished it off last night with a loaf of fresh Zingerman's Rustic Italian bread and various cheeses. Jeff was a real lifesaver. She headed to the telephone to order the pizza.

After dinner, Anne cleared the kitchen table and pulled out her con law text. Jeff walked by but doubled back when he glanced at what Anne was reading. She looked at him curiously as he sat down at the table across from her.

He said, "So, what are you finding out about our activist courts?"

Anne shook her head. "My head is so packed with cases and law. We just got a handout on a guy named John Hart Ely. Apparently, Professor Fletcher thinks he has the right idea about how our courts should interpret the Constitution."

"I've read some of his stuff. It's in one of our tracts. We think the Supreme Court, and all the other federal courts, have no business creating rights that are not even mentioned in the Constitution. The Founding Fathers never intended for the federal government to be so intrusive. I've got a copy of that tract, if you are interested."

"Just how much do you people know about John Hart Ely?"

"Some know quite a bit about him. Also that lib Lawrence Tribe."

"Amazing."

"Not everyone is fixated on black helicopters, Mom."

"Yes. I'd like to see it—the tract. Actually, I've been thinking quite a bit about some of your ideas, and to a great extent they—you—are right. I guess I sympathize with you."

Jeff's eyes widened and he regarded her for a moment. "Hopefully, we can make a difference."

"Well, I hope so, too. Uh, I've been meaning to ask you. What are you folks trying to do, exactly? You seem awfully busy with working on their stuff." Anne chuckled, "You're not really planning a revolution, I hope."

Jeff's face lost a bit of color and he paused before speaking. "I'd rather not say, exactly. Remember? I swore to secrecy, and while I've told you what I'm doing… Heck, Dad hasn't even told me, yet, exactly how the operation is planned."

"Operation what? Take over the country?" Anne chuckled again.

"Don't laugh. It's serious. I suppose I can tell you a little—at this point, anyhow. But the fact is, I don't know where, or exactly when, or even how… yet. It's all top secret. Only Dad and a few others know. They are worried about infiltration by the FBI."

"I told you Bradley's brother is FBI?"

Jeff's back straightened. "Holy crap, Mom. I hope you haven't mentioned anything to Bradley Fletcher. He might—"

Anne cut him off. "Actually, I think he knows a little and suspects more, but doesn't really want to know—if you know what I mean." Anne lowered her eyes. "To tell the truth Jeff, that's one reason I haven't seen him. I was afraid he might think he needed to turn you in if he found out too much."

Now Jeff's neck seemed to strain forward and the veins on either side began to protrude. "Mom!"

The telephone rang.

"Hold on, Jeff. I think it's Linda. She said she would call." Anne stepped out to the living room, since the phone on the end table was actually easier to get to from where she was sitting than the phone on the opposite kitchen wall. Linda often called the land line (she had learned Anne did not keep her cell at hand when she was home). Anne tried to make sense of Jeff's reaction but didn't really have time. She picked up the telephone. "Linda? Yep. Pretty good. Just a lot of work. You wouldn't believe…"

When Anne finished talking she set the receiver on the base and noticed that the phone was sitting a little funny—like something was under the base. A pen, perhaps. She lifted the base and heard something drop to the glass table top. She picked a screw up and saw that it had fallen out of the base of the phone. That was odd. The thing was brand-new.

Jeff walked into the living room. "What are you doing Mom? Don't tell me your fancy phone's already broken. I told you not to buy Chinese crap."

"A screw just fell out, that's all."

Jeff walked over and took the phone. "The screw is stripped."

"How could that be? It's brand-new."

"Wait a minute."

Jeff headed out to the garage where he had a bunch of tools. He came back a moment later with a tiny screwdriver.

❧

SEVERAL MILES FROM THE KREIG HOME, BILL FLETCHER HAD been listening on a headset when Anne answered the phone. Cindy Cooper was also listening, and Bill noted with more than a little discomfort that Cindy gave him a long glance when his brother's name came up. A rush of acid once again made its way up his esophagus.

One of the technicians manning the controls in the van was watching the graphical representation of the voices being picked up. "We just lost a transmitter."

Bill snapped his head around. "Did they find it?"

The technician threw his hand up.

Cindy Cooper mumbled something and then cleared her throat. "It's possible, sir. I did have trouble getting the last phone back together. But I don't see how they could know it was tapped. More likely, sir, is that I screwed up the receiver somehow. I had to really squeeze it. There wasn't much room in that case. They found the loose screw, but probably nothing else."

Bill wondered what in the hell was going on. After a moment, he said, "Okay, for now we will go on the assumption that it malfunctioned. Keep monitoring the others. We'll know if they found it soon enough."

Tim Bannister said, "We got something, anyhow." He burned it to a disk which he popped out of the computer and held in his hand. Tim had been in the agency when Bill's partner had been caught taking a bribe. He knew that Bill's career had been unjustly affected. He faced

Bill and stood mute, as if mulling over a great conflict. His eyes glassed over. "You want it, or should we send it in?" He meant that he could also transmit the file via a satellite link.

"I'll take it." Bill plucked the DVD out of Tim's hand and slid it into the breast pocket of his sport coat. He told himself he wanted to listen to it again. The patriots were apparently planning some sort of take-over. *But a takeover of what, where, when?*

The truth of the matter was—Bill didn't know why he wanted the disk.

Was it to save, or expose, his brother? Suddenly he noticed every-one in the van looking at him. He tried to snap out of his thoughts and concentrate. "As soon as possible, I want that bug fixed. I'm also going to call in the NSA and get some of their long-range equipment. This case just got a hell of a lot bigger. Keep listening. If Hartman shows up at the bomb plant, I want Hartman and Jeff picked up as soon as you can get your ass to a judge for warrants. These bastards are going down."

"Will do, boss."

❧

ANNE WAS IN STUNNED DISBELIEF—HER THROAT WAS CON-stricted in anger. Jeff was holding the phone in one hand and a small circular object in the other. He had already crushed it. He gently cradled the phone down and waved her to the back of the house. She followed her son to the middle of the backyard. He leaned to her and cupped his hands around his mouth and covered her ear.

"Mom, it has to be the FBI. This is a bug. Probably others in the house. We will keep talking, even a little about the patriots. Be nor-mal. I don't want them to know we've discovered the tap." Anne was somewhat taken aback by the steady way Jeff was responding to the situation. He glanced around as if searching for someone. "Let's get back inside. Relax. Everything will be okay." He led her by the hand back into the house.

Anne's head was spinning, but her blood was boiling. She wanted to rip the heart right out of that phony law professor and his brother. She saw it now.

He had been using her to get to Jeff.

Why, he had probably known about or even planted the transmitter! No wonder he had told her he was willing to see her at the risk his career; it was all a setup! That bastard!

Jeff stopped just before they reentered the back door. He again cupped his hands around Anne's ear and spoke in whispered tones. "I just remembered. This couldn't have come at a worse time. I can't explain everything, but one of Dad's adversaries in the patriots, a guy—Nate Smith—the Vice Commander, wants a violent revolution. He wants to do terrorist shit like the Oklahoma bombing. Anyhow, Nate has called an important meeting for tonight. Dad and Miles were supposed to go. And me." Jeff stroked his chin with the palm of his hand, apparently thinking as fast as he could. "At the moment I'm not confident of my own phone. I have to get to them so we can talk face to face. Something is funny. This is too much—way too much—coincidence."

Haunting memories of divorce, of lost ambition, of bleak, sterile vistas, cascaded into Anne's mind. Like a room with walls covered with bookshelves, filled from floor to ceiling, Anne's mind felt as if a tornado had whipped through and sucked every book into its swirling rage—sending everything around and around in a churning vortex—tearing covers and bindings, ripping free whole chapters, crumpling and scattering pages in knee-deep piles of mangled books. Anne's head swayed under the weight of ponderous reflection. Each book represented a portion of her life, an area about which she felt some closure, even basic equanimity; now there was utter confusion, pure chaos. Her first instinct was to protect her son. He hadn't broken any laws, as far as she could tell. Next, she had to protect herself. Any legal trouble would ruin her chance to finish law school. Then she had Hartman to think about. He was still the man with whom she had borne their only child. And finally there was Bradley.

She wanted to pull out that bastard's fingernails.

Jeff again spoke into her ear. "Mom, I need your help in getting me out of here. I've got to warn Dad and Miles. I'd use the computer in the fort, but undoubtedly the house is being watched and I can't risk it until night. I need you to help get me out of here. And remember. Be *natural*."

Anne could feel her legs weaken and wobble slightly. Her knees buckled and she began to fall. Jeff caught her and struggled slightly to hold her up. "Mom, are you okay?"

Anne stared at him.

"Okay. Dumb question. Here, come over and sit for a minute. We can't go in the house until you're normal." Anne put her rear on the arm of a concrete two-person bench sitting under a big maple tree; there was a puddle of water on the seat from the rain earlier in the day.

Anne fought off a laugh—a big, hysterical laugh. "Be natural, be normal," he'd said. *Oh sure! No problem!* Lives were at stake. Careers were on the line. Someone wanted a violent revolution. Hartman and Miles… did he say Miles? My God. Everyone's life hung on Anne Kreig's shoulders. *Be normal?*

"Mom, will you help me? We are trying to build a better country. We love America and can't stand to see it go down. Without us, you know where it is going… You could put me in the trunk of your car and drive out of here. They won't follow you, I hope, since they are after me."

Jeff had a way of making the most distasteful thing seem the right thing to do. They wanted to form a more perfect union. Well, it wasn't the first time that mantra had been used. But it begged the question. Could a revolution actually benefit her country? There was no way to know.

Sitting under the tree, Anne looked skyward. She saw birds flitting from branch to branch. There was a gentle breeze blowing, and the tree was swinging to and fro. Few leaves were left. Yet those seemed determined against all odds not to succumb. That summed up her life, didn't it? Lines from Hamlet inexplicably came to mind, as fresh as if she had read them only a moment ago—

Was she to suffer the slings and arrows of outrageous fortune, or to take arms against this sea of troubles? Would she die in the face of the heartache and the thousand natural shocks that her flesh was heir to? She had already suffered, at one time or another, the oppressor's wrong, the proud man's contumely, the pangs of dispriz'd love, the law's delay, and the insolence of office. In death she would relive and be haunted by all of it. So, why not take up arms?

Perhaps, Anne thought, conscience *does* make cowards of us all... But still, she had the will to do what was right.

She glanced again at the leaves dangling on the tree limb. Would they make it? Would she?

Did it matter?

No, by God. It didn't.

This was going to be, truly, an enterprise of great pith and moment.

Jeff snapped her from her thoughts. "Mom, I know this is complicated, but we wouldn't be doing it if we didn't think it would help the country. If Dad gets captured—Nate Smith is a crazy man. We have to stop him."

It was an easy decision. Anne put her hand to Jeff's ear. She said, "Go to the garage from the inside door and get in my trunk. No, wait. Get in *your* trunk. It's so small they won't think you could possibly be in there. In a few minutes I'll come out. But first I'll call Linda and tell her that I'm coming over and that I'm driving your car since mine is having troubles. Oh... And... And also because you are staying to watch TV or something."

"Good thinking."

With that, and her son, Anne determinedly walked into the name of action.

❧

CHAPTER 31

NATE SMITH WAS SITTING IN A PLAIN WOODEN CHAIR situated in the bay window of his safe-house in a formerly middle-class but now run-down section on the outskirts of Detroit. The heavy curtains were badly stained and drawn open only a few inches. Nate carefully brushed back the curtain a few more inches to see out at a better angle. A relatively new model car had just passed, moving very slowly, and had stopped at the end of the block. Nate fingered the grip of his Ted Yost 1911 that was firmly secured by his inside-the-waistband holster; his left hand reached to his belt where a pouch held two magazines.

A paper corporation had purchased the house five years ago, following repossession from the original owners, long since laid off by General Motors. The house was purposefully kept in the general condition of the surrounding homes, which is to say it was in disrepair. Walking up the cobbled steps required more than a little care.

The car continued down the street and Nate took his hand off the grip of his gun. He let the curtain drift back to its original position. It still gave him a view of the fallen leaves swirling around in the wind. Leonard Williams, who had been at the house since the failed attack on the warheads, was retrieving from the nearly antique Frigidaire refrigerator a couple of brews. That's all the fridge was good for anymore; the damn thing barely kept even the beer cool. It was still relatively early in the day to start drinking, but this occasion deserved a measure of celebration.

⥸

BILL FLETCHER HAD BEEN PICKED UP BY AN UNMARKED CAR and driven from the Kreig surveillance to an unmarked and otherwise unremarkable FBI surveillance van in one of the countless nondescript, light-industrial areas in and around metropolitan Detroit. The area consisted of 16 square blocks, each little more than a couple hundred yards long. The target building sat in the middle of the block and was surrounded by similarly sized tool and die shops. The rest of the area was filled with metal fabricators, stamping plants, and assorted machine shops. The streets were dirty and oil-covered from the frequent and sooty diesel trucks. Beyond the industrial sector, on all sides, was run-down housing. Many of the homes were boarded up, and a few had been burned, some to the ground, during the nationally popular (among the media) Detroit Devils' Night.

Bill was just getting briefed by the FBI agents at the scene. They still hadn't tracked down the anonymous tip, but indications from some of the highly sensitive equipment in the van confirmed the presence of chemicals typically associated with a bomb plant. The anonymous tip had indicated that the three leaders of the attack on the warheads were supposed to show up and join three armed men inside. Bill had emphasized extreme caution since he feared a trap, and he was in a surveillance van parked at one corner of the block. With him were Cindy, Tim, and two communication analysts ("techies" who were also trained and armed special agents). Parked immediately behind them was a car with three additional SWAT agents. At each of the other three corners of the block, Bill had placed a car, each containing two additional SWAT members. These nine SWAT agents, plus Bill, Cindy, and Tim gave Bill a fairly potent team should things get messy.

The agents had set up a high sensitivity receiver that could pick up a conversation from up to about 300 yards; if they got really lucky, it was possible to pick up a conversation even through a single-pane window. So far, however, nothing of significance had been learned. There was one window and one door in the back of the building. The front was a modest office that appeared barely large enough to house one manager, a secretary, and a small waiting room; it had two windows that faced the street. The building had a side door as well, and Bill had watched it with some concern.

Suddenly one of the communications agents called for Bill to come to the window of the van.

Bill took the field glasses and peered through one of the building's front windows. "It's our shooter (their name for Hartman). Let's see who else joins the party."

❧

ANNE PULLED OUT OF THE DRIVE WITH JEFF IN THE TRUNK. The FBI agent in charge reported that Anne had left the scene in Jeff's Mustang, but that she had left alone. Only one team was present, so they had to decide whether to tail Anne or stay and watch for Jeff. Presumably, Jeff was still in the house, so they stayed put.

Anne headed directly to Miles's house with Jeff in the trunk. It was only a few miles, and she tried to make it as quickly as she could. She also tried to avoid potholes, since she knew they would seem like huge craters for someone scrunched into the trunk.

Linda was raking leaves in her front lawn as Anne pulled up the drive.

Anne quickly got out of the car and went around to the trunk. She looked across the lawn to Linda. "Is Miles here?" The trunk popped open and Jeff crawled out, stretching his arms and legs as if they had been cramped up for weeks.

Linda, standing ramrod straight in the middle of her lawn, eyes wide and mouth dropped open, rake still in hand, said, "What the—"

Anne cut her off. "No time to explain. Is Miles here?"

"No, he left about five minutes ago. Some meeting—"

Anne was already out to the middle of the lawn and had Linda by the hand. "You are coming with us!"

The three piled into the Mustang and Anne threw it into reverse and punched the accelerator, jolting everyone forward in their seats. She snapped the car out on to the road. All heads then jerked backward as she pressed the accelerator to the floor. The wide tires spun and squealed on the now-dry pavement.

Anne glanced in the rear-view mirror in time to see Jeff turn his head back to observe the long black slick of smoldering rubber left on the pavement and the wisps of smoke gently raising into the air. She wanted to smile but gritted her teeth instead.

Anne raced to the meeting place, taking directions from Jeff as they went. Linda was in the back seat, jostling and sliding back and forth with every bump or sharp turn, eyes and mouth wide open, still. Jeff turned around to face Linda.

"First thing, put on your seat belt."

Linda glared but snapped it on without objection.

"Second thing. What has Miles told you about what we have been doing?"

Linda's face screwed up. "What? Who's doing… What?"

"I don't have time to give you the whole picture, but basically, Miles and I are in the patriots. My dad is the leader. We are supposed to be at a meeting tonight but it appears the FBI wants to arrest us. So we are trying to get to Miles and my dad before the meeting and get them out. I'd call them on their cells, but I don't trust them right now."

Anne glanced in the rearview mirror and saw Linda's face blanch, which was impressive given that she was black.

"What? My Miles is wanted by the FBI! Oh my God I'm going to have a heart attack! Since when? Why? What has he done wrong? Oh my God!"

Anne had to virtually yell since the noise of the racing engine and squealing tires was making it hard to hear, *"Linda, relax! We are going to get to Miles before he makes it to the meeting!"* She didn't say that they were also going to get Hartman if they could. She continued, "Technically, he hasn't really done anything, but if Jeff is right, the FBI mistakenly thinks he is involved in an illegal militia."

Full color returned to Linda's face and her eyes narrowed. She studied Jeff a moment and then looked to Anne. "Then step on it!"

After approximately 20 miles the surrounding tool and die shops told them they were getting close. Anne slowed to a crawl as all three kept a lookout for potential FBI surveillance vehicles and a way to approach the building by way of an alley or through a series of interconnected parking lots. After a few minutes they found an alley that dead-ended at a small stamping plant. A short piece of pavement connected to a truck delivery route for a tire wholesaler which was two blocks to the front of the bomb plant. Jeff had Anne stop at the end of the alley and he got out and walked along the truck path and disappeared around the wholesaler's building.

Jeff returned after about 10 minutes. "The FBI has the building surrounded. I could just make out a small sign on the lawn. It's called West Side Tooling and Die. They have cars on the two corners I could see. I'm sure the others are covered. We can't get any closer."

Linda said, "If we can't get closer, we stand a good chance of missing Miles. He could easily approach from one of the three sides."

Jeff touched a finger to his chin. "But this is the most likely route, if he comes from Ann Arbor." Jeff shrugged. "Nothing else we can do. We will just have to wait and see if we get lucky."

Anne happened to glance to her right, down another alley that ran behind the shops and out to one of the streets. Something went past her field of view fairly quickly, but she was pretty sure it was Miles's new red pickup. He had customized it with a front-end flame paint job of the type seen on old WORLD WAR II fighters.

Anne was about to say she might have just seen Miles when she got an idea. "Jeff, take Linda's phone and call West Side Tooling and Die; if they still have a phone, tell Hartman, assuming he's in there, to make a run for it—to us. The FBI won't expect some guy just bolting out of the building—and he can probably make it past everyone." She didn't say that she also hoped Miles would see the ensuing commotion and keep on driving.

Jeff got the number for West Side Tooling and Die and dialed. The phone began to ring. And it continued to ring…

Jeff said, "Come on… Come on. Answer the damn phone… Come on!"

◆

HARTMAN HEARD THE PHONE RINGING UP FRONT, BUT HE was damn near in a state of shock as to why Nate would call a meeting at such a place. He had been pacing around just waiting to chew into Nate when he arrived. They didn't need any homemade bombs damn it! Terrorism was not their bag. Obviously, this was some game Nate was playing.

But the phone in front was still ringing.

Hartman said to one of the three bomb makers, "Phone ever ring here?"

"No."

"I'm going to go answer it." As he headed to the front offices alarm bells started going off in his head.

"Hello—"

The line went dead.

Hartman held the receiver for a second, and toyed with the idea of leaving it off the hook. He set it on the telephone cradle and shook his head. Something was definitely wrong.

◆

JEFF HAD GROWN IMPATIENT AND WAS SECOND GUESSING whether he had dialed the right number. He punched redial and prayed.

◆

HARTMAN WAS ALREADY OUT OF THE FRONT OFFICES WHEN he heard the phone ring again. This time he quickly moved to pick it up.

"Hello?"

"Dad! Mom's house was bugged. The FBI is outside the building right now. What's going on?"

"This is a freaking bomb factory!"

"It's a set-up. You have to get out. Front door. Across the street and between the buildings. Two blocks. There is an alley, we are on the right. The FBI is on all four corners, so move!"

❦

BILL WAS STILL PEERING THROUGH ONE OF THE BUILDING'S front windows when one of the techies tapped him on the shoulder and pointed to a computer screen that displayed the conversation Jeff and Hartman had just had. Bill reached into his coat for his radio. And as he did...

Hartman burst through the front door of the building, running full tilt across the street on which their van was parked, quickly disappearing between the buildings. Just seconds later, a fancy red Ford pickup stopped at the front of the building.

"Jesus!" Bill could see their cover was somehow blown. But how? Well, it didn't make any difference. They had to move fast. Bill barked orders over the radio. Quickly, the car closest to the front of the building raced ahead to the middle of the block and screeched to a halt. Agents burst forth and chased after Hartman. One FBI car stationed at the back corner raced around to the red truck. Two SWAT agents jumped out and pulled Miles from the side of the truck facing away from the building. Miles struggled a bit from the shock of what was happening, and both agents were forced to focus on Miles instead of the front of the building.

Things were happening too fast. Bill was too busy coordinating activities to notice two men with M16s come to the front windows of the building. They opened fire.

Hearing the gunshots and seeing the scene on the video monitor, Cindy, Tim, and the three SWAT agents rushed out of the van and car. Bill ordered the techies to say behind, observe, coordinate if necessary, and call backup. Bill was the last out and he stopped on the first step of the van, making sure he was shielded by the door. He peered around to look to the front of the building.

Two of the three SWAT agents stationed behind the van raced to get behind a parked car about 50 yards closer to the building from which the bad guys were shooting. The third SWAT member circled around the van and disappeared from view. *Good,* Bill thought, he was attempting to flank the shooters and engage them from the side. Suddenly one of the SWAT members racing to the parked car reeled backwards, apparently hit.

Instinctively, Bill took a step down from the van and away from the protection of the door…

He felt something hit his chest, under his left arm. It made him look toward the side of the building, where there was an access door he had been watching earlier. Except that now it was open, and under a bearded face and wild eyes of fire was an M16 that had just pushed a 60 grain bullet down its 20 inch barrel at just over 3100 feet per second.

Bill tumbled forward.

❧

CINDY AND TIM HAD RUSHED ACROSS THE STREET FROM THE shooters to a building that had a waist-high brick wall running in an "L" shape from its parking lot to its front door. Shrubbery grew along both sides of the wall. They both dived behind the wall and, more than less, into the shrubbery. Cindy quickly righted herself and extracted a branch that had jammed its way up her right sleeve. She was aware of Tim off to her side, also extracting himself from the branches of the shrubbery. He was cursing something.

"What the hell is this stuff? You'd think they could plant nice soft flowers."

Cindy cracked a slight smile. She drew her Springfield Professional 1911-style .45 caliber semiautomatic. Cindy's gun frequently placed two-inch groups at 50 yards. She loved that gun and practiced with it obsessively. While the average FBI agent will fire 20,000 rounds in a career. Cindy fired that many every year.

FBI special agents had been taught to carry their weapons with a round in the chamber, the hammer cocked, and with the safety activated—so called "cocked and locked." Cindy drew her gun and took a kneeling position behind the brick wall, resting the butt of her left hand on the top of the wall. Her left hand wrapped around her right hand, which gripped the weapon. She carefully peered over the wall. Her peripheral vision picked up Tim, to her left. He was doing the same with his 1911.

Two shooters from inside the building apparently had illegal (for civilians) M16A2s, which is to say the guns were distinguished from the legal AR-15 by virtue of having the option of selecting between two firing modes: semiautomatic, which meant that the gun would fire every time the trigger was depressed, or burst, which would fire three shots every time the trigger was pulled.

The shooters had the M16s on burst and they were keeping up a pretty steady fire at the SWAT members behind the red pickup and the car. Several times the SWAT agents tried to raise up to get a shot with their short-barreled M16s, known as the M4. Every time, they'd been met with bursts of deadly lead. Two bad guys, even really good bad guys, can do only so much, however, and Cindy and Tim went unnoticed.

From their place of cover behind the wall, Cindy and Tim were about 45 yards from the shooters. Cindy practiced often at a distance of 25 yards, and she'd been known, at that distance, and from a draw, to put three rounds in one ragged hole within two seconds. Most of the time, however, she practiced at seven yards, which FBI statistics show is the maximum common distance for armed encounters.

Cindy said, "You go right. I'll take left. On my mark."

"Don't miss," Tim replied.

Cindy mumbled to herself, "Not a chance," as she lined up the three dots of her sights on the middle of a forehead.

Cindy said, "You got him?"

"Yup."

"Okay. On three. One. Two. Three…"

They fired double taps.

Cindy's target sprouted an arching fountain of blood. He instantly dropped out of sight. The other shooter was doused in blood. Tim had missed, however, and the blood-soaked shooter ducked down.

Cindy swore.

Still, the SWAT agents recognized what had just happened and they leapt to action, charging from opposite sides of the pickup and the car to the sides of the building. The shooter stayed out of sight long enough for the SWAT members to complete their move, and when he reappeared and opened fire toward the truck, all four SWAT agents stepped from the side of the building—just enough to get an angle into the window. The shooter was instantly cut down in a flurry of lead.

That left one *known* bad guy.

And everyone knew he was the one who had shot Bill.

Cindy prayed that he would *not* come out with his hands up. It was time for an eye for an eye. and she wanted the bastard for herself.

For a moment the men just stood their ground, mesmerized by what was taking place. Cindy, however, instantly realized the last bad guy likely had a brain and was heading out the back door. Of course, she knew that would put him in the path of the two agents who were covering the back of the building. But *she* wanted this bastard, and consequently she took off in a dead run across the street. Tim yelled after her but she ignored it. She raced past the front of the building (where the SWAT agents were now carefully approaching the front door) and between the bomb plant and the adjacent building. As she approached the back of the bomb plant, she moved up against the wall, her Springfield 1911 in the low ready.

Cindy's heart was pounding out of her head. She could actually feel the beating in her ears! Her chest was heaving. She willed her hands and arms to be still. Slowly, she approached the back corner of the bomb plant. She knew the other FBI agents would have their weapons trained on the door and any windows. *Damn!* She suddenly couldn't remember if there were any windows! *Come on, think...*

Yes!

There was one.

Between herself and the door. And the door was approximately in the middle of the building.

Suddenly there was the distinctive popping from another M16 on burst. She dared a peek around the corner. Every muscle tensed. Her gun was still in the low ready. She told herself to relax her grip; her hands were getting fatigued.

She could see the barrel of an M16 sticking out the window. And it was only 10 or so feet from where she stood! Out of the corner of her eye she saw another agent wave to her. He was signaling for her to get back. Undoubtedly, backup was near, and they had no reason to take more chances than they already had. This asshole wasn't going anywhere.

But he had killed her mentor—shot, she told herself. He had been shot. She had no idea if it was fatal.

Then the bastard got smart and switched to semi-auto fire. That made him more accurate.

Cindy heard the pop of the M16 and then she watched as the top portion of an agent's head disappeared in a hail of skull fragments, brains, and blood.

The killing of President Kennedy immediately came to mind.

It was a virtual replay, except this was the agent who had just waved for her to get back.

That was enough! Cindy raced around the corner and crouched as she passed under the window and the barrel of the M16, which was still pointing out toward the other agents huddling behind their cars. She reached the door and, without pausing, pushed the latch down and yanked the door out. Quickly she raced through the door—her training had taught her that doors are killing funnels—and she threw herself to her knees, sliding on the oily concrete floor behind the first piece of machinery she could see. As she slid, however, she brought her Springfield up from the low ready and lined up the sights and inserted her forefinger into the trigger guard.

The shooter reacted quickly, but he was surprised, and thus a split second behind. Also, he had to pull the M16 back through, and then down from, the window.

Cindy's mind and body were on autopilot. Abstractly, she knew that it was a race for life. Who would be the first to bring the weapon to bear? Who would shoot accurately? Who had trained the most? Who had "muscle memory" from thousands upon thousands of repetitions?

And on whose side would be lady luck?

In no more than two seconds of deafening reports—smoke and fire spitting from the muzzles of a .45 semiautomatic and a .223 assault rifle—the matter was decided.

Decisively.

Cindy stood and felt her body with her left hand—her right holding her gun steadily on target. There didn't seem to be any unwanted holes.

The same couldn't be said for the sorry son-of-a-bitch leaning in a crumpled heap against the inside wall, his gun caught ominously under his limp body. Blood was spurting, intermittently, from two holes in the center of his chest. The hole smack dab in the middle of his forehead had initially spurted blood but now merely bled in a steady, but weakening, stream.

Cindy started to shake uncontrollably.

Then she threw up.

↦

ANNE SAW HARTMAN COMING—AS WELL AS THE TWO agents some ways behind. Jeff had already wedged himself in the back seat with Linda. He had the door open for Hartman. Anne had the engine racing and the clutch to the floor. Her stomach was in a knot and her palms were sweaty on the steering wheel. Couldn't he run any faster?

Hartman dived in and Anne slid her foot off the clutch. They didn't have to worry about closing the door. It slammed shut so hard Anne thought it might tear right off. She laid rubber the entire length of the alley. She was getting to like the 5.0 part of Jeff's Mustang.

Once they were away from the scene, and apparently not followed, Anne eased off on the imitation of Jeff Gordon. She looked in the back seat via the rear view mirror and almost broke out laughing. Linda's eyes were still as big around as grapefruits, her hair frazzled every which way. It was Whoopi Goldberg with her finger stuck in a light socket.

Hartman, on the other hand, was humorless, all business, calm, and staring straight ahead. Then, as if he had reconsidered something, he turned to Anne. "Thank you." Anne turned to meet his gaze. His eyes… they were so full of… something… they were red around the edges. Were they just a little watery? There was something on which she couldn't put her finger. In any event, this was definitely not the man who had divorced her.

Anne tried to keep an eye on the rearview mirror as she drove. Hartman turned toward the back seat. "Jeff, I don't know what happened back there." His eyes darted quickly to Linda and then back to Jeff. "We have to assume Miles has been captured along with the rest of those people. Nate Smith obviously wanted us out of the picture. He's probably going to take command. The FBI will assume we are behind this place. We have to hide and retake control—somehow. They will start looking for this car. Scratch that; they are looking for this car."

Anne said, "Why don't I drive you right to the police?"

Hartman seemed stunned.

Anne continued, "I'm not kidding. You can prove you were set up, and merely being the leader of the patriots doesn't mean you've committed any crime." She knew that might not be totally true, but she was looking for any way to solve the escalating crisis. She continued, "And the police can find this Nate guy and put a stop to… whatever."

Hartman ran his hand across his chin and appeared to be thinking. "Look, Anne, you are probably right, so far as this episode goes. But there is a larger issue here." He paused again, carefully selecting his words. "There is going to be a takeover of the U.P., a revolution. It's planned to start in a couple of days. The question, and this largely depends on you, is whether it will be bloody. Jeff and I need your help. We have to hide in the fort while we contact a bunch of people and tell them what's going on. We need some time to do that and to make sure our plans are on track. Right now, we are the only ones who stand between Nate Smith, who set us up just now, and who knows what."

Jeff said, "How are we going to do that? We have no idea where he is or what he intends."

Hartman said, "You can be sure it involves something that explodes and that innocent people will die. But we will need your mother's help so we have time to figure out what he is planning."

Just what I wanted, Anne thought, her heart aching with concern. If she helped, she could save lives, presumably. And possibly her son would come out of this without a criminal record. If she refused, and drove to a police station, then apparently this Nate character would be on the loose. Bradley jumped into her mind. That jerk! He was behind this. Her stomach felt like it was one of those rubber bands on toy airplanes made of balsa. You can twist the propeller round and round, twisting and knotting that rubber band, with knots knotting on knots... Yep. That was her stomach, all right. How was she going to get through this day?

But what if Bradley had nothing to do with this? Oh she wanted to talk to him! To find out. To ask his advice. He would tell her whether he was for or against her. And she needed to know at least that. Of course, if he'd been involved in targeting her son, that would be the end of their relationship for sure. Oddly, however, she felt a peace at the prospect of losing him.

But she didn't intend to lose her son. She glared at Hartman. "Tell me what you need."

❧

THE FBI AGENTS AT THE KREIG HOUSE GOT A CALL TO ENTER and arrest Jeff. They searched the house, the barn, and the surrounding fields. Jeff and Hartman both would have had a heart attack if they had seen how close an agent came to stumbling on the metal "ring" that opened the door to the fort. One agent commented on the cool dune buggy, and another noticed the small junction box near the ground on an outside wall, but said nothing, thinking it must have been for the barn light he had seen above the entry.

Anne ditched the car in the woods a couple of miles away from her home. No one was sure the car had been identified, but there was no sense in taking any chances. Anne, Linda, Jeff, and Hartman trudged through fields and woods to the back of Anne's property.

To the general surprise of the FBI agents watching the house from the field across the street, the garage door opened and Anne drove off with a passenger they identified as her friend, Linda Larson. There was immediate confusion about what to do. Technically, they had no legitimate reason to stop Anne or Linda. It was her son they were after. Further, with the shoot-out, they were temporarily without a ranking officer who knew much about the investigation. So, rather than make a mistake, they simply watched Anne drive away.

Hartman and Jeff hid in the woods until dark and then made their way to the barn and into the fort.

Nate sent an encrypted text message to all leaders explaining that Hartman was, regrettably, out of the loop. Consequently, he was assuming the role of Commander. Nate added that Hartman had obviously been lying, since he had been secretly operating a bomb-making facility that the FBI had just discovered.

Nate ordered the rest of the operation to begin immediately, as previously planned. Colonel Riggins was to put his men and women in motion: transport planes were to begin flying and the air wing's helicopters were to begin their trip to the decommissioned KI Sawyer Air Force Base. The A-10s were also to defect and make their trip to KI Sawyer, where they would be quickly retrofitted with the Russian missiles.

Across the state of Michigan, approximately one million deer hunters were already packing and getting ready for the two-week firearms deer season set to begin this second week in November. It was the most clever part of the plan. A good percentage of those armed hunters had no interest in deer.

❧

CHAPTER 32

Jeff awoke with a start. His eyes flickered several times and then opened. His head jerked up and he tossed open the heavy wool blanket in which he was sandwiched. He coughed a couple of times to clear his throat. He'd slept on the fort's cold and damp concrete floor.

Hartman groaned and turned over, away from Jeff. He curled up in a fetal position and wedged his hands between his knees. He had elected to use the entire blanket, official U.S. Navy issue, doubled over, to shield himself from the floor. He was shivering. Without moving from his fetal position he said, "For Heaven's sake, you think Anne could have given us a few more blankets… and pillows."

"She would look pretty conspicuous if someone saw her bringing pillows to the barn for the horses. A couple of blankets she could do."

Hartman coughed; it was grossly productive. The cold was clearly affecting his sinuses. "Yeah, I guess. But no running water, no toilet, a tiny space heater that's damn near useless—" His head still on the blanket, out of the corner of his eye, Hartman saw a candy bar wrapper and a few crumpled pieces of paper on the floor next to the trash can. "And trash all over the floor."

Jeff rubbed his stiff neck. "It's not like this place was intended to be a hotel room."

Hartman grumbled something Jeff didn't catch. Jeff sat up Indian-style. He was still trying to rub the stiffness out of his neck. "What are you going to do? I'm sure by now Nate has told everyone you're wanted for the bomb factory. He's probably taken over. What do you think he's going to do? What the hell does he have up his sleeve?"

Hartman got to one knee and wavered slightly. "Whoa," he said, as he touched one hand to the floor. He paused a moment and then stood, still a little wobbly. "I've got to get out of this dungeon to where I can get some cell reception. I've probably got 50 messages, voice and text. Soon as I return some calls and find out what Nate's done, I'll figure it out."

"Makes sense. Just be careful. I'm sure the FBI can't break my enhanced encryption program, but I can't guarantee they won't locate you by your call. So I'd wait to make calls to be safe. And when you do, we should get out of here."

"Jeff, I've got to find out what's going on."

Jeff considered it for a moment. He still had a software program from his hacking days that could be used to mount a brute force attack on Nate's computer to find his system password. If Jeff could update it and perhaps load in some things about Nate's life… He said, "Dad, I've got an idea."

❧

ANNE ARRIVED TO HER CONSTITUTIONAL LAW CLASS SEVeral minutes early. Nervous but determined, she held out her hand and watched it shake. "Steady now," she whispered to herself, clenching her hand into a white-knuckled fist. She had already gone to Bradley's office, and Beth had said he was not in. Then she had called his cell and gotten no answer. Either her luck was bad, or he was avoiding her.

Students started to trickle in, and then they arrived in a wave. The class was full. She didn't want to confront Bradley in front of an entire class, so she took her seat. A moment later, Bradley entered and walked straight to the lectern.

Bradley started right in on his lecture and Anne didn't hear a word he said. She desperately wanted to confirm what she feared: that his only interest in her was to investigate Jeff. Six months ago news like that would have killed her. But not now. It took all of her self control to sit quietly. The urge to march right up to him in the middle of the class and demand an answer was nearly irresistible.

Just then the Associate Dean burst into the class and quickly walked over to Bradley. Anne couldn't hear what he said. His back was turned to the class as he spoke to Bradley.

But Bradley's face told the story. It was clearly bad news. Bradley went white and even seemed to lose his balance as he reached out and steadied himself on the lectern. The Associate Dean stepped forward and also steadied him.

Suddenly, Bradley looked directly at Anne.

Immediately, she felt his piercing eyes cut to her bone. Without thinking, she jumped up, sending her textbook, pen, and note pad crashing to the floor. She rushed to his side. She grabbed on to him and was frightened by how weak he felt. He had always been so strong in her arms. They had always caressed her and had given her a feeling of security. Now, oddly, it seemed reversed.

The Associate Dean spoke First. "Bradley, should I get you a doctor?"

"No… No. I'm okay."

"I'll drive you to the hospital."

Anne said, "Hospital?"

"My brother was shot last night…"

Anne's heart leaped to her throat and she began to shake, again. She recalled her own narrow escape from the FBI. She had been so singleminded at the time… Now she recalled hearing muted pops—gunfire. That might have been Bill getting shot! My God! If Bradley knew she had been there! A wave of heat swept over her body and her legs threatened to buckle. To fight it off, she clenched her teeth and tightened her grip on Bradley's arm. *Screw the Associate Dean!* She embraced Bradley in a manner that bespoke a significant relationship. "Bradley, I'll drive you. My car is right outside the classroom."

The Associate Dean stood back. His big bushy eyebrows were raised so high they seemed to be touching his scalp. Anne shot him a hostile glance and his eyes popped out of his head.

Without waiting for a reply, Anne gripped Bradley's arms and
pulled him into the hallway. She grimaced. He felt like a limp doll as
she held him by an arm and began to direct him out to her car. His legs
moved, but a bit more slowly than hers, and they refused to support
his entire weight. She was puffing and sweating by the time they made
it out to curb. Thank God she had lucked out with a parking spot right
outside the law school. She stuffed him into the car.

They got to the nurses' station just in time to be told that Bill was
in surgery down the hall. They ran down the corridor and made it to
the doors leading to the operating room just as a body was wheeled
out of surgery. They both stopped dead in their tracks. Anne's heart
was pounding from the run. The nurse who had been pushing the
cart paused to make a notation on a clipboard just outside the operating room doors. The only thing Anne could make out were the letters
"gsw."

Anne stepped forward and read the name on the chart attached to
the cart.

It was Bill.

And his head was covered by a sheet.

A doctor walked into the hall and made a notation on Bill's chart.
His back was to Bradley and Anne.

"He's my brother."

The doctor turned around. His expression was emotionless. "I'm
sorry. I'm the surgeon, Dr. Lippart. He never regained consciousness. When they brought him in last evening he was in surgery for six
hours. Apparently, it took a while for someone to contact you. About
two hours ago he developed complications. We did everything we—"

"It's okay, doctor."

The surgeon nodded and walked away.

A wall of suffocating guilt descended on Anne. She had stopped
her excessive breathing, but beads of sweat were forming around her
mouth and in her hairline. What could she say? She was sure he would
eventually learn that she had been at the shooting. Yet, she wasn't
absolutely sure that she had been there when Bill was shot. But did
that technicality make a difference?

Bradley startled Anne out of her thoughts. "Anne… I'm so glad you are here." He pulled her into his arms, put his head on her shoulder— and started to cry. Anne reached up and ran her fingers through his hair. They were both startled by the nurse's brisk voice.

"I take it you are family?"

Bradley pulled his head from Anne's shoulder. His face and eyes were red with tears. "Yes. I'm his brother."

"Well, I don't know how this happened. It's not supposed to. But new people are always screwing up. Anyway, someone from the ambulance just brought this in. Said it got accidentally kicked under or behind— I forget what she said—some equipment." She held out a plastic bag containing the tattered remains of a blue sport coat that had obviously been cut off the body and was drenched in blood. "Anyway, this is personal property and if you take it I won't have to try to cover for some fool's mistake in not getting it into inventory."

Anne was stunned that Bradley took it. It was potential evidence of a murder. She knew it should have been taken by FBI forensics. Obviously, he still wasn't thinking.

He said, "Thank you." The nurse hurried off down the corridor. Bradley opened the bag and seemed to absently rummage through the pockets of the jacket. He pulled a DVD from an inner pocket. He held it up and examined it. After a moment, he slipped it in his own coat pocket. He grabbed her by the hand. "I've got to talk to you. And I've got to get out of here—my head is spinning and I feel like I'm going to be sick."

❧

OUTSIDE, BRADLEY FELT HIS STOMACH SETTLE. IT HAD GOT- ten awfully stuffy in the hospital—the smell of sickness, beeping monitors, and the sight of Bill…

The change of environment was helping. It was a typical fall day in Michigan. Multicolored leaves were scattered about; their fragrance was strong in the cool and crisp air. His mind, however, was still numb.

Anne said, "Bradley, I know about everything."

"What?" *What the heck was she talking about?*

"You must not tell anyone. I have to have your promise that what I am going to tell you—you will keep secret. If you can't promise, let me know—right now."

Bradley stared at her, unable to figure out what was going on. His brother was dead, and this woman wanted him to keep some secret. Was she *insane*?

Anne stepped around in front of Bradley and grabbed him by the arms. Her face was stiff, the muscles of her jaws, taut.

"Yes, okay, okay," he said, as much to get her out of his face as anything. Bradley's head was beginning to feel as if it were in a vice. And Anne was twisting the handle.

Anne said, "First I have a question. I have to know something."

Bradley didn't know how much of this he could take. "I'm so tired Anne. I can't handle this." He began to lean away but she tightened her grip on his arms.

Her face was set. "Do you love me?"

Bradley felt his legs begin to buckle—again. Anne kept her tight grip and supported him. "Anne, that's not fair to ask me right now."

She tilted her head to the side slightly. Her eyes softened but remained determined. "I'm sorry about the circumstances. I can't help that. But I think you just answered me. Let's go." Anne let go of his arms and walked briskly toward the emergency parking for the hospital. Bradley paused to let her get a few steps ahead, and then followed.

The short drive to Bradley's house was in total silence. He couldn't think of anything to say. Apparently, neither could she. When she pulled up to the curb at his house, she stared straight ahead. He really wanted to say something. To talk. But his mind was all gummed up. Nothing seemed to make any sense. He got out of the car and watched Anne drive away. When she was out of sight, he remembered the plastic bag in his hand and the DVD in his pocket. What in the hell was he doing with this stuff? Why had that nurse given it to him? She must have broken every rule in the book. Oh well, he would have to give it to someone in the F BI first thing tomorrow.

❧

T HE C-130S WERE BEGINNING TO LAND AT KI SAWYER AIR Force Base, 15 miles south of Marquette in Michigan's U.P. The civilians in the joint military/civilian use complex were excited to see so much weaponry unload. Naturally, they assumed that it was some kind of training exercise. No one even thought to make any calls to check up on it. And even if they had, Colonel Riggins had pushed the paperwork through. Moreover, the only danger Riggins had feared was getting stopped before his planes took off. Once they were in the air and on their way to KI Sawyer, he knew his team would make it.

Defending the Michigan–Wisconsin border would actually be quite easy. Most of the border runs down the middle of a river with very few bridges that cross it. What isn't largely impenetrable due to water is mostly impenetrable due to rugged terrain and dense forest. A patriot force some 300,000 strong would have no difficulty turning back anything likely to come his way for at least a week. He also had dispatched forces to back up about 10,000 patriots who would hold the only other ways into the U.P.: the Mackinac and Sault Ste. Marie bridges.

The rest of Riggins's plan called for the ability to locate any encroaching formations with airborne radar. His Apache attack helicopters and the A-10 Thunderbolt IIs would then move in to intercept. If necessary, he could quickly air lift heavy weapons to problem areas.

The entire operation was, from a military standpoint, a no-brainer. Riggins knew it would take some time for the United States to mount a counteroffensive (if it did so at all) and that he needed only to inflict light casualties to create enough public outcry to stall the counterattack. Further, once it became known that the local population desired and welcomed his forces, and that *everyone* in the U.P. was armed, the federal government would have no choice but to relent and grant the Upper Peninsula its desired independence.

At least that was the plan.

Meanwhile, Nate Smith had been in the Upper Peninsula for a couple of days, personally visiting his core groups of "hunters" to make sure they all knew what to do and to ensure their allegiance to him. He had traveled to the U.P. in an SUV with boxes full of the very latest high-powered explosives. Further, there were three identically loaded SUVs heading to other locations. They would provoke and energize the population to revolt. Obama had gotten violence to spark revolutions all over the world. This time it would be in service of a just cause.

❧

CHAPTER 33

ANNE WALKED ACROSS THE GRASS, MEANDERING between tombstones. She could see that Bradley was delivering the eulogy. Bill was survived by his wife and two children, who were standing to one side, facing Bradley. Anne couldn't tell whether the little ones were crying, but she knew if they were not doing so outwardly, they surely were inwardly. They seemed young; one was probably about 10, and the other maybe seven. Anne felt as if a thousand knives were piercing her heart. Tears welled up in her eyes and began to run down her cheeks. For a few minutes, her own problems seemed less important.

Yet Anne was incessantly tormented. How could Bradley love her and participate in investigating Jeff? He couldn't, of course. But what if he merely knew that an investigation was underway? She could probably live with that. But what if he had used, and taken advantage of, her love? And what did it matter anyhow? He had told her he didn't love her.

Anne could not identify the rest of the people gathered around Bill's grave. Probably, they were FBI agents and their families. Bill and Bradley's parents had both passed away some years ago. There was no other family.

Anne kept her distance, watching from a small rise. She was just close enough to hear Bradley's voice, but not what he said. After about 10 minutes, he stopped talking and everyone began to congregate. Some were crying. Anne felt the tremendous weight of not knowing whether she had contributed to Bill's death. A sharp pain gripped her chest; maybe it was a heart attack that would kill her right then and there. Anger welled up—but it was anger at herself. She clenched her fists and dug her fingernails into her palms until deep red indentations appeared. One nail, sharper than the others, broke through the skin. She didn't notice blood oozing from the wound; a couple of drops trickled from her hand and landed on her shoe.

The group started breaking up and people headed toward the cemetery entrance. Anne started down toward the grave. She tried to wipe the tears away with a tissue, but it was quickly soaked with tears and blood. Anne noticed the blood, looked at her hand, and cursed. She reached into her purse for another tissue and saw the blood on her shoe. "Damn!" she blurted, too loudly, gaining several indignant looks from the gathering around the grave.

Bradley looked as well, and their eyes met. His eyes were like beacons bringing in a wayward ship. The next thing she knew she was standing in front of him. She couldn't remember walking the rest of the way down the hill.

"Bradley, I'm—"

"It's okay." He opened his arms.

Anne lunged into his arms. She clutched the dark wool of his sport coat with both fists. He opened his arms… was he trying to tell her something? She so wanted him to love her. Was it possible?

"Bradley—" She hesitated. There had to be a good way to ask this. "There is something I need to know…" She couldn't think of any way to put it other than directly. "Did you use me to assist the FBI in investigating Jeff?" Anne tensed in anticipation. Her world teetered on his answer.

He looked into her eyes. "Of course not."

Relief rushed through her body. But she was watching his eyes and face very carefully. She perceived some pensiveness. The muscles in his forehead seemed taut.

Bradley glanced toward the ground. "I knew Bill was investigating, but before I could ask you—well, everything happened. And that stupid nurse gave me his coat. There was a DVD inside. I played it."

Anne tensed. "Yes?"

"It's you and Jeff discussing the patriot operation or takeover. And you specifically mention that I was trying to be blind to the whole thing. Anne, this implicates all of us in varying degrees. I was going to turn it over, but now I'm having second thoughts. Just my name on something this hot could sink my career. I'm praying this is the only copy."

So it was his career he was concerned with. It felt as though Bradley had just shoved a long, sharply pointed stainless steel ice pick into her heart. She abruptly turned her face and pushed herself away from his hold. Her mind raced, trying to decide what his words meant, trying to find an interpretation that wasn't so painful. Unfortunately, the ice pick that had ripped into her chest and pierced her heart told her what she didn't want to know.

"Anne, even before this tape, I suspected Jeff was involved with the patriots, just from some things he said. But I didn't know he was a suspect in the failed attack on the nuclear warheads until—"

"What? *My son was involved in that?*" Bradley had just taken a hold of that ice pick and twisted it around.

"I don't actually know. But they were looking for the person who put together some monitor-scanning device they believe was used to intercept the delivery schedule."

That made sense. She knew about Jeff's hacking device. But it was just incredible that Jeff would have anything to do with trying to steal devices of mass destruction.

"I wanted to call and warn you as soon as Bill told me, but…" Bradley looked down. "Then he came by and told me he made a mistake in telling me and he wanted to make sure I didn't mention anything to you. And that was just before—well, if I had contacted you, it could have looked like we both were in on this craziness. We're talking federal crimes."

"I've some news for you, Bradley." She figured she might as well tell him. What did it matter? Her heart was broken…yet, what he had just explained seemed to make sense. Things were happening too fast for her mind and emotions to stay on the same page. She quickly blurted it out: "I drove the getaway car. I was at the scene where your brother was killed."

Bradley's face began to quickly lose color. He paced back and forth a few times. His voice took on an edge, "That means, Anne... hell, I don't know what it means. But you were there?"

"I was driving the car to get Hartman and Miles out of a trap. Jeff made a call into the building, which it seems was a bomb plant being used to frame Hartman, Jeff, and Miles. Hartman came running out and we escaped. Apparently, some shots were fired."

"By who?"

"I don't know. Not by any of us. We were just trying to get out of there."

"Do you realize what this could do to me? This could all but implicate me in this patriot crap. And— No. I can't believe it—" Bradley uncharacteristically ran his hand through his hair. His face was ashen. "I could be implicated in my own brother's death!"

Anne hadn't thought that far along. *How could he be implicated?* He was overreacting. *She* was the one in trouble. It was *her* fingerprints that would be in the car—not his. What the hell was he worried about? "Bradley, you're overreacting. I'm the one in trouble. Not you."

Bradley glared. "Oh yeah?" There was an edge in his voice. "Well, if losing my job and having a relationship with someone charged in a patriot murder isn't trouble, I don't know what is." He turned and walked away.

Anne watched him go the 100 or so yards to the entrance of the cemetery. He stepped through the open gate and disappeared.

Anne felt like a zombie as she drove home from the funeral. Had she reacted too harshly to Bradley? Maybe he was struggling with what to do just as much as she was. With somewhat calmer emotions, she could imagine herself and Bill standing on either side of Bradley, each pulling one of his arms in the opposite direction. A lump formed in Anne's throat. Damn, she had been too hasty with Bradley, and now, possibly he had had enough of her ticklish emotions.

The lines of Hamlet came back to her again. Maybe it wasn't such a great idea to oppose the slings and arrows of outrageous fortune. She was battling against the thousand natural shocks that flesh is heir to—but was, with a pale cast of thought, flying, headlong, to other pains she knew not of…

⟿

*T*hank *God,* JEFF THOUGHT. NATE STILL HAD HIS HOME COMputer running and on line. Jeff had just sent the command to access Nate's system.

The request was denied for lack of a password.

Hartman grumbled, "What are you doing?"

Jeff gave his dad a guilty look.

Hartman responded with a raised eyebrow and a drawn out, "Jeeeff?"

Jeff concentrated on his computer screen, in part to avoid looking at his dad.

"Jeff, what did you do?"

Might as well tell him, Jeff decided. *Face the music, as they say.* "Well, we did set up the communications via email so that, if we had to, we could try to hack Nate's private key." Jeff glanced at his dad to see his reaction. Hartman looked troubled, but not overtly hostile.

"Are you saying you put in one of those horse things?"

"Well, not exactly. Not directly."

"Shit," Hartman grumbled.

Jeff said in surprise, "What?"

Hartman mumbled sheepishly, "Maybe I miscalculated. I should have let you install one of your horses into the cell phones. I guess you were right. I don't want Nate to kill anyone. And now it's more real to me."

Jeff smiled inwardly, "You mean push has come to shove?"

Hartman gave Jeff a blank stare. "Can you get into his system?"

"Yes, eventually."

Hartman stepped in behind Jeff to watch the computer screen. "I remember your saying it would take a hundred years or some such thing to break your encryption code. We have only a couple of days, if that, before someone stumbles on that damn metal ring and finds us, or before Nate destroys the whole damn world."

"Mathematically, that's correct. To try all of the possible keys for a defense grade cryptosystem, even if you had a computer that could try something like a billion keys per second, and you had a bazillion such computers, bla, bla, bla. You get the point."

Hartman said, "So we're screwed." Jeff noted it wasn't posed as a question.

"I'm not going to try to break the encryption. That's just not realistic without a few linked Cray supercomputers. Macs are fast, but not *that* fast. What I'm going to do is different. I didn't expect to get into Nate's computer on my first try. I was just hoping Nate hadn't shut his system down or turned off the software that allows remote access." Jeff had previously made sure all of the patriot leaders had their home computers properly configured for communications with each other and the server on which Jeff and Miles had posted all of the public keys. "A password attack is really the best chance we have of finding out what Nate is up to. Until you can risk making some calls. And, to be honest, I can't *guarantee* that the system we put in is totally secure."

Hartman exhaled, "Harrumph."

Jeff looked over his shoulder at his dad. He knew what his dad was thinking. "Yeah, I doubt he's told anyone who's an ally of yours what he's up to. So, if I can break the password that restricts access, we can get into Nate's computer."

Hartman asked, "What's a password attack?"

"Well, basically, it's a guessing game. There is no magic hack that discovers a password. You have to guess it or find it somewhere on his computer, such as in a separate password collection or generation program. But even those programs will have passwords that have to be guessed. So, basically, you are back to square one. Say he has a sophisticated password generation program like I use. There is no way I'm going to break the passwords generated by a good program. But I might be able to guess the password he used to get into *that* program.

Somewhere he has to have a password he can remember that makes some sense to him. If he can remember it, and if it makes sense to him, it has to be related to his life. If we know enough about his life, we might be able to guess his password."

"You mean we need to know what he likes to read, watch on TV, stuff he likes to do? Guns he owns. Stuff like that?"

"Exactly." Jeff was surprised his very non-computer-literate dad was catching on so fast. "That's why hackers rummage through trash. Remember? That's how Miles and I broke into IBM. Someone had thrown away a disk full of passwords. People throw away magazines that can tell us their interests. They throw away receipts of what they buy. Boxes from stores. Maybe a box from REI or Williams-Sonoma, or maybe some fancy tea. Maybe a bag from an exotic coffee. Beer six-packs. Stuff like that."

"My bank ATM password is the year I was born." Hartman stopped pacing and rubbed his chin in worried contemplation.

Jeff cringed. "Ah, Dad, that's about the worst password you could use."

"I see."

"Anyhow, I've got an old password-breaking program that does nothing but throw possible passwords at a computer."

Hartman rolled his eyes. "But how in hell does it know what to try?"

Jeff wondered if his dad might be able to provide some insight into Nate's life. That could be big. Jeff looked over his shoulder at his dad. "It uses a novice word list—that is, people who are not likely to understand the basics of password strength. It searches for names of sports teams, cars, common pet names, music groups, colors, names of the computer used. It tries things like 'dad' and 'daddy,' all of the Star Trek words, names of obscure philosophers, job-related stuff like 'memo,' 'project,' 'pres,' 'sec.' It also runs through the first three digits of the social security numbers for whatever state I tell it—"

"Wait a minute. How do you know what those numbers are?"

"Easy, the first three digits are always assigned according to the state of application. Michigan numbers run from 362 to 386. I happen to remember that New York is 050 to 134. Obama claims he was born in Hawaii yet his social security number is from Connecticut. And we know that he never lived in Connecticut. So that's fraud too."

Hartman scratched his chin. "Hmm. Figures. I never realized that about social security numbers."

"Not a lot of people do. But it's all quite easy to get ahold of. Anyhow, it's a pretty comprehensive list."

"Then we should get in."

"Not necessarily. First, there are a jillion possible passwords it checks. If you can tell me more about his life, I can focus the program on a smaller number of possibilities. When I set up the access protocol on Nate's system, I took the precaution of allowing unlimited attempts at a password when the requests come in from my system. Normally, software that controls access allows three tries and then cuts you off. We can do a brute force attack, but even so, it could take a long time."

Jeff turned back to his screen. "Think, Dad; what can you tell me about his life?"

Hartman rubbed his chin and glanced around the room. "I know he reloads .45 ammunition."

"That's a start. We can run words like 'caliber,' 'brass,' 'primer,' and such, and combinations of those words with numbers that relate to guns." Thinking of his mom's illegal semiautomatic rifle he said, "Like 'ruger14.'"

Hartman quickly added, "Well, his .45 is some custom brand."

"Okay, give me some custom brands…"

❧

WHEN ANNE ARRIVED HOME FROM THE CEMETERY, SHE LET Roni and Cara out the back door to do their business, and she headed out to feed the horses. When she got to the barn, she partially closed the sliding door to darken the interior of the barn and to cast a shadow over the area in the floor where the hatch to the fort was located. Quickly, she walked to the hatch and opened it.

❧

O UTSIDE, TWO FBI AGENTS WALKED TO THE FRONT DOOR OF the house. They knocked, and after a couple moments, decided to walk around to the back door.

⋗

A NNE HAD THE HATCH OPEN AND WAS TALKING TO Hartman, who was standing on the ladder so his neck and head were above the opening. Hartman said, "Anne, I'm hungry—we're hungry and thirsty as hell. We've been down here with nothing to eat or drink! We also need money and a vehicle. We have got to get to the U.P. fast—"

Roni and Cara were outside the garage and started barking like crazy. "Quiet!" Anne cut him off and strained toward the opening, through which the sun's rays were cascading into the barn.

"What, the dogs are barking?"

"Shush!" Anne kept her eye on the door to the barn.

⋗

O NE OF THE AGENTS HEADING AROUND TO THE BACK OF THE house had encountered both dogs and was trying to remain motionless. He had heard about the rawhide caper but had not taken the time to properly arm himself. The other agent had headed around the other side, closer to the barn, and saw the barn door part way open.

⋗

H ARTMAN SAID, "IT'S JUST THE DOGS, ANNE. PROBABLY A squirrel or something."

"No, they don't bark like that at squirrels." Anne turned her head away from the opening of the barn door. Hartman absently glanced toward the opening. Anne noticed a slight change in his expression and turned her head back toward the door.

Anne didn't see Hartman reach up and push her away from the hatch as he jumped down the ladder into the fort. The hatch closed with a distinctive metal clank and sent dust flying. Anne lost her balance and fell backwards into a bale of hay. She was just about to scream Hartman's name when the agent appeared in the sunlight and shadows at the opening to the barn door.

"Ma'am?... Are you okay?"

Anne's heart leaped into her throat. She tried to say everything was fine, but no words came out. She was sure the agent knew what was going on. This was it.

The agent stepped in through the sunlight and walked over to where Anne was struggling to right herself. She was brushing off the particles of hay when he reached her.

"Ma'am, you better get some dressings on those cuts. You are bleeding pretty badly. If you don't have anything, I think we have a first aid kit in our cruiser."

Anne hadn't noticed that her wrists were bleeding from having scraped on the floor and sharp pieces of hay. "Um… yes. I mean no, I'm fine. I have stuff in the house. Thank you. I must have tripped over something feeding the horses."

The agent's head tilted slightly. He did not respond. There was something about the way he was looking at her… "Ms. Kreig, I presume?"

"Yes."

"I'm Special Agent Richard Andrew of the FBI. I'm in charge of some ongoing investigations in this area. I'm taking over for Bill Fletcher. I believe you know his brother, Bradley. He is one of your law professors, if I'm not mistaken."

"Yes, that's rrr—" Something seemed to be caught in her throat and she forced a cough. "That's right! What—" There it was again, caught in her throat. Her throat felt so tight. She forced another cough. "What can I do for you?" Anne knew she was looking pretty bad, but there didn't seem anything she could do about it. At least, for the moment, he didn't seem to have caught on. Or had he?

"Well, first off, you could tell me how you fell way over here…" He pointed to the floor at their feet. "… while feeding the horses way back on the other side?" He pointed over to the horse stalls.

Anne swallowed hard. She had to think fast. "Oh, I just meant I was in here, meaning the barn in general, feeding the horses. Of course I wasn't feeding the horses over here." She stared him in the eye, praying that she had enough control to get out of this mess. "That's a silly question, Mr. Andrew." She faked a smile to gloss over the purposeful insult that, she hoped, would break his train of inquiry. "This is where the stacks of hay are. See?" Anne waved her hand around at the numerous stacks of hay. This time she gave him a cross expression, as if scolding him. She was trying everything—and anything.

The Special Agent glanced around as if scanning for something. He stared at a stack of hay just a few feet away. He seemed to be thinking. He said, "We are looking for your son, Jeff. I understand he lives here. Have you seen him?"

"Yes." *Thank God,* Anne thought. He seemed to have given up on his train of thought and was moving on.

Richard Andrew pulled out a note pad from his breast pocket and began scribbling something. "Okay, when was that?"

"Yesterday, just after he got home from work. He hasn't been in the house since then."

That apparently wasn't the answer he expected. His eyes seemed to study her. Oddly, she felt pleased with herself. The fact was, she hadn't lied. He had not asked where she last *saw* Jeff. It was true that he hadn't been *in the house.*

"Is it normal for him to leave and not return without telling you where he is going?"

"Yes, it is." Again, Anne mused, she was telling the truth.

"Ms. Kreig, please take my card and let me know when you hear from him or when he comes home. We need to ask him some questions."

"Can I ask about what?"

"No. Good day to you. Thank you for your time."

❧

JEFF AND HARTMAN HAD BEEN WORKING NON STOP TRYING TO brainstorm possible pass phrases for Nate's computer. They had run through every gun they could think of, every caliber of ammunition, brand of ammunition... They tried "Ted Yost" with the numerals 4 and 5 in all positions around the words: 4ted5yost, yost45ted, tedyost45, etc. They tried every brand of gun powder used to reload ammunition, and nothing had worked. Jeff had been pretty sure the gun idea was a winner. It seemed almost certain Nate's main password would be related to firearms, but now he was having doubts.

Hartman was pacing around again and it was driving Jeff crazy. He needed his dad to concentrate and, more importantly, to allow him to concentrate.

Hartman stopped pacing and stood in the corner of the fort. He glanced at the floor.

"Jeff, since when do you eat candy bars?"

Jeff concentrated on the computer screen. "I don't. Must be from Miles." As soon as he said it, however, he knew it wasn't right. Miles wasn't into candy, either.

Jeff didn't see Hartman reach down and pick up the crumpled wrapper. He said, "3 Musketeers."

Jeff turned around. "What?"

"It's a 3 Musketeers bar."

That didn't make any sense. It couldn't be from Jeff or Miles. So from where in the heck did it come?

Hartman crumpled it back up, stepped back a few feet, and made a nice high arching shot into the center of the basket. He announced as a TV broadcaster, "A three-pointer from downtown!"

It hit Jeff like a ton of bricks.

Nate had missed a short little toss several months ago. He looked straight at his dad. "It's from Nate."

Hartman tilted his head as if in contemplation and said, "Great. Just great. We need information about his guns and we get a candy bar."

"Dad, give me that wrapper, will you?"

Hartman fished it out and walked it over to Jeff, who straightened it out stared at the label. 3 Musketeers... He said, "Dad, we never thought of a Revolutionary War musket." He was thinking of what numbers might be associated with muskets.

He typed "musket1776" into the password program and watched the screen...

"I'm in!"

Hartman rushed over beside Jeff to watch the screen. Jeff was typing and hastily moving the mouse.

"Jackpot, Dad! Nate definitely does not understand computers. His password, would you believe it—guess what it is..."

"I have no clue."

"Musket1776. And, thankfully, he saved a copy of all of his correspondence. It's in a folder carefully disguised as 'patriot email.' Let's see..."

Jeff's blood went cold.

As expected, Nate had ordered commencement of the revolution. That wasn't the problem, since Hartman was planning to give the order in any event. To spark the revolution, however, Nate planned, two days from today, to simultaneously bomb three bridges and a tunnel. He would be taking care of the "main event." The email messages did not identify the targets by name. They didn't need to.

Anne came back in a few hours with some food and drink wrapped in horse blankets. Hartman and Jeff told her they had to get to the U.P. as soon as possible. They explained Nate's plans and the obvious need to get word to law enforcement personnel to stop the bombings. The problems were vexing. How were they going to notify the FBI, stop Nate, take control of the revolution, and exonerate themselves? And how were they going to accomplish all that from a tiny, damp, cold room under a barn?

❧

CHAPTER 34

ANNE CALLED BRADLEY FIRST THING IN THE MORNING. As Bradley's phone was ringing, Anne got the most eerie feeling—knowing (well, she was pretty sure of it) her phone was still tapped and her conversation would be recorded. At the same time, however, the strange feeling underscored the significance of what she was trying to accomplish.

When Bradley answered, Anne explained that she had a troublesome question with a case she was reading, which was again true, and asked him to meet her in his office, if he was going in, that is. Apparently, Bradley got the drift and agreed.

⮿

BRADLEY HUNG UP THE PHONE AND WALKED OVER TO THE kitchen table, grabbed his cup of coffee, and promptly poured it down the drain. He didn't need anything else to stimulate his nerves. What the hell was this about? Anne wanted to meet him at his office this early? Bradley looked at the clock. It was 7:05 A.M. He didn't like it. Not at all. And he also didn't like the fact that her line was being monitored by the FBI.

As Bradley approached his office he saw that Anne was waiting for him. Briefly, he wondered if she was being watched even now. He unlocked the door and nodded for Anne to go in. Bradley followed and then re-locked the door. He led Anne through the secretarial office and through the inner door to his private office. He walked around behind his desk and felt a bit of relief when Anne took a seat in front of his desk. He had been afraid she might get personal.

Anne said, "We need your help."

"We?"

"Yes, we." There was an indignant tone to her voice. Her eyes were on fire.

"You had best be careful with whom you associate."

Anne's face hardened. "Don't be a fool, Bradley. I don't like this situation any better than you. But *I'm* doing something about it."

Who the hell was she? Bradley tried to put on his best professorial tone. "Well, I'm glad for you. But what is the situation to which you are referring?"

"Look—Oh, forget it! I'm sorry I bothered you." Now, with a suddenly anguished face, Anne jumped up and headed for the door. She was into the secretary's office before Bradley even got around his desk. Damn, she could move when she was angry! To Anne's obvious frustration, however, that was as far as she got. The door was locked and by the time Anne had fumbled with the dead bolt Bradley reached her and grabbed her arms.

"Let go of me, you jerk!" Anne ripped herself from Bradley's grasp and fell onto the secretary's desk with a crash, sending papers and files flying, and a coffee cup full of pens and pencils crashing to the floor. Bradley lunged after her and grabbed her legs, holding them and thus keeping her from falling all the way off the other side of the desk. Anne kicked once to try to break Bradley's hold. It didn't work and she seemed to calm. Bradley had wrapped both of his arms around her legs and was holding her firmly.

Anne started to cry but choked it off. "I'm okay… You can let go."

"Anne, I was just trying to keep you from hurting yourself."

"I know. It's okay."

Bradley pulled her legs until her butt was at the edge of the desk and gently set her feet to the floor. He straightened up and found himself inches from her face. The hostility was gone, but her eyes had an unusual look. Bradley felt a shiver down his spine as he realized that what he saw in her eyes was a combination of pain and strength. It amazed him how she could project strength even while her eyelashes and cheeks were still wet from tears. He wanted to kiss her. But he was definitely not getting romantic vibrations from her.

"Bradley. Listen to me. Lives are at stake. And you may be the only person who can save them. Now are you willing to help or not!"

Bradley swallowed hard. He had never seen her like this—she commanded respect. "I'm listening."

"Hartman and Jeff—" Anne stopped abruptly and Bradley turned his head as they both heard the dead bolt on the door begin to open.

Jesus, Bradley thought, *That's Beth.*

"Anne—"

It was too late. The door swung open and Beth screamed.

"It's fine Beth, it's—"

"Oh my God, Bradley!" Beth was clutching her chest. "You scared me. I'm sorry Anne. I'll come back later." White-faced, she turned and started to walk away.

"Beth! Wait!" Bradley ran out to her. "It's fine. Anne and I had a little accident with your desk. But come back. We will go into my office."

Anne was already in the inner office and this time she was seated *behind* his desk. Bradley walked in and smiled at her. He assumed her taking his chair was a sign of affection. He liked the change. Bradley sat in one of the guest chairs and casually crossed his legs at the knees.

"Perhaps I could do this myself," Anne said, hand massaging her purse strap, "but Hartman and Jeff felt it would be more likely to receive prompt response if it came from you." She raised her chin to make eye contact. "Also, if I do it, the FBI will be down on my house like bees on honey. And that can't happen quite yet."

"Go on." What Bradley wanted to do was scoop her up and run away with her. Run a long way away. She did this to him every time. Even when she was mad.

"Jeff cracked the email of the person who tried to frame them with the bomb-making facility—"

"What?" Bradley jumped up and began pacing in front of his desk, his eyes to the floor.

"It sounds crazy. You are going to have to trust me. Hartman had no idea he was walking into a trap. He thinks a guy named Nate Smith tipped off the police and called the meeting so Hartman and Jeff and Miles would get caught."

Bradley stopped in his tracks. "I don't get it. Why would—"

"Because Hartman wants a peaceful take-over of the Upper Peninsula. Nate Smith has been vying for control for some time, and he wants to do it with terrorist-type acts. Jeff got into his email and he is planning to blow up the Ambassador Bridge, the Detroit-Windsor Tunnel, the bridge to Canada at Sault Ste. Marie, and the Mackinac Bridge."

"Good God." Bradley shook his head and began again to pace. He straightened his bow tie several times.

Anne said, "We need you to go to the FBI to stop him."

"What?" Bradley knew he was beginning to sound like a broken record. He stopped in his tracks and snapped his head around to face Anne. "If I do that, I would have to tell them where Hartman and Jeff are. It could also implicate you. And it could implicate me!"

Anne's face seemed to contort and her skin lost some color. She began again massaging her purse strap. "Couldn't you just tell them about Nate? Hartman and Jeff are going to try to get to the U.P. to stop him… Bradley, Jeff is my son!" Tears began to form in Anne's reddening eyes.

Bradley stepped around the desk and bent to one knee so his face was level with hers. A tear threatened to drip from the bottom of her eye, and he reached up with the thumb of his right hand and swabbed it away. "Come on, Anne. How realistic is—"

Bradley's intercom buzzed and he stopped short to answer it. Beth rarely used it, preferring to simply walk in and talk to him. So something was funny. Perhaps it was Anne's presence that deterred her.

"Yes, Beth."

"There are two FBI agents out here to see you. I asked what about, and they won't tell me. I told them you were in a conference and would be a little while. They are going to wait in the hall."

Bradley's heart skipped. This meant trouble; he knew it was about the DVD. It had to be. The terror in Anne's eyes confirmed it. Time. He needed *time*. He had planned to go to them to explain that he had mistakenly been given some of Bill's effects by the hospital. He had taken the DVD home and played it. Hearing Anne and Jeff talk about the patriots as they mentioned his name in virtually the same breath had had a chilling effect that caused him to do nothing. Now, he wished to God he had called the FBI. With them coming to him, it would look entirely different.

Suddenly he had an idea. It was not a crime to avoid talking with the FBI, so long as they didn't have a subpoena. And Beth would have mentioned that if they had presented one.

"Quickly." Bradley motioned to Anne to follow him to the back of his office. She stood still. Obviously, she didn't realize there was a door that led to the back stairs used only by professors when the law school was first built. It was a sliding door that looked just like part of the wall, except that it had an old, discolored bronze latch. It wasn't meant to be secret; it just was not patently obvious to a casual observer.

Bradley slid the door open and nodded for Anne to go first.

⌾

BETH COULD SEE THAT THE TWO FBI AGENTS WERE GETTING impatient. They were pacing back and forth, walking into and out of her office. She initially gave them a blank face. When it seemed they might just walk past her and into Bradley's office, she said, "Bradley never responds. He just finishes whatever he is doing and then comes to the door to greet his guests."

Then everyone heard what sounded like a door slide shut. Beth saw they would not wait much longer, so she said, "Just a minute," and walked in to Bradley's office.

As soon as she did, she knew she had made a mistake.

Both agents pushed past her into Bradley's office. One of them quickly saw the latch to the sliding door and rushed over to it. He slid it open. The other agent came over as the first agent was stepping into the darkness.

Beth automatically did what secretaries have been doing from time immemorial. She protected her boss. "Wait! Take the elevator outside. It's faster. You will cut them off!"

Both agents looked at her as if trying to determine her veracity. She tried to seem natural, yet excited, just as one would expect under the circumstances. She looked back into their eyes… and held her breath.

The agents paused, and then proved themselves to be lousy judges of character. They bolted out of the office and rushed to the elevator. Beth watched them get in and punch a button. Relief, and a sense of triumph rushed through her body. It felt good, really good, to help the man who treated her so well. She turned around so they wouldn't see her smile as the elevator doors, with a rhythmic, twitching motion, slowly…inched…their…way…closed.

❧

BRADLEY AND ANNE REACHED THE BASEMENT HE KNEW SO well from his college days. They dashed away from the stairwell. Bradley held Anne's hand to lead her. They raced around several old boilers, which had once heated the law school, to a corner of the room that had another set of steps descending to a manhole cover. It brought back vivid memories of sneaking down here to play dungeons and dragons when he was an undergraduate. Bradley shook off the memories, grabbed an iron bar hanging on the wall of the steps, and popped the cover. It was heavier than he remembered. He rolled it to the side.

Anne said, "No way am I going in there!"

"Don't argue with me. For God's sake I just ran from the FBI. *Get in that hole!*"

Anne took one apprehensive look into the darkness and stepped onto the metal rungs that formed a ladder. Bradley waited for Anne to reach the bottom, then lowered himself, taking care to replace the manhole cover as he descended into the cool dampness of a complex series of old steam tunnels which meander under the University of Michigan Central Campus and the City of Ann Arbor.

❧

RICHARD ANDREW HAD ALREADY MOVED INTO HIS NEW Detroit office as the replacement SAC for Bill Fletcher. He had taken, temporarily of course, a small vacant office while Bill's things were being removed. The temporary office had no windows to the outside and was hardly large enough to fit a modest desk, a lateral filing cabinet, and one visitor's chair. He had read one of the maintenance requests made by Bill to check the ventilation system, and now he knew why. It really was stuffy. He loosened his tie and shifted forward in his chair to let some air circulate across his back and under his thighs.

He was trying to put all the pieces of the puzzle together. Bradley Fletcher had run—no, that didn't seem possible; he must have been confused about something. Two of Richard's agents had stopped by his office to find out if he had any information about the missing DVD. A nurse they had interviewed claimed that someone from the family had demanded she turn over the coat that had been taken off Bill's body in the ambulance. But whatever had happened, it seemed very strange.

Also missing were Anne Kreig, her son, and Hartman. Richard shook his head. It was a curious cast of characters to be missing at the same time.

Then, oddly enough, there were several reports from the Upper Peninsula of a few drunken hunters brandishing rifles and military-looking weapons. One local trooper even reported he had seen an anti-tank weapon, for crying out loud. Richard smiled. The poor trooper had probably seen one of the large versions of the Colt AR-15 rifle; the one by ArmaLite called the AR-10 that was chambered for the more powerful .308 instead of the .223. To appear even more menacing, it likely had a 20 inch barrel fitted with a flash suppressor and a bayonet lug, as well as serious-looking scopes, one attached to the top of the receiver and another, for close-in work, attached to the extended hand guard but offset 45 degrees. All illegal nowadays, of course, but it was nothing he was going to get all worked up about. He had more important matters at hand.

Nothing was particularly unusual, given that it was deer hunting season. Skittish folks were always seeing things that, upon investigation, turned out to be quite normal. Like the time, a dozen or so years ago, when Russian tanks were reported invading Michigan. Turns out, they *were* Russian tanks—various models being shipped on uncovered flatbed rail cars to various bases, some as mementos, some for target practice, and even a few for study.

There was a memo by Bill discussing a complaint received several months ago about some door-to-door crazies in the Upper Peninsula. The man who called had said the people were canvassing for "Yoopers who wanted their own nation." Bill had largely written it off, given the periodic resurgence of the drive for statehood by residents of the Upper Peninsula. Still, it seemed like an awful lot of things involved the U.P.

The telephone rang and Richard answered it. One of his agents had just taken a call from a concerned citizen about an unusual amount of military activity at KI Sawyer Air Force Base. Apparently, the citizen was former Air Force and had noted that activities on the base didn't look normal.

Well, what the hell was normal?

Richard decided to make a few calls to find out whom he needed to contact to alert the Air Force of possible trouble.

❧

BRADLEY CAREFULLY PUSHED UP AN EDGE OF THE MANHOLE cover and saw that they were directly under the middle of State Street, right in front of Espresso Royale Cafe. He quickly ducked down and let the manhole cover rattle closed as cars roared overhead. They would definitely be conspicuous if they got out here, but the thought of descending again into the darkness was more than he could take. He told Anne they were going up, then he waited for quiet, signaling a break in traffic before he raised the manhole cover and pushed it off to the side. Quickly, they climbed out onto the street surface. There was still a trickle of cars that had to stop momentarily as Bradley, standing in the middle of the street, struggled with the manhole cover. He finally got it on end and rolled it over the hole, where it crashed into place with a clang. Several students and others on the sidewalks gawked. Bradley quickly wiped the grime from his hands on his worsted wool pants and he and Anne skipped out of the street onto the sidewalk, which was uncomfortably devoid of student and general traffic. Bradley felt as if he and Anne had around their necks huge signs, Las Vegas style, proclaiming over and over with flashing bulbs: "WE JUST RAN FROM THE FBI … WE JUST RAN FROM THE FBI … WE JUST RAN FROM THE FBI …"

They stood for a moment to give their eyes time to adjust to the bright sunlight. Bradley was shocked by how dirty they were. Head to toe, they were covered with greasy black smudges.

Anne smirked. "Oh, you look good."

"Rather professorial, don't you think?" Bradley smiled. He hadn't been able to read his watch in the darkness and was shocked to find that they had been wandering around for nearly two hours. He hadn't remembered the tunnels that well from his college days, and it also appeared that the tunnels were little used anymore, since most of the lights were either off or burned out. As a result, they had been forced to feel their way in almost total darkness. They had frequently bumped into overhead pipes and tripped over occasional metal boxes and valves near the floor.

And through all of it, Bradley reflected, Anne had remained calm, polite, and determined. There was something different about her, black-smudged face and all. There was a power, an assurance, that he liked. It was attractive, even sexy. But there was not time to ponder such niceties. "Where is your car?"

Anne gave him a blank look. "Outside your office."

Bradley frowned. "Great, we can't go back there. And we can't go to my house for my car…"

"Let's get a cab!"

"Good idea." Bradley saw a cab come around the corner and he stepped out into the street so it would see him when it got closer. He was holding his hand out to signal it. Suddenly he felt someone grip his arm and yank it down, and at the same time pull him by his coat back into the sidewalk. Startled, he quickly realized it was Anne.

Her face was now full of tension. "What if the FBI has already notified the police and the cabbies to look for us? We can't take a cab. I have another idea." Anne was watching two college students ride down the street on mountain bikes.

"Anne, we are not going to steal a couple of bikes."

She turned and smiled. "No, dummy. We can borrow them."

"Right. Without the intent to permanently deny the owner of possession, there is no larceny."

"That's not what I mean, either. Loosen up, will ya? Come on. Trust me." Anne headed down the sidewalk.

Bradley followed after her, shaking his head. What in the heck was she thinking?

Twenty minutes later they were fitted with helmets, stiff-soled shoes, and shiny new mountain bikes from Cycle Cellar, a local bike shop, long closed but now reopened, catering to the enthusiast. Stan Lanskier, the beefy, six-foot-four owner with a warm, Teddy-bear personality, was all too happy to supply the equipment to Anne, who had briefly explained the circumstances surrounding their dire need.

For nearly an hour they pedaled along dirt roads and across fields to the back of Anne's property. From there, the woods were too dense and covered with fallen logs to continue riding, so they walked the bikes toward the barn.

When they got close to the edge of the woods, which stopped about 50 yards from the back of the barn, they could see a car parked along the road leading to the house. It had to be FBI, since Anne's house was the only one in the area. Unfortunately, the bushes lining the sides of the road prohibited them from being able to tell whether someone was in the car.

Anne said, "The agents could be anywhere. We could make a run to the barn, but that is risky. Either we wait until dark, which is how Jeff and Hartman had to get to the barn, or we move over to that tree line that runs up the property." Anne pointed and motioned with her hand. "That gives us an almost completely covered entrance to the side door of the house. From there, we can use the back door route to the barn, which provides decent cover from the dense shrubs on both sides of the walk."

"Seems like that is a lot of moving around. I think the safer bet is to wait until dark."

"But we don't have much time."

"If we get caught, it will be over for sure."

"Okay, you're right. Let's wait."

They both backed away from the edge of the woods and found a small clearing about a hundred yards into the woods. FBI agents would have to walk well into the woods, and the sound of snapping twigs and rustling branches would surely signal their approach. Bradley leaned his bike against a tree and took Anne's and leaned it against his. He reached out for her hand. She gave him her hand and stepped up close to him. Since he was taller, her head tilted back so she could see his face.

Bradley said, "This is kind of corny—and I really feel like it should be a romantic moment. But I guess I'm a law professor through-and-through, and as we were riding here I was thinking—for all my talk about the Constitution and how great it makes this country—as a citizen, I have a duty to the Constitution that is higher than to myself. I have to take actions I believe are in my country's best interests, even if it opens me up to censure. Otherwise, I'm no better than the two-faced lawyers, judges, or legislators who serve themselves first."

Anne said tenderly, "It's not corny."

A shiver raced up Bradley's spine and his skin prickled with goose bumps. He knew this was a turning point in his life. "You know, Anne…" Bradley sat down in the bushes and pulled at a long blade of grass. He snapped it out of the ground and examined its torn roots. "I grew up and went to the finest schools, got the best jobs, published books that put me at the top of my profession and made me fairly wealthy. And it was just handed to me. It has been handed to all of us. A gift. I never got shot at in the Mekong Delta. I never huddled in a foxhole in the middle of winter with German artillery shells tearing my friends into shreds, hearing their screams of pain…" Bradley paused, imagining.

Anne reached up and tenderly touched Bradley's face. The warmth of her fingers was so soothing. He continued, "If I can do something now. Maybe help stop Nate Smith. Save lives…" He glanced up at Anne and saw that her eyes were red and full of tears just waiting to break free. "It makes me feel like—maybe for the first time in my life I feel like a *real* American."

"Even if it helps the patriots?"

"What are the patriots all about, Anne, if it's not love of country? Sure, there are some crazies like Nate. But most are just like the Tea Party. They simply want to bring the nation back in line with the Constitution."

"Well, Mr. Professor. This is quite a change."

"There comes a time when talk is not enough. The politicians and media have long recognized that we have, as John Barlow said recently, government by 'Hallucinating Mob.' The citizens are too easily swayed by nonsense."

Anne nodded. "Like the gun issue—the government's own statistics showed that concealed carry laws reduced crimes in every state where they were enacted. Yet the Hallucinating Mob, as you call it, led around by the nose by the last two reprobate presidents and the ultra-liberal press, decides that law-abiding citizens can no longer own guns. I mean, *really?* Have a damn brain! Common sense, as well as the actual facts, tell you that allowing law-abiding citizens to own and carry firearms makes criminals think twice and, simultaneously, enables citizens to protect themselves when the punks make the wrong decision." Anne paused and looked out toward the house.

Bradley was mildly taken-aback. "I didn't realize you were a gun advocate." *And intense about it,* Bradley thought. Here was a side to Anne that he hadn't seen. The professor in him forced him to play devil's advocate: "I hate guns. They are designed to kill. What can be redeeming about that?"

Anne shot him a piercing look. "I didn't realize you were part of the Hallucinating Mob. I just told you, but you ignored it. Lawfully carried guns save innocent lives. Period. There can be no—and I mean NO—argument about it. The facts are incontrovertible. Read Professor John Lott's book, *More Guns, Less Crime.* Look, Bradley, a gun has no moral stature. It makes no decisions—plays no favorites. There were a couple of times when I needed, and was damn glad to have, a gun to scare off punks. I think it's probably impossible to reform punks, but they can certainly be deterred or even corrected by citizens with lawfully carried guns."

"But that's why we have the police and courts."

Anne rolled her eyes. "Tell that to Ronald Goldman, Nicole Simpson, Bill Cosby's son. Everyone would like to think we don't need to protect ourselves, that the simple existence of laws and the police are a sufficient deterrent. But it's not so. The facts are the facts."

Bradley loved a good argument. And Anne was giving him one. He decided to try the gun-grabber's favorite line. "But isn't it worth banning guns if it saves even one life? Surely, Anne, you don't value your gun over keeping some innocent child alive."

Anne suddenly had a look of triumph. "That's a clever argument. But it again ignores the facts and also makes my point—not yours."

"How so?" Up to now, Anne had pretty much toed the party line of the gun-rights activists. He thought he had this winning blow in his repertoire. Now she was telling him his *coup de grâce* was actually hers.

"As I told you, the FBI's own statistics prove that concealed carry saves more lives than it costs. My ownership and concealment of a gun is likelier to save my life than harm someone else by accident or ill intent. The same goes for guns owned by law-abiding citizens." Anne paused to glare squarely into Bradley's eyes. With a seriousness he had never seen in her, she continued, "Surely you don't value your distaste for my gun more than you value my life. After all, isn't concealed carry worth it, aren't guns in citizens' hands worth it, even if only one life will be saved?"

She'd turned his argument right back around. When you had argued and thus conceded a line of logic, if it were accurately turned around on you, well, that was that. You were beaten. Yet, it was a defeat that didn't really hurt. In fact, Bradley did not like guns, but he had always placed his personal likes and dislikes behind him when it came to matters of the Constitution. Truth was, the Second

Amendment was the trump card. It clearly assured the individual's right to keep and bear arms, as the Supreme Court in *Heller* had made clear. The intent of the Founding Fathers was clear to anyone taking an honest look at what they said and wrote on the subject. The right to self defense was the palladium of freedom. Indeed, taking the argument that the times had changed, it could persuasively be argued that, since the Constitution was written at a time when women could safely walk about at night and before the widespread advent of carjackings and the myriad random and senseless acts of violence, if anything, law-abiding citizens would be assured *increased* latitude to own and carry arms.

Bradley stood. Anne had been standing—one leg propped backwards against a tree. He stepped to within inches of her face. Her fog of depression and dull eyes were *long* gone. Her eyes were ablaze with intelligence, resourcefulness, and drive.

There was a fallen tree just at the edge of the small clearing. Bradley stepped away from Anne and led her by the hand to the tree. He sat down and pulled her down next to him. "I want to make love to you in the worst way."

Anne shifted nervously; her eyes blinked.

Bradley quickly added, "But not now. Not yet."

She seemed to relax.

"I have something to accomplish first. But then, young lady…"

❧

HARTMAN AND JEFF WERE SURPRISED AND RELIEVED WHEN they saw Bradley and Anne climbing down the ladder. They were certain their hideout would not last, as agents had twice walked right over the top of the trap door. The four started to brainstorm. Time was running out.

❧

CHAPTER 35

THE NIGHT WAS AS DARK AS A SOCK DRAWER AT DAWN. Tim Bannister and his partner, Cindy Cooper, couldn't see a damn thing. This was their first night shift and they had been cursing the lack of night-vision binoculars. They were sitting in an unmarked car about 300 yards down the road from the Kreig home. They were in radio contact with an FBI surveillance van about a quarter of a mile away, sitting on the opposite side of the house.

Suddenly, the radio crackled. The agents in the van reported strange sounds, unknown origin, were being picked up from the bugs in the house.

Tim said, "What the hell is going on?"

Cindy said, "Hell if I know… Maybe a cat?"

"No. They have dogs. But, if something is going on, I want you to check it out—carefully. I'll be right behind. No heroics this time, okay?"

Cindy nodded and stuck out her tongue.

Tim put a cross look on his face. This was no time to be funny. He was pretty certain there was no one in the house. The noise was most likely caused by the house settling, curtains swaying from the furnace going on or something similar. So all would be safe. Yet, he didn't want Cindy taking matters into her own hands, *again*.

Cindy put her hand on the latch to the car door and seemed to tense. Tim was just about to tell her to relax when—

The radio crackled from the surveillance van: "Someone is in there. Get in there right away!"

Cindy threw the car door open and took off like a puppy snapping free of its leash.

"Cindy!" But Tim immediately saw that it was too late. She had already been swallowed up by the darkness.

◆

BRADLEY HAD CREPT TO THE HOUSE AND QUIETLY LET HIM-self in the back door. He was groping around in the dark, praying he didn't bump into anything that one of the bugs would pick up. He knew FBI agents were listening for any noises or conversation. The house was so quiet. Anne had given both dogs to Linda. All he could hear was a mantel clock ticking, the furnace kicking on and off, and his heart beating like mad.

Finally, he found a kitchen chair. He carried it to the front room, careful not to bump one of its legs into anything. He set the chair down and headed to the library where Jeff had said he kept his skeet shotgun locked in a gun case. When he got to the gun case he cursed. In all the stress, he couldn't remember where Jeff had told him to find the key. Not knowing what else to do, he headed toward Jeff's bedroom.

It took a full five minutes, but he finally found the dresser, the wallet stand and, bingo! The key. Carefully, silently, he headed back to the library. Sweat was dripping from his chin and he could feel beads of sweat sliding down the crevice along his spine.

At last. He had everything in the living room, in front of the picture window…

◆

HARTMAN WAS STANDING ON THE LADDER WITH HIS HEAD just above the floor of the barn, holding the hatch with one hand, listening. Jeff, Anne, and Hartman had been waiting patiently, sort of. Now, however, the tension was more than Hartman could take. He momentarily closed the hatch to ensure that no one would hear him except Jeff and Anne, who were standing below. *"What the hell is taking that guy so long?"*

Jeff said, "He is probably just being careful. Maybe he can't find the key. Damn, I hope it's where I told him."

"Great, just great," Hartman muttered and slowly raised the hatch a couple of inches, just far enough so that he could hear.

Anne whispered, "I know him. He is just being careful."

Jeff whispered back, "I hope he doesn't get shot."

❧

BRADLEY STOOD BEHIND THE DRAWN CURTAINS IN THE front room. The tension was making sweat pour off his face. He wiped his forehead with his shirtsleeve. The cotton of the shirt became instantly soaked and stuck to his arm. He was glad he hadn't eaten in a long while because his stomach was quivering with nausea.

This was it; he was about to set in motion a series of events that would change his world. Forever. His reputation, his career, and even his life, were about to be placed on the line. Funny thing was, incredible as it seemed, he was confident of his new direction. All these years he had blindly progressed through his career, believing his own bull about the law. It had taken the events of the last few days to wake him to reality—so stunning it felt like his face had been hit with a baseball bat. He was done with the bullcrap legal system that pretended to adhere to precedent, to the law and logic of past decisions. In reality, court decisions more frequently reflected the untrammeled statesmanship of individual judges. The whole damn thing was a crock. It made him madder than hell to think he had spent his career in blind devotion to the concept of legal analysis, when analysis too often had nothing whatsoever to do with the law.

No. The patriots were right. Anne was right. Hartman was right. The current system was headed for total disaster. America had lawmakers who lied more often than they told the truth, and it had a citizenry capable of discerning the difference if only the liberal media gave the whole truth.

With that, Bradley grabbed the kitchen chair, swung it back and forth like a discus thrower getting ready to go into his twirl and, when he felt he had sufficient momentum going forward, he let go…

❧

AS CINDY RACED TOWARD THE HOUSE SHE IMMEDIATELY SAW what had made the crashing sound. A kitchen chair lay in the middle of the front lawn and glass was strewn everywhere. She rushed up to a shrub on the walkway to the porch and kneeled, studying the hole in the picture window to see whether she could determine what had propelled the chair through it. It had to be a person—that chair was way out in the front lawn… But she couldn't see anything.

Suddenly, a shotgun blast rang out from inside the house. Cindy lunged away from the picture window and her concealment. She hit the driveway like a gymnast, did a quick somersault across the drive-way, and landed behind a large boulder on the grass. She immediately assumed a double kneel position, drew her Springfield to the guard position (finger off the trigger and along the side of the trigger guard, gun pointed down approximately 45 degrees), and carefully peered around the far end the rock.

Three more shotgun blasts rang out from inside the house.

Cindy knew she had to get in there to find out if anyone was shot. She reached for her radio and realized it had fallen out when she somersaulted across the drive. Fortunately, Tim would be close behind. And that thought made her wonder if she should wait for him. House entry was not, generally, something to be done solo—at least if one wanted to live. But she was confident of her skills. And seconds of delay could mean life or death to innocents. Cautiously, she got up on her legs and crouched behind the boulder. She put her head down and sprinted for the garage door.

❧

T IM BANNISTER CURSED AS SOON AS CINDY BOLTED FOR THE
garage door. He had just tried to radio her. Obviously, she hadn't
heard him. Then he saw why. In the middle of the driveway was a
small dark object, barely visible in the dim ambient light created by
a lamp post in the middle of the front yard. He was pretty sure it was
her radio. Immediately, Tim got a terrible feeling in his gut. It always
happened when he knew something was going very wrong.

Tim knew Cindy wouldn't go in by herself, so she was obviously
expecting him to be close behind. Quickly, he radioed to the two backup agents in the van to cover. He waited to allow them to get into position, and in seconds they radioed the ok. He headed toward the house,
his heart full of dread.

Seconds later he heard a second series of blasts from a shotgun.
Cindy wasn't in sight. She was probably already inside. That meant
that the shots might have been aimed at her! Tim raced for the same
boulder Cindy had used moments before. He looked around and saw
a side door to the garage. It was open. "Oh Christ, Cindy." He got up
and raced for the open door.

❦

B RADLEY WAS CONVINCED HE HAD DONE HIS JOB. NOW HE
had to make sure he didn't get shot. He knew the agents would be
coming. And they would have weapons drawn. They had every reason to think that he was not out of ammunition. He looked around
the kitchen and decided the best thing he could do would be to place
the shotgun on the breakfast bar that jutted out into the room and
was, therefore, the first thing one would see when entering. He set it
there and went to the kitchen table and sat down with his hands on his
head. Now he could only wait. And hope the first agent on the scene
wasn't trigger happy…

❦

T HE COMMOTION COULDN'T HAVE COME TOO SOON FOR
Hartman, Jeff, and Anne, who were all bunched up on the ladder—waiting and waiting. With each passing moment they were

getting more and more irritated with one another. Finally, the second series of shotgun blasts rang out. Immediately, Hartman threw open the hatch and he and Jeff burst forth and uncovered the dune buggy. Anne rushed to the barn door and opened it as quietly as she could. Anne jumped into the driver's seat of the dune buggy and Hartman and Jeff lined up to push from behind. Just as they were passing through the door Jeff stopped pushing and ran to a corner of the barn. Hartman grunted as the dune buggy quickly lost momentum. "Jeff, what in hell?" Then he saw. Jeff had grabbed his bow and a quiver of arrows from a couple of pegs in the wall. Hartman frowned. He would have preferred a couple of AR-15s, each with four or five 30-round magazines. Jeff came running back and tossed his bow and quiver full of arrows into the back of the buggy. One Glock 27 and a bow would have to do.

They again started to push. With Anne at the wheel, they continued to push through the fields, thankful for the wide, bouncy tires and the light weight of the tubular frame. After about 40 minutes of sweating they figured they had covered about two-thirds of a mile. That was probably far enough to be out of earshot, so they fired up the engine. Anne was still at the wheel, so she took the first agreed-upon rotation for driving. The plan was to stick to back roads and traverse fields when the roads stopped or turned in the wrong direction. Thank God for GPS iPhones!

As Anne drove along, Hartman considered two problems and developed a splitting headache. The first problem was that the Upper Peninsula was at least seven hours away, particularly if they came from the western side of the state so as to fool anyone expecting them to come straight north along the I-75 corridor. And it would be daylight in about nine hours. The second problem was that they had not the foggiest idea what they were going to do if, and when, they got there.

❧

Back at the house, Bradley thought he heard what could have been the sounds of an agent approaching. He thought about simply speaking out, but he wasn't sure how that would influence a trained agent. When, after all, did they take a suspects's word when their own lives were in danger? So he decided to simply remain quiet.

✧

CINDY WAS SLOWLY MAKING HER WAY ALONG THE WALL OF the family room that separated the garage, where she had entered, and the kitchen, where she saw a light. Careful to move with balance and without crossing her feet, she silently advanced. Her training had told her to keep her eyes, muzzle, and target all in line. Accordingly, she was raising and lowering her gun along her line of sight, covering all potential areas from which a threat might emerge. She was terrified, but also excited. Her heart was racing. For some reason she remembered the day she had decided to join the FBI. She had been sitting in her apartment, studying for her Masters degree finals and there, on the television, was the burning inferno of Waco. And even before the fires were out, commentators were calling for heads to roll in the FBI. Right then and there she had decided to join. Something was tragically wrong with her country, and how better to serve it than to join a truly injured organization? As she came to the opening that led to the kitchen, she hoped she hadn't made a mistake.

✧

TIM HAD COME THROUGH THE GARAGE, THE MUD ROOM, AND was in the family room when he saw Cindy aggressively burst through the opening to the kitchen. She trained her gun and screamed, "Put your hands over your head. Don't move!" Tim tried to quickly analyze what was happening. Was the person she was confronting armed? Had he fired those shots at her? Was she acting on the assumption that he was right behind her?

Tim raced tip-toe across the family room and stopped at the opening to the kitchen. Instantly, he was confused. Cindy was squared off in a strong Weaver stance, pointing her gun toward... what? He couldn't see. There was a damn kitchen breakfast bar in the way.

Then he saw it.

The barrel of a shotgun was resting on the top of the bar, pointing in the direction of Cindy! His pulse immediately went off the chart. This was a life and death situation. Tunnel vision began to take over. Worse, he couldn't see who was holding the gun. It must be a second person Cindy, somehow, didn't see.

Cindy started talking to someone, telling someone to lie on the floor.

She was not going to get ambushed by some jerk. No damn way. Now! He lunged into the opening of the kitchen, his gun already aimed in the direction of the shotgun.

Suddenly, Tim felt as if he were in a carnival fun house with the floor moving and shifting under him. It seemed as though he was watching the room through a movie camera that was jiggling and bouncing around. Everything turned into a blur of confusion. Then he saw the shotgun. What was going on? There didn't seem to be anyone holding it. But a figure was moving forward—on Cindy. Tim heard someone fire a double tap.

"Oh my God!" he cried.

❧

BRADLEY HAD BEEN WAITING AT THE KITCHEN TABLE WHEN he saw a young woman slowly come into view and then quickly move the rest of the way into the kitchen, momentarily training her gun on an area along the wall that she had apparently not been able to see a moment before. She wore a blue jacket marked with clear yellow letters "FBI." After quickly checking the blind area along the wall, she retrained her gun on his chest. *"Oh shit,"* was all he could think.

Quickly, however, she started barking orders for Bradley to lie on the floor with his hands behind his back. As he stood to move forward from the table and lie down, he heard movement off to his right and two quick sounds, sort of like the "pop" made by a bicycle tire blowing out. He turned his head and saw another agent with a gun pointed at him. He realized, at that instant, that the strange sounds were made by a gun discharging.

Bradley froze, not knowing whether he'd been hit, and not knowing whether he would be hearing more such sounds. All he could feel was a severe burning sensation in his chest.

The next thing he heard was the woman agent screaming something at the second agent. Then everything went black.

❧

CHAPTER 36

DANIEL ROSEN, MD, WAS ON THE LAST HOUR OF HIS 20-hour shift as the emergency-room doctor for the University of Michigan Hospital. The handsome, curly-haired intern was tired. He was convinced that, were it not for his very serious commitment to bicycle racing that helped him stay fit and thus alert, given these horrid working conditions, he would be malpractice waiting to happen. Dan was leaning against the intake counter chatting with one of the more attractive hospital employees when the call came in on the speakerphone from the ambulance. The emergency-room technician got it down on paper and also began pulling off the vital signs from the digital, direct-link electronics. What he heard made him wonder if the ambulance would get here in time. Gunshots to the chest and shoulder. Massive bleeding. Heart rate erratic and presently at 67. Blood pressure dropping. Originally 125/80, now 90/70. One of the ambulance technicians had said this was a FUBAR.

Dan had graduated two years earlier at the top of his class at Michigan State University Medical School. His first choice upon graduation had been to intern right where he was now, one of the finest teaching hospitals in the nation. Long hours of memorization had paid off in earning his distinction in school. It has also paid off several times in his practice.

He turned his thoughts to the incoming patient. From the information he had—the pattern of blood pressure, with the maximum and minimum pressures growing closer—

Suddenly, something jogged in his mind. He tried to think of what it meant, but fitness or not, after 20 hours on shift, his mind was beginning to turn to mush. He went off to prepare himself for surgery.

Fifteen minutes later, the patient, one Bradley Fletcher, was wheeled into surgery. The ambulance crew had cut off his clothes. X-rays showed bullet fragments all over the chest cavity. Quickly, Dan scanned the skin of his chest. Two holes. He listened with his stethoscope to the heart. That was odd, and worrisome. The normal pumping sounds were muffled, distant. Carefully, they turned him over. No exit holes.

A nurse reported the patient's blood pressure to be 85/75.

Dan started to panic. This man was dying, but he wasn't sure why. He was going to need to crack him open right away.

Then he noticed that the victim's neck veins were distended. *What the hell?*

Then it clicked. Beck's Triad: muffed heart sounds, narrowing of blood pressures, enlargement of neck veins. That was it!

"Nurse, aspiration needle. *Quickly!*"

Dan took the huge needle from the nurse and aimed at a point between the ribs near the breastbone. He plunged it in and blood shot fourth from the top opening of the needle like a geyser.

❧

BRADLEY WAS BEGINNING THE SLOW PROCESS OF REGAIN-ing consciousness. At first he blinked his eyes several times, trying to see through a hazy fog. His mind was still filled with a nightmare where he had jumped off a cliff and was falling and falling, all the while frantically reaching out for tree branches that were there to grab but wouldn't end up in his hands. And so he just kept falling. He turned his head and a pain shot through his body. It also burned off some of the haze and, for the first time, he realized that he was in a hospital room. The scene at the house came back—and the odd popping sounds. He felt his pulse increase. He recognized, now, that those sounds had been from a gun and that he had been shot. *God in Heaven!* But at least he was alive. He blinked again and scanned the room. It was an intensive care unit. He had several tubes in his arms and there were machines above his head. How had this happened? His head was still a little fuzzy. Hadn't he taken every precaution? He slightly rolled his head to try to clear his thoughts. This was an exclamation point, a turning point, from which he would go in his new direction. He rolled his head again. His mind was clearing. He would prevail. Nothing was going to stop him from making a decisive impact on fixing the law and his country. Anne! A longing for her rushed through his body. Where was she? Did they get free? Could they stop Nate? God, they had to. What time was it?

Bradley reached with his right arm for the button to buzz for the nurse and pain again shot through him, this time from his shoulder through his entire body. For the first time he realized that his shoulder and chest were wrapped in bandages.

A middle-aged nurse walked in with a smiling doctor.

Bradley said, "I need to talk to someone from the FBI. What time is it?"

The nurse checked several electronic instruments and stepped up to the head of the bed. She lingered, closely studying Bradley, and then turned and headed toward the door. She spoke as she walked, not bothering to look back. "You shouldn't be talking to anyone for a while. But they want to talk to you, too. It's four in the morning."

The doctor stepped forward and checked Bradley over, mumbling to himself as he poked and probed. He seemed satisfied and backed away. "I'm Doctor Carey. You're lucky to be alive."

One of the overhead monitors began to beep with increased speed. Bradley didn't doubt what the doctor had said, it was just something to actually hear it. Bradley tried to get his mind off his sudden brush with mortality and he decided to study the doctor. He was tall, blond hair, middle-aged, but still clearly a ladies' man. "I was wondering what happened to me."

"You were treated by one of the best interns on my staff, Dr. Daniel Rosen. You caught him at the end of his shift or he would be here. He saved your life."

"Really?" He wanted to ask why the boss doctor would be on shift at four in the morning, but he let it pass. His head was still muddled, he assumed, from all the drugs.

"You took two bullets. The first entered your chest wall just below the pectoral muscle. As it began to expand, it hit one of your ribs and was deflected downward, where it tore through the bottom portion of your right lung and came to a stop in the muscles of the back. The second bullet was the one that created more immediately life-threatening problems. It was right in the center of your chest and tore through the sternum, where it largely disintegrated into several smaller pieces, each of which created separate wound channels. The main portion of the bullet, however, pierced the aortic arch, a huge vessel coming off the heart. Blood began spilling into the pericardial sac, the pressure from which began to squeeze the heart. In effect, your heart began to drown in its own blood. Fortunately, Dan noticed the symptoms and aspirated the pericardial sac immediately."

"Obviously, I need to thank him."

The doctor nodded. "I'll send in your visitors."

Bradley watched the doctor walk around the corner and then heard him say something to someone apparently just outside the door. A second later, a short, neatly dressed man entered. At first glance, Bradley thought he must have been in his late forties. He had a slight paunch at the waist.

"Hello, Professor Fletcher. I'm relieved that you made it through surgery in good shape. I'm Richard Andrew of the FBI."

Bradley's heart jumped into his throat. Talking about talking to the FBI was suddenly different than *actually* talking to the FBI. The latter involved the prospect of going to prison. He swallowed hard, and a pain shot through his chest. It cleared his mind a bit. "Mr. Andrew, you must wonder what I was up to in Anne Kreig's house."

Richard Andrew shifted on his feet. "The question did occur to me."

"You must believe what I am about to tell you. It is vitally important and many lives are at risk."

"Your antics got my attention. I normally do not wait around hospitals at all hours of the morning."

"A rogue element in the patriots is about to bomb the Ambassador Bridge, the Detroit/Windsor Tunnel, the bridge at Sault Ste. Marie, and the Mackinac Bridge. They are using vans that will stop for engine trouble. They also plan to block traffic somehow to cover for the stopped vans. The good patriots just uncovered the plot and are taking steps to protect the Mackinac Bridge. You need to concentrate on the others."

Richard Andrew's face screwed up and his eyes began to blink repeatedly. His skin seemed to lose color. He stood there in silence for several moments, as if trying to sort out all of the data. His voice cracked slightly as he spoke, "I'm going to take your word at face value. The story is too farfetched to be an attempt to deceive me. The doctor tells me you would have difficulty fabricating a story so soon out of surgery and the effects of anesthetics. But, professor, if you are lying, I will personally make sure you find yourself in the iron motel for a nice long stay."

Bradley felt himself flush with guilt, which was strange, since he was telling the truth.

Richard Andrew returned a couple of minutes later with another agent. "Professor, if we are to believe you, we need a couple more questions answered."

Bradley nodded.

"You didn't mention how you got into the Kreig home without our surveillance team seeing you, and you didn't explain why you made such a commotion. Why not simply call us and tell us?"

Oh crap, Bradley thought. He hadn't realized that his very presence in the home spoke volumes about the fact that he wasn't telling everything. But if he explained those circumstances, he would implicate himself and Anne. No. He had to stick to his guns and ride it out. "You are just going to have to believe me. I am not presently at liberty to explain the circumstances surrounding my presence in the Kreig home nor my chosen method of getting your attention. Let us just say that, if I had it to do over again, I would have selected a means

PAGE 470   ◦   CAMERON REDDY

that would not have resulted in my getting shot." Bradley smiled, but inside he felt guilty as hell.

Richard put a finger between his tight shirt collar and his neck and he ran his finger back and forth several times, pulling the shirt away from his neck. He glanced at his assistant and then back to Bradley. "Okay, then. Tell me what you can."

↭

RICHARD ANDREW WALKED OUT OF BRADLEY'S INTENSIVE care room and instantly recognized the danger posed; on such short notice, he seriously doubted he could get SWAT and bomb teams everywhere they needed to be. Simply put, there were not enough assets to simultaneously protect four locations spread over those distances. In all likelihood, he could get units to the Detroit-Windsor tunnel and the Ambassador Bridge spanning the Detroit River. There was no way he could get teams to the Mackinac and Sault St. Marie bridges before daybreak. Canadian authorities would have to protect the Sault St. Marie bridge. The Mackinac bridge would be left to local law enforcement and, he presumed, if Bradley was correct, the patriots. Lord, wasn't *that* the business—he had to root for the patriots. He wondered whether it meant Hartman or those at Hartman's direction. But Hartman had been in the Detroit area a couple of days ago, and then he had disappeared. He was probably already in the U.P. or was heading there. He made a mental note to put out an all points bulletin.

↭

CHAPTER 37

ANNE FOUND THAT DRIVING THE FIRST LEG OF THE TRIP to the U.P. and the Mackinac Bridge was quite enjoyable. For the most part, Hartman and Jeff had been able to direct her along paved, two lane roads. Occasionally, they found themselves racing down dirt roads and spraying stones and dirt as they rounded corners. It was a mildly foggy night, and the dune buggy's four lights, two normal headlights and two high-mounted beams, created an eerie sensation, like something out of a horror movie where the hero must approach a castle shrouded in fog and lighting. Fortunately, the fog wasn't so dense that they had to significantly limit their speed. Anne could see the road just fine, and she pretty consistently maintained sixty-plus miles per hour. Her real fear, as evidenced by Hartman and Jeff straining their eyes at the tree line on either side of the road, was the very real possibility of deer wandering into their path. At these speeds, it could be fatal for more than the deer.

Anne's hair was blowing in the cold wind and it gave her a rush of excitement. At the same time, however, she wondered what in the hell she was doing. How had she gotten involved this deeply? By God, she was helping the patriots! The gun-toting crazies so often associated with angry white supremacists—racists!

Yet, Anne was helping her son and her former husband; *they* weren't racist. Actually, they seemed pretty much in tune about where the country had gone, and where it was heading. Being honest and forthright in speaking about "politically incorrect" issues didn't make someone a racist. Disagreeing with people of a different heritage or religion didn't mean you looked upon them as inferior beings. How had we gotten so tongue-tied?

Anne certainly questioned the patriots' plans; could they really bring about change? She thought about it for a moment and decided it didn't matter. Whether or not their plans would succeed, at least one thing was abundantly clear: Nate had to be stopped.

The urge to get to the U.P. increased. She pushed aside all the intellectual ruminations, gripped the steering wheel a little tighter and focused on making the road underneath race by. She was surprised that she wasn't shivering to death. The light coat she was wearing shouldn't have been nearly enough to keep her warm, what with a sixty-mile-per-hour wind blowing in her face. She smiled. It had been years since she had felt this kind of intense physical rush of adrenaline.

Hartman was sitting beside her. He had been mostly quiet since they got underway. Only occasionally did he confer with Jeff about the route.

Anne wondered how Hartman felt. Something for which he had worked, for so long, was threatening to fall apart. If the bombings were successful, the government might be so angered it would mount a military campaign to unseat the patriots. In such event, there was no way the patriots, even backed by an armored cavalry unit, could ultimately prevail. That was the folly of Nate's idea. She knew Hartman's plans counted on surprising the federal government and being in a position to threaten losses if challenged. Under those circumstances, he did not expect a challenge.

Not that long ago even the thought of Hartman raised her hackles. He had played a part in destroying her. But now she felt sorry for him. She negotiated a couple of sharp turns and quickly brought the buggy back up to speed. Hartman had been insensitive to her needs during their marriage. But she no longer blamed him. It had been her weakness that allowed him to walk on her. Neither did she blame herself. She just refused, any longer, to blame Hartman.

It was ironic, really. Here she was careening down narrow roads at breakneck speed, and for the first time in years she really felt as if she had taken control of her life. She could now accept personal responsibility for where she was, where she had been, and where she was going. She pressed the accelerator a bit harder and the needle on the tachometer bumped up slightly. The pitch of the engine whined just a little higher.

Damn, it felt good to go fast!

The miles went by and soon they were getting close to Petoskey and the end of their gas supply. They would have to pick a main road and risk stopping at a gas station. Anne was still at the wheel, principally because she was driving so effectively. Hartman had begun in earnest to assist Jeff in studying the map to pick the best routes. So far, they had been able to limit traveling across fields to a minimum. They had been lucky. Hopefully, it would hold out just a little longer.

❧

Tom Shaw was a volunteer fireman who had grown up in Iron Mountain in the U.P. but had moved south to find a job. In Traverse City he found work and enough beautiful country to satisfy his needs. A strapping physical specimen, he loved driving around with the array of emergency lights attached to the top of the cab of his Ford F-150 pick-up. It was unusual for him to be out driving around at this hour, but he and his team of volunteer fireman had just gotten back from putting out a small fire in a field sparked by embers rising from a poorly designed chimney. He was listening to the police channel on his scanner when he heard the all points bulletin.

"All right!"

He loved this stuff.

Tom lived off the beaten path, down an old county road that was rarely used anymore, mostly because the new state road went by just a quarter mile further west. He was almost home when he saw headlights approaching in his rearview mirror. Except it wasn't just headlights. This vehicle had cab lights of the kind you see on off-road vehicles or rally cars. He had almost figured out what is was when it closed the distance very quickly and blew past.

What the? They've got some kind of death wish, he thought to himself. A dune buggy? Flying down this road at this time of night? With two or three passengers? The only one he had gotten a look at, however, was a middle-aged man in the passenger seat. Long dark sideburns, dark hair… "Blazes! That must have been the guy on the police channel!" He grabbed his radio handset.

↝

JEFF WAS JUST COMING OUT OF THE GAS STATION WHEN HE saw the police cruiser racing down the road, lights flashing. It was about a half mile off, but it was closing fast. Damn!

Jeff raced to the dune buggy. Apparently, Anne and Hartman had also seen the cruiser's lights. Anne had the engine revving when Jeff dived into the back. She popped the clutch and threw gravel so hard Jeff could hear it ricochet off the gas station and its gas pumps. When they hit the blacktop, the tires bit, squealed, and lunged the dune buggy forward.

Hartman had taken the iPhone and was barking directions to Anne. *We're done,* Jeff thought. How in the heck were they going to outrun police that have radios? That happened only in movies. Jeff was lying on his back, bracing himself against the sides of the cargo hold as Anne yanked the buggy to and fro. He watched the moon glow brightly, serenely.

The police cruiser was closing. The siren was getting louder. Hartman continued to bark directions. Anne suddenly turned off the paved highway and onto a dirt road, and then she seemed to almost immediately turn down another. The violent turns tossed Jeff about the cargo hold as if he were a pinball in an arcade machine. With that last move, however, the sound of the siren seemed to grow quieter. That was a good sign. Hartman had obviously directed her to run on dirt roads where the dune buggy's fat and buoyant wheels, with deep treads, would easily outrun the car over rough surfaces and around any corner. She navigated a couple more corners like an experienced racer. He could feel the buggy weave out to the edge of the road and then dig into an arc that would pass within inches of the inside corner, only to continue the arc back out to the far outside of the road. It was certainly fun, he thought, but most certainly it would be short lived. The siren was still wailing in the distance—though with each corner Anne traversed, the wailing became more faint.

Finally, they seemed to be on a straight stretch and Jeff decided to pick himself off the floor and see where they were. He could still hear the siren, though it was again probably at least a quarter of a mile back. Maybe a half-mile.

Glancing forward, between his mom and dad, he was surprised to see the pitch blackness of a lake directly ahead. He knew from its size that it was Lake Michigan. *What in the heck?* They were north of Harbor Springs and racing down a dirt road that led to a boat launch on the lake. He had been down this road several years back with a friend who liked to fish salmon on the lake.

His heart sank when he remembered it was a dead end.

"Dad! This is a dead end!"

"I know. Hold on!"

Anne yanked the wheel a full quarter of a turn and the dune buggy threatened to go up on only two wheels. Jeff saw dirt and sand spray everywhere. The centrifugal force nearly threw him out. Jeff thought his heart would stop when he saw Anne heading right for the sunken wood pylons that surrounded the road near the beach. They were intentionally spaced narrower than a car.

Then, suddenly, Anne straightened the dune buggy out and was running alongside the pylons, which were only a foot or so to the right of the dune buggy. The siren was getting louder and the road was coming to its end at the water's edge.

Jeff watched his mom and dad. They were communicating something to each other--probably recognizing that they had, quite literally, run out of road. Only a hundred yards away loomed the glistening waves of Lake Michigan.

Anne said, "Jeff, hold on!"

Anne yanked the steering wheel nearly halfway around to the right—steering directly into the wood pylons! "Whoa!" Jeff screamed as the dune buggy's left-side tires dug into the sand and threw the vehicle into a violent turn. Just when Jeff could tell the tires might lose their grip, he felt the right side of the dune buggy raise up. And before he even had a chance to realize what was happening, the buggy's right side dropped back down. Suddenly, the sound of the police siren began to fade away. To his surprise, he was back on the floor of the storage compartment.

Jeff raised his head and peered out… "What the?" They were racing along the water's edge, occasionally splashing through the shallow remnants of a receding wave. He looked back and saw, in the outline of the headlights of the police car, only two tire tracks through the string of pylons—but both tracks were from the left side of the buggy!

Anne was still gripping the steering wheel and sending plumes of water skyward each time a tire clipped the tip of a receding wave.

She was wearing a very big smile.

↮

T WO SWAT TEAMS HAD BEEN HASTILY CALLED IN, ASSEMbled, and dispatched from the Detroit Police Department. The sun was just moments from peeking over the horizon when the teams arrived at the Detroit/Windsor Tunnel and the Ambassador Bridge. Captains Charlie Saunderson, who was leading the bridge team, and Leslie Wilson, leading the tunnel team, were in immediate radio contact with each other. Charlie stood at the base of the bridge on the Detroit side and cursed. He radioed Leslie. "I've got a problem already. An accident on the Windsor side has traffic heading to Canada jammed and at a total stop."

Leslie barked back over the secure link, "Same here. Tunnel is jammed. I've already called in a chopper to get some of my people over the water. I just hope to God Canada and Customs can do something."

"The perp is going to be somewhere in front of us. May already be off the bridge. What do you suggest?"

"Set up a stop both ways. Evacuate everyone, but check everybody for traces of explosives. Start a vehicle by vehicle search with the dogs.

I'll bet they didn't use a van just to throw us off. Where the hell is the bomb unit?"

"No idea. Mine isn't here yet. I'll get started. Out." Charlie shoved the radio onto his belt rig and started shouting orders. He had a bad feeling about this. They needed to have gotten to the scene an hour earlier… And where the hell was his bomb squad?

⊸

In Canada, at Sault Ste. Marie, despite the attendant difficulties of communication with a foreign government, Canada's RCMP (Royal Canadian Mounted Police) SWAT team deployed far more quickly. There were also fewer vehicles on the bridge. Accordingly, the staged accident, brazenly enacted right in front of a SWAT vehicle, was not at all deceptive. An SUV was spotted, and when the driver got out and began to run away, the SWAT team knew what to do. Immediately a large, specially designed tractor/truck with a huge, thick blade as tall as the truck itself, pulled onto the bridge and raced at the SUV. It rammed it from the front with so much force that it completely collapsed the driver and passenger compartment.

It seemed an eternity for the driver of the tractor, but the SUV was finally pushed all the way to the foot of the bridge on the American side before it exploded. The force was sufficient to lift the tractor's huge front end into the air several feet, and the tractor's momentum carried it right into the huge crater formed by the blast. Fortunately for the driver of the tractor, and for the bridge, the crater was wider than it was deep, and except for blown ear drums, both survived relatively unscathed.

⊸

Charlie Saunderson heard it first. It was a deep rumble and seemed to come from about a quarter-mile downstream. He knew what that meant. Despite the urgency of his own assignment, he took a moment and glanced downstream. There was a swell of watery froth at the surface of the river. With the oblique angle of the sun, still very low in the sky, the water seemed to take on a dark, reddish brown color, as though it was mixed with mud. Suddenly his radio crackled.

"Charlie! Station—" Leslie's voice abruptly broke off. But she must have dropped the radio because for a couple of seconds he could only hear muffed screams. Then it went dead.

Charlie radioed his team somewhere over the crest of the bridge. They were moving from car to car, truck to truck, as quickly as the two dogs could sniff. Nothing yet. Twenty more seconds ticked off. The bridge was just too damn jammed with vehicles and people.

It occurred at the far end of the bridge, near the Canadian side. The effect of the blast was dramatic. There was a flash of white, red, and orange light. A split second later a concussion wave blew nearly everything off the bridge except a couple of trucks. Charlie was killed instantly by the concussion and his limp body was thrown into the river like a discarded rag doll. The suspension cables snapped at the same time that a tremendous shock wave raced along the road surface. It was like taking a rope and whipping it so that the wave travels along the length of the rope until it reaches the end, where it snaps. The rolling shock wave broke up the concrete and asphalt surface and blew fragments in all directions—with nearly the same deadly effect as a fragmentary bomb. Anyone not thrown off the bridge with the initial concussion, including many people still alive in their vehicles, was torn to shreds. Vehicles, and everything else that was still on the bridge and not very securely attached, were whipped into the air like so many toys.

✦

CHAPTER 38

ANNE PULLED THE DUNE BUGGY UP TO A SMALL FORMA-tion of rocks which jutted out onto the beach. Her arms and neck ached from a long night of tense driving. She rolled her shoulders in a shrugging motion to loosen the muscles. Her hands were stiff, too; she pulled off her gloves and rubbed each hand in turn. She was thirsty as hell but her stomach was too knotted to register hunger. For the first time all evening she shivered from the cold. She stood to get a better view. In the distance she could see the faint outline of the Mackinac Bridge, which was shrouded in early morning fog. Just barely, she could also see the cars and trucks moving on the bridge. It was impossible to see St. Ignace some five miles across the Straits of Mackinac. Anne pointed toward the bridge.

Hartman nodded and then frowned. "Must be that the bridge authority hasn't been informed."

Jeff stood up in the back of the dune buggy. He stretched out his arm past Anne's face. "But look, there are flashing lights on the Mackinaw City side. Police cars. It's a checkpoint. I can't tell if there are any patrol cars on the other side."

This far north and this early in the morning, traffic was usu-ally light, so an accident had not been planned. Instead, Jeff had explained, Nate's plan was to stop the van about a mile onto the bridge, at the location of the suspension anchors. The driver would simply lift the hood to feign engine trouble and walk away. The electronic fuse would take several minutes, and the driver would be picked up by a car going in the opposite direction.

Hartman raised himself over the windshield and scanned about. "We made it in time, it appears."

Jeff quipped, "Thanks to Mom'eo Anne-dretti." Hartman smiled and groaned. Jeff and Anne laughed.

The pun relaxed Anne a little. She was amazed that Jeff could maintain a sense of humor in these circumstances. Quickly, however, she went back to trying to figure out what was occurring on the bridge. As she did, she could feel Hartman's eyes on her. She wanted to turn and meet his warming gaze, but she fought off the urge. Instead, she smiled inwardly. "And I don't see anyone on the beach in front of us, so whoever was after us back there," Anne nodded toward the direction they had come, "either thought we were just locals or they assumed we would approach the bridge from a road."

Hartman pointed to some densely packed pine trees running parallel to the beach almost all the way to the bridge, "We might not be able to see if someone is waiting for us just off the beach."

That was true, Anne considered. "The more important point, gentlemen, is whether the authorities already on the bridge can identify and stop Nate's bomb. If they can, then our job is done for us, and I can turn this buggy around."

"I doubt it, Mom. Nate will see the police. He's likely to load the bomb in another vehicle."

Hartman nodded. "He probably never had it in a van."

Now Anne was confused. "But doesn't he need the size of a van to pack enough explosives?"

Hartman again shook his head. "Not necessarily. Plastics are much smaller and could fit in a trunk."

My God, Anne thought. Now what in the heck were they going to do if they couldn't identify Nate's vehicle? It would put them at the same disadvantage as the police and the FBI. It would be a guessing game—against the clock. Frustration began to well up. To come this far, to have risked so much—was it all for naught?

A depressed silence overcame everyone. No one moved for more than a minute. Pain cut like a knife into Anne's chest. Within the last several hours she had felt more alive than at any point in her life. She had been living on the edge and loving every second of it. But now, at this climactic moment, she was staring at abject failure. Old feelings of despair and hopelessness came crashing down on her. It felt as though someone had tightened a rope around her chest; she labored to breathe.

Suddenly Jeff piped up, "Over there!" Jeff's outstretched arm pointed to a spot about a half mile from the entrance to the bridge, at a road that ran alongside the beach but was obscured for most of its length by the dense pine trees. There was about a 200 yard stretch where the trees thinned and the road was visible. An old Ford Explorer SUV was making its way to the bridge. That had to be Nate. Sport utility vehicles had become a rarity in the last several years. Only Ford Motor Company still manufactured anything close to the size.

Anne's distress vanished as quickly as it had appeared. It was as if someone had fired off the starting gun. The adrenaline rush returned. Her mind focused.

Hartman said, "50 bucks it's him. I just have a feeling." He looked at Anne.

Anne turned her head toward the back of the dune buggy. "Jeff, can you climb onto the bridge?"

"I don't know, but I'll sure as hell try."

"Hartman, give him your gun."

Hartman started to unhook his holster. Jeff said, "No, Dad. You're way better with a handgun. I'm much better with a bow."

Hartman glanced at Anne, obviously looking for direction. She didn't like the idea. But, Hartman would be useless with the bow, and it was better to have two people effectively armed as opposed to one. "Okay, take your bow. I'll drop you under the bridge and we will try to head off the Explorer." Anne looked back and forth from Hartman to Jeff.

Hartman yelled, "Let's go!"

Anne pressed her foot to the floor and the dune buggy's turbo-charged Chevrolet Corvair engine roared to life. Cranking out in excess of 175 horsepower, Jeff's specially tuned dune buggy launched sand and water 40 feet into the air. As they raced toward the bridge, the tires threw up huge fantails of water as they skimmed waves.

The Mackinac Bridge is supported by suspension cables only for the middle two miles of its five-mile length. For approximately one-and-one-half miles from each shore line, the bridge is like any other; it is supported by legs reaching to the sandy beach or, further from shore, into the water and down to the floor of the Mackinac Straits. Surprisingly, at the point where the bridge passes over the end of the beach, just at the water's edge, the surface of the road is only 10 to 12 feet above. The support structure underneath the road's surface, a labyrinth of steel cross-members anchored to the steel-reinforced concrete legs, is reachable by someone with a ladder or, in this case, a dune buggy on which to stand.

At least that was what Anne was hoping as she raced past historic Fort Michilimackinac to the bridge. As she neared the bridge, she slammed the brakes and the tires dug into the wet sand, ripping trenches in the silky smoothness of the beach. The dune buggy skidded to a stop directly under the bridge. With his bow and quiver across his back, Jeff reached up to the first steel girder and pulled himself out of the buggy and up underneath the bridge. From there, he climbed over to a large I-beam that was flared enough at the ends that he was able to walk along the inside flare. He headed out, ducking and climbing over cross members. Anne and Hartman watched Jeff long enough to see that he was going to make it; then Anne floored the gas pedal, causing the dune buggy to fishtail a full 180 degrees on the top layer of wet sand and race back in the direction from which they had come. Watching Jeff, Anne's heart had swelled with pride. Now, her chest again tightened with fear.

The entire beach area surrounding the bridge is fenced off; presumably, this is to keep the thousands of tourists who visit the bridge and the adjacent Fort Michilimackinac from doing exactly as Jeff had done. However, Anne had noticed there was a large gate in the fence, about midway between the bridge and the fort. She prayed it wasn't locked. If it was, they would have to circle to the far side of the Fort before they would be able to get off the beach and onto the road. That, of course, would take more time. Already, the SUV was making its way to the makeshift road block set up by the police…

❧

NATE'S PULSE WOULD HAVE BEEN A DEAD GIVEAWAY. So would the sweat on his brow, that only moments before he had wiped away. Of course, he had no way of knowing that the FBI, let alone Anne, Hartman, and Jeff, were on to him. Just the same, the surprising checkpoint at the entrance to the bridge made it clear that the authorities were looking for someone. *Thank God,* he thought to himself, as he pulled up and rolled down his window to speak to the officer, *that I took the precaution of using a Ford Explorer instead of a van.* He was never so glad that he hadn't trusted the security of his communications.

"A problem, officer?"

"No. Just some kook on the loose that just might be coming this way. Anyone in back?" The officer glanced into the rear of the SUV.

This was the part Nate most feared. He hoped this officer was not the suspicious type. The several boxes in the back of the SUV, some stacked on the back seat and others in the back storage area, were open and topped off with various antique kitchen appliances, knick-knacks, and old winter clothing.

"What's all that stuff?"

"You wouldn't believe what the trolls get rid of in garage sales. I can make a fortune with this stuff back in Houghton. I have a road-side stand and I sell this stuff right back to the idiots! Make triple my money, too."

"That's great," said the trooper, laughing. "Good luck." He waved Nate on. Nate glanced in his rearview mirror and saw that the officer was still chuckling as the next vehicle pulled up to the checkpoint.

❧

ANNE DROVE TO THE FENCE AND HARTMAN JUMPED OUT and raced to the gate. He had his back to her and was apparently shaking something. After a few seconds, he turned around, shoulders slumped.

"Come on! We'll just have to go around the fort! Come on!"

Hartman ambled back toward the dune buggy.

"Hartman, move your tail!"

He picked up the pace and jumped into the dune buggy. She glared at him and got a sheepish look in reply. Now was not the time to argue, however, so she punched the gas once again and wheeled the buggy back out to the beach, where she could go around to the other side of the fort, plow through some tall grass and shrubs and get onto the road. As she turned left and headed up the beach and across the bumpy grass and shrubs, she had a dreadful sense that they would not make it in time.

❧

AS PLANNED, NATE DROVE OUT TO THE FIRST POINT AT which the huge suspension cables were anchored, about a mile from the start of the bridge, and about a half mile past the point at which the bridge passes over water. This spot, if obliterated, would bring the whole thing down.

Casually, despite a pulse that had never slowed from the encounter with the officer at the checkpoint, Nate stopped the SUV, got out, and walked to the front. He opened the hood and then walked around to the back and lifted the tailgate. He stood for a moment, eyeing the electronic timer that would set off two dozen boxes of high explosives. He glanced down the length of the bridge, looking north, to see whether his ride to safety was on its way. He didn't want to start the timer until he could see his man. Then, a few moments later, out of the fog at the center of the bridge, he saw the Ford F-150 with both headlights, but only one fog light, illuminated. He reached down to begin setting the timer.

❧

Anne could see they were not going to make it. From their vantage point driving along the road to the bridge, they could occasionally get a glimpse of the bridge through the trees. The SUV had its hood up and tailgate open.

"Anne, if we go on the bridge now, it might blow with us on it."

Anne tossed Hartman a quick glance and kept her foot to the floor. She was approaching the left turn that would take them up to the police who had established their checkpoint just this side of the toll booths. She veered out to sweep through the corner. She was going to take it at speed and wanted a big, easy arc around the corner. As she started into the turn she was already wondering how she'd do this without getting shot.

Anne took the corner a tad too fast, and the dune buggy squealed and partially slid sideways at the tightest part of the arc through the corner. Hartman screamed, "Anne! My God!" But all four wheels remained planted on the ground.

She straightened it out and put her foot to the floor. There was less than a hundred yards to the police, who were now starting to run around. Things were happening fast. The police seemed to be in a panic. She was searching for someone with a gun who might have it aimed her way.

Hartman was squirming around in the seat. "We're not going to make it! Stop! We can talk to them!"

Anne pressed her foot so hard to the floor that her leg was starting to hurt. If she could just make this thing go faster!

Ahead, an officer began waving his arms, presumably signaling her to stop.

"Anne, for the last time. There is a road block. You can't run it without getting shot!"

She glanced quickly at Hartman and saw that his face was beet red. What the hell was he thinking? They had no choice but to run the road block and get onto that bridge. In the confusion and intensity of the moment, he must have forgotten one thing. One *very* important thing.

Their son was on that bridge.

❧

JEFF HAD BEEN ABLE TO MAKE QUITE GOOD TIME, WALKING along the length of the I-beam, occasionally climbing over cross-members. Every once in a while, to get his bearings, he would climb from the inside of the I-beam to the outside and grab the cement ledge that formed the edge of the road surface. It was tricky, as the fall backwards was a doozy, but it was the only way he could keep an eye on the bridge and find Nate.

Finally, with a bit of luck, he climbed to the outside of the I-beam, peered over the edge and saw Nate stop the SUV about a hundred yards further toward the center of the bridge. He quickly climbed back underneath the bridge. *This son-of-a-bitch is done,* he thought to himself as he shimmied along. Just a few more yards. It all reminded him, rather ironically, of that day in the woods not so long ago...

When he reached the point where he figured to be directly across from Nate, he stepped from underneath the bridge and pulled himself as silently as he could up onto the road surface. Fortunately, light traffic covered the noise he made as his clothes brushed across the cement and as his bow, once, to his horror, clanked against the bridge. He peered over the railing. Nate was waiting for something. He was staring north toward the center of the bridge.

In one last motion, Jeff pulled himself to the road's surface, reached behind and over his shoulder, pulled around the bow and strung an arrow. He took aim at Nate's chest.

"Nate! Get back or I'll shoot!"

Nate turned to face Jeff, who was momentarily stunned. Nate was crying! His eyes were bloodshot and puffy. Tears hung from his eyelids. Suddenly Jeff's mind was flooded with images of the deer he had killed a year ago—eyes wide with confusion and terror—pleading, beseeching for Jeff to let him live. He could never again kill such an animal.

His arms began to shake.

"Go away little boy. You and your toy don't scare me." Nate began to move his right hand toward his waist.

◆

ANNE AND HARTMAN BLEW PAST THE POLICE AT THE CHECK-point, with an officer diving out of the way at the last instant. Anne never saw anyone shoot, but she thought she heard a couple of reports to her left. Of course, unless you have a good deal of practice, hitting a moving target with any kind of firearm (the Warren Commission notwithstanding) is a little like hitting the lottery.

◆

THE SOUND OF GUNFIRE CAUSED JEFF TO JUMP AND NATE'S whole body to jerk. Nate turned his head to the left, toward the gunfire. When he turned, his torso opened up slightly, and Jeff could see Nate reaching for his gun.

Screw those sad, beseeching eyes.

Jeff steadied his hands and let the arrow fly.

◆

ANNE AND HARTMAN SAW THE DRAMA UNFOLD IN FRONT OF them as they raced along the bridge. Anne felt a huge rush of triumph as she saw Jeff release the string of the bow and the nearly immediate appearance of the arrow sticking out both ends of Nate's chest. They were almost there. Jeff was already waving as Anne began to hit the brakes.

◆

LEONARD WILLIAMS HAD BEEN NATE'S INTENDED RIDE TO safety. He, too, had watched the drama unfold. "Well, that little…" he said to himself as he drew within range of his own Colt 1911 semiautomatic, "… is going down." He stopped the f-150, fired a double tap, stepped out, and headed to the back of the suv to make sure Nate had been able to do his job.

❧

ANNE'S BLOOD TURNED TO ICE AND HER HEART SHATTERED into a million crystalline fragments. It was the worst nightmare imaginable. Anne was too stunned to react, even as she and Hartman were splattered with the blood of their own son.

Hartman, however, reacted quickly by drawing his gun and firing. It seemed to Anne that several of his shots hit home, as the big man twisted a couple of times as he climbed into his truck. Even so, he promptly executed a u-turn, and raced back to the north, seemingly oblivious to Hartman's continuous firing and the front, side, and back windows of the F-150 blowing apart from at least a dozen hits.

It took the arrival of screeching police cars to jolt Anne and Hartman from their shock. Jeff was unconscious and Anne was afraid to check for a pulse. He was bleeding profusely and had obviously been hit by two gunshots.

The first officer on the scene approached with his gun drawn. Anne saw him. "My son has been shot by that man." She pointed at the vanishing truck. Hartman had quickly holstered his gun as soon as Leonard had driven out of range. The officer, apparently satisfied that he was in no danger, approached and examined Jeff.

"This your son?"

Anne nodded. Hartman said, "My son, too."

"He's alive. But I don't know for how long." And with that, the officer jumped up and ran to his squad car. He reached in and grabbed the radio handset; Anne could hear him calling for a helicopter.

Oh my God, Anne thought. *He's alive! Oh God save him!* Then her skin turned cold. She remembered the bomb. It would go off any second. "Hartman, the bomb!"

Hartman's eyes were glassy and he seemed to be in shock. He said nothing.

Anne knew she couldn't waste another second. She raced toward the SUV. Just as she was opening the driver's door she felt someone grab her from behind. It was Hartman.

He said, "Let me." Now, his eyes were clear and bright.

Anne felt his strong arm pull her away from the door. Hartman got in, started the engine, threw it in drive, and hit the accelerator.

"Hartman!" The SUV raced toward the north end of the bridge. That was the wrong way! It was almost four miles to the end of the bridge, whereas, had he turned around, as she had intended, the distance was only a mile. Clearly, the chances were better heading south. Yet, as soon as she had screamed, she realized it was no use... Then, oddly, the SUV swerved violently into the oncoming lane and then swerved back toward the northbound lane.

"What the—" started an officer who was standing behind her.

But Anne knew. She and Hartman had talked about it years ago when it had happened with a Yugo. Except then, it had presumably been an accident. No one had ever figured out how the car had managed to flip itself high enough on the guardrail to get caught by the wind and be blown off the bridge. But of course, Hartman intended exactly that.

"Mother of Jesus," said the officer as the SUV hit the railing, caromed up its passenger side, caught the wind, and pitched over the edge, out of sight.

For Anne, time stopped.

Suddenly, the bridge was cloaked in an eerie silence... that was deafening to Anne. On a span of less than a quarter mile, and in a span of about 60 seconds, her son had been shot, probably to death, and her former husband had just sacrificed himself. All the pain of the past vanished. What was left was a body that could feel nothing. There was a vast hollowness that emitted no fear, no pain, no joy, no sadness. Just nothing. Absolutely nothing. She knew her heart should be broken, pained, laboring to beat; but it was as if it weren't even there. Anne realized she wasn't even breathing.

Then it exploded.

"*Holy Mother Mary!*" an officer screamed. Instantly, a great fireball spread out from under both sides of the bridge, lapped over the railings, and rushed over their heads like a thundering jet only feet above. The heat was intense and Anne reflexively ducked and raised her arms to shield her head. Others did the same. People screamed.

And then it was gone, the explosion choked off in its own fury. Anne could feel a lingering sensation of heat in her cheeks. She was coughing as if she had tried to breathe but there was no air. Her lungs burned. She noticed that the officer on his knees next to her had singed hair sticking out under his hat. He was also hacking and coughing.

The bridge began to shake. It swayed back and forth several times. Again people screamed. After a moment the bridge was still.

Anne turned her attention to her dying son.

❧

CHAPTER 39

Washington, D.C.

D IRECTOR OF THE BUREAU OF SOCIALLY CORRECT
Activities, former Senator Elmer Kennison, glanced around
the Oval Office. There, sitting behind his walnut desk,
was that pompous ass of a president, Jared Wallmire. In the several chairs and couch were General Matthew Leighton, Chairman, Joint Chiefs of Staff; Todd Barnstorm, National Security Advisor; and Secretary of Defense, William Turner. The pansies all seemed nervous. That, of course, was simply because they were not as good at the game of politics as Director Kennison. Barnstorm was playing with a pen. Turner was twiddling his fingers. The General was rapidly tapping his foot. The president gave each person a harsh glare that was intended, Kennison was sure, to put everyone in their place. Well, he could just screw himself as far as that was concerned. He was sure not going to put former Senator and now BSCA Director Kennison in any place, by God.

The president stood, rubbed his hand on his jaw, and paced back and forth behind his desk. His face was gaunt. This was shaping up well. A worried president is an easier president to manipulate.

The president said, "Okay, gentlemen, what do you make of this situation? I just got a call from an army colonel who claims his armored cavalry unit is in Michigan's Upper Peninsula, along with 300,000 strong and heavily armed patriots. I've got a bridge and a tunnel blown up, with God knows how many casualties. What the hell is going on? And why didn't we see this coming? I need to respond quickly. And can someone tell me how the hell one of our own units got involved—without anyone catching on?"

With some degree of satisfaction, Kennison noted that the Secretary of Defense squirmed uneasily in his chair.

Todd Barnstorm raised his hand to catch the glance of the president. "First off, Mr. President, I've been in contact with the FBI and they have picked up a law professor who tipped them off to the bombings. Apparently—"

The president's face drew tight and he stepped toward Todd. "What? How the hell would a law professor have inside knowledge? And if he had it, why would he disclose it? And what do you mean by 'they have him picked up'?" The president's voice was so high-pitched he sounded like a whining child.

Todd cleared his throat. "His name is Bradley Fletcher, from the University of Michigan Law School. He is in the hospital, sir; he was shot by one of our agents—"

The president stepped back, raised his hand toward the ceiling and interrupted. "Shot by one of our agents? What the hell?"

"Yes, sir, I cannot explain it, at least right now. I don't have all the details. And frankly, many of them are not relevant to the discussion here—"

Kennison flinched. He knew that was a mistake. The president boomed, "Damn it Todd! I'll decide what's relevant and what's not. You just answer my questions." Kennison could barely mask his enjoyment. He put his hand to his face and tried to make his broadening smile appear as a yawn. This was too much. That quack of a professor, whom he had debated, and embarrassed, on national television.

Barnstorm briefly explained what had happened at the Kreig home. By now, the president had calmed and retaken his throne. He was shaking his head. Todd continued, "The SAC waited at the hospital for him to come out of surgery and got the information about the planned bombings. The professor claims the bombs were set by a rogue element in the patriots. And the story seems to check out.

As you know, the Canadians successfully pushed the bomb off the bridge at Sault Ste. Marie, and the bombing at Mackinac was apparently thwarted by the patriots themselves. Though I don't have all the details on that yet."

The president appeared to consider Barnstorm's statement. "If what you say is reliable, that may tell us something about these people. They may not be looking for a fight."

Damn, Kennison thought. That was not the direction he wanted the conversation to go. General Matthew Leighton, Chairman, Joint Chiefs of Staff, came to the rescue. "Uh, Mr. President, it's my advice that we hit these nut heads hard, and quickly. We can't be letting every damn group run around and claim u.s. territory for themselves. It's not negotiable." Kennison wanted to voice his support but dared not, at least yet.

Todd Barnstorm shook his head vigorously. "They aren't looking to negotiate, Mr. President. If that colonel was telling the truth about his armament and the number of patriots—300,000 armed men is more than we have in our entire military. It appears the patriots simply took over. It's a *fait accompli.* And they did it so peacefully."

The president nodded, and Leighton seemed to exhale, deflate, in defeat. No one else seemed willing to comment. This was bad. Kennison couldn't take the chance Barnstorm's ideas would prevail. Kennison spoke up, "The hell they are peaceful, Mr. President. Unless you call blowing up a bridge and a tunnel peaceful. These are a bunch of racist, hate-mongering, un-American terrorists. If we move now, with a few fighter bombers, we can root 'em out in no time. Furthermore, I know that idiot professor. He is nothing but an alarmist and a right wing radical. The patriots probably don't have half what they say. Probably not a tenth." With a full scale battle with the patriots, Kennison knew he could ride his stringent restrictions on dissidents and gun confiscation all the way to the White House. This would make even more Americans receptive to his notions that America needed an even bigger government—a government with a serious capital "G."

Barnstorm was on his feet. "But that wasn't them! Mr. President, if you could prove the patriots set the bombs, there would certainly be public outcry to go in after them militarily. You could sustain some casualties and keep the public's opinion. But if the bombings were from a rogue element, and the patriots were responsible for saving the Mackinac Bridge and also warned us, through the professor, about the other bombings, then attacking them would be political suicide!"

The president nodded, ever so slightly. The little shit Barnstorm still had the president's ear. Damn him! Kennison needed to fix that once and for all. "Mr. President, I speak on behalf of the people, and I, Senator-Director Kennison, have no doubt they want these radicals pounded into submission. I implore you to examine the level of character we are dealing with. These are animals, and animals cannot reason. They must be hammered with impunity."

The president got up and walked to the window. Kennison wondered if he should push just a bit more. Probably, he decided, but before he could get the words out of his mouth, the president spoke. "I'm going to wait until some of this can be sorted out." Kennison's face flushed with anger. This president was a coward. Damn! Kennison glared at the little twit Barnstorm, who responded with a confused look. The president continued, "And if they dig in they dig in. We still have the firepower to handle it." He turned to Todd. "Get me the facts on what happened on that bridge. And in the meantime," he swung back toward the general, "get some satellite and eyeball reconnaissance."

❧

COLONEL RIGGINS KNEW THAT THE FIRST THING TO OCCUR would be a few overflights to "test" his defenses and perform a little recon. The specially outfitted Apache attack helicopter had a large round object above the center of its rotors. It looked almost like a large donut. Inside, however, were some of the most advanced electronics in the world. This was one of the new AWACS (Airborne Warning And Control System) specially designed for the Apache, which is perfect for the system, since it can drop in and out of sight much more readily than a Boeing 707, the traditional platform for the AWACS.

Riggins had two AWACS-equipped Apaches up, one to the west, and one to the north. He was not surprised when he received confirmation from his western AWACS that it had just spotted two rapidly approaching jets. From the signature on the radar, they were identified AS F-16s. Riggins chuckled. This is exactly what he had expected. He promptly ordered two A-10s up to meet them. Ordinarily cannon fodder for F-16s, in this instance he intended his A-10s to administer a lesson in Russian avionics.

❖

LIEUTENANT COLONEL ROBBY SMITH FLASHED A THUMBS-up to his A-10 wing man, Captain John Fresco, just before he taxied out to the runway. Within moments, Robby was engulfed in the roar of his General Electric TF-34 high-bypass turbofan engine, generating just over 9,000 pounds of static thrust as he thundered down the runway at KI Sawyer Joint-Use Air Base. It was always an adrenaline rush. The G-force of take off, while mild compared to air-superiority fighters such as the F-16, still amplified the sensation of Robby's heart pounding in his ears.

As soon as Robby and John had formed up at 10,000 feet and logged into the AWACS fire control system, they headed straight at the incoming F-16s. With the exceptionally long range of the Russian missiles, the A-10s would not even have to find the F-16s on their own radar, which is always a tricky task. The AWACS would notify the A-10s of the range of the F-16s and would "paint" the F-16s for the targeting mechanism of the Russian-built missiles. The A-10s would simply fire the missiles and turn around.

They were just about within range of their missiles when the AWACS picked up two more F-16s following at a range of 200 miles, but closing very fast.

Robby smiled. He and Captain Fresco would be able to fire their Russian R-77 long-range air-to-air missiles well before the F-16s would find them within range of their U.S.-made weapons. He and John were going to have to get just a little closer to the first wave of F-16s before they could fire and turn to put the second wave of F-16s at their "six."

Robby was watching his weapons display that relayed the view generated by the AWACS. He could feel the tension in his back and he had to tell himself to relax. Tight muscles were never a good thing for flying a fighter aircraft. So far, so good, however. Just a few more seconds and the first two blips on his monitor would be within range.

Suddenly he saw the "lock-on" light turn green for his R-77s. Immediately he fired both missiles and called out to his wingman. A moment later, he heard John call out that he had fired his two R-77s and was beginning his 180 degree turn toward home.

Robby watched his screen. Under his flight suit, he was soaked in sweat. He knew that if the first two blips didn't disappear, they would quickly find him and fire their own weapons. And with two more F-16s right behind, he knew it would be all over except for the shouting.

And then the first two blips vanished from the screen.

"Thank you, Lord," Robby whispered to himself, relief rushing through his sweat-soaked body. Quickly, he got ready for the second phase of the air battle. He flicked his weapons switch to activate the aft radar of the R-73 short range missiles. His only worry, now, was to entice the second wave of F-16s to drive right up his "six" and go visual for a kill. It would get very dicey if the F-16s decided to try longer-range shots with their highly reliable, radar-guided AIM-120 AMRAAMS. It would be less dangerous if they went for a visual kill with their guns or the short-range AIM-9 missiles. The AIM-9, or "Sidewinder," as it is popularly known, is an infrared seeker. The A-10 was designed to loiter over a battle field where infrared ground-to-air missiles might be used against it. Accordingly, the General Electric turbofan engine was specifically chosen because its "bypass" air mixed with and cooled the exhaust plume, making the aircraft less visible to infrared detection.

Of course, the strategy went against everything learned in fighter school. Your "six" was exactly where you didn't want the enemy. Robby could feel another onslaught of sweat begin to break out on his forehead. He fought the urge to turn into his enemy. The two blips were getting closer and closer. The only consolation was that it was beginning to look as if they were taking the bait and would move in for visual. "These damn Russian missiles better work as advertised," he said to himself as he fingered the firing control. He knew he was getting dangerously close to the range for the F-16s' Sidewinders.

Suddenly his threat warning went off and he knew one of the F-16s had obtained a "lock" on him and had probably fired one or two Sidewinders. "Damn!" he yelled, as he pulled hard on the stick to put his lift vector on the attacking F-16.

This was exactly what he had not wanted: a fight with one of the world's most advanced air superiority fighters. He was dog meat unless he could use these damn Russian missiles—and fast. But first, he had to fight off that (or those) Sidewinder(s).

In the world of BFM (Basic Flight Maneuver), putting your lift vector on the attacking fighter creates the most problems for the attacker to solve. By turning into the Sidewinders, Robby was hoping to make the missiles approach his jet at something close to a ninety-degree angle. This would reduce the window of opportunity for the missiles to find him. The missiles, and he was still assuming there were two, would have to solve the mathematics of flight speed and direction vis-a-vis the speed and angle of his plane moving across their fields of view. To put it another way, it is much easier to run up behind a slower car, than it is to hit that same car as it races across an intersection in front of you. The latter situation forces a perfectly timed approach to the intersection. And at this moment, Robby wanted things to be difficult for the other guy.

Fortunately, it seemed as if it was working. He was pulling at his maximum corner velocity, giving him the highest turn rate. The Sidewinders would have to be perfect.

Suddenly Robby saw two white trails off to his right and then the flash of two explosions. Robby's heart stopped and his skin tingled. His entire body shook as the 25 lb./11.36 kg Annular Blast Fragmentation (ABF) warheads erupted, sending a barrage of shrapnel against his aircraft. He heard the thumps as the fragments hit and tore into the soft portions of the aircraft. Fortunately, the essential functions for the A-10 were in "hardened" areas designed to take considerable small and medium arms fire. Robby quickly scanned his controls and breathed a huge sigh of relief. There was no critical damage—though the Sidewinders, designed as proximity bombs, had technically hit. They were able to take out thin-skinned aircraft by exploding in close proximity. They were not designed to take out an A-10.

Now the second problem. The approaching F-16 would be lining him up for a gun shot with the M61 Vulcan 20 mm cannon. And a lumbering A-10 would be like a fish in a bucket.

Robby reached across his body with his right arm and grabbed the "handicapper" bar on the left side of the cockpit. With that leverage, he twisted himself around almost 180 degrees so that he could see the attacking F-16. Thus contorted, Robby felt the coolness from various portions of his wet clothing. He could again feel his pounding heart in his eardrums.

The F-16 was closing in.

Robby reached down and toggled the fire switch for the R-73s. The aft radar immediately beeped and flashed, indicating that it had a lock. He punched the fire button and both R-73s released from their rails.

Momentarily, the R-73s flew backwards at about 300 knots (the forward speed of the A-10). Within a split second, however, they accelerated to zero air speed, thrust-vectored themselves to positive air speed, and honed in on the nose of the F-16.

The F-16 pilot must have seen them coming, because he pulled into a hard turn. Unfortunately, it had only the effect of creating a larger target area for the highly maneuverable R-73s, which a moment later rammed into the underside of the F-16 about midway back from the cockpit.

After the ball of fire dissipated, Robby could see the parachute of the pilot. It made him smile. He wanted to destroy the aircraft—not the American.

Robby pulled the A-10 back around to a level heading. He was greeted by the smiling face and thumbs-up sign of John Fresco, who had run through a nearly identical scenario. Robby's body shook one last time and then relaxed. The pounding in his ears dissipated. He signaled a return to KI Sawyer. Along the way, he mouthed a silent prayer. He prayed that no one had been harmed, and that his actions would ultimately benefit the flag of the four fighter aircraft just blown out of the sky.

∾

Bradley Fletcher was just finishing lunch in his room at the University of Michigan Medical Center. A pretty nurse, Janet Adams, who Bradley figured couldn't be a day over 25, was checking on some of his monitoring equipment. Janet was Bradley's favorite, not because of her looks, which were aplenty, but because she was the most efficient and professional of all the nurses who attended him. Janet was standing next to the telephone, when it rang.

"Answer it for me, please, Janet." Bradley hated having to reach over to the table. Any movement of his arms—no, make that any movement of any part of his body—caused considerable pain.

Janet scooped up the telephone with the same certainty and grace that characterized everything she did. "Bradley Fletcher's room… Yes…" But, instead of immediately handing the phone to him, she seemed to be mesmerized. The color drained from her cheeks. She turned to Bradley and slowly extended the receiver to him. Her eyes, pupils dilated, were as big around as silver dollars. Terror knifed through Bradley's chest.

Anne was dead—

The revolution had begun—

The revolution had failed—

He was being indicted—

Before Bradley could assess what other tragedy might have occurred, Janet handed him the receiver.

Deadpan, she said, "It's the President of the United States."

Bradley was startled, but not shocked. In fact, he had hoped something like this would happen, though he hadn't thought he would get a chance to talk directly to the Big Guy. He studied the receiver held out by Janet, but he did not immediately take it. His mind was racing. He had to make the right argument. Lives could be spared. Perhaps, a nation could be saved. He swallowed hard and grabbed the phone. "This is Bradley Fletcher…"

"Professor Fletcher, this is the President. I am calling from the White House and I want to put you on the speaker phone with some of my advisers to discuss what you have been telling the FBI. Are you up to it?"

What a funny comment, Bradley thought. As if he would say he was feeling just a bit peaked and could the president be so kind as to call back in a little while?

He said, "Yes, Mr. President, I'm fine. What would you like explained?"

"Why don't you start by recounting what you told the FBI?"

Bradley quickly explained.

"Uh, Professor, this is General Matthew Leighton, Chairman, Joint Chiefs of Staff. Can you confirm the level of their military strength or the numbers of patriots who are armed?"

"No, General. I'm sorry. I only know what I was told. One Armored Cavalry Unit and about 300,000 armed patriots."

"Bradley, this is Senator Kennison, Director of the Bureau of Socially Correct Activities—"

"Nice speaking with you again, Senator."

"Yes, well… you have been alarmist in the past, as I recall from our televised debate. What first-hand knowledge do you really have that these racists intend anything other than to commit terrorist acts?"

God, Bradley thought, *why does Kennison have to be one of the president's advisors? Of all the idiots.* He said, "Senator, Mr. President, I think it's pretty clear, first off, that the patriots have planned this very carefully and are quite serious. This is, I have come to believe, very much a middle America thing. Rightly or wrongly, our policies, many of which have been driven and proposed by the good Senator, have pushed middle America to the right. Those in the U.P., for example, support the takeover—"

Kennison broke in, "That's crap. These are a bunch of racists—terrorists!"

The president said, calmly, "That's quite enough, Senator. Professor Fletcher, continue."

"Nate Smith is your terrorist, Mr. President. He has carried out a coup d'état that has left Hartman Kreig scrambling to regain control of the patriots. That should be evident from what happened on the Mackinac Bridge, as well as by my very existence here to warn the FBI, and to talk candidly with you."

The president said, "So, what was the point this Nate Smith had with his bombings? What was he trying to do? The only logical explanation is that he wanted to provoke an armed response."

"Believe it or not, Mr. President, I think he actually hoped to incite, stir up, a violent anti-government rebellion—across the entire nation. Frankly, the guy was trying to emulate the Arab Spring, Castro, and others who used violence to set off revolutions."

"But that obviously hasn't happened. How could he be so stupid as to think it might?"

"Well, Mr. President, the United States is not fed up with its form of governance as embodied in the Constitution. Americans do want to cut the size and intrusiveness of the federal government. But only because it has swelled far past the support of its foundations, not because of any hatred of those foundations. In this sense, then, the entire patriot movement and its planned takeover have a resonance that a large majority of Americans find appealing."

"Then why an Armored Cavalry Unit and, we have just learned, at least a couple of Air Force A-10s, which somehow took out four

F-16s I had ordered to reconnoitre the U.P.? Why 300,000 armed patriots?"

"No kidding? I had no idea. How did A-10s—"

"At the moment, that's classified. But they did. And frankly, that's why I decided to call you. They obviously have a few tricks up their sleeves, and I don't want to walk into any more traps. I'm assuming it was a message for me to listen to you. Well, it got my attention. I'm listening."

"Unquestionably, sir, virtually every member of the patriots would have preferred to use the vote. But with what your predecessor did and with ACORN padding the voter rolls and the census, the most expedient means was to build a trim, uncluttered, constitutionally adept house—and to build it right next door."

"Right in our face."

"That's the point, no doubt."

"Well, I'm inclined to believe you. The takeover of all government buildings in the U.P. went without a shot fired. A few police agencies responded, that we know of so far, and in each case, the patriots apparently called in backup that surrounded the police. Again, however, no shots have been fired, that we know of."

"Mr. President, if I can be so bold as to suggest—"

Kennison blurted out, "Mr. President! How can you believe this co-conspirator in terrorism? He is guessing, lying, covering up!"

The president spoke again, but this time his voice was muffled, as if he were facing away from the telephone. And he addressed someone who had not been disclosed as being in the room with the president. "Amy, remove this idiot from the room. He is, at this moment, a threat to national security. I want him out of here. And if he gives you any trouble, you have my permission—No, I order you to shoot him. Is that clear?"

"Yes Sir. Senator, this way—"

"This is an outrage!" Bradley could hear scuffling. "Take your hands off me you insolent little girl!" More scuffling. Then the sound of handcuffs ratcheting closed and the calm voice of a woman mixed in with the screams of an irate senator. The woman was explaining what have become known as an arrestee's "Miranda rights."

After a moment, the president spoke again. His voice was strained, but calm. "Professor, what are your suggestions?"

"In effect, sir, you have three choices. The first is to fight and kill Americans in the process of taking back control of the u.p. No doubt, from a military point of view, though the General would know better than I, but I would assume that it could be done. Of course, if I read the sentiment of the nation properly, this option will generate even more hatred of the federal government."

"We don't have any polls out yet. But you are convincing me."

"The second option is to let them have their country. This will cost no lives. In addition, the patriots intend to enact a constitution and bill of rights identical to our own. Those documents will serve as a good example, or test ground, for their ideas. The rest of America could observe and benefit from their experiences. Perhaps they will fail, but I doubt it."

"That's a tough pill to swallow."

Bradley knew what the president meant by that. There would still be many in the u.s. who would view him as weak if he let that occur. "The third option, Mr. President, you could encourage them back into the fold by taking steps that mirror their intentions. And I believe you will find that most Americans will support your actions. This is really your best alternative, I believe, from a political standpoint. There will be some fall-out, certainly. But the support you see for what has occurred, and will likely see once the polls come out, will demonstrate the viability of this option. Specifically, you would need to repeal the Un-American Act, the Advancement of Affirmative Action Act, and the Religious and Cultural Sensitivities Act, for starters. You will have to issue an Executive Order compelling the federal government to recognize the Second Amendment as interpreted by *Heller*. You need to abolish all other federally mandated 'special interest' set-asides. Return decision-making authority to the states by abolishing the Department of Education and gutting numerous other federal regulatory agencies. Dramatically limit the powers of those agencies that remain. You'll need to pledge to appoint federal judges and Supreme Court justices who will not act as some type of super-legislature. Finally, you must return to the former owners all of the companies you and Obama have taken over. The UAW will lose its false position of power, you and the Democrats will lose your base of power, but that is the right result for the right reason. In short, stop all attempts to play Big Brother where the states and the people are fully capable of making their own decisions—"

"Hold it a moment, Professor." The president's press secretary had stepped into the room and was beckoning the president, who stepped away from Bradley to confer. After a brief conversation he stepped back and said, "We just got a CNN poll. It appears by a two-to-one margin, Americans think the U.P. has just as much right to form its own country as did the original 13 colonies in 1776. Moreover, it appears that Montana, Utah, and Texas have all voted to secede from the union if I use further force against the U.P." The president was silent for a moment and then added, "Well, for crying out loud."

Bradley let the president linger with his thoughts for another moment. Then he said, "It was the colonists' goal then, sir, as it is the U.P.'s goal today—they only want to form a more perfect union. It's just sad that it had to be done by force of patriots."

❧

CHAPTER 40

FROM HIS HOSPITAL BED, NEAR DEATH AND IN EXTREME agony, Jeff made a plea to the nation that was carried on every network and seen around the world by over 200 million people. It was from the heart, tearful, and so clear in analysis that its force was sufficient for Congress to immediately convene and carry out, in 30 days, the most sweeping legislative revisions in the world's history. The president signed it, knowing that failure to do so would be immediate political suicide. And thereupon, Colonel Riggins surrendered in a jubilant ceremony.

With the federal government off the back of the states and out of the business of meddling with matters the Constitution left to the power of the people, the state of Michigan, in cooperation with Canada, was able to rebuild the Detroit/Windsor tunnel and Ambassador Bridge under budget and in record time.

⤙⤚

CHAPTER 41

DEAN BRADLEY FLETCHER WAS SITTING IN HIS NEW office overlooking the law quadrangle. It felt really good. He glanced around the room and smiled. *Maybe that picture would look better sitting in the far corner of my desk*, he thought. He stood up and leaned way over to move the picture across his very large desk. As he set down the picture, he changed his mind and drew it near. He studied the smile of the President of the United States of America. He pulled the picture out of its frame and read the handwriting on the back. Of course, he knew what it said. He just liked reading it:

> To Bradley Fletcher, Distinguished Professor of Law,
> Many heartfelt thanks. You have served your country with dignity.
>
> Sincerely,
> President Jared Wallmire

Bradley was snapped out of his reminiscing by the buzz of the intercom. It was Beth.

"Dean Fletcher, your wife is in the lobby."

"Good. Please send her in. Thank you, Beth."

She strode in and gave her husband the usual—a deep, sensual kiss.

"Bradley, we have to make it a quick lunch. I'm beginning a trial in Circuit Court this afternoon."

"I understand completely. Anne Kreig, PLLC. It has such a nice ring to it."

"Yup, it's been good so far…"

They headed out of Bradley's office and down the hall to the stairs. The elevator was still too cranky and slow, and for some reason Bradley just couldn't bring himself to get it fixed.

When they reached the ground floor, Bradley stopped and pulled Anne around to face him.

"Are you still upset about Jeff?"

Anne cast her eyes to the floor, and Bradley put his hand out and gently raised her chin.

"Yes… I guess I am… I just had such high hopes."

"I know. So did I. Come on, lets get some lunch." And with that, they headed toward the light streaming through the painted glass doors of Michigan Law School.

They walked along State Street toward their favorite lunch spot, the Red Hawk Bar & Grill. They were startled by a car horn from behind. Reflexively, they both jumped back, away from the street. They turned to see who it was.

Jeff was smiling from behind the wheel of his new Ford Shelby 5.0 Mustang (other automobile companies were beginning to make big, powerful cars, but Ford was ahead of the curve). Jeff pulled up alongside the curb. "Cindy and I were just going to lunch. You two hungry?"

"Hi!" Cindy Cooper yelled.

Anne said, "If you two love-birds can make it quick. We're going to the Red Hawk."

"Sounds great! Let me park this beast and we'll be there in a minute."

Bradley and Anne watched Jeff and Cindy continue along State Street, hunting for a parking place, the deep, bubbling growl of the engine fading as the sport's car continued down the road.

Bradley said, "Criminy, a young guy like that loses out for a seat in the United States House of Representatives and you would think he would be upset."

"Not Jeff. He ran just as a tune-up. He really has his eye on the governor's mansion in Lansing. Besides, he's got a wedding to attend to, and he and Miles have their hands full with their computer consulting business. I understand they just got a contract with the downsized Energy Department. Something about computer security…"

Finis.

About the Author

Mr. Reddy received his BA from Michigan State University and his law degree from The University of Michigan Law School (but his blood runs Spartan green!). A graduate of Gunsite Training Center and numerous firearm and self defense classes, he has taught the lawful use of deadly force for over 10 years. Mr. Reddy's interests include golf, table tennis, swing dancing, cross country skiing, cycling, playing guitar, building acoustic guitars, woodworking, and impersonating the Big Bopper on karaoke night. He currently lives in Ann Arbor, Michigan, with his two miniature schnauzers, Elsie and Ellie Mae.